# Life Line

**Also by James Sloan Allen**

*The Romance of Commerce and Culture:
Capitalism, Modernism, and the Chicago-Aspen Crusade
for Cultural Reform*

*Worldly Wisdom:
Great Books and the Meanings of Life*

*William James on Habit, Will, Truth, and the Meaning of Life*
*(editor)*

*Aloha:
The Surprising History of an Idea and a Culture*

# Life Line

## A Novel of Romance and Rebirth

James Sloan Allen

ISBN: 978-0-578-55772-4

Cover art and book design by Rachel Davis

*To the people and places I have loved,*
*with gratitude*

# Contents

# 1

## Onto a Bridge of Dreams

It had been a memorable day. One of many on this romantic adventure. Both of them felt this, if in different ways. And they were thinking they would carry their own images of this sublime place, and other cherished memories of India, with them forever.

In that felicitous mood, Rebecca and Alex left behind the Taj Mahal, its gracefully symmetrical white marble domes, arches, and minarets, bathed by the hazy afternoon sun in an amber glow and reflected in the long narrow pool that divided an expansive manicured garden. Hand in hand, they joined droves of other visitors departing the shrine through the grandiose doorway in the garden wall. Then, bantering about love and beauty, truth and illusion, they crossed the broad outer grounds to a smaller passageway leading through the exterior wall to the street.

Outside, they paused to brace themselves for the trek back down the congested roadway to their car and driver waiting a hundred yards or so away. Tourists in flowered clothes and floppy hats, laden with cameras and curios, surged in groups to and from buses parked on the side. Others crowded around makeshift stalls that lined the street, haggling with merchants over souvenirs. Merchants beckoned buyers to their stalls with promises of low prices and superior artifacts—"Best deals. Best Taj marble! Malachite! Lapis lazuli!" Touts threaded through the mass proffering trinkets and photographs—"Ten rupee! Five rupee!" Ragged children flitted from one cluster of tourists to another pushing postcards and beads and small marble boxes into prospective customers' hands—"Stones. Marble. Same as Taj. Five rupee! Three rupee!" Beggars scuffled here and there extending emaciated arms for alms. Soldiers roamed on casual guard duty.

"Ah, tourists Ah, humanity," Alex muttered.

Rebecca raised an eyebrow and gave a knowing laugh. Exchanging affectionate smiles, they started off.

Moments later, a clamor of shouting voices erupted above the normal hubbub. It came from behind them near the exit. A loud POP! POP! POP! followed. Alex and Rebecca jerked their heads around. A figure in camouflage khakis raced in their direction shoving people from his path. A soldier sprawling on the ground cried out for someone to stop the runner. As the figure rushed past, Alex impulsively lunged at him. The runner swerved and swung a pistol, striking Alex on the shoulder and firing a shot that kicked up a whiff of dust near Rebecca. Alex lost his footing and fell. He had knocked the gunman off stride but hadn't upended him, and the fugitive merged into the throng. Two shouting soldiers raced by in pursuit.

Gathering himself up, stunned but unhurt, Alex met an alarmed expression on Rebecca's face. Before they could speak, more loud voices broke out in frantic, unintelligible words, and then in sporadic English: "BACK! BACK! GET BACK! GET BACK! GET AWAY!" They saw another pair of soldiers desperately trying to clear people from the exit gate area where, against the wall, a large military back-pack lay slumped. Alex grasped Rebecca's arm and pushed her in front of him into the horde of panicking tourists running away.

The blast came as a booming clap of thunder, too deafening to be heard distinctly. It consumed all sensations in a cacophony of sound. It split the air and shook the ground. It disintegrated brick and rock. It pulverized pavement. It swallowed the street in dust and smoke.

Shattered stone, spikes of metal, and splintered wood flew in all directions. Tour bus windows burst into shards as the buses buckled under the force. Hats and purses and parcels soared into the sky. Curios and cameras sailed and clattered down. Artifacts broke apart, and semi-precious stones scattered into the dirt. Bodies tumbled like dolls. Bones fractured. Blood sprayed. Severed limbs spun high and dropped like sticks.

Mayhem spread in a tidal wave. Tourists, touts, and merchants fled in terror. Running, screaming, trying to get away, trying to hide. They hurtled down the road or rushed away from it, pushing, shoving, stumbling, falling. Makeshift shops not blown apart by the explosion crumpled beneath the rampage. Frenzied feet trampled fallen bodies. Fallen bodies struggled to get up or to crawl. Many bodies did not move at all.

The pandemonium finally subsided, and an eerie semi-silence descended. Through the acrid smoke and dust that clogged the air, nothing could be seen but disarray, and nothing could be heard but moans and whimpers.

Blinking her eyes open, Rebecca had no sense of where she was. The force of the blast had thrown her down and jarred her unconscious briefly. Gradually she became aware that she was lying askew on her side. She nebulously remembered shots and chaos after they had come through the gate. Trying to move, she found herself partially pinned under something. And a pain shot down one leg. Turning her head and blinking hard to clear her eyes, she discovered that the "something" was a body.

She tried to wrench free but couldn't. A burning sensation seized her leg. Gritting her teeth against the pain, she managed to roll onto her back. Then she collected her strength, rooted her elbows in the dirt, and pushed herself part way up. Now she could see that the body lying across her, face down, was Alex.

He didn't move. His back and head were bloody. She gasped and spoke his name. No sound. Again. Nothing. She spoke more loudly. "Alex?!" Still no response. "Alex!" she cried and nudged him with her hand. "Say something!" Nothing.

Fighting against his weight and her pain, she inched herself farther up to get closer to his face. The portion of it she could see was spattered with blood, and his eyes were closed. A shock of fright tore through her, and a scream sprang from her throat. "ALEX!"

She twisted part-way around searching for help. Through the murky air, a surreal landscape of carnage materialized. Bodies lay everywhere. Some moved limbs in slow motion. Others lay still. Cries and moans were growing more pronounced and profuse. In the clouded distance a few figures flitted about like ghosts. Others staggered aimlessly as if sleep-walking.

"Help! Helllp! Helllllp!" she yelled, waving at anyone standing upright. But her voice was lost in the rising swell of cries, and her flailing arms became part of a surreal dumb show.

She tried again to slide out from under Alex, gripping the ground with one hand and gently pushing against him with the other. It was painful, but she succeeded. Sitting up, she noticed that her clothes were wet with blood on one side from her ribs on down. She switched her eyes to Alex's face. It was still. She waved her arms again and cried for help to no one in particular. No one responded.

The surreal scene was becoming more animated. Torn and bleeding bodies were tottering around. Children were wailing. Soldiers and police officers were shouting orders. Medics were carrying stretchers and attending to the injured seemingly at random.

An eternity elapsed before anyone came to her. At last an Indian soldier responded to her cries. "Help him!" she pleaded, pointing to Alex as he arrived. "He's not moving." She grabbed the solder's arm, discerning a medical insignia on his sleeve. "Please! Help him."

He knelt down to feel for a pulse in Alex's neck. "He's alive," the medic said in mildly accented English without looking at her. It had not hit her that Alex might *not* be alive. The words brought fright, then momentary relief. The medic summoned a stretcher and proceeded swiftly to wrap Alex's wounds in strips of gauzy bandages to stanch the bleeding, disregarding Rebecca's pleas for a prognosis.

Still ignoring her as he finished his work, the medic told the stretcher bearers, "He has head and back wounds and has lost much blood. Put him with the other criticals." Turning to Rebecca, he said, "Now, let me see this," and he examined her side and leg. Rebecca gaped as the stretcher bearers carted Alex off.

"Will he be all right?' she implored, indifferent to her own injuries.

"I do not know," he answered rather distantly. He removed some shards from her side and leg, wrapped her wounds, gave her a shot of anesthetic, told her she had a serious leg wound but it would heal, and summoned another stretcher.

Hearing him also say she should be put with non-criticals, she stammered plaintively, "Please, please, can't I go with him? I have to!"

Reading her tormented face, he relented. "Take her over there," he told the stretcher bearers, pointing to the area where Alex lay. "But she can't go to the hospital yet. Criticals first."

As they carried her away, she wagged a hand toward where she saw Alex's stretcher at the end of a row of them on the ground. They laid her down next to him and told a soldier standing guard that she could remain there but couldn't go with him. Then they ran back into the carnage.

A few feet from her, Alex lay on his stomach facing her, his head covered down to his eyes in bloody dressings. She wanted to get closer. Despite the pain, she rolled off the stretcher and dragged herself to him. Coming within inches of his face, she saw that his mouth, misshapen from lying heavily against the ground on the stretcher, dripped saliva. Yes, he was alive, she assured herself. She wiped his lip with her finger.

With her eyes fixed on his immobile features, she began to sense the chaos around her dissolving. The cries and shouts trailed off. And a quiet isolation seemed to enclose the two of them. She thought she saw a hint of movement in his eyelids. A twitch. A flutter. Was it really there? The eyelids opened. Just a slit. But enough for her to detect a speck of whites. He could hear her. He could see her. Or she thought he could. She moved still closer to him.

"Alex. Alex! Can you hear me?" she whispered. The eyelids moved again. He had heard her! She knew it. She strengthened her voice. "Oh, hear me, Alex. Please." A slight motion appeared on his lips. She was sure of it. He was trying to speak. Yes. He was trying to speak. She was certain. He had seen her, and heard her, and was trying to speak to her. She bent over and put an ear near his mouth and listened intently. And she thought she heard his voice make the sounds, "vvvv yuuuuuu . . . ."

That was all she could make out. Had he said "I love you"? Or was it only a breath? She kissed her fingertips and touched his lips with them. She drew back. And she saw a tiny upward curl at the corners of his mouth. He was smiling at her. She knew it. He was smiling in answer to the kiss. Then the curl ebbed away. The slit in his eyes closed. And his face became immobile again. But she had seen them, hadn't she? The eyes? The smile? And she had heard it, hadn't she? The words? Or had she imagined it all? Was it only in her mind? Part of a dream? What was happening ?

"Take that one over there, but not the woman" shouted a voice nearby, jarring her back to the scene. Two soldiers hefted Alex's stretcher and headed toward one of several military ambulances that had now assembled.

"Wait!" she called out. "Take me too. I must go with him." The soldiers ignored her. She could only watch as they slid Alex's stretcher inside with a few others and slammed the doors. And she could only follow with her eyes as the ambulance rumbled off, its siren drowning out for her all other noise, piercing the air with a wail that gradually faded but did not die as she closed her eyes tight and clung to its sound. She listened to it longer than she could have heard it. But she listened anyway. Inside.

She was still listening to the phantom siren when someone near her said. "You go now." Detached and drowsy from the anesthetic, she was hardly aware of being carried to another medical vehicle and riding off to the hospital. Her mind saw only that fleeting smile on Alex's face, and heard only that endless siren, and the ethereally whispered "vvvv yuuuuu . . . ."

She was sinking into a dream-world, unsure of everything, disbelieving all that surrounded her as a nightmare. She started vaguely feeling that she was going onto some bridge of dreams and would awaken in her own life before all of this had happened.

But, she woozily asked herself, which life would it be? Would it be the life she had come so unexpectedly to share with Alex for the past few months in New York, when they were probing their differences and talking about all kinds of things, and opening themselves up to each other and discovering the deepening intimacy that had then brought them to India? Or would it be the life just before that, when she had felt lost in an inexplicable abyss of emptiness after . . . that frightening night? Or would it be the life leading up to *that night*, when an unconscious listlessness had slowly, over uncounted months, infected her? Or would it be her life even before that, when for as long as she could remember she had been so composed and productive, comfortable and contented, and had married Richard in the same way? Yes, that could be it, she wondered dreamily. It could be that everything since her old comfortable and contented life had imperceptibly drifted into listlessness and had then died *that night*, and on down to this nightmare—had all been a bad dream. And that when she awoke she would find herself in that customary old life. And nothing after that would have happened—*none of it!*—and she could go on as before, and everything would be as she had wanted it to be. Is that what she wanted?

No, she thought. Not that. That's what had started it all, wasn't it—her *old life*, her *comfortable and contented life*, her *perfect life*? Which had started to slip away, and had then come to a dramatic end one night at home about six months ago, in a panic. After a divorce made in heaven.

# 2

## A Perfect Life

*(Six Months Earlier)*

**D**ivorces *are made in heaven.* Some wag had said that, she remembered as she sat stretched out on the sofa in her Manhattan living room looking idly through the window at the leaves fluttering in Central Park while a soft spring evening descended. Who was it? Oscar Wilde? Sounds like him. A catchy half-truth. A teased cliché. But her divorce was like that, she said to herself. Made in heaven.

After all, they hadn't really loved each other. Or not any more. Not in the way that lovers think they do. And not even in the way that old married couples do after the passion wanes and yet they belong to each other as one and lose part of themselves without the other.

It was different in the beginning. It always is. *Beginnings beguile us with possibilities. Beginnings give us a new life. With no new beginnings, we die inside.* She remembered reading something like that in Wordsworth—"the budding rose," and so on— and she'd heard lesser versions as blather from psychobabblers and males on the make. But she'd never heard anyone say that beginnings can go on and on, suspending us in possibilities, and then just end. Like this. Her life with Richard. So easily.

It had begun no less easily. She had let his eyes catch hers at a cocktail party. Not something she would normally have allowed herself. Don't make eye contact with a man you don't know, unless . . . . That's the rule she'd learned long ago. It's an invitation, and you usually regret it. She didn't know why she'd let it happen this time. She wasn't deliberately sending an invitation. Not that she thought of herself as irresistible. Her face was a bit too round, her legs a bit too short, her form a bit too fleshy. At least that's how she saw herself. She would have chosen to be sleeker, more statuesque. But the thought didn't preoccupy her. And when the natural smile on her sensuous lips lit her face, she radiated the rosy sensuality of a Renoir portrait. That's what people told her—she had a Renoir-like beauty. She was flattered, although she didn't really believe it. And she'd unintentionally smiled a little when Richard had come toward her through the party crowd that night. He couldn't resist her. He didn't try.

She was used to men coming up to her, even when she didn't make eye-contact or smile. "It goes with being an attractive woman. But don't count on it for much," her mother had cautioned her in adolescence. "Just be gracious, and remember who you are." Her mother—intelligent, perceptive, wary, loving, and thoughtful Adrianna Winters, a long-time teacher who had taught her daughter well, and whose husband had left her nearly twenty years ago for a younger woman.

Adrianna Winters had given her daughter a temperament like her own, and that Renoir beauty. And both parents had given their daughter an agile mind, a wry wit, and a literary bent. But it was mainly to her father, professor of literature Justin Warren Winters, that, as he liked to remind her, she owed her name. He had taken it from Daphne du Maurier's once-popular novel *Rebecca*. Or rather from the movie by Alfred Hitchcock, with a young Laurence Olivier playing the aristocratic Maxim de Winter, and a girlish Joan Fontaine playing the nameless ingénue whom Maxim marries to forget his dead wife, named Rebecca. Professor Winters didn't think much of the novel as literature. But he enjoyed the mystery in it, and he delighted in the movie with its nifty Hitchcockian twists. "The whole drama turns on a dime," he would point out in his animated professorial style, "when the imperious Olivier looks down at the cowering Joan Fontaine, who is whimpering over what she believes to be his unquenchable love for the beautiful, intelligent, sophisticated, Rebecca de Winter, and he incredulously spits out at her: *You thought I loved Rebecca!? You thought **that**!? I **hated her!!!**"*

Maxim de Winter had come to hate Rebecca for her willful, unfaithful, and malevolent character, and he had accidentally killed her in a fit of rage. But Justin Warren Winters liked the name, shared in part with his own. It had euphony and weight to it, he said, and it carried an evocative, if ambiguous, allusion to beauty and intelligence and sophistication that their daughter could play upon all her life. Adrianna Winters had liked the name for itself, despite the questionable Hollywood allusions, and she had reminded her husband that the fabled Rebecca of the Bible, Isaac's wife, was another intelligent beauty with a streak of deceit in her.

And that is how Adrianna and Justin Warren Winters' only child got her name: *Rebecca Winters*. An eccentric legacy, her parents granted, this name invoking a mysterious fictional villainess, and maybe a manipulative Biblical wife, both women of beauty and intelligence, willfulness and intrigue. But these parents were rather eccentric people. And they made a fond family joke of their daughter's literary identity. True to her blood, Rebecca Winters took to her name for its nice sonority, and for its ambiguous allusions, even though she didn't intend to live up to them all.

So Rebecca Winters owed her allusive name mainly to her father, whom she had adored for his deft intellect, winning charm, playful wit, and unwavering affection for her, and for whom she had mourned when he had died five years ago, but whom she could never forgive for leaving her mother. He had probably identified too much with the likes of Maxim de Winter, she had speculated. Like Maxim, in mid-life her father had married an ingénue, who naively worshipped him, like Joan Fontaine in the movie, and as Adrianna Winters was not the type to do. Why her father needed that youthful adulation, Rebecca could never understand.

Carrying her peculiar family heritage amusedly, and wearing her physical attractions modestly, Rebecca Winters had managed her life well. Conscientious, self-controlled, composed, and sensitive, like her mother, she had achieved what she wanted to achieve, caused rare hurts, proffered many kindnesses, suffered few sorrows, and become comfortable and contented. She had also easily let men into her life, on her own terms.

Richard, who had wended across the room that night, had been the best of these men. He was handsome, she had thought. Nice features, if a little ungainly in manner, but the more disarming for that. They had talked and laughed with the contrived conviviality of party-goers. She liked his understated charm and unpretentious intelligence. He liked her radiance and intelligence and self-possession. And then they had acted out the script. Casual sociability had led to easygoing romance. Easygoing romance had led to congenially living together. And congenially living together had brought easy marriage. "Should we do it?" Richard had asked one rainy Sunday afternoon while they were reading the *New York Times* in their Manhattan apartment. "Why not?" she had answered, contented with herself and with him. So they had married, with the airy, agreeable inertia that had borne them along from the beginning.

And the beginning had gone on and on like that. They had enjoyed each other like familiar pictures on the wall. Pictures that fill a space. Nice to look at. Then in time you don't quite see them anymore. And there, in that comfortable setting, the beginning had suspended itself, and started to end. The possibilities gradually dissolved into the air, and invisibly leaked out through cracks around windows and doors, leaving nothing disturbed. Familiar pictures on the wall. But no more possibilities.

Rebecca wondered now why their life together—she refused to label it a "relationship" in the pop psychological jargon she despised—hadn't gone deeper, or higher, or somewhere. Maybe it was because they were too much alike, too conscientious, too given to routine, too agreeable, too comfortable, too emotionally passive. The beginning had gently seduced them, but they hadn't known where to go from there. Children had never fit in, either. Their lives hadn't had room. Or their hearts hadn't. Some possibilities demanded too much.

Their careers had always come first. Richard had spent more and more time at his law firm. Dinners with clients. Nights. Weekends. Trips out of town. They had spent less and less time together. But she hadn't complained. Her work was her life, too. It always had been, more or less. Ever since childhood when she had started to read voraciously—and had almost always earned A's in school and on through college and some graduate studies at Yale. Hard work, intelligence, and her bookish penchant had led her to become a respected acquisitions editor at a New York publishing house, spending her days and many nights reading, searching for good manuscripts to publish, books that she could be proud of, books that would last. All of that had made her life go well for her, and had made work the center of her life. Rebecca and Richard both wanted to be good at what they did, and routine carried them the rest of the way.

By tacit agreement, and for more reasons than they needed, both of them had played out the beginning until it had suspended itself and seeped away. Then he had found someone else. He might have wanted more than Rebecca could give after all. Or he might have simply wanted to *begin* again, seduced by new possibilities. It would not have been like him to say. And not like Rebecca to ask.

Six years. Now it was over. About the same way it had begun and gone on. Agreeable inertia. "It's time, isn't it?" he had asked one day about their separating. "Yes, I guess it is," she had answered, conceding to an inevitability that she didn't resist or question. Just like that, or something like that. The same way they had decided to marry. And now a divorce made in heaven. That's how she remembered it.

But they would always be "friends." The kind that most formerly married couples could never be. They knew they could do it because they still had their early congeniality, and no scars of conflict. They were meant to be friends, they had decided, and probably nothing more. Somehow, that was enough.

"We'll *do* lunch," Richard had said with his customary civility as they had parted for the first time as "friends" not long ago when the divorce came through.

"Yes," she had responded smiling. "We'll *do* lunch." And they knew they would.

That summed up their lives together. And it was all right with her. Pictures on the wall. A divorce made in heaven.

⌒ℓ⌒

But now, lounging on the sofa with a book on her lap in the apartment she shared with Clarissa, her gray tabby snuggled at her feet, Rebecca Winters started asking herself—*Why?* Why was it all right? Why didn't she care? Six years of life with Richard, and she had let them go, contented to *do* lunch. No pain. No anger. No loss. No sorrow. Nothing. Why?

An impression of herself began forming in her mind. She saw that she had never truly felt deprived of anything—except perhaps her father after he left. She had always had what she wanted, or what she thought she wanted. Affection. Security. Friends. Achievement. And what she didn't have she didn't want. Or she thought she didn't want, which can amount to the same thing. That made her life easy. It also made her easy to like. Easy to work with. Easy to live with. Easy to leave. Just as it made it easy for her to leave Richard. Nothing seemed to ruffle what her hometown friends, with adolescent needling and envy, had once tagged *a perfect life.*

But on this languid May evening, with her eyes vacantly watching the leaves shifting in the breeze outside, alien emotions began bubbling up in her. She couldn't identify them. The sensation was new, and disquieting. It wasn't the sense of an ending, or an admission of failure in marriage. It was something else. More nebulous.

Was it that she'd never been alone like this before, at this age, on the threshold of forty? She had usually had a man in her life who had made her comfortable and hadn't asked too much of her, a man who was there, but who had let her live her own life. Like Richard, the only one of them she had married. Yes, being alone like this was new. It's different for men, of course, she reflected. They never stay alone long. But that's because men need women more than women need men. She had read somewhere that men don't survive alone as well as women. Most widowers re-marry or die fast. Most widows don't do either, living happily enough with their memories and independence and friends. But she hadn't needed to read that. She'd have guessed it. And she had implicit confidence that new, *comforting* men would come her way, and she would marry again if she wanted to—defying the insulting statistics she had read about women over forty getting married

So, why this disquietude? Now? Or had it been coming on for a while? As she thought about it, she recognized that she had increasingly sensed something vaguely amiss. What was it? A mild dissatisfaction? A kind of discontent? A dim apathy? Yes, that was more like it. But for how long? When did it start?

Going back over the recent past, Rebecca found traces of something like apathy or listlessness leading from the spring back into the winter and on to the fall. A thought struck her. She blinked. September 11th, about nine months ago. Could that have caused it? Sure she had been scarred by the events of that day, like all New Yorkers, who had experienced those events more immediately and deeply than most people elsewhere. Shock and dismay, then disbelief and disorientation. And she knew that such events can leave lasting residues and even induce an obscure depression. Was that what had happened to her? Was that what her apathy and listlessness were? An obscure depression after September 11th? She wouldn't have been the only one. Or had the apathy started before that?

She looked outside over the trees and searched her memories beyond September 11th. It had been a normal summer before that. Light work load. A few days in Maine with Richard. But, yes, some of those feelings were already there, weren't they, if indistinctly? A barely discernible sense of creeping indifference to work and to Richard and—to everything. Why? Trying to follow the thinning traces farther back, she lost sight of them when they faded away a year or so ago. Had they started then, she asked herself, or had they only then become visible?

So what had happened? And why? Somewhere in the past, for some reason, she had begun losing her way into indifference, or something like that. Then had come September 11th, and the indifference had become a subliminal apathy, and possibly depression. Was that it? It's possible, she thought. She was almost proud of her self-analysis.

But even if that were all true, she concluded, it wouldn't explain the mood now. This is more than all of that. It feels more disquieting and more—empty. Why? What does it mean?

She closed her eyes, and a hazy image began assembling in her mind. She saw herself holding a book, turning a page. A commonplace sight for her. But coming closer, she saw it was a book about *her*. Her life. Examining it, she saw that the open pages were—blank! No, not entirely blank. A line here and there. But eerily vacant. She mentally thumbed backwards and forward through the spectral pages. They were blank, too. A chilling intimation gathered in her mental fog. A blank life? Past, present, future? Not blank of everyday incident but . . . . Is that what all of these things mean?

She heard a voice sigh: *What if my whole life has been wrong?* Her literary memory identified the words. They came from Tolstoy's Ivan Ilych before he screamed for three days on his deathbed because he had discovered that his *whole life had been wrong*—placid, contented, and terrible. A babble of voices now began murmuring in her head. She couldn't make them out, except for snippets from books and people . . . . *He saw the jungle of his life, and he saw the beast . . . . The horror, the horror . . . . With a whimper . . . . What did it mean to her, this thing she called life?* And others. A dissonant, mournful chorus. Why? A judgment on her for having things too easy? For not suffering? For being who she was? She clamped her hands against her ears to shut the voices out. But she couldn't. They came from within.

Then amidst the unsettling voices, through the fog, she saw an abyss opening. And inside it another image took form. It was her own face, slowly dissolving and receding into another dissolving face and another and another, and another, over and over and over into an infinity of lonely emptiness, and empty loneliness. Her amorphous fears froze into palpable fright. This was no apathy or depression, her weakening consciousness told her. It was some kind of . . . panic. Was it the panic they say can strike anyone during terrifying events or psychological traumas, spreading out in temblors that erupt in quivering flesh, immovable limbs, cold perspiration, and blind terror in the eyes; the panic that once you live through its paralyzing deer-caught-in-the-headlights helplessness you can never feel quite the same about yourself again, or even believe that you are who you thought you were?—was this *that* panic?

For the first time in her nearly forty outwardly accomplished, unruffled, contended years, Rebecca felt her self-control fraying into brittle strands, as though her very self was crumbling. She couldn't move. She couldn't think. She didn't know who she was. And then, from somewhere inside, a gulping sob welled up and enveloped her, until her mind went dark, and consciousness drained away.

# 3

## *Dilemma*

When she woke up the next day, everything had changed. And nothing. The paralyzing panic had gone, but the emptiness remained. And with it the aching sensation that Rebecca didn't know who she was.

She had always had such mastery of herself, of her life. Whenever she had stumbled, which was rare, she had always tightened her grip, lifted herself up, and played over the travails. That gave her control. She hadn't wanted it any other way. It was her nature. Rebecca Winters, who had shared some of her fictional namesake's will power, along with a measure of her imponderable character, if not her deviousness. But now, lying in bed staring at the ceiling in the early morning light, obscurely conscious of having come to bed sometime in the night after awakening damp and weak on the sofa, Rebecca felt she had lost everything. Including herself.

Can you actually lose yourself, your life, like that? she wondered—simply by looking inside and seeing almost nothing? And can you find nothing inside just because you have managed the surface too well, and let the inside go to dust, grain by grain, and let that dust blow away, leaving a lonely hollow, and then one day you fall into it? How could that happen? Could it be because you refuse to feel deep feelings or care enough about anything

19

for fear of losing control? Is that what had happened with her marriage? Is that what had happened with her work? Is that what had happened after September 11th? Or had she never really felt very intensely about anything in the first place?

Oh that's all so corny and clichéd, she scoffed. Her editorial instincts knew better. Sure, Tolstoy might put this kind of stuff in a story—she recoiled at recalling the threatening voices of last night. That's literature. This is life. But what was she going to do? She needed self-control now more than ever, to keep from falling into that abyss, or whatever it was, inside of her. But if self-control, or some such thing, had unwittingly opened the abyss, wouldn't more of the same deepen it?

Such banality. Does emotional extremity do that to you? she asked herself. Fear and despair, passion and love—they all breed banality because we can't do them justice in words. Probably. But that's how she felt. She had sunk into both emptiness and banality, with no way out.

An absurd condition. It wasn't a *problem*. Problems have solutions. She saw no solution possible here. It was more a pre-dicament, or a conundrum, or a paradox, or a dilemma. Yes, that's it, she told herself. A dilemma. There's no solution to a dilemma. It stares you in the face with the sardonic grin of an irresolvable conflict that won't go away no matter what you do. So, if living the life she had lived had somehow created her absurd condition, and yet she had to cling to that life to protect herself from that condition, that's a dilemma for sure, isn't it? A classic *absurd existential dilemma* at that. Banality or not.

Rebecca's mind was working now. This had always been her therapy. She could turn disturbing facts and disconcerting thoughts and troubled feelings into abstractions. Abstractions were detached, manageable. She had insisted she would never go to a psychotherapist. Psychotherapy is the ideology of emo-tional exhibitionism, she would say. And psychotherapists are emotional voyeurs who want you to believe mental health means wearing your heart on your sleeve. Not for her. She could analyze herself if she needed to.

Practicing her own therapy, she found that the mental exercise and semantic clarity were helping to pacify her. And she decided that having some control was better than having none, whatever the consequences. What other choice did she have if she was going to go on at all? So she shut out the unanswerable questions, filed away her *dilemma*, and sluggishly climbed out of bed for a day she didn't welcome, in a life that had inexplicably all but ceased to matter. After glowering in the bathroom mirror at the lined face and dark eyes that peered out at her, she got in the shower and let the hot water gush and the steam billow and their medicinal beneficence sink in, thinking, if this is denial, so be it. Denial can be therapeutic.

When she left her apartment for the office an hour later to begin a new week, she appeared to be herself again. But she knew she wasn't.

"Are you OK?" Rebecca's colleague and friend Meredith asked, leaning against the half-opened office door that afternoon. "You seem very down. Withdrawn. More than I've ever seen." Meredith had an instinct for such things. She could pick up a mood swing at fifty yards. And she often went after them like a social worker on the case of an abused child. She had detected something amiss in Rebecca for months. It had grown visible in Rebecca's periodically slow reactions and occasionally distracted manner, and in fluctuating dedication to work. A few others in the office had seen such things, too, but had dismissed them as the result of overwork or other minor lapses in a well-ordered life. Meredith couldn't do that. She had wanted to find out the cause so she could provide a cure.

Rebecca had casually deflected Meredith's subtle probes,

chalking them up to her friend's solicitous nature. Meredith was nothing if not a friend. She wasn't much of an intellectual, although she was intelligent. Her interests ran to the ephemera of pop culture, light fiction, and celebrity biographies—the world of changing fashions. But Rebecca liked her for her high spirits, her good heart, and her devoted friendship. Everyone should have a Meredith in her life, Rebecca had often thought. And with genuine affection, she had reciprocated Meredith's friendship, bestowing many small favors and frequent attentions. But nature drew a line between them where Rebecca's self-protection took over. And Meredith knew this better than Rebecca.

On this day, Rebecca admitted to herself that Meredith had been right. Something had been amiss with her for a long time. And now the bottom had fallen our of her world. But what was she going to say about it to this sensitive, inquiring, and devoted friend? Contriving a reasonably responsive expression, Rebecca finally replied to Meredith's question, "Oh, preoccupied. Lots of work to do."

Seeing through the evasion, Meredith said cheerily, "You need a break. Let me take you out for a drink later. There's a new wine and cheese place on 48th and Madison. It's very 'hot.' Neat looking. Tasty light food. It'll revive you."

Meredith had antennae for these things, too—what was "hot" in this city of incessantly changing fashions in restaurants, in clothes, in the arts, in people. And when she put her mind to changing a mood with a dose of fashion, there was no defeating her. You could defer defeat, but not avert it.

Rebecca deferred. She wasn't ready to socialize. "Sorry. Can't tonight."

"Tomorrow?"

Knowing it would be both futile and rude to put Meredith off indefinitely, Rebecca thumbed through her desk calendar for a suitably late but politely early enough date. She settled on Friday, despite her dislike of weekend crowds.

"Friday?"

"Busy schedule, eh? If I get a better offer, I'll let you know. Otherwise, Friday it is. For a drink after work and dinner? And how about a movie?"

Rebecca obligingly jotted down the engagement, and Meredith left her to herself. But Meredith could tell something was seriously wrong. She saw it in Rebecca's drawn face and vacant eyes, and heard it in her abnormally flat voice. Meredith saw this the next day, too. And the day after. And the day after that. Rebecca stayed in her office most of the time, emerging to exchange cordialities and business talk that couldn't be avoided. Meredith took note but said nothing more about it.

Some other colleagues also asked Rebecca what was ailing her, but she shrugged them off. And Meredith offered them the explanation of a long-needed vacation, which Rebecca had not taken, except for maybe a week here and there, for as long as anyone could remember. Rebecca's boss, the editor-in-chief, Henry Randolph, even came by Rebecca's office—after a meeting where she had come in late, as never before, and had then said hardly a word, equally unprecedented—to ask if she would like some time off now that they were entering the slow summer season. "I might," she answered, surprised at his uncharacteristic attentiveness. "But not now. I have too much to do." He seemed gratified that work still came first for her despite his display of sensitivity. But work didn't really come first for her now. Work hadn't prevented her crisis, and couldn't end it. And yet, what good would it do to take time off? At least at work she had the office to distract her from what she had come to fear most—the images of her empty life, and the questions she found herself asking over and over in the night: What had gone wrong? How? Why? And what was she supposed to do about it? Yes, she would stick to the routine of work if she could.

⁂

Friday, after the business week was over, in the chic bistro Meredith started digging, aiming to open Rebecca up and banish her troubles.

"Rebecca, you can't deny that something is bothering you. What can I do?

"Nothing. Just be your lovably inimitable self."

"You're evading again. What is it? The divorce? Closing in on forty? Being alone? This seems so much worse than what I've seen in you before. You've got to let it out. Talk about it. And why not to me?"

Rebecca looked at her friend. Here is *one good* thing in my life, she said to herself—loyal friends. How good they can be. Still, she felt lifeless inside and afraid of the cause. How was she going to satisfy Meredith's good-hearted curiosity without revealing that? She didn't want to lie. But she didn't want to tell the whole truth either. She didn't even know what the whole truth was. A strategy came to mind. She could confess a little, and try to make a joke of it. Could she pull it off?

She started by explaining as matter-of-factly as she could that the divorce wasn't causing her malaise—she used the word *malaise* as a concession to truth and to satisfy Meredith. "You know that the divorce was perfectly amicable," she said. "A divorce made in heaven." Rebecca spoke these words with forced jocularity, concealing the bleak echo they brought her of that abysmal night. Meredith laughed, pleased that Rebecca could make light of it. And Meredith said she knew there had to be more to the *malaise* than the divorce from Richard. She had seen it coming on for too long.

"But that's just it," Rebecca continued, trying to convey candor while skating over the darker truth. "I don't know what's wrong. It's amorphous. Made up of a lot of things. Going back a long time probably. And then . . . . Well, I've kind of fallen into the dumps. And I don't yet see how to get out." She was venturing as close to the truth as she could while still avoiding it, chasm that it was. "But I'm working on it. And you'll be the first to know when I figure it out."

Meredith responded with friendly urgings for Rebecca to plumb deeper. "Have you considered that 9/11 could have something to do with how you feel? I know people who have been depressed ever since and can't shake it."

Rebecca paused. "That has occurred to me. And there might be some of that going on. But I don't think I was affected more than most New Yorkers. And besides, that was last fall. It couldn't account for the *malaise* now. But let's not dwell on such things," she said perking up her tone determined to change the subject. "*You're* making me depressed. That's not what you're supposed to do." She said this with an emphasis and a slight smile that gave Meredith encouragement and told her that Rebecca would resist further probing tonight.

"Right," Meredith responded. "I mustn't do that. And it could be just a garden variety mid-life crisis. Make the most of it. Be good to yourself. You need diversions and fun and new people. By all means a new man, or a woman, who knows?"

Rebecca smiled again. And seizing the chance to redirect the conversation to a topic that would amuse Meredith and let her be helpful, she said, "Here's something you *can* do for me." She reached into her bag and took out her pocket calendar. "You can fill me in on someone I agreed to have lunch with as a favor to Sarah Rose. You probably know him, since you know everybody."

"The new man—as prescribed?"

Rebecca shook her head. "No, no. It's business. Sarah asked me to meet one of the authors she represents who has a book idea he wants to pitch. She said she'd set up a lunch for the three of us. I wasn't enthusiastic, but she's a good soul so I gave in."

"Sounds like a set-up to me."

"Sarah wouldn't do that."

"Oh, how sweetly devious friends can be. Especially literary agents."

"Bite your tongue." Rebecca flipped through the calendar and stopped. "His name is Alexander Rodgers. He's written articles and a couple of books on culture and politics. You know anything else about him?"

Meredith took the bait. She searched her memory.

"Alexander Rodgers? Hmmm. Ah, yes. But where? . . . Ah, that's it. I met him at a party last winter. He was talking with Harold Schapiro of the *Times*. They were making fun of our entertainment culture and such things. He's quite good looking. Tallish and thin."

"How *do* you keep track of such data?"

"A mental file. But he also made an impression on me. He seemed peculiarly detached. Aloof. Like he thought everything around him was a charade. It wasn't that he came across as a snob exactly, and certainly not a dour academic. More of a jaded intellectual playboy. Where are you having lunch with them?

"You *would* want to know that." Rebecca reexamined her calendar. "A place called Indochine on 57th Street."

"Good choice. A fancy new Vietnamese/French. Tropical Asian exotica with a French flair."

Rebecca sighed, not much drawn to *tropical Asian exotica*. "Thanks for the character portrait and the other vital facts. You are a trove."

"Anytime. Provided I get a full report to keep my mental file up to date," Meredith joked. Then, with the subject of new men on the table, she decided to take a shot. "I know another guy you should meet. Todd Hilton. He's dreamy-looking, and he's got all of the best credentials and connections, and his future is golden in the business. *And* I heard that he's getting divorced—I never thought his wife was up to him. So you'd have something in common right away, and he'd go for you in a minute. You'd have a great time. You could be a perfect couple. How about it? Let me introduce you."

*Something in common?* Rebecca didn't think so. *A perfect couple?* Hadn't she heard that said about Richard and her? She forced a laugh. "Thanks for the thought. But no matchmaking. I'm not very good company these days anyway, and I don't feel like making the effort."

"Don't be so hasty. Todd would be a super catch for the right woman. You could be it. And there aren't that many fish out there worth catching."

"I don't want a *catch*. I . . ." Rebecca hesitated. "I don't know what I want. But it's not a man. Besides, I've already met Todd Hilton. Not long ago at some gathering. Yes, he's attractive. Nice teeth. He grinned a lot. But he's all corporation. He was holding forth on 'product' and 'e-pubs' and 'tie-ins' and 'synergy'. I never heard him say the words *author* or *book*. That's all I remember. But he wouldn't remember me."

"So you're ahead of me. But don't kid yourself. He's terrific. If you change your mind, I can make him yours. Meanwhile, I'll keep an eye out for other candidates."

"Don't go out of your way."

"It *is* my way."

Shifting the conversation away from herself again, Rebecca pointed out a couple of overdressed nymphets across the room. As she expected, Meredith had ripe observations to make about them, culminating in an ingenious interpretation of the delicious vulgarity of contemporary couture, the delightfully short shelf-life of fashions in contemporary culture, and the pathetic predictability of male desire and folly.

"You really must compile a book of such nuggets," Rebecca said, pleased to see Meredith's imagination safely occupied.

"Oh, my files are overflowing."

From there, people-watching and badinage, stimulated by Meredith's discerning eye and witty commentary, carried them through dinner. Later, after the movie—a romantic comedy that

Meredith had chosen to cheer Rebecca up—they shared acerbic critiques of the admirably acted film but implausible screenplay.

Rebecca kept her mental blinkers on and her performance running smoothly from the beginning of the evening to the end. She had always been good at this kind of thing. It was control. And she was persuading Meredith to believe she was getting control of her *malaise*—or so she persuaded herself. Meredith was not wholly persuaded. They parted with a sisterly embrace and went home—Rebecca satisfied with her performance but fearing that the abyss inside could swallow her anytime, Meredith uncertain of what Rebecca was feeling and what would come next.

And when Rebecca later closed her eyes in bed, images of emptiness returned. Not the blank book this time. Instead, a dim light began flickering across her mind. A movie projector showing a broken film. No picture. Black and white. White and black. Running to the sound of clatter. Her eyes ripped open.

She lay in the pale yellow light of the street lamps reflecting through the window shades from the street. She was used to this nocturnal world, often reading manuscripts in bed and then seamlessly falling asleep. But since that panicked night, these late hours had grown disquieting, leading her from the manageable working day into an anxiously threatening darkness. And now, lying there, her eyes wide open, watching the reflected headlights from passing cars momentarily sharpen and then shift the shadows of the room, and hearing the accompanying low rumble of tires on the road, she saw the ceiling above her become another empty screen with an old projector showing a broken film. Like the one in her mind.

She shuddered and shut her eyes tight. But the screen of her mind continued flickering. She wanted to shout to the projectionist, Fix it! Turn it off! And it came to her that this could be how deranged people get started carrying on loud conversations with themselves on the sidewalk—talking to the shadows, and their fears, alone, late at night.

Finally, she was able to mentally drag her desk calendar onto the flickering screen. Examining the items in it, she slowly left the ghostly film and lost herself in the dates and names and obligations, counting her sheep. And eventually they led her into a saving sleep.

# 4

## A Way Out?

*

A weekend of fitful work broken by brief diversions, and bad-gered by bouts of lonely fears and struggles with searching, unanswerable questions delivered Rebecca to another week at the office with manuscripts to read, letters to write, and meetings with colleagues on book prospects and books in production. This was a role she could play, even if she didn't want to do it. And it was almost therapeutic. Like denial.

But it took more will than she had expected. She was noticeably distracted. Her memory slipped. She misplaced things. She showed up very late for another editorial meeting, to be greeted by Henry's ostentatious throat-clearing. And again she spoke little at the meeting, deferring to others whom she said had a better grasp than she did of the topics under discussion.

Henry was bewildered. "I can always count on you, Rebecca, for a sharp on-target appraisal of anything," he had once told her. "You're our point-woman and compass." But he had noticed uncharacteristic dips in her energy over recent months. Now he began thinking that maybe she did need time off, no matter what she thought.

"I've got it!" Meredith announced as she pushed open the door to Rebecca's office Wednesday afternoon. "I'm going to organize a cocktail party this Friday after work in the fabulous lounge down the elegant winding stairway at Brasserie 57. I turn forty exactly six months from then—paving the way for you, by the way—and I thought we should start giving our Thirties a last hurrah with a summer celebration. It'll be great fun. You have to come. It'd help you be your old self again. Your drinks will be on me. You might even meet someone irresistible."

*Be your old self again.* The phrase resounded in Rebecca, as did many others these days. What does it mean? *Old self?* Self-deception? Unconscious emptiness? That's her *old self*, isn't it? That's not who she wanted to be. But she didn't want to be who she was now, either, trapped in her *dilemma.* Would bubbly talk about impending birthdays with acquaintances and strangers in another fashionable restaurant help her find a way out of it? Not likely. But very New York. She started to frame a civil rejection. Then she thought better of it. Meredith was trying to be kind, and Rebecca didn't want to disappoint her friend, who had no doubt contrived this event largely for her. They would turn forty within a month of each other, and this was one of Meredith's typically spirited gestures of friendly affinity—and attempts at therapy. She should go. It would make Meredith happy. And it probably couldn't do herself any harm. It would at least give her an escape from her dilemma for a while. After all, the weekend promised *nothing.* Rebecca shrank from the word. She said she would come.

The phone rang, and as Rebecca reached for it Meredith left the office giving a thumbs up. It was Catherine Ravitch, a rising professorial star at Barnard College who had written a popular book on feminism that Rebecca had acquired and brought out to wide critical acclaim and respectable commercial success. They had become casual friends.

"How are you?" Catherine asked.

"Fine," Rebecca lied. "And you?"

"Are you sure? You weren't quite yourself when I saw you last."

Did everybody see it? Rebecca asked herself. Even before the worst of it? Was she the only one who hadn't seen it before? She had thought she was deceiving everybody. But they weren't deceived. So, was she an object of pity? She couldn't stand that. But what could she do? What could she say? Except perhaps, as with Meredith, to offer a partial admission masking the deeper truth.

"Just tending to a garden-variety mid-life crisis, as a friend of mine calls it. Any psycho-horticultural advice?" she said with what she took to be convincing candor and deflecting wit. "And don't give me Dorothy Parker's—'You can lead a whore to culture . . .'"

"I wouldn't have thought of it," Catherine laughed.

"Fat chance."

"I could give you a few cases of life-crises in literature."

The ploy was working. Now they could talk about literature. "I'm all ears."

"When Dante found himself in a 'dark place' of middle life, he went to Hell."

"Oh, thanks."

"But he wound up in paradise."

"I'd never make it."

"Or there's Tolstoy's Anna Karenina. She took a lover."

"She had a bad marriage and wound up throwing herself under a train."

"OK. Not so good. But there's her brother-in-law Levin, who resolves his life-crisis by turning to God and the spirit and the peasants."

"He never convinced me."

"How about Ivan Ilych? He . . ."

"Don't mention him," Rebecca spoke up before Catherine could finish.

"Well, try Thomas Mann's Aschenbach. He goes to Venice."

"Where he dies in a cholera epidemic."

"But blissfully on a beach—for the love of beauty."

"That's comforting."

"Moving on, there's Updike's Rabbit Angstrom. He just runs away."

"Catherine. Enough! You overwhelm me with your morbid erudition. You make me prosaically normal by comparison."

"So it worked."

"A grim therapy."

"That's literature for you. But all kidding aside, Rebecca, I hope you are feeling better. And I called to ask you a favor."

"What can I do for you?" Rebecca responded welcomingly, relieved to be off the hook again.

Catherine explained that her younger sister, Gena, had just graduated from college in the mid-west, where their family lived, and was now in New York searching for a job in publishing with no success. She was smart, hard-working, an A student, likeable, bent on proving herself professionally. She would be happy to start at the bottom. Did Rebecca have any suggestions? Engaged by the prospect of helping her friend, Rebecca offered to talk to Gena and make some inquiries. Catherine thanked her, adding that Gena could use any guidance.

"I'm in your debt for those dreadful literary role models," Rebecca said, keeping up the ruse of jocularity.

"I'll try to come up with more, if you'd like."

"Not for me. But that could be your next book."

"Such an ingenious editor. How deftly you needle your authors."

"So when will you get me the manuscript?"

Catherine laughed. "The pressure, the pressure."

"The horror, the horror," Rebecca replied with mock gravity.

"You think Kurtz was going through a mid-life crisis?"

"A novel interpretation. Make a note for your book."

Ending the banter, Catherine said she would have Gena call right away. The phone rang only minutes after they hung up. It was Gena. She quickly impressed Rebecca with her articulate intelligence, eagerness, and maturity. And Rebecca wanted to give her a boost. Rebecca said she would ask a few people and let Gena know what she learned. Then they could take it from there.

As soon as their conversation ended, Rebecca set herself to the task. It took her mind off other things and gave her a satisfyingly selfless purpose. She spoke to the director of Human Resources at her firm, who knew of no openings for a neophyte, as she put it, but, at Rebecca's urging, said she would look further into it. Then Rebecca called Henry to make an appeal. One of their most **p**rominent and **p**roductive young academic authors, she told him, has a **p**recocious and **p**romising sister willing to work for **p**eanuts for an o**pp**ortunity to **p**rove herself in **p**ublishing—she stressed each alliterative **P** to get his attention. She said she thought they should do what they could for her, adding the remark that this emphatically alliterative request alone should earn his consideration. Encouraged by the apparently renewed spirit, if arch manner, in Rebecca's voice, Henry said he would endorse hiring the young woman on Rebecca's recommendation, *despite* the shameless alliteration, if they could find a lowly enough place for her to start. Rebecca lauded his big heart. Then she spoke to the head of Human Resources again, assuring her that Henry was on board if they could carve out a little niche for Gena somewhere. An editorial assistant would be the right thing. Of course, Rebecca would want to meet Gena before they created a job, but she was already confident of her.

By the end of the day, Rebecca informed Gena of the situation, trying to keep her expectations low, but nevertheless eliciting expressions of surprise and exclamations of thanks—as well as mention of the complimentary things Catherine had said about Rebecca. There probably wouldn't be anything more to report until next week, Rebecca wound up, but they agreed to meet at Rebecca's office in the meantime to become acquainted.

The most gratifying task of the day completed, Rebecca left the office feeling better than she had all week. And it occurred to her that she might have chosen to help Gena not just because of Catherine but because Gena reminded her of herself at that age. So able and eager. Then she remembered Meredith's stabbing words—*be your old self.* Meredith's phrase and the questions it spawned about where *her old self* had gone wrong brought her back to her dilemma. And they led her to hope nothing like that would happen to Gena.

Or does everyone go through this kind of thing at some time? she wondered. When you lose your way and find yourself in a patch of life where nothing makes sense—where you are, how you got there, and how to get out? Is that the garden variety mid-life crisis? But other people don't suddenly feel as though they have lived no life and have no life to live, do they? They don't collapse in panic, do they? And if they do suffer this, or something like it, how do they get out of it?

She called to mind Catherine's literary examples. What were they?—take a trip, take a lover, kill yourself, or just run away?

Trips and running away don't work, or not for long. You can't escape yourself. Well, maybe Aschenbach did, but look at what happened to him. As for Dante, Rebecca already was in a kind of Hell, but with no salvation in Paradise on the itinerary. Besides, salvation requires religious faith, and she'd never had it, thanks to her skeptical, free-thinking parents and her seemingly untroubled life. And even if she could take up religion, wouldn't it be false to do it now? "Never trust fox-hole conversions," her father had warned her. "Especially in yourself. They're one of God's tasteless temptations to test our will. If you want religion, do it in good times. That's the honest way, if there is one." That was about the extent of her religious training—irreverent theology and personal ethics. And she couldn't give it up.

A lover? Not likely. Not now. She would have to pretend to feel things she didn't feel. Not just physically but in every way. Or could a man change that, banish the emptiness and fear and lead her out of the dilemma? That is pathetic, she scolded herself. So predictable. A venerable remedy for loneliness, but it never really works, and can leave you worse off. Think of Anna Karenina.

Kill yourself, as Anna finally did? You can't go wrong with that. It has a clean finality to it. It's a definitive way out—even from a dilemma. She suspected most people contemplate suicide sooner or later. They say most adolescents do—and a fair number act on it. The first encounters with real life in those years can make you bitter with failed expectations, grotesque humiliations, and hopeless dreams, making suicide a bold gesture of existential rebellion against a fallen world that you know very little about.

A girl a year older than Rebecca in a neighboring town had done it. Killed herself. In tenth grade. The girl's social clique had turned on her, claiming she had become fat and ugly and now dimmed their luster. They threw her out, and pilloried her socially. On a lonely Saturday night, she got into a full warm bath, swallowed a handful of her mother's sleeping pills with a large glass of her father's rum diluted with Coke, and slid effortlessly under the water to sleep. Rebecca hadn't understood why anyone would do that. How anyone could get so undone. Now, for the first time, she understood. She wasn't an adolescent with a cruel social clique to blame. But she understood. Should she do it? Not tonight. But she had to find a way out.

⁓

The stylish lounge and bar at the base of the brasserie's grandly modern circular staircase was buzzing with Friday revelers when Rebecca descended it just after six o'clock. She hadn't expected so many people to be there on a summer weekend. Shouldn't they be out in the Hamptons? Meredith, who had left the office early to play hostess, promptly came up to her offering a glass of wine and leading her to a large gathering in one area of the lounge where Meredith joked about birthdays and introduced a few people, and from there they moved on to a pair of men on the side talking and eyeing the crowd throughout the lounge.

"This is Jeremy Blevin," Meredith said, "whom I lured here from London as my date on his way to California. And I think you have met Todd Hilton." Todd Hilton grinned.

Rebecca shot Meredith a swift visual reproach. So that's what she's up to. Oh, Meredith, she thought, you are nothing if not persistent. But Rebecca decided to go along, telling herself she should do it for good-hearted Meredith, and to try to forget herself for a while. Besides, there was nothing waiting for her at home—that baleful *nothing*. And before long, enticed by vague hopes, welcomed by convivial company, and braced by Meredith's generous refills of wine, Rebecca found herself more involved in social life than she had been for weeks.

It turned out that Todd Hilton had indeed separated from his wife some time ago and was awaiting their divorce. His estranged wife was now staying in their Bridgehampton vacation house while he was batching it for the summer in the city. "Alas," he feigned a sigh through a grin. He did grin a lot. But he was more engaging than Rebecca had remembered him. Not all corporate and pompous and oily. He could talk about more than "tie-ins" and "synergy" and such, and he could do it with intelligence and wit. Although obviously quite fond of himself, he also gave Rebecca all the attention she could have wanted, if she had thought of wanting any. He was rather charming after all, she conceded. Or was it the wine?

Her submission to Meredith's friendly scheming, and to the wine, and to the conviviality did make Rebecca forget herself. And, when the cocktail party was over, that submission led her into an evening of dining in the restaurant with Meredith and the two men. The dinner went on and on, carried by wine and conversation. And the thought crossed Rebecca's mind that she might be "getting out" after all.

After dinner, Todd Hilton graciously offered to escort Rebecca home. She did not decline. She even unthinkingly acceded to his request for a nightcap. In her living room, partly from the wine—more than she was used to but had allowed herself as an experiment in escapism—partly from the search for ways out of her emotional wasteland, she indulged his mildly amorous compliments and physical proximity. Then came an unexpected kiss.

As if waking from a dream, Rebecca shook off the effects of the wine and the evening. She pulled away.

"No. Todd. Please." She said both firmly and plaintively. "I'm sorry. This isn't right. I shouldn't have. I don't know why. Please, I'm sorry if I . . . Forgive me."

Baffled and visibly wounded, Todd Hilton sat up and rapidly composed himself. He wasn't used to this, he said proudly. Perhaps he had misread the signs. He apologized. But he didn't want anyone who didn't want him. If she decided otherwise, she could give him a call. He gave her his card. And he grinned as he left the apartment, as if to play over the incident, or as if the evening were only beginning for him.

Rebecca sat on the sofa feeling a chill. Could she have thought *that* was the way out? She had even dismissed it only hours earlier. No, this evening she hadn't actually *thought* at all. Could she have been one of those women who invite men into their lives to feel good about themselves or to escape from themselves? She had never imagined herself that way. Could she have done that with Richard? But, if she had, it hadn't worked. Or had it worked for a while? Anyway, Todd Hilton was no Richard. Whatever her motives, conscious or not, how could she have made such a blunder? Was it the wine? No doubt. But there had to be more to it than that.

Dozy from the wine and the hour, Rebecca fell asleep quickly. On awakening late the next morning, she groggily brought herself to life with vague memories of last night. What was that all about? Crawling sluggishly out of bed nursing a headache and ashamed of letting herself go so far at that party and with that smarmy, self-important male, she told herself that at least she had avoided the haunting images for one night. Still, she added besotted socializing to her mental list of predictable, but ultimately futile, ways out of her dilemma.

She drank some juice and coffee and puttered around. Then, still stung by shame, she pulled herself together and called Meredith to thank her for the party, to apologize for getting tipsy, and to deflect the inevitable questions about Todd Hilton without faulting Meredith's intentions.

"You were right." she answered with as much nonchalance as she could muster to the first eager question. "He's an impressive guy. But he's not for me. And I'm not for him."

"Why do you say that? You seemed to be having a good time. What happened?"

"Let's say we exhausted the possibilities in a single evening."

"I don't believe it. You can't say that."

"Yes, I can. In fact, I let the evening go farther than it should have. You were sweet to try. But, please, Meredith, no more Todd Hiltons. Maybe somebody else sometime, when . . . I'm ready." But she didn't know what that would mean.

"You don't expect me to do nothing when I see a friend in need, do you?" Meredith responded with a measure of self-mockery.

"God forbid. I would never expect that. Or want it. But I'll let you know when I know what I need. Meanwhile, my dear, let me wish you a happy half-year birthday again."

Dearest Meredith, Rebecca repeated to herself after they had said goodbye. Meredith saw so much, and tried so hard, but sometimes understood so little. And now Rebecca felt herself hungering to confide in someone else. Catherine's dismal literary anecdotes came to mind. But Catherine was too young and too much of an intellectual to empathize and understand. What about her mother, whom she visited occasionally in Connecticut, and whom she could talk to freely, and who seemed to understand more than Rebecca ever told her? No. Rebecca was too confused and ashamed. Ashamed? Why should she be ashamed?—except about last night. The parent-child syndrome? Parental expectations of perfection that children feel they have to meet, whether their parents have those expectations or not? No, she didn't think that was it. Still, for some reason, she felt ashamed to talk to her mother about her *dilemma*. She would see her mother soon. But she wasn't ready yet.

There was Sarah Rose. She was older, as close to Rebecca's mother's age as to her own. They had talked many times about many things since becoming professional friends ten or more years ago. Rebecca had been quite drawn to her. Although Sarah belonged to Rebecca's professional world, she was a motherly type, unpretentious, sensitive, insightful, and caring. Rebecca admitted to herself that maybe this is what she needed. And they were having lunch to catch up before their later meeting with Sarah's author, Alexander Rodgers.

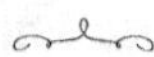

"You look especially nice today," Sarah greeted Rebecca as she sat down in a restaurant on 21st Street and 5th Avenue where agents and editors often congregated.

"Thanks, Sarah, but you're too generous. It arouses suspicion." Rebecca smiled, but not quite naturally.

"Generosity is the least we have to fear from man or beast—didn't Auden say that?"

"I think his word was 'indifference,'" Rebecca answered good-naturedly.

"Ah, yes. It's truer to life. More like Auden. So, how are you? When we last got together you seemed kind of distant. You denied it, but I didn't believe you."

They *do* know, Rebecca said to herself. Everybody knows. Is it a conspiracy? I *am* pathetic. "From generosity to accusations before the *hors d'oeuvres?*" she retorted with feigned affront.

They shared a friendly laugh and ordered lunch. Rebecca inquired about Sarah's grown children, now into their lives after college—a son in New York aspiring to be an actor, "still regularly getting rave reviews as a waiter," Sarah joked, and a daughter working as a publicist in Los Angeles. "The curse of show business has fallen over my family," Sarah said with arch resignation and transparently veiled pride at her children's ambitions and independence.

After other pleasantries, Sarah began describing a handful of book proposals that she had been discussing with her authors. Rebecca registered a certain interest, but she had to contrive much of it. None of this mattered to her as it used to. Sarah sensed this and stopped talking. She saw more than distraction in Rebecca now. She looked Rebecca straight in the eye.

"All right, Rebecca. Let's get down to it. You're not just distracted. You're depressed. What's wrong?"

Having all but openly solicited the question, Rebecca did not shrink from it. She had to make herself do it, and after a short silence drew herself up unsure of where to start or how far to go.

"Oh, I don't know, Sarah." She held her eyes on the small flower vase in the center of the table, stroking the petal of a rose in it with one finger. She spoke slowly. "Have you ever had a time in your life when you peered into yourself and didn't like what you saw? No . . . when you didn't see anything?"

"I've tried to avoid such risky ventures," Sarah replied with a tone of companionable self-deprecation.

"I'm not kidding," Rebecca lifted her eyes to Sarah's. "I mean just . . . nothing. As though nobody's there."

"I can't say I have, not exactly," Sarah said seriously.

"Well, that's what's happened to me. I can't explain it. But . . . it's frightening."

"That's it? You feel like *nothing*? Are you sure it's not over-work, boredom, aging, your divorce, or any of the standard causes of depression at this time of life? Or even the attack on New York and the sorry condition of the world?"

Rebecca fidgeted. "I'm not sure of anything anymore. But I think it goes beyond any of that."

"Forgive me for asking, but have you tried the conventional cures—novelty, rebellion, travel, adventure, romance, and so on?"

"You're not the first to ask. And, yes, I guess I made a foray. It only made things worse."

"Have you considered motherhood?"

"What? Me? I've never thought much about having children. And it's not something you just do on your own, or most women don't. Besides, I doubt I'd be good at it. And certainly not now. You have any other, less complicated, suggestions?"

"You'd be better at it than you think. Or how about a shrink?"

"That's *your* role, isn't it?" Rebecca gave a wan smile.

"You can't go to your friends for therapy. Too much baggage on both sides. Let me give you my therapist's name. A terrific woman. Margeurite Sendak. She's seen and heard everything. And, for one thing, she's helped several people I know deal with the aftermath of September 11th. Maybe. . . ."

Cutting her off, Rebecca said, "*You* see a shrink?"

"Doesn't everybody—except you? I go only when I have to talk to someone about things that are bothering me. I don't make a fetish of it."

Sarah wrote the name and phone number on a slip of paper and handed it across the table. Rebecca took it.

"You'll be amazed what she can do for you. Much more than I ever could. And think how good that will make *me* feel."

Rebecca slid the paper into her purse thinking Sarah was an exemplary Jewish mother—doling out kindness and guilt with velvet gloves. But the therapist would be a last resort. Or close to it.

"Oh, another thing you can do for me," Sarah added, playing to Rebecca's natural decency. "I meant to get to this earlier. It's about the lunch we're having on the 12th with Alexander Rodgers. As I've told you, I want a new book out of him, and he has an idea for one. But now I've got a conflict. Will you go ahead and meet with him anyway? I'm sure you'll find him entertaining."

Taken aback, Rebecca stalled. "Oh, Sarah, I don't think so. Can't we put it off until you can be there?"

Sarah pressed. "Please, Rebecca. You won't be bored. He's very intelligent, a good writer, and one of the most interesting people I know. But he is malingering and, well, rather unpredictable. You could move things along."

Rebecca recalled the evening with Todd Hilton. Not another meeting with a man arranged by a friend, even for professional reasons.

"Be a pal, will you?" Sarah persevered. "I'd really appreciate it. You might inspire him."

Rebecca faced Sarah without speaking, remembering that Sarah had been through her own doses of troubles. Her son had been into drugs for a while, and her husband had died of cancer two years ago. But she hadn't asked for pity. There was nothing *pathetic* about Sarah. Rebecca respected that, and it made her doubt herself the more. How could she refuse Sarah's insistent request without seeming selfish? Sarah was a generous and valuable friend. Rebecca managed a small smile.

"If you insist, Sarah. I'll do it. For *you*. But don't expect me to be a muse for this guy. Or even *a-musing*." The pun came automatically.

"Aha! A bad pun. You sound nearly like your old self again."

*Old self?* Not that. Meredith's nagging phrase once more. It *is* a conspiracy. But they've got it wrong, Rebecca said to herself. There is no going back—to the *old self.* And yet, where is a way out? They embraced and promised to speak again after the scheduled lunch.

# 5

## *Flâneur*

Rebecca was still trapped in her *dilemma* and felt like she was almost sleepwalking through much of her daily routine when noon arrived on the day slated for the obligatory lunch. She resignedly freshened her makeup, combed her brown above-the-shoulder-length hair, snatched up her purse, and took the elevator to the street where she pushed through the revolving doors into the unusually warm damp June air. Walking as briskly as she could tolerate in the heat, she remembered what Meredith and Sarah had said about Alexander Rodgers. But she didn't care about that. She just wanted to get through lunch as fast as she could.

Sticky from the humidity, she was feeling less than cordial when she entered the cool, tropical restaurant invoking colonial Saigon—white-tiled walls adorned with marbled mirrors and period photographs, ceiling fans rotating slowly, palm trees arrayed among rattan chairs and linen covered tables. The maître d' ushered her to where a middle-aged man with graying hair and a tanned, lean face exuding an urbane air sat with a tall drink at a banquette along the wall. He got up as she came near.

"Ah, you are Rebecca Winters? I'm Alex Rodgers."

He extended an arm across the table and they shook hands. She said a single word: "Hello." Before she could sit down in the outside chair, he said, "Oh, please. You must sit on the banquette side. So you can see the room. I was only sitting here so I could see you when you came in."

"It doesn't matter."

"It does to me," he said with a gentlemanly smile. "I'd be uncomfortable if you had to face the wall."

"If you say so," she replied indifferently. He stepped out from the banquette, pulled the table aside, and directed her around it, moving his drink and taking the outside chair for himself when she was seated. An odd touch of gallantry, or affectation, she thought.

"Will you have a drink?" he asked. "Forgive me for starting. I just had to have a gin and tonic while I sat here in old Indochina amid the palms, with the first heat of summer in the air outside."

"I'll have a mineral water," she said without inflection.

A disciplined professional, he speculated. "With or without bubbles?" he asked.

"Without," she answered. He signaled a waiter and ordered a large bottle for the table, thinking, "Not even bubbles?" Ordering a Vietnamese beer for himself, he finished the gin and tonic and said to her, "I hope you don't mind if I continue my summer inauguration."

"Go ahead," she said coolly and began examining the menu.

"You like Vietnamese food, I hope," he resumed affably. "I admit that coming here was my idea."

"I haven't sought it out."

"It has many virtues. Not heavy and greasy like Chinese and Indian. And refreshing flavors, lots of mint and cilantro. Here they do Vietnamese with a French touch. Colonial style. Perhaps not quite authentic but the best way."

"Thanks for the review," she responded without raising her eyes from the menu.

"Well, as a great anthropologist once observed," he said blithely, "*food is not just good to eat, it's good to think.*"

"All foodies believe that, don't they?" she remarked with a polite smile, closing the menu and laying it on the table. "I'll just have the chicken salad," she told the waiter, who had returned with the drinks.

"That's all? Could be a mistake," Alex said lightly, and ordered summer rolls and coconut mint shrimp for himself, thinking that she is not going to be the easiest lunch companion.

"You must tire of lunches with authors and would-be authors," he ventured, probing her mood, which seemed distant, and a little testy. Had he got her on a bad day?

"I don't do it all that often," she said casually. "Publishing isn't what it was when Bennett Cerf used to while away afternoons schmoozing with authors in fashionable restaurants. Nowadays we rely more on e-mail and faxes."

"That's rather a loss, isn't it? To the civility of publishing?"

"Possibly. But it saves time and money."

"Well, thank you for consenting to take the time to come here, especially after Sarah canceled." He decided she wasn't inclined to chat. But the testiness in her voice sounded more unnatural than habitual. It was a nice voice, resonant and supple, and he heard more fatigue or preoccupation or something else in it than irritation. Her comely face also appeared a trifle wan, and the distance in her eyes suggested sadness. No, it wasn't her day. Still, she might soften and warm up. He hoped she would, and possibly for more than professional reasons.

"Sarah has said such glowing things about you," he went on, "that I wanted to meet you before writing up a book proposal for you. She said you'd probably be willing if she twisted your arm a little. I'm glad she succeeded. Even though she had to cancel."

"Sarah's a good friend," Rebecca said diplomatically, taking a sip of the mineral water just served. "What have you got in mind?"

"A novel, of course. Doesn't everybody?"

"I hope not," she muttered, idly wiping away with her thumb a trace of her lipstick on the rim of her glass, acknowledging to herself that she was being unnecessarily abrupt.

"It'll have romance and adventure and philosophy," he continued—rather theatrically, she thought.

"You mean something like a Harlequin Romance as written by Tom Clancy and Fyodor Dostoevsky?" she quipped, making an effort to be sociable.

"Ha! Close. But more like, oh, say the Bronte sisters meet Kafka and Somerset Maugham." She chuckled. "Anyway," he continued, "it's about a character, an anthropologist maybe, who thinks about food and everything else"—he smiled broadly—"but who has lost interest in his life. So he cuts himself adrift and goes off to some exotic part of the world where he has adventures and then falls in love with an exceptional woman, and together they start a new life. I'm thinking of calling it *Metamorphosis*, but it'll be closer to Ovid's than to Kafka's—no cockroaches."

His tone and manner were cavalier, and they annoyed her. She didn't entirely know why. She rolled her eyes, partially concealing this by taking another drink. What am I doing here? she asked herself.

"Look, Mr. Rodgers," she said evenly, putting down her glass.

"Call me Alex," he cut her off genially. "I know, I know. It's an old story. A string of clichés. But there are only so many stories to tell. Twenty-two, I think the scholars say."

The waiter arrived with their food. Alex exaggeratedly inhaled the scent of the cilantro in the summer rolls and the mint with the coconut shrimp. "Heavenly. Your must have a taste."

"No thanks. I'm fine." She poked at her salad.

"Well, where was I? Yes, an old story. Doesn't all of world literature come down to some twenty-two story lines? Recycled over and over. You could put every story ever told on a computer and have it sort out the variations, and you'd still come up with only about twenty-two plots—and you've probably read them all."

"I'd have to think about it," she replied, uncertain how to handle him. Part of her wanted to be curt, instructing him on the shallowness of his book idea and on the economics of publishing novels. But it wouldn't be like her to do that. She wasn't prone to slash. Still, she wasn't quite herself anymore. And she wasn't managing her act today as well as she knew she should. Besides, she was doing a professional favor for a friend. She should be gracious and allow his book idea to sink on its own. These thoughts put her more at ease. Gave her more control.

She looked up and said pleasantly, "In fact, there are people who would reduce all stories to two types, comedies and tragedies—those with happy endings and those with unhappy endings. And I'm sure you know the joke about there being only two types of people—those who divide everything into two types and those who don't."

He laughed. The joke and her change of tone encouraged him. She went on with a somewhat strained cordiality, ignoring his request to use his first name. "Story lines aside, Mr. Rodgers, what, may I ask, motivates you to write such a book?"

"Please, it's Alex," he repeated. "Oh, it's another old story. I'm tired of making a living without living a life, as the adage says. Filling my days with seemingly worthwhile pursuits and accomplishments, but still coming up empty. This may not happen to everybody, but it happens to me from time to time. Could be pathological. In any case, writing this self-indulgent novel will give me the change of life I need, at least for a while." He shot her a rather self-deprecating expression.

Rebecca had the discomfiting sensation that he was talking about her. Did *he* know, too? Does it show? Had Sarah told him?

"The truth is, of course," he picked up, noticing a reaction, "it matters less how you live your life than how you feel about it. How you look at it. Don't you think? That might be trite, but it's true."

"So, you rely on the *trite* and *true*?" she jabbed affably, slightly abashed at the bad pun.

Boosted by her making such obvious and rather good

natured fun of him, he laughed again. "Only when I'm at my best. Anyhow," he returned to the theme, "I want to write about someone who breaks out of his life and starts over. What about you? Haven't you ever wanted to do that?"

She gulped and almost choked.

"I mean write a novel about *the meaning of life.*" He stressed the pompousness of the phrase for comic effect and waited for an answer while he concentrated on his lunch.

His words had caught her off guard. They sounded all too familiar. What was going on? And who was he to be asking her about such things? He had no right. Even if she had known what to say, she wouldn't have told him, not here, not now, a stranger who seems to be mocking everything.

She collected herself and answered tersely, "No, I haven't." But, determined to be cordial, for Sarah, and to keep the conversation pointed away from herself, she added civilly, "If you'd like me to look at a draft proposal, send me a synopsis and a sample chapter or two. Then I'll talk to Sarah about it and take it from there. But beware of the shop-worn topic. Doing it fresh won't be easy." Pushing the conversation still farther away from herself, and hoping to flush out a more promising book idea, while getting him to do the talking, she asked, "Now, why don't you tell me what else you've been working on."

Bending to her evident preference for professional topics, he breezily sketched his current writings—a magazine piece here, an essay there—and vented his opinions on contemporary art and culture. While he spoke, she admitted to herself that he was an arresting talker, amusing and erudite, self-effacing if theatrical, and more lively than most authors she knew who have personality only in print. At the same time, he was, as Meredith had reported, oddly detached, as if somehow removed from everything. She didn't know what to make of that. It had annoyed her at first because he seemed to lack seriousness. But while he talked, and she grazed through her lemongrass-seasoned chicken salad, she felt herself unexpectedly easing, her body relaxing, as if she were becoming a bit detached, too, from herself.

He could see it. She *was* softening. And when she lifted her face, and the low tropical light brushed over it, the traces of tension and fatigue he had seen earlier melted away, and he thought he saw taking form in front of him a living Renoir portrait. Yes, he said to himself, she looks like Renoir's Mona Lisa, the portrait of Tilla Durieux, which he had admired many times at the Metropolitan Museum—luminous blue-green eyes, rounded roseate cheeks, and full sensuous lips with their gently uplifted corners suggesting a slight smile that had been born with her. And all radiating an innate warmth. He had to resist staring. Casting a glance at Rebecca's left hand, he saw no wedding ring. He didn't expect one since Sarah had mentioned a recent divorce—while also praising Rebecca's intelligence, professionalism, and generosity—when proposing this lunch, but the act was habitual when he was in the company of a lovely woman. Now he wondered if the divorce could account for the strained manner, testiness, and emotional reserve he had seen earlier.

Hoping to keep her Renoir warmth alive, he cautiously asked if he could put a mildly personal question to her. She resisted spontaneously. But then she made herself assent with the proviso that she might not answer it. Accepting the terms, he told her that because her "elegant and evocative" name, Rebecca Winters, almost exactly matched that of the title character in the du Maurier novel and Hitchcock move *Rebecca*—a favorite of his, he said, for its adroit mystery and sophisticated style—he wanted to know if her parents had intended this. Impressed by his intuition, and deferring to his gentlemanly manner, she related the story. He liked it, and her way of telling it. And he took the further step of asking how she liked being named for a devious fictional character. Not wanting to appear defensive. She joked that she had all of her namesake's malevolent qualities. He laughed and said he doubted it. At least she was performing well now, she thought, in a defensive sort of way.

By the time they had finished their coffee and were preparing to leave, attracted as he was by her beauty and intelligence, urged on as he was by curiosity and challenge, and emboldened as he was by her apparent softening, he had a proposition ready.

"I have one more request to make of you, Ms. Winters, if I may," he said with playful formality.

"Yes?" she responded warily.

"There's a stunning Indian art exhibition opening next week at the Asia Society. Could I persuade you to go see it with me?"

She was startled. This was no social occasion. It was business—for her, despite the largely non-professional conversation. Or had Sarah planned it for other purposes as well, just as Meredith had speculated? And Indian art? She started to say no. But he had anticipated that and acted first.

"Please don't say no. Consider it a professional consultation. It might help with my book proposal. And we can go to an Indian restaurant afterwards. Make an adventure of it. Think of it as a trip to India with no jet lag. An evening of top sights, good food, and you're home by nine, if you wish. And maybe you'd inspire a better book."

Why, she thought, would she do that with this flippant author who, for all she knew was simply on the make? But she didn't immediately decline. "You are something of a con man, aren't you Mr. Rodgers?" she said with a trace of amusement but still disregarding his repeated requests to use his first name.

"I wouldn't deceive you. I promise. It'll be enrapturing, and enlightening, and take you away."

"An exotic escape? You evidently go for those."

"Sure. Wouldn't want to live without 'em. But I don't confine myself to the exotic. I'll take escape any way I can get it."

"That's rather childish isn't it?"

"Not at all. Or it keeps the child in me alive. And culture depends on it. After all, most restaurants give us escape, don't they? And so do art and religion."

"A debatable assertion."

"Good idea! Let's debate it amidst art and religion at the Asia Society, and finish in an excellent Indian restaurant nearby. An escape with stimulating conversation, philosophical enlightenment, and good food."

She scowled at his overwrought attempt at persuasion. "I don't . . ." she started weakly.

Cutting off a rejection, he retreated to diplomacy. "Please. May I call you later and try once more? That would give you a chance to think about it—and get used to the idea."

Get used to it? What did that mean? And yet, in spite of herself, she didn't dismiss his second request. She didn't know why, except that it would please Sarah if she accepted. Rebecca said he could call, and gave him her card.

He received it with a hearty smile. "I'll not abuse the privilege."

The waiter brought the check, and Rebecca picked it up with one hand while taking her wallet from her purse with the other.

"Oh, this is mine," he said, reaching for the check. "You're already doing me the favor of being here."

"It's business," she said emphatically, pulling a credit card from her wallet.

He backed off. "Next time's on me."

She registered no response.

"Thank you so much for the lunch and conversation," he said as they went outside. "Far superior to e-mails and faxes. Now you *must* call me Alex. And may I call you Rebecca? I do so like the name. And the story."

She gave him a slight nod with a small smile. They shook hands and parted

Waiting for the light at Park Avenue, Rebecca could hardly believe she had virtually agreed to see this frivolous man again for such faint professional reasons. Well, he'll never write that novel. As Meredith had said, he's an intellectual playboy. Still, he did have a provocative mind, a nice face, and an easy charm. But what did he really want from her?

After watching Rebecca disappear into the flood of lunchtime pedestrians, Alexander Rodgers noticed that he had a couple of hours before meeting one of his "sources" for a magazine article he was writing on contemporary architecture in New York. He decided to walk. He often did this in the city. Walking and watching and thinking. The city was good for that. The ceaseless waves of traffic, the rivers of people, the general hurly-burly sweeping everything along made it easy to be alone, without being isolated. To be an observer, a voyeur, secretly observing the swirl, eyeing curiosities, and thinking about—anything. He sometimes looked at himself from afar as a *flâneur*, that creature of the modern city whom he thanked Poe and Baudelaire for immortalizing, endlessly wandering up and down the streets and avenues, swimming with the flow, a fish in the urban sea, anonymous, unnoticed, but noticing. A *flâneur* who had never truly connected with anyone.

Or not many. Alexander Rodgers had some friends. And he had enjoyed his share of love affairs. But most of those had fizzled. The women had tried too hard, or had given too little, or had expected too much. He had even been married for a while. Until one day his wife had said: "The trouble with you. Alex, is that you don't need anyone. You're so removed, so indifferent. Nothing seems to affect you. I'm not like that. I want someone to need me more than life itself." And then she was gone.

She didn't really know him. The others didn't either. But she was half right, he had conceded. Maybe he didn't need anyone. Not like that. And yet, he denied that he was *indifferent*. Detached, perhaps, but not indifferent. Indifference is cold. And he wanted *to burn always with a hard gemlike flame, to maintain this ecstasy—that is success in life.* He'd recited Walter Pater's line many times, because he wanted to believe you could burn with that hard gemlike flame and still be detached.

This isn't a contradiction, he liked to tell his friend Conrad Goldman, a skeptical psychotherapist. It's the Buddhism of everyday life. Detached ecstasy, ecstatic detachment. It delighted Alexander Rodgers to think and say things like that. And to live his own life, in his own way, even with its discontents, whatever anyone else thought of it.

This *Buddhism of everyday life* had also nourished in him by now a certain cynicism about the world and other people, which he cloaked in a debonair *joie de vivre*. He indulged his appetites excessively, spurned conventions brazenly, and burned his bridges willfully—with *detachment*. And his heroes had always been loners, or close to it, although they usually paid a hard price. Lonely cowboys, like Shane in the movie, and those rueful characters in country songs, free but lonely, all part of the American myth of the male individualist without attachments, without a past, or with a past hidden in shadows—Jay Gatsbys all. Taking a little license, he admired Melville's Bartleby for the same reason, for stubbornly refusing to submit to the world's demands, for being willing to lose everything, because Bartleby could say to every request made of him, however reasonable it might be, "I prefer not to," even if it finally took him to his grave. He also applauded Dostoevsky's Underground Man for proving with random self-destructive acts that he couldn't be "played like a piano key," and Don Quixote for inventing a new life in middle age, often making a fool of himself, while nevertheless proving the uses of ideals. Alexander Rodgers' personal mythology had many fictional heroes, adopted as he chose. And he emulated them all, in his way.

But walking off that afternoon, a *flâneur* plying the urban sea, he was not thinking of himself or his personal mythology, or about the city around him that he loved. He was thinking of the woman who had just left him. Cool and distant as she had been most of the time, she had an arresting appeal to his searching eye, to his inquisitive mind, and to his *ecstatic detachment*. He couldn't fathom her. She had a quick intellect, a sharp wit, and an easy graciousness when she turned it on. And there was that Renoir face with its inborn Mona Lisa curl of a smile. Anyone with that much of a Renoir portrait in her had to have a lot of natural warmth. Nature's sensuality. And she couldn't suppress it, or not completely, although she had tried.

But that wasn't all that attracted him. She also emanated an aura of ambiguity, enigma, and mystery. This came through an air of remoteness, verging on sadness, that hung over her, a recurrent avoidance in her eyes, and a supple voice that he guessed could modulate a word in a dozen intonations, saying far more than the words themselves. He suspected that her mind didn't miss a thing, and that her emotions went deep into tangled banks. And yet she exposed only a fraction of what was in her. Why? Would he ever know?

# On a Bridge of Dreams

(Continued)

Rebecca awoke befuddled in a huge, stark room. Groggily squinting around in the thin light, she saw beds arrayed side by side from wall to wall. Three or four white-coated figures moved about among them. A dank medical scent suffused the air. Where was she? Why was she here? Then it began coming back to her in a kaleidoscope of images. The Taj Mahal. The explosion. The bedlam. She bolted up, but quickly fell back with a stabbing pain.

One of the white-coated figures approached her bed. "Awake?" asked the doctor in a refined Anglo-Indian accent.

"What? . . . What happened? Where am I?" She slurred the words.

"A bomb. Terrorists. You are in a hospital in Agra."

"My God!" She shut her eyes. Images rushed into her mind of the shock and loss in New York on that September day not much over a year ago now that had changed the world. And here she had come half-way around the globe into another cataclysm. But this time she hadn't remained at a distance from it to suffer only emotional wounds, as she had in New York. She had been physically thrown into the tragedy's midst. Alex! His name shot through her mind. Where was he? She strained to see if he lay in one of the beds beside her. Patients wrapped like herself lay on both sides. Their long hair told her they were women. "Where is he?" she asked the doctor urgently. "My friend. He was wounded. Please. Is he all right? Where is he?"

"Let us attend to you."

"Please! I must know," she coaxed.

Ignoring her supplication, the doctor raised the sheet and examined the dressings that patched her side and bound her leg down to her knee. She didn't remember getting them. But she didn't remember coming to the hospital either. "Some fragments," he said. "but not too deep, except in your leg. We removed them and stitched the wounds. You will be in some pain, and it will be difficult to walk for a while, But you will recover." He gave her another shot of anesthetic.

"Terrorists?" she asked haltingly, trying to gain some poise. "Who?"

"Probably Hindu or Moslem fanatics. Over Kashmir. Or other grievances. They have been killing each other and innocent victims for centuries."

Her thoughts reverted. "Will you help me find him?" she stammered to the doctor. "Please. An American. Alexander Rodgers. Please!"

"I don't know of him. We have so many people here injured in the attack. From so many places. We do not know who they all are. I will inquire. But you will have to wait. I will find him when I can."

"Please! I must know."

"Yes. Yes. When I can," he repeated. "Now you rest." And he left, against her entreaties, to attend to other patients.

Rebecca wanted to leap out of bed and find Alex herself. But she could hardly move. And she was growing woozy again.

Some time later, she awakened to a room quieter than before. She sat up as well as she could, wincing at the pain. Through the *dim light of bare bulbs dangling from the high ceiling and reflected in the darkness now outside windows, her eyes fell upon the bed on one side of hers, where a pallid face poked from the sheets, and then onto the next, where a woman lay in a body cast, then onto another, and another, on down the row of shrouded, seemingly sleeping, forms, and on to the nurses' station where a fluorescent desk lamp glared into an empty chair.*

*Where are they? Don't they care? And where is he? Is he alive? Why don't they tell me? Oh God! she thought. Any god. Don't let him die.*

*Any god? She had never believed in any god. But Alex did, didn't he? No, not really. Gods were like romance to him. An imaginative invention that embellishes life. The two of them had argued about such things many times. Religion as art. Illusion as truth. Life as fantasy and melodrama. The romance of it all. Did he ever take anything more seriously than that? He said he did, but . . . . And that's how it had begun with him. Arguing about all of that.*

*Drifting in and out of sleep, she kept reliving a mélange of sights and sounds and feelings. They took her back again to her last sight of Alex, with his shadowy smile and whispered word, then back to the happy day before that at the temples of Khajuraho, and earlier to the palm reader in Varanasi and to the other palmist they had visited in Atlantic City, where Rebecca had surprisingly agreed to come to India with him, and on back to that evening in June when for unknown reasons she had gone to meet him at the Asia Society.*

# 6

## *Shiva's Dance*

Afine June rain was laying a slick on the sidewalk of upper Park Avenue when Rebecca got out of the cab in front of the Asia Society. Dispensing with her umbrella, she quickly made her way to the entrance and went through, unsettled in her feelings and wondering why she had let herself get drawn into this misadventure.

After her lunch with Alexander Rodgers, Rebecca had returned to the office that day to find Meredith predictably poised for an interrogation. Did Rebecca "like" him? Were Meredith's impressions of him accurate? Was Rebecca going to see him again? Rebecca reminded her that it had been only a professional lunch for a friend. But to humor her, Rebecca had granted that, as usual, Meredith had hit the mark. He was kind of an intellectual playboy with an air of detachment. And she didn't know if she could take him seriously. But, yes, she did find him somewhat interesting. And, she acknowledged with studied indifference, that she probably would see him again since she had promised to look at his draft book proposal. Meredith had been glad to hear this, although she hadn't seen much in Rebecca's response.

But Rebecca had never revealed feelings very conspicuously. And lately she had revealed almost no feelings at all beyond a disconnected vacancy. Meredith would have to wait and watch for more.

Sarah had been grateful to Rebecca for having lunch in her absence with Alex, as she called him, and she had been happy to learn that Rebecca had given him her card and was expecting a call. This gave Rebecca the minor satisfaction of doing something for Sarah. But Rebecca didn't shrink from telling Sarah that she doubted this author was very serious about his so-called book, or about anything else, for that matter, unsettling her some. "I told you he's rather unusual, didn't I?" Sarah had responded. "Possibly a bit flaky. But he's talented, interested in all kinds of things, and great fun. I adore him and thought you would enjoy his company. And, as I said, your influence could spur him on, able editor that you are. Just give him some time, will you?" Rebecca had said she would talk to him and see.

He had called later that week and had persuaded her to have a drink with him after work at a nearby hotel bar to give him a second audition, he cracked, for his book idea and for winning her company for an evening in India. She had hesitantly but surprisingly consented, for Sarah, or so she had told herself yet again, and he had met her there chary of her uncertain emotions, not wanting to give her a ready excuse to withdraw and reject his earlier invitation. So he had tried to put her at ease by subduing his usual glib, loquacious style, and by playing carefully to her mood, which was again rather distant but wavering, not cold. The conversation had touched on his book proposal—in progress, he assured her—on books she had acquired, on people they knew in common, on events of the day, and on the still nearly ubiquitous subject in New York over the past nine months, September 11th, which she said had affected her in ways she could not quite describe, and which he said had aroused in him an intense, if amorphous, anger that had erupted erratically and still simmered, and they both said they preferred not to dwell on it anymore. By the time his second drink, and her first, were gone, and she had declined another, he had thought it prudent to let her say good night without imposing himself further. But before letting her go he had suggested giving her his book proposal during the "exotically escapist" evening at the Asia Society and an Indian restaurant afterwards, if she would accept his invitation. It would be an early evening he had guaranteed her, in the mid-week if she would like. Eased by his civility and restraint— or was it merely contrived "charm"?—although still discomfited by his occasional flamboyance, and for Sarah's sake once more, or for some other nameless reason, she had accepted.

⚬────⚬

Alexander Rodgers came up to Rebecca from the Asia Society bookstore off the lobby feeling quite proud of himself for the minor victory of attracting her here. He greeted her amiably, apologized for the weather, and thanked her for braving it.

"No one's fault. Nature's tears," she muttered as he helped her off with her rain coat.

Her words startled him. "Nature's tears?" he repeated. "Poetic, but a doleful view of life."

"Only a phrase, not a philosophy," she replied, unsure why she had said it, and a little sorry, as she shook raindrops from her hair.

He tried to read her while they checked her coat and umbrella at the cloak room. Ambiguous again. Testy? Or Playful?

"I didn't ask if you like Indian art," he said, changing the subject as they started toward the gallery.

"I don't know much about it. I trust I'll find enlightenment tonight." She smiled slightly, brightening her manner.

"Aha. That's the spirit. And this is the place for it." An

improvement, he said to himself. The give and take. Testy, perhaps, but also playful. Still, a quirky mood.

"I don't know much about it either, really, or about anything else for that matter. Knowing too much about anything takes the bloom off your ignorance and leaves only wilting expertise." He was giving himself a freer rein tonight than at their last meeting. And, hoping his levity would loosen her further, he went on animatedly, as she cast him a dubious expression. "Of course, you have to know something in order for your ignorance to bloom at all. I guess that rather defines a dilettante. And I plead guilty—although dilettantes get a bad rap in our over-specialized world."

The glibness and loquacity again, she reflected. And, yes, he probably is a dilettante.

He pressed on without waiting for her response. "But I love the sensuous grace and sublime mystery of Hindu and Buddhist art. It's all about life and death, good and evil, infinity and the order of the universe. Nothing trivial or contrived for effect alone."

Now he criticizes triviality and contrivance? she said to herself. Can a dilettante do that? "But some of it is so repetitious," she observed. "The same images over and over. And too many arms."

"They're images of infinity, especially in Buddhism, to take you out of yourself, show you the unreality of things, reveal that life is just a bridge of dreams to the extinction of nirvana. It's religion and art as escape. We came to debate that, didn't we?"

"Did we?" Taking the bait, she went on. "Aren't you trivializing both religion and art?"

"Escape isn't trivial for Buddhists or Hindus. It's the purpose of life. Nirvana. Extinction. And I might say that debating such things is inevitable here."

"You get that fatalism from Eastern religions, too?"

"It's not fatalism. It's common sense. And Buddhism and Hinduism aren't fatalistic. They let you make you own fate, again and again in many lives."

She didn't answer. He seemed to be talking in circles. Then it occurred to her that maybe she had made her own fate again and again, in this life, and hadn't seen it. Do we all do that, she wondered.

They entered the main gallery and approached a pedestal holding a three-headed bust representing, so they read on an adjacent plaque, the Hindu triumvirate of Brahma, Vishnu, and Shiva.

"Another virtue of Hinduism," he continued breezily. "It embraces all gods. Nice idea, don't you think?"

"I'm afraid religion has never spoken deeply to me." Her voice had a reflective, not dismissive, tone to it.

"Why not?"

"Oh, probably because my parents were skeptics who didn't trust most of religion's influence on people—the arrogant certitudes and self-righteousness—and I inherited their skepticism and distrust."

"Understandable. But religion's not a bad thing if people use it right. Like art. Not for absolute truth—which it cannot give—but as an imaginative invention that serves life. God doesn't have to be anything more than a metaphor for a power we can't possess, a perfection we can't attain, and a hope we can't live without—or some people can't. Art and life would be far poorer if that kind of god didn't exist And any god worthy of the name should be willing to accept that."

She raised an eyebrow, which he found as alluring as it was skeptical. "You prepared this philosophical vignette?" she said, with gentle rather then sharp mockery, refusing to take him any more seriously than he took himself. He thought he saw a sliver of a smile, or was it just the curl of her Renoir lips caught by a small pin spotlight high overhead?

"I want to keep you entertained," he remarked, convincing himself it *was* a smile. They moved on to a small group of people clustered around a five-foot high brass sculpture depicting a slender male figure balanced gracefully on one leg slightly bent at the knee, with the other leg raised and crooked forward almost perpendicular to his body, his four lithe arms arrayed in delicate dancing gestures, hair flying out to each side, and the entire form encircled in a vertical ring of flames.

"Shiva is the most prominent Hindu deity today," an officious woman standing next to the sculpture was explaining. "And his most common emblem is the phallic lingam, an image of creation. But he is also the Destroyer of Evil, and the God of Dance. He often destroys evil with fire and dances in victory. Here you see him holding a flame in one hand while dancing on a demon that he's slain—possibly a symbol of illusion—within a circle of fire."

"A perfect image of art and religion," Alex said quietly. "God dancing."

"Shhhh," Rebecca whispered, listening to the speaker explicate more of the iconography—a drum in one hand to make the sounds of creation, the other hands banishing fear and offering refuge for the soul, the wavy hair flying in the dancer's spin and suggesting the headwaters of the sacred Ganges where Shiva was born. When she finished and directed her flock to the next artwork, Rebecca stepped closer to the sculpture.

"They must mass produce these," she said. "You can buy them in art stores. Or is that another sign of infinity?"

He saw a faintly amused smile fleet across her face.

"Could be," he agreed. "But now you know the other symbolism in it—Shiva dancing in triumph of good over evil, life over death."

"And brutal truth over seductive illusion." She said this as if talking to herself, thinking how easy it is to be seduced by illusions, and how brutal truth can be. But again, she rather regretted saying it.

"That's a lugubrious interpretation." She *is* in an odd mood, he thought, and they rejoined the group now examining the sculpture of a portly human figure, with an elephant's head, doing a jig.

They listened to the woman describing how Ganesha had acquired his elephant's head after Shiva, his father, had errantly cut off his human head and replaced it with an elephant's, and then, from remorse, had made Ganesha a god of many good things—luck and prosperity, letters and learning, and overcoming obstacles—so now worshippers invoke Ganesha at the beginning of any enterprise. "He also dances," the woman added. "Not in victory like Shiva, but jovially. You can see why he is such a popular Hindu god."

"Why the broken tusk," a questioner spoke up, and while the answer came, explaining how Ganesha had used it to write as the scribe of the *Mahabharata*, the speaker and her listeners moved away. Alex and Rebecca let them go, and Alex asked if she had seen Terrence McNally's play *A Perfect Ganesh*. She said she hadn't, and he summarized its witty tale of a Western tourist in India searching for the perfect Ganesha figure to bring good luck. "We should all have one," he concluded with a grin. "At least as a metaphor—for good luck, overcoming obstacles, and auspicious beginnings."

She remembered her beginning with Richard that had gone on and on to nowhere. "Maybe so," she muttered.

They lingered near the figures of Shiva and Ganesha, exchanging comments on the dancing Destroyer of Evil and the dancing Bringer of Good Luck. Alex claimed indisputable evidence here of art and religion as kindred inventions to embellish life. Rebecca questioned his treating serious things so whimsically. Meandering on, they paused at images of Hindu deities in divine poses and in loving embrace, of Buddhas in imperturbable meditation, and of Bodhisattvas in sublime beneficence. Their conversation meandered with them as they talked about the diverse religious uses of art, the humane ingenuity of polytheism, and the wise psychology of Buddhist detachment.

Rebecca found her earlier discomfort dissolving, although she remained unsettled by Alex's glib and theatrical manner. But she admitted to herself that her mind was engaged in a way that both stimulated her and took her out of herself. Alex sensed that she still had an edge to her and also carried an air of remoteness hinting at sadness that he could neither fathom nor dispel. At the same time, she could be so mentally agile, and so subtly expressive, and so unintentionally alluring that he became more entranced all the time.

When they discovered that they had circled back to the entrance, Rebecca noted what a small exhibit it was. Alex assured her that he had arranged this to satisfy her obvious penchant for efficiency and to fulfill his guarantee of a short evening. She uttered a polite sarcasm, and they agreed that, in any case, the artworks were exquisite, if not created as "art." He told himself that, so far, the evening had been a success.

The rain had stopped when they got outside, leaving puddles along the curb, but the sidewalks were mostly dry, and the air was fresh.

"Do you mind if we walk?" he asked. "It's not far to the restaurant."

She didn't object, and they strolled down Park Avenue between walls of staid apartment buildings channeling into a corridor of soaring office towers that Alex remarked had mostly been built in the Fifties and Sixties with prosaic glass and steel monotony that had given a bad name to modern architecture—except for the Lever House and Mies van der Rohe's classic Seagram's building—and had helped precipitate the post-modernist reaction against it all.

"An architectural tour?" She lifted her voice to not sound condescending.

"I want you to get your money's worth," he replied confidently. "And I happen to be writing a piece on the subject. Do you find this part of the city inspiring or boring?" He gestured to the vertical cityscape in front of them.

"Park Avenue? I wouldn't want to live here."

"Neither would I. But like it or not, it's quintessential New York. And I can't resist it. You know, I once had a taxi driver, in the days before they became recent immigrants who can't speak English or find their way around, who told me he had been driving a taxi in New York for thirty years and had never left the city in his life, and that he never wanted to. 'This city'll make ya crazy,' he said. 'But if they ever tear it down I wanna' be here to go wit' it.'"

"Curious sentiment."

"I took it as a avowal of love. Don't you think that's enviable, to love the city where you live and work, driving the streets that much?"

"Maybe he was just at home here and he knew his way around."

They turned at an intersection onto a side street.

"I'd rather think it was true love," he continued. "The kind you have for someone who is good to you, even though they give you a hard time. That guy was cursing the traffic, but at the same time he was alive to everything around him, and loving every minute of it."

"Some people might say he loved the power he had behind the wheel."

"That's kind of sad. Are you one of them?"

"Well, I've ridden in too many taxis to be sentimental about the drivers."

"Is that one of your—what did you say?—'brutal truths' that crush 'seductive illusions'?"

"You're turning my words against me."

"Not really. I recognize the brutal truth. But I'll take 'seductive illusions' every time."

"That can be hazardous."

Suddenly, midway up the block, a car barreling from behind them swerved to the curb and caught a puddle of water, arching a well-aimed splash that struck Alex along the side and spattered

Rebecca. Stunned, they watched the car careen ahead, laughter crackling from inside, and then stop at a red light. Alex spontaneously took off after it shouting, "Hey! You morons! What the hell do you think you're doing!?"

Reaching the car, he glimpsed the New Jersey license plate and banged on the trunk. "You owe the lady an apology, you uncivilized cretins!" he yelled. The back door opened and a young male voice slurred, "lezz git the fucker." But before anyone could get out, the light changed, the door swung back and slammed, and the car shot across the street accompanied by more laughter, and disappeared into the shadows.

"You need help there?" a deep masculine voice called out from a Mercedes that had pulled up behind and stopped alongside Alex.

"Oh, thanks," Alex answered, catching his breath. "Kids from New Jersey showing off on their night in the city. They splashed us." He motioned toward Rebecca, who was cautiously nearing them.

"Bastards!" cursed the man in the Mercedes. "I saw them weaving up Park Avenue from where I was at the stoplight across the street and figured they were chasing trouble. They all ought to be shot on sight."

"That'd certainly simplify the criminal justice system," Alex said, brushing himself off. "Thanks again for stopping."

"Sure," the man answered, and after more curses at the delinquents drove off down Lexington Avenue.

"What was that all about?" Rebecca asked tensely, shaken more by Alex's impulsive act than by the incident itself.

"Oh, one of those events that makes you question city life and human nature—and that loving taxi driver I was talking about."

"You must be crazy. You could've been killed!"

"Not likely. But I couldn't help myself. Are you all right?"

"Yes, if a little damp and rattled qualifies."

"Damn! I'm so sorry. I'll have your coat cleaned."

"No, no. It'll be fine."

"Well," he said, renewing his aplomb, "let's not let anything *dampen* the evening more. The restaurant will redeem it."

Rebecca was still noticeably jangled when they sat down a few minutes later in a room of warm orange walls, colorful prints and polished brass. "Sophisticated exotica," Alex had labeled it. But she paid little attention to the décor.

"Would you care for an Indian beer?" Alex asked, trying to be nonchalant. "It's the best thing with Indian food. Kingfisher is light, but Taj Mahal comes in a tall bottle with a picture of the Taj Mahal on it. It's hokey but suited to our evening in India."

"I've never cared much for beer," she replied coolly. "I'd prefer a glass of white wine."

"Of course. You should have what you *prefer. Ah, Bartleby. Ah, humanity*," he mumbled. "And let's order some breads and appetizers, okay?"

"Go ahead. But I'm not very hungry. That altercation rather took my appetite. And what do you mean by the reference to Bartleby and humanity?"

"I assure you it's a compliment," he said off-handedly, and began to order the drinks and some poppadums, parathas, naans, chaats, and chutneys.

"What were you trying to accomplish out there?" she returned to the subject edgily.

"Not much. Except not to let animals like that get away with gross incivility."

"Sounds like a macho gratification."

"I doubt the macho part, but gratification, yes. Behavior like theirs is evil and ugly."

"You equate evil with ugliness?"

"We all do, in one way or another."

"That's a very aesthetic morality."

"There's more aesthetics in morality than people admit. The Greeks thought the good is beautiful and the beautiful good. And Nietzsche said: *One thing is needed: to impose style on your character. A great and a rare art.* That makes style the highest morality. Could be true."

Alex's self-satisfied tone nettled her as much as his words. "You're trying to sound like Oscar Wilde," she muttered. "Those are more poses than principles."

"Ah, *la nuance*," Alex said with a subtle smile. "You're deft at drawing them." The drinks and appetizers arrived, and he thought it best to move the conversation to more prosaic and congenial topics. "But I apologize for upsetting you," he said solicitously. "Let's forget all that. Can we? Do you like spicy food?"

"Not very spicy," she answered, and repeated that she hadn't much appetite anyway. Was she being rude? she asked herself. Was she overreacting to that street incident? Yes, she decided, she was doing both. Why? Because she didn't like his histrionics? Or was it because she was fragile these days, fearful of things? Or did these go together? Half regretting again that she had subjected herself to this flamboyant, unpredictable man, she wasn't sure how to proceed. But she recognized that it wasn't all his fault. She *was* overwrought. And she told herself to relax and be civil. She sat back and had a sip wine. He thought he saw her face soften in the warm lighting.

They ordered a mild crabmeat masala with a tamarind cream sauce for her and a spicy chicken Jalfrazie for him, along with a poori. After pouring some beer into his glass, Alex held up the tall bottle, displaying the small picture of the Taj Mahal on its label. "Have you been to India?" he asked.

"No, I haven't." She took a swallow of wine. "Have you?"

"No. One of my regrets, which I intend to remedy this year. Oh, that reminds me." He pulled an envelope from inside his jacket pocket. "Here's the draft proposal I promised—no chapters yet, just a synopsis. Don't read it now. Wait until you have nothing better to do."

"A risky invitation" she said, more amicably now that she had calmed herself. She slid the envelope into her purse. He sensed that she was warming once more. Maybe now he could get closer, and learn what lay beneath her enigmatic exterior.

"I was charmed by how you got your name," he began. "Now, may I ask you to tell me more—about your life story, and what you do besides read manuscripts and indulge the occasional narcissistic author in conversation?" He appealed to her with a self-deprecating look.

She nearly flinched. But she told herself to blunt his curiosity by responding as casually and briefly as she could. So she gave him a concise sketch in an off-hand manner of how she had grown up in Connecticut as the only child of academic parents, attended Yale, gone into publishing, gotten married and later been harmoniously divorced. Then, side-stepping a question about her divorce, she took the offensive and asked for *his* autobiography—"but I expect more of the writer's flair and detail from you," she added, hoping for a time-consuming, possibly entertaining, monologue.

Submitting to her apparently sincere request, and honoring her evident disinclination to talk about herself, as they started dinner he outlined his biography, with a few elaborations. He said he had been the late child of parents who had lived in the suburbs of Chicago and who had both been very successful in that city's commercial real estate, and who had both died by the time he was forty-two. He had also had an older brother who was killed in an automobile accident when he himself was a child. After his own rather restless adolescence, he had come to New York for college and graduate school, then entered into a short, misbegotten marriage, along with a stint of discontented college teaching. And for the last dozen years he had engaged in a somewhat fragmented but occasionally satisfying career in journalism and freelance writing in this city that he had loved at first sight. Then, pointing out the noteworthy coincidences that both he and Rebecca had, in effect, been raised as only children and had both gone through abbreviated marriages and therefore had quintessentially American stories, he wound up with a flourish, quoting Nietzsche on living dangerously and sending "your ships into uncharted seas," and Pater on burning always "with a hard gem-like flame," and how such ideas had made him change his life several times, and how he needed to do it again now, as he had already told her. And he finished with an apology for falling short of her standards of autobiographical economy.

"No apology necessary. I didn't ask for economy. And I half-expected erudite quotations and theatricality. But," she concluded, seeing him now a little differently than she had before, "I'm sorry for the loss of your brother and parents."

"Thanks for the thought. And I hope you don't consider my use of what you call 'erudite quotations', pretentious."

"Oh, no. You're a liberal education." She was trying to be pleasant.

"Your patronizing me. But you do it engagingly. And since you brought it up, and you are patiently indulging my dilettantism tonight, may I offer you my theory of 'erudite quotations'? It's not academic. It's more like the art of clichés."

Glad to have him do the talking, she encouraged him to continue. He suspected she was less interested than her inviting words and tone implied. But he didn't let that stop him.

"How gracious you are," he began. "OK. I think of erudite quotations as 'pithy thoughts,' 'nice phrases,' and 'good clichés' that we use as a kind of dramatic punctuation. You know how grammatical punctuation gives clarity and drama to sentences by keeping things straight, setting rhythms, and punching climaxes?"

"I thought you said this wasn't going to be academic," she answered with a natural smile.

"It isn't. Just wait. Pithy thoughts, nice phrases, and good clichés punctuate our lives rather like that. They enhance experiences and intensify moments. And they aren't only erudite words. They include the songs that we fall in love to, the artworks that we worship God with, and the twenty-two story-lines—or however many there are—of world literature, that we use to tell our tales. They all give our lives more drama—and sometimes show us what is most important to us. That's the art of clichés, in anything."

Rebecca did not agree but was unsure whether to respond or just let him carry on. She decided to challenge him, but in a friendly tone. "Ingenious. But aren't you confusing clichés with things that are original and authentic and powerful? Clichés are the opposite. They're formulas. At most they give a phony drama to life because they produce ready-made, hackneyed, homogenized responses. And this deadens us instead of enlivening us, because it takes the place of fresh thoughts and feelings."

Alex was pleased to have stirred such a reaction. "Spoken like an astute and seasoned editor who scorns clichés. But maybe it's a matter of semantics. What I mean is that good clichés—particularly nice phrases—can capture and distill an idea or a feeling or an incident in a way that we can use over and over to enhance and lend drama to our lives. They become life-serving metaphors. We call them clichés when they get repeated and well-known. But by whatever name, I think they stay alive as long as they can *punctuate* our lives.

She was still not persuaded. Of course, she could admire good literary lines. She had even memorized some. And it dawned on her that a few had come to haunt her nights against her will. But he wasn't talking about that kind of thing, was he? He seemed to be playing with words, making a game of clichés and art and religion and of everything else for the fun of it, to *enhance* and *lend drama* to his own life.

Provoked again by this penchant of his, she said,: "You know . . . *Alex* . . . ." She had not addressed him by his nick name before, and she did it with an emphasis that subtly mocked, while finally adopting, the informality he had urged. "You say clichés enhance and lend drama to life. You say you want to *burn with a hard gemlike flame.* You say you prefer illusions to reality. You say religion is art. You say ugliness is evil. You know what you are? You're not a dilettante, you're an aesthete. Like Oscar Wilde, you want to live for aesthetic pleasures and watch the drama of your life from the outside. Even chasing that car on the street probably comes down to that."

Her words had taken on a cutting edge again. She hadn't intended it. But she had let it happen. He was being all too glib. Too willing to mask reality with illusions and histrionics and clichés. That was it—he refused to see things as they are and wanted to play at life. But *she* saw things as they are, didn't she? Now? She saw them in herself. Although she didn't know entirely what they were. And as she spoke, Alex heard in her voice as much defensiveness as criticism. She wasn't simply irritated with him, he told himself. She was protecting herself. From what? He couldn't let the argument end here. He would try one more tactic.

"You make that accusation sound very grave," he said cordially. "But I've heard it before. And it's plausible. Still, it doesn't do me justice, if I might say so. Take those phrases, metaphors, and clichés I was talking about. They're not merely aesthetic playthings. As I said, they can inspire us. Think of Don Quixote. He turned the literary clichés of medieval chivalry into a life of honorable knighthood, then he became a metaphor himself, even a cliché, that has inspired countless actual lives. Or take those reproductions of Shiva dancing. They're clichés of Hindu art because they are so commonplace. You said so yourself. But to believers they aren't only that, they're animating metaphors of god dancing victoriously. And how about your own borrowed literary name—doesn't it give you a certain metaphorical identity that adds something to your life? None of these things is about aesthetics and illusion and pleasure alone. They're all about *enhancing* and *lending drama* to real life. And I should add social manners to the list. Aren't manners social clichés that embellish social life with civility and beauty and pleasure?"

Not really following this free-flowing monologue, she didn't answer. Deferring to her reaction, he decided to leave a subject that was wearing thin and possibly getting away from him. "But that's enough of this. I can be such a boor. Let's have another drink and talk of other things, *shoes and ships and sealing wax, and cabbages and kings, and why the sea is boiling hot, and whether pigs have wings.* Sorry. Sometimes nice phrases just leap to mind and I can't resist 'em." He gave her an abashed look.

She raised her eyebrows at the Lewis Carroll line. But, appeased by his evident retreat, however theatrical, from these unwieldy topics, she ordered another drink. He construed this to mean he had withdrawn with timely valor and prevented the evening from regressing. He had hoped to engage this mystifying woman, not to estrange her. She had found herself alternately engaged and estranged. Now they were both ready for a simpler conversation.

By the time they left the restaurant, they were exchanging casual observations on the food and ambiance, and Alex joked about whether they were reciting dead social clichés or honoring live ones. She laughed politely, and he teased her that even this laughter was a reliable social cliché. She conceded gracefully. And as they waited for a taxi on Lexington Avenue, he read her renewed sociability as an opening to offer a new invitation.

"Rebecca, would you be willing to consider another adventure with this reprobate aesthete? Nothing exotic this time.

Whatever you would like to do. Wherever you would like to go. You might reform me—to my lasting benefit."

What a showman he is, she thought. Playing with ideas, art, religion, life. And yet, the evening had not been dull. Some of it had actually given her a lift. Her uncertainties brought a new surge of ambivalence about him, and an equivocal response to her lips. "Why don't you call me next week." Once more, her tone was warmer than her words. But they still betrayed a return to some of the guardedness that he couldn't understand.

"Another negotiation? But I'd be delighted to call," he replied chivalrously, sensing that this was the only commitment he would get from her tonight. "I warn you, though, I might conjure up something in the mean time. The possibilities are infinite."

"Your Buddhist view of life?" she kidded as the taxi pulled up.

"Why, Rebecca Winters! You *are* enlightened." He grinned and opened the door for her.

The grin brought a memory of Todd Hilton. But this grin had a less self-satisfied and an almost sweet quality. Or was Alex Rodgers simply a better performer? "Thank you for the . . . *enlightening* evening," she said with a hint of sarcasm and a softening smile, "despite the sidewalk machismo and your . . . eccentric ideas on clichés." He playfully vowed to restrain his *sidewalk machismo* but confessed an inability to restrain his *eccentric ideas*. Then he said good night with a modestly theatrical bow. The door closed.

As he watched the taxi drive off and then turn out of sight at the intersection, he was hoping a romance was about to begin. Not only an amorous conquest. At the late age of nearly fifty, he wanted his life to have more texture to it than that. He wanted sensations, emotions, events that gave him delectable moments, hours, and days, and that left lasting residues, a past to be cherished. He liked to quote Proust's last line in *Swann's Way* on this, one of those phrases that *punctuated* his life: *The memory of a particular image is but regret for a particular moment; and the houses, the roads, the avenues are as fugitive, alas, as the years.* That's what our lives are, he would say. Fleeting, evanescent, fugitive moments that leave their residues in memories. So we must capture these moments and cling to them as they pass. Sensations to savor. Pleasures to taste. Feelings to hold. Ideas to contemplate. Phrases to quote. Images to remember. What is life but this?

"Alex," his friend Conrad, the psychotherapist with an-ever-ready-free-diagnosis, would say in various ways over drinks at their favorite bar, "you think you experience everything for your own detached satisfaction. But you don't fool me. You don't want to live in the real world. It's all a defense for some profound failing in you as a human being."

Alex would always respond with a hearty laugh and reply with words like: "Thanks, Con. Your barroom therapy is worth everything I pay for it. And it comes in handy at cocktail parties. But what you don't grasp is that reality is over-rated, especially by people like you."

Alex and Conrad had bantered like this since college days. It had made them candid friends. Alex admitted that Conrad was not wholly wrong about him. But he liked to make light of Conrad's theories, often arguing that Freud would take Alex's side because "psychoanalysis is mainly about the power of fantasy, what we imagine and think and feel, what we want and fear, more than it is about the *real world.*"

"No, Alex," Conrad would retort. "It's about getting people to live in the real world instead of escaping into their fantasies and wallowing in their imaginations and feelings and frustrations and fears." And so, with perennial variations, their genial jousting would go.

Now, relishing the prospect of more delectable moments with Rebecca Winters, this on-and-off Renoir portrait with an argumentative mind and an enigmatic heart, Alex hailed another cab. And went home down town with his delectable anticipations.

⁂

Rain was falling again, pelting her windows overlooking Central Park, when Rebecca climbed into bed. The clock showed ten-thirty. How did it get to be so late? No, that's not late. Not in New York. She opened a book and read fitfully. Finally, feeling sleepy, she gave up and switched off the bed-side lamp. Now, dreading the images that had come to haunt her bedtime hours, she tried a new defense, taken from earlier that evening. They're only metaphors, she told herself, and they're getting to be worn clichés. They shouldn't cause fright. Or, she caught herself, are they the kind that *he* was talking about, the kind that change life and never die?

Who is this man? she asked herself. A peculiar character. A dilettante. An aesthete, for sure. He hadn't denied it. Flippant, self-indulgent, histrionic, probably untrustworthy, possibly dangerous. Not her type. He made her uncomfortable half the time. And that madness on the street! Still, he wasn't boring. And there were moments . . . . Should she see him again? The *possibilities are infinite*, he had said for effect. She recoiled at the thought, recalling some fruitless *possibilities* of her past. But why was he, in his nonchalant way, trying so hard to . . . do what? Was she just a challenge for him? A game? Very likely. And she didn't want any part of that. No, he wasn't her type at all. But . . . .

7

# The City and the Night

"Rebecca, this is Alex Rodgers." The call came at her office late Monday morning. "Am I getting you at a bad time?"

Her morning routine broken by the unexpected voice, she answered with friendly sarcasm. "No. I just sit here looking out the window waiting for the phone to ring."

"A comedienne. And on Monday morning. I like it. Well, I'm calling to collect on that promise you made last week."

"Promise?"

"To talk about risking another evening of urban adventure with me—on your terms, and barring sidewalk brawls, of course."

She wasn't prepared for this. She had tried to put him out of her mind, and when her thoughts had strayed to their evening together she had wavered over her impressions of him and over whether to see him again socially or only for professional reasons. She did have his attempt at a book proposal, which she hadn't looked at. But she was caught off guard this morning. She tried another jest.

"You're an eager collector of purported debts. Have you worked for the IRS?"

"Ha!. It's just that I have a proposition, no, a proposal, no, no, an invitation to offer."

Disarmed by his faltering, almost boyish, manner, she hesitated. Should she head him off or wait to hear what he had to say? If she waited, it would be harder to decline. Did she want to decline? She waited. Her silence encouraged him to try to close the deal.

"Here it is. A friend of mine has offered me a pair of tickets to the revival of *42nd Street* for Friday night. He said he couldn't make it and that my personality is better suited than his is to fantasies of show business success like that in the show anyway. He's a psychotherapist and likes to joke about mental health and character flaws at my expense. But never mind that. Would you come? Please don't say no."

She hesitated again as her mind wove through a thicket of questions. What should she do? What did she want to do? She hadn't much liked going out in the city on weekends for years. Too crowded. Can't get a cab. Tourists in the summer. Bad weather in the winter. Weeknights were better. She preferred to spend weekends with good company at home or at someone else's home, or with a good book or reading manuscripts, letting the young and the restless and the out-of-towners pry their way into hit shows and vie for tables in "hot" restaurants, working to have fun. Her thoughts flitted back to that last weekend night out—Meredith's cocktail party, and its aftermath. She cringed. She couldn't let that happen again. But her weekend nights were not as appealing as they used to be, either. The blank screen flickered across her mind. Now, here was Alexander Rodgers. His blithe and theatrical style still unsettled her, and she again questioned his motives for pursuing her. Was he just a self-important male on the make—like Todd Hilton? Could be. And yet, there was something about him that . . . .

"Are you still there?" he asked after the long pause.

"Yes," she answered vaguely.

"Is that 'yes I am here' or 'yes I will come to the theater?' Or should I start over?"

"You shouldn't ask so many questions before you get an answer to the first one," she lightly reproached him.

"Forgive me. I guess I'm over-eager. A juvenile trait I've never grown out of. But where does that leave us?"

She took a breath. And, as if hearing someone else speak, she answered, "Yes, I will come."

"Terrific!" he exclaimed. "Could we have an early dinner near the theater? Would you like to meet at your office or at the restaurant?"

"So many questions again," she replied, still rather distantly but more amiably. "At the restaurant, I suppose. I was planning to work at home, as I sometimes do on Fridays in the summer."

"Ah, could I pick you up at home, as a chivalrous gentleman would do?"

"It's up to you."

"I'll pick you up at home about 5:45, OK? In the meantime, don't bother with my book proposal. I wouldn't want it to intrude on the evening."

"Fair enough." She hadn't in fact given his proposal any thought and was happy to put off reading it, suspecting that it might give her trouble. She told him her address on Central Park West in the Eighties and put down the phone with a quiver of ill-ease at submitting to his persistence, unsure how she should deal with him. But the ill-ease mingled with an indistinct curiosity. To quell the distracting sensations, she concentrated again on writing a letter rejecting a manuscript lying on her desk. Then she scanned her schedule for the rest of the day. And the rest of the week. The ill-ease and curiosity persisted.

***

The doorbell rang at a twenty minutes to six. Always ready in advance for any engagement, business or social, Rebecca unhurriedly opened the door.

"Hi," Alex said cheerfully, "I hope you don't mind if I'm a trifle early. I warned you about my over-eagerness. Self-restraint is not my strength."

She offered a small smile and invited him in. Her manner was somewhat removed but not cold. And he chose to think she was trying to be subtly welcoming. A mystifying but beguiling combination. And as she stepped back under the vestibule light, the orange silk dress she was wearing took on a luster that brought out the full Renoir warmth of her face. Alex felt a rush of heat. He was certain she caused that without trying, and probably without feeling it herself. But he wanted to think she sometimes felt it. It had to be in her nature. And he wanted to reach it.

"I'll get a jacket." She crossed the living room to a hallway.

"It's warm out," he called to her as she disappeared and he walked in to survey the living room lined with bookshelves and furnished sparingly but impeccably. Oriental rugs lay over hardwood floors. A glass coffee table between a pair of Barcelona chairs held a vase of flowers. A long beige sofa ran beneath the windows overlooking the street and Central Park. Magazines bedecked matching end tables under stylish lamps. Everything appropriate. Nothing out of place. Like her. A cat sidled into the room from the hallway. Alex followed its slow progress brushing against a bookcase and then weaving around a chair until it levitated onto the sofa and curled into a spot where, resting its head on a front paw, it peered at him through half-closed eyes, watching, judging.

"So you are a cat person?" he said as Rebecca reappeared.

"I have a cat, if that's what you mean. I don't have a dozen of them." Her pleasant expression and supple voice undercut the abruptness of her words.

"I stand corrected. They say you are master to a dog. But you're servant to a cat. Is that true?"

"It's true of cats."

"You don't strike me as the servant type."

"I'm not. But I know when I'm overmatched."

He laughed. "What's it's name?"

"I call her Clarissa. I don't know what she calls herself." She smiled.

They left the apartment, and he was thinking how her curt words came this time with a note of humor—a cutting edge with an undercutting tone. A new mood? Or was she getting comfortable with him? Anyhow, he rather liked it. Even the edge. Part of the enigma he hoped to unravel.

To her this mood or manner was just a variation on the deliberately good-humored defensiveness she had developed lately to shield herself from probing questions at work, and from her own fears. But she was also girding herself for this "adventure," which she had acceded to uncertain of how it would go and how she was going to feel about it.

The pre-theater dinner passed in casual talk. When it turned to books, Alex said his tastes in literature ran more to classic novels than to the contemporary. "The great age of fiction," he declared, "lasted about a hundred years or so down to the early twentieth century, didn't it? After that, most fiction is littered with trivialities dressed-up in skillful writing, and with defective human beings absorbed in themselves. Self-conscious artistry and narcissistic psychology."

"You're a literary critic." she responded.

"Just opinionated. But honestly, I'm not a good judge of literature as art because I go for the ideas and images and 'nice phrases' rather than the books themselves."

She smiled and said she shared his literary tastes to the extent that she loved classic novels for their rich and varied characters and for the dense historical and public world they often depicted. But she added, "I wouldn't debunk modern fiction as you do. It can be deeply moving and even profound. Still, as an editor I don't handle much fiction. I'm more at home with non-fiction."

"Why is that?"

"It's not as . . . subjective and has more . . . focus, you might say. Easier to get a hold on."

"So why did you agree to look at my novel proposal?

"As a favor to Sarah." Her voice dropped as she thought of how she hadn't wanted to do it, and that her work didn't matter to her as it used to anyway. He picked up on the change in tone.

"I might as well abandon my idea," he sighed with feigned dejection, sensing that she was drifting away. "It's very subjective and unfocused. And, despite my 'classical' tastes, I'm afraid it has all the modern qualities I complained about. I'd write a nineteenth-century novel if I could, but it's too late. I'm a prisoner of my times."

"Aren't we all," she replied rather distantly. He saw a glimmer in her eyes but he suspected she was only partially with him.

They left for the theater talking about the decline of the Broadway musical and the virtues of revivals. After settling into their seats and the curtain had gone up, they listened to Harry Warren's brassy songs in this classic show about an ingénue understudy who becomes a star one night in a Broadway musical when told to play the lead role, and they watched troupes of tap dancers clatter in unison around the stage. But their minds wandered, and along different paths.

Rebecca returned to their dinner conversation and to some of her favorite novels. Lines from one of them bubbled up. *She always had the feeling that it was very, very dangerous to live even one day . . . . But what did it mean to her, this thing she called life?* Virginia Woolf's Clarissa Dalloway, for whom Rebecca had named her cat. She tensed. Nice phrases? Pithy thoughts? Good clichés? That's what he would say. In any case, now they were part of her recurring nightmare. And she didn't want to hear them. Their *punctuation* was too darkly dramatic. She shook them off, telling herself not to let her mind wander. She should concentrate on the show, listen to the music. Live music should not be merely a backdrop for daydreams, or nightmares. She gave herself to it, and it brought her a welcome mental diversion.

Alex let his thoughts play over the pleasures of being out in the city, at the theater, in the night. He relished it all. It invigorated him. And he was glad to be with her. She kept him off-balance with her keen mind, dry wit, vacillating moods, and that Renoir smile.

When the curtain fell on the last act, they joined the crowd pressing toward the exits, show tunes humming in the air. "*If you can't hum the tunes, I don't want to hear it.* Didn't some old-time Broadway producer say that?" Alex asked as they edged through the congestion outside.

"No doubt," she answered, the sprightly melodies still in her ear. "It sounds like a theater adage. And not bad advice."

He persuaded her to cap this New York evening with a drink and dessert at the rooftop restaurant of a hotel just north of Times Square. A few minutes later, after exchanging reviews of the show and comparing classic Broadway composers, they were standing on that rooftop looking down at the lights of Broadway and the river of cars flowing south into Times Square.

"I didn't know this place was here," Rebecca remarked, looking down over the railing.

"One of the surprises of New York. It's a different city up here. At ground level the city is all dull storefronts and offices, crowds and traffic, and the shadows of featureless buildings. But up here in places like this it's a city of fantasy. Like Oz."

"Oz?"

They sat down at a table against the railing lined with flower boxes and ordered drinks and two tiramisus.

"Yes. You know the modern city was the inspiration for the Emerald City of Oz." Alex resumed. "Not New York exactly. Probably Chicago. Frank Baum wrote *The Wizard of Oz* while he was working there creating imaginative window displays for department stores. Those windows were a novelty then, at the turn of the twentieth century. People flocked to see them as sidewalk theater. Baum's Oz was the fantasy of the modern city. And when you see the city from up here, it's all Oz. Soaring towers, whimsical spires, flashy ornaments, bizarre gargoyles, and below, tiny people and cars darting about like toys. And at night, with the lights, it's magic on top of fantasy."

"Another urban lecture?" she said good-naturedly.

"Chosen for the occasion."

The waiter arrived with a Sambuca, iced tea, and the desserts. "New York at night is as romantic as Paris, don't you think?" he went on, taking a bite of tiramisu.

"It depends on what you mean by 'romantic.'"

"Ah, we can pick up where we left off last week."

"Where was that?"

"I think you were faulting me for being an aesthete and other discreditable things. Anyhow, I'd be happy to tell you what I mean by romantic or romance—if you can tolerate another of my rambling meditations and 'eccentric ideas,' as you put it."

"I can try," she said affably.

"That's all I could ask. Well, I'd say that romance is a way of looking at things. Another of my *trite and true* notions, to quote you again—you see, I listen to what you say."

"It was a lapse of taste on my part." She shot him a fleeting smile.

"It fit the occasion, as good clichés do. But back to romance. There it is, out there. See—the romance of the city." He stretched an arm out over the railing and declaimed as he pointed to the sights: "The glittering garishness of Times Square down there, the Empire State building in the distance with its vulgar changing nighttime colors, the spire of the Chrysler building piercing the sky with its arrows of light. It's all art, fantasy, romance. Oz and Eros."

She chuckled obligingly. "From Oz to Eros. Sounds like a hip sexy course at the New School."

"Ha! But I don't mean sex. I mean the Eros that Freud talked about and that Auden celebrated in his wonderful poem on the death of Freud. You know it?"

"I've read it. I don't remember it much. I like Auden. But I've never been a great admirer of Freud."

"No? Well, forget the textbook Freud of Oedipal conflicts, phallic imagery, sexual repressions, that stuff. They're not the best Freud. Not Auden's Freud. Not the Freud of romance."

"Romantic Freud?"

"Yes. It's the best way to read him. And now, will you indulge me in a fractured poetry recitation?"

"More 'erudite quotations'? Performing selections from your greatest hits tonight?" she joked and leaned back against her chair. "Carry on."

"I'll summarize and be brief—I know you like brevity, and I wouldn't want you to leave before the show is over. Auden says that above all Freud urged people not to fear passion but to accept it and be emotionally honest and free and relish the energies of life and to love the night for all of its mysteries and delights. And he winds up the poem with the idea that when Freud died the energies of life mourned, and—here's my favorite part, the last line—'Sad is Eros, builder of cities, and weeping anarchic Aphrodite'. That's moving, don't you think? This is the Eros and Aphrodite I think of in places like this, at times like this. But not sad or weeping. I think of them as Auden did— building the city and loving it; and reveling in the night."

She paused before speaking. His romanticized Freud, even graced by Auden, didn't ring true for her. "A rather masculine fantasy of creation, isn't it?" she said. "Eros, the male sex god as the creator, and the female sex goddess—what is she, 'anarchic Aphrodite'?—she's an anarchist? That makes her destructive not creative."

"A feminist critique, eh? But don't blame me. Blame Auden. And you're being too literal. Eros is just creative energy in general—kind of like Shiva. And Aphrodite is the passion, the love—sometimes anarchic—that we should openly embrace instead of denying it with timidity and excuses. Auden's words are better. Anyhow, I like to think that the city at night comes from Eros and Aphrodite in Auden's sense. It's their creation, metaphorically, out of vitality and love. That's the delectable fantasy and romance of it. And that makes it romantic, like romantic love."

"You've lost me again."

"Everybody knows romantic love is a kind of fantasy," he went on without pausing. "Stendhal said it's like 'crystalliza-tion'?—when we fall in love we see our beloved sparkling with crystals that aren't truly there, but they're there for us—it's a way of looking at things. That's the fantasy of romantic love—and a metaphor for all fantasies. And who would want it otherwise?"

"I know people who would. But even if that image fits romantic love for some people, what you're saying could be a formula for self-deception in life. You can romanticize anything like that, wrapping it in fantasies. But then you don't see things for what they are. And you live in illusions." She felt a trace of edginess creeping into her.

"Your *brutal truths* conquering *seductive illusions* once more? But you misunderstand what I'm saying."

"I think *you* misunderstand," she responded unexpectedly. "I have no quarrel with romance and fantasy. They have their places. And surely New York can be romantic. But you seem to want to turn everything into romantic fantasies and aesthetics. What about bad things like villainy and human suffering, and good things like friendship and work and achievement and the public welfare? They're not just fantasies or aesthetics or 'a way of looking at things.' They're all very real, and they affect our lives. You'd have us live in illusions and for the sake of what?—pleasures of the moment? Like being on drugs."

The words poured from her with an intensity that startled them both. She didn't know where it came from. Yes, she had always steered clear of men with notions like his. She had thought them self-indulgent, dreamy, irresponsible, dishonest. Not that she had known anyone quite like him. But she had encountered semblances. And yet, she could not have predicted her reaction. It wasn't that she was particularly surprised to hear him go on this way. He had implied such things before. Could it be that he had now touched something too sensitive in her? Or that she was growing more resistant to some of the things he was saying? Sipping her iced tea, she examined her feelings.

He waited, choosing his words, determined to explain himself, and hoping to reassure her. He spoke cautiously.

"I seem to have stumbled down the same path that I did last time. Let me try again. The shrink who gave me the theater tickets criticizes me for the same things you do. I don't go to him professionally, mind you. He just gives me a bad time for free over drinks or dinner. And his friendship means a lot to me. But I tell him that although we have to live in reality, we need more than reality to make life worth living—or more than the reality that we bump up against every day. That's all I mean by fantasy and romance, like art and ideas and nice phrases, and so forth. They don't wholly take us out of the world as much as they help us find things in the world to live for. This isn't dishonest or delusional. There is even a kind of mental discipline in it. That sounds pretentious. But think of the Zen teachings about how to see beauty in a raindrop on a leaf or in a falling blossom. If we don't know how to do these things, we're not entirely alive. Or I wouldn't be. Romance, fantasy, aesthetics—they go together, and they're also real."

Rebecca didn't respond. She didn't believe what he was saying any more than she had earlier. At least she didn't want to. But he seemed to genuinely believe what he was saying. She had more tea, feeling obscurely confused and uncomfortable. No, it wasn't only his "eccentric ideas" that bothered her. Could it be that he was circling around something that she didn't want to think about, much less defend? He noticed her discomfort.

"Would you like more tea or some Sambuca, or anything else?"

"No, thanks," she murmured.

He sensed that she was withdrawing again into the distance that lay like a shadow in her eyes. He wanted to bring her back. And somehow draw her out. But how? A story came to mind. "Will you allow me one more little anecdote?" he asked tentatively.

"Poetry or fantasy?" She spoke with a wary civility.

"Neither. A true story."

She said she would listen.

"It's about a woman I interviewed years ago. I was working on a piece about Vietnamese immigrants. She had come here with the first batch after the war and was working in a restaurant in Los Angeles. She was intelligent and quite attractive, but her face bore deep lines of a sorrow that pooled in her eyes. I told her she looked sad, and she replied with words I have never forgotten. She said, 'I am always sad.' What a thing to say! *I am always sad.* I asked her why, and she explained it was because she had been separated from her family during the last chaotic days of the war in Saigon, and had managed to get out. Since reaching America, she had been working to survive and save money to go back and find the loved-ones she had left behind. Maybe she did go back. I don't know. But her phrase—*I am always sad*—stayed with me. Not because of the tragedy she had suffered, which was unquestionably *real.* But because she would probably always be sad, just as she said, no matter what happened to her, and she would be sad because she had let sadness consume her life. She had become—forgive me for saying it again—her way of looking at things. I don't deny that terrible events can cause real sadness like that. The death of my brother did that in my family. And September 11th did it on a grand scale in New York. I know people who have felt a kind of sadness ever since that day. I've felt it, too. But I will not let that or any other sadness consume me. At the same time, refusing to let sadness, or other negative feelings cloud your life doesn't mean you deny them or reality. It means you have learned to manage your emotions and perceptions to your advantage. That's the Buddhism of everyday life."

Although his lips flickered with a smile, he had a serious expression that she had not seen before. It gave her a measure of ease, despite the facile remark about Buddhism. He certainly likes to hear himself talk, she thought. And to play with words. But, she said to herself, maybe he is sincere. Maybe he isn't just the blithe aesthete and histrionic fantasist he pretends to be. And in some ways he could be talking about her, couldn't he? Had she let sadness or something like that consume her? She was again both disconcerted and curious.

"A poignant story," she said. Then, as if prompted by an unwilled inner force, she went on. "But this insistence of yours on seeing things as you *want* to see them, seeing the 'romance,' as you label it, in everything . . ."

"Not everything," he interrupted.

"Yes, yes, all right. But could it be that you are actually running away from things that you don't want to see, including things in yourself?" Her voice dropped, and a new twinge of uneasiness coursed through her. She knew she was talking about herself as much as him. Not that she had taken up fantasies, but there were things in herself that she didn't want to see. And now she suspected this of him, too. Or was she just projecting? How unlike her to probe. But he had provoked it. Was that his strategy? Leading her out on a limb where she couldn't defend herself and might fall off? Now she wanted to take back her words or wished he would toss them off with a joke.

"And you said you had no use for Freud," he kidded.

She resisted saying that Freud had nothing to do with it, but was relieved that he had made a joke of it.

Still, he didn't let it go. Her openness surprised but also emboldened him. The story had paid off. And he continued. "My friend the shrink agrees with you here, too. And no doubt you are both right. But in one way or another we're all running away from something, aren't we? The wolves snap at our heels from every side. I'm sure no one would accuse you of being a fantasist or aesthete or anything like that. But your cautiousness in conversation, and your tendency to withdraw, even your wit, are probably a kind of escape, or rather a defense. From what, or against what, I don't know. Would it do any good to ask?"

Rebecca caught her breath. She had let the conversation go to far, or get too close. And he had turned it against her. That *was* his strategy. That's how it felt. She wanted to leave. But she couldn't do that without betraying herself in flight. She drained her iced tea and leaned back in her chair again, fingering the base of her glass and gazing away from him toward the lights of Times Square, trying to conjure up a *good line* to save herself from having to reveal things she didn't want to reveal, or to think about. A defense? Yes. But she needed it.

He could tell she didn't want to answer. He *had* gone too far. He was losing her.

"Never mind," he said softly. "I shouldn't have. It's late and I don't want the evening to end like this. You've been so . . ." Wanting to convey more solicitude than words could do, he slid his hand across the table and laid his fingers gently on hers, unsure how she would react. She brought her eyes back to him. But she didn't pull her hand away. And he thought he felt her fingers move against his. For a suspended moment they looked into each other's eyes. And there, with the glimmer of the candle on the table and the glitter of the city lights around them, they believed they saw in each other's eyes hints of kindred fears and common yearnings. Then the moment passed.

"Yes," she said, lowering her eyes and slowly withdrawing her hand, glad that he had let her off the hook and uncertain what had just occurred. "I really must go. I've got work to do tomorrow."

"On Saturday?" he asked incredulously. "That's a mistake."

"You don't let up do you?" she said genially.

"Chronic curiosity and unconstrained impulses. Flaws, I know."

"Will it comfort you if I say I'll be going to my mother's house in Connecticut in the afternoon?"

"Oh, immensely. Your mother? I'm fond of her already, for your name. What's hers?"

"Adrianna."

"Good names in your family." He paid the check over her protests to split it. Then they wended through the tables to the doorway leading inside. "Wait," he said at the threshold, taking her arm. He moved them both around to face the kaleidoscope of lights. "Please. One more homage to Eros, builder of cities, and to anarchic Aphrodite."

"You do like theater," Rebecca sighed, more pleasantly than she would have expected.

"It's all romance. My defense against something, you know." He smiled and they stepped inside.

⌁

Alex persuaded Rebecca that he should escort her home properly like a gentleman with no intention of anything more. The cab ride to her apartment took them from the bustle of midtown up along Central Park West where a few couples were idling home arm in arm, some late-night joggers were running beside the park, and dutiful dog owners were completing the last daily round of walking their pets. When the cab pulled up at the curb, Alex asked the driver to wait. He got out, held the car door for Rebecca, then closed it and walked with her across the broad sidewalk toward the apartment house, thanking her for engaging in this urban adventure with him, and for so graciously putting up with his ramblings and theatrics. She stopped outside the entrance and gave him a sleepy smile. Succumbing to her warmth, he raised a hand and brushed her cheek lightly with the back of his fingers. Then he felt silly for doing it. A sentimental adolescent gesture. He wanted to kiss her forcefully to efface it. But he didn't.

How boyish, she thought. Almost shy. Kind of sweet. For all of his histrionics.

They said good night, and she went inside. Alex got back in the taxi, and as it headed south, he opened the window, reclined in the seat, and stretched an arm outside to feel the warm June air rush between the splayed fingers that had touched her hand and cheek. The lights of other cars and neon signs became a blur as the taxi flew down the avenue and then into mid-town. A youthful exuberance and the thrill of romance intoxicated him.

"Thank you Eros, builder of cities, and anarchic Aphrodite," he breathed into the wind, "for the city, and the night."

# 8

## Against the Grain

Rebecca had always rather enjoyed her occasional Saturday mornings in the office. Nobody around. No interruptions. She could put things in place without distractions, and then be alone in fresh decorum to finish manuscripts, write letters, plan the calendar ahead. And she disliked coming in on Mondays to undone work and disarray. Not like Meredith, who thrived on disorder and the adrenaline of catching up fast. Being organized, in control. That was Rebecca's way. A good Saturday in the office did that for her, especially after working at home on Friday. Or it used to.

This Saturday, as usual, she sorted out the tasks to be done. What to read, what letters to write, what to set aside for later. But this time she couldn't quite focus. Last night kept intruding. The sometimes congenial, sometimes discomfiting conversation. The touches. The fleetingly revealing eyes. What had they seen in each other? What did it all mean? What did she want it to mean? Was he just playing at his *romance*? Or was he doing more than that, as occasionally he seemed? Those questions had taken her to sleep last night, sparing her the dreaded visitors of her restless bedtime hours—the blank book and flickering screen. Today those questions returned.

Shuffling through a pile of papers, she saw an envelope with Alexander Rodgers' name on it and the word *Metamorphoses*. His book proposal. She had laid it aside. Now she pulled out the pages. Only four? Skimming quickly, she tracked the theme of an alienated bon vivant who damns conventions, dabbles in pleasures, travels the world, falls into intrigues, has a love affair, and then . . . . What? Her eyebrows shot up. It stops with an ellipsis? No climax? No ending? Why did he give me this, even as a draft?

She tossed the pages onto her desk. It was just as she had suspected. He wasn't serious about this, or probably anything else, after all. Merely playing. Don't trust him. She pushed him from her mind and went on with her routine weekend labors. But her concentration kept faltering with conflicting emotions. One of these, she faintly recognized, adding to her perplexity, was a dim disappointment. But disappointment with what exactly she could not have said. When the phone rang a few minutes later, it broke into the quiet vacillations of her morning.

"Hi. It's Alex Rodgers. I hope I'm not interrupting the progress of culture too much," he said with cheerful mockery. "But I wanted to thank you again for last night. And to remind you that weekends weren't made for work. What *are* you doing, if I may ask?"

Already obscurely disaffected, she grew piqued at his flippancy and condescension and answered coolly, "For one thing, I read your draft."

"Oh, that was a mistake," he said jocularly. "But at least that will give me an opportunity to lure you away to talk business sometime soon. When?"

His frivolity strengthened her suspicions of him and increased her agitation. No, she couldn't trust him. He was too cavalier and self-indulgent. But . . . there were those moments of revelation last night. And she would have to deal with his proposal sometime. Despite her suspicions and agitation, somehow she was not altogether sorry he had called. She reached for her calendar.

"Are you still there?" he asked.

"You want to do that comedy routine again?" she answered genially.

"Ha! You're always ahead of me."

Ignoring his remark she said, "I'm just checking my calendar."

"Good! I'll patiently await the results."

She saw a tight schedule of deadlines and appointments and engagements spilling into the next week, as well as a three-day conference over the weekend. They were not all equally obligatory. She had committed to some of them to fill her days and nights with activity. But she wasn't about to admit that. She was almost relieved that she could say fairly honestly that she would have scarce free time for a while. She wanted to . . . what? Untangle her emotions? Distance herself? She wasn't sure.

"The next couple of weeks are jammed," she said as matter-of-factly as she could. "And I have a conference in Boston next weekend."

"That bad? Not a single free evening?" She's backing away again, isn't she? he said to himself. No one has *no* time to see someone for two weeks. Why was she doing it, after last night? Had he misread her? Could it be that silly book proposal? He was framing a question when she spoke, more cordially than before.

"But there is a retirement party for Carlton Sprague, head of Mega Publishing, on Thursday. If you are going to be there, we could talk then or maybe afterwards."

The offer and tone bolstered him. "Not exactly what I'd hoped for. A party? And it's a life-time away. But if it's all I can get, I'll take it. Sarah will arrange an invitation. And I'll plan to steal you away at the end. Where is it going to be held?"

"At the bar on the fourteenth floor of the Ritz-Carlton hotel just north of Battery Park. It's planned there as a gesture of support for the revival of lower Manhattan after 9/11."

"I applaud that." To coax her further out of her chilly working mode, he switched subjects. "You said you're spending the rest of this weekend with your mother. Is that a pleasure or an obligation?"

"It's not obligation."

"I'll bet she's a good conversationalist, and is very opinionated."

"True."

"Do you see her often?"

"Every couple of months."

"May I ask her age?"

"A youthful seventy."

"And your father?"

"He died a few years ago. But they had long been divorced."

"I'm sorry."

"It's history."

Although Rebecca was not cold, it was clear that her professional self did not want to chat. Or her private self had withdrawn. He repeated how much he had enjoyed their evening together at the theater and afterwards, and thanked her again for going along with it all. She responded politely, with her own civility, but not as warmly as he would have liked. He heard remoteness in her voice. And he signed off wishing her a happy weekend with her mother and saying he would look forward to seeing her at the party.

Alex hung up the phone puzzled. Why had she withdrawn? Had the office got its fangs into her? Had he offended her? Or was it just another of her mood swings, or whatever they were? He should probably expect them, he consoled himself. But even if he expected them, and was sometimes intrigued by them, would he ever understand them? Or alter them?

Still agitated, Rebecca tried to put him and her muddled

feelings behind her by diving into a manuscript about the great lovers of literature and of history that she had promised to read this week. But the lovers wouldn't come off the page. It might not be the author's fault, she admitted. It was hers. She couldn't concentrate. She felt restless. Not like her *old self* on Saturdays—Meredith's words rang hollowly once more. She knew now that her absorption in work had begun invisibly waning a year or more ago, and had grown gradually more visible until that paralyzing night. But there was some other vague distraction stymieing her, too. An hour later, she gave up and left the office, hoping the Connecticut countryside would clear her head and quiet her agitation. She had decided a week earlier that it was time for her mother's company. They had spoken on the phone. But now she needed more.

"Hi, Addy," Rebecca said as cheerfully as she could while embracing her mother at the train station in Westport. Rebecca had known her mother as "Addy" since childhood, when she had repeatedly heard her father call her that and figured her parents should be "Daddy" and "Addy." It became another Winters' family tradition. And Addy and Rebecca—one with an endearing nickname, the other with an allusive given name never vulgarized into the likes of "Becky"—had long ago become friends.

"You look tired," came the kindly maternal response. "Lovely, but tired. You've been working too much."

"Not really."

"Well, you'll have a restful weekend. And you'll tell me everything that's on your mind."

"What makes you think there's anything in particular on my mind?"

Rebecca knew her mother could always see through her. But that had become more reassuring than invasive. Adrianna

Winters never used her intuitions against her daughter. And mother and daughter had developed over the years a companionable closeness that renewed itself with every meeting. That made conversation easy—and sometimes unnecessary.

"So," her mother began as they later reclined on chaise lounges in the shaded garden behind the house with tall glasses of iced tea, Adrianna's spiked with rum, a libation Rebecca declined, "how are you adapting to your life as a single professional woman again?"

Rebecca balked. This was the first time they had seen each other since the divorce. She knew her mother would ask. But already? "You do go straight to the heart," she said feigning injury.

"Why pretend?"

"Courtesy?"

"You want me to *curtsy* around your feelings?"

"*Curtsy*? You're shameless. Or maybe I should say you're being *cutesy*."

"Ooooh. You didn't get such bad puns from me."

"Who else?"

Rebecca was used to her mother's repartee. And her bad puns. Levity came naturally to Adrianna. It was one of her strategies for putting people at ease and drawing them out. And it had helped open the door to unthreatening candor between mother and daughter, whether they chose to go through that door or not.

Yielding herself to her mother's affectionate needling, Rebecca went on. "As I told you after the divorce, it's not much different. Richard and I had drifted apart, or rather we had drifted into a kind of closeness that asked little of either of us. We remain close like that. Friends. And work fills the time, as it always has." Her voice faded and she took a drink.

Rebecca's words carried enough of a stock reply, and her tone conveyed enough lack of conviction that Adrianna studied her daughter's face for clues before continuing. She saw there more of what she had observed earlier, which she had politely dubbed tiredness, and which she had discerned less conspicuously as an unnatural disengagement during Rebecca's visits of the past six months or so.

"You don't say that with your normal confidence, my dear. What's wrong?"

"You won't let up, will you?"

"Should I?"

When Rebecca didn't answer, her mother proceeded. "If I didn't know you so well, I might guess that you hear the proverbial clock ticking and want a family, or that you want to spend your golden years with a good man." She gave her daughter a warm smile.

"Thanks for the *memento mori*." More of her mother's tactics. Light-hearted baiting. "No, it's not that. You know I'm not one of those children of divorced parents determined to replace the lost family. It's . . . I don't know." The words echoed into her glass as she had more iced tea.

"Well, this is a first! Rebecca Winters doesn't know what she wants? At the ripe age of thirty-nine? You'd better tell me about it."

Her mother was applying the tempered pressure that she surmised Rebecca actually wanted from her. Wanting it or not, Rebecca knew there was no use trying to hide or evade. Adrianna would get through eventually, even if she kept silent what she found. And today Rebecca wanted to open up, at least a little.

Rebecca drew a breath. "Something very strange and rather frightening happened to me, Addy," she began, her eyes fixed on the glass in her hands. "I don't know quite how to describe it. And I don't know what to do about it." She put the glass to her lips and drank slowly.

"Oh? What?" her mother asked sympathetically.

Rebecca rested the glass on her lap and held it with both hands.

"I can't say when it started, but it came to a head a few weeks ago. It wasn't because of the divorce. Or not because I was hurt by it. It was the opposite. I didn't really care about Richard, or the marriage. That sounds unlikely. But somehow it was true. I didn't think about it at the time. It all seemed so easy. Then one night it hit me. I didn't care about *anything*. Not deeply. And I didn't feel anything. I hadn't for I don't know how long. I didn't understand why. I still don't. But the worst of it was that suddenly I saw my whole life, past, present, future, all of it, *empty*. Everything I'd ever done added up to nothing. It was like a hallucination. And then," she took another drink and forced out the words, "I collapsed in a kind of panic. Not depression. *Real panic*. The trembling. The paralysis. And I literally fainted, passed out. Since then, I've gone on with my life, but it's not the same. I . . . don't quite know myself anymore. The panic took part of me with it. It's all so . . . baffling and . . . ." Her voice trailed off.

"Rebecca, dear." Her mother reached out and touched her arm affectionately. "I'm so sorry. Why didn't you tell me earlier?"

"There was nothing you could do. And I needed to try to figure it out. But I haven't made much progress. Much of the time I feel empty, lost. Nothing like that's ever happened to you, has it?"

Adrianna had never heard Rebecca say anything remotely suggesting emotional problems before. But she had seen signs of strong emotions in her daughter as a child and youth that Rebecca had seemed to resist or suppress. And Adrianna had suspected that Rebecca was hurt more by her father's leaving than she had admitted, even to herself. So, as Adrianna had watched her daughter skate through life with such seeming ease, and with such disciplined self-mastery, she had wondered if one day the ice would crack and Rebecca would break through into what lay beneath, and not even know why. Adrianna had even seen indications a few times over the last year or so that the ice could be cracking. She hadn't wanted this, god knows. No mother would. But with this strong-willed, emotionally protective daughter she figured she couldn't do much to prevent it. The only questions were, if it happened, how would Rebecca handle it? And where would it leave her? And what could Adrianna do? Now it occurred to Adrianna that it might be good for Rebecca to hear her mother talk about her own life. Adrianna had regrets that she had hidden, and feelings she had never fully bared. Perhaps revealing them would help.

"I can't say that I have been through what you describe," she began softly. But I've had my share of losses and regrets. Shall I tell you one of my greatest regrets?" she asked, deciding to take a motherly tack. Rebecca looked at her with raised eyebrows. "Not having had more children," Adrianna went on. "Our lives in teaching—your father's and mine—didn't encourage having more. Besides, you were enough. But now, I wish I'd had more of *you*." She smiled a smile showing where Rebecca had got hers, trying to brighten Rebecca up.

Losses? Regrets? Everyone has them. Rebecca knew her mother had been hurt and gone through some difficult times after her father had left. But Adrianna had risen above them, as Rebecca had expected. And over the years, mother and daughter had talked mostly about good times and common interests, and the rising arc of Rebecca's successful career. They had never talked at length about her mother's life, much less about her mother's losses and regrets.

"A mother's bias," Rebecca said modestly. "But I didn't know you felt that way about children. Still, if you're advocating motherhood, I don't think it's for me. Certainly not now. It's not just that I'm too old. I don't have anything to give, and I wouldn't want to depend on a child to fill an empty life."

"I'm not saying you should do it," Adrianna replied. "But you'd be surprised how much you can care about a child, no matter what. The devotion comes from nowhere. And it never leaves. Or maybe I was just fortunate to have you." She gave that warm maternal smile again.

Acknowledging the sentiments with a fond expression, Rebecca returned to regrets. "If you could do it all over again, your life," she asked, "what else would you have done differently, besides have more children? Assuming you were the same person you are and not someone else."

"True confessions? You've never gone in for that."

"You haven't either."

"You've never asked."

Is that true? Rebecca asked herself. It must be. She was not one to dig into peoples' lives, including her mother's. And her own. She swallowed and said, "Should I have? Well, I'm asking now."

Pleased that her gambit had provoked Rebecca's curiosity, Adrianna answered carefully. "Like most people, I'd change many things. I've never bought that old Edith Piaf bravado, *je ne regret rien*. It's selfish. And false. We've all made mistakes and hurt people, and ourselves, and we should regret that and want to undo such things. And anyone who denies regrets is a self-serving or self-deceived liar."

"So, what regrets do you have, say, about your marriage to Daddy that you haven't told me? What would you change if you could?"

Adrianna was ready. She chose her words to have the right effect. "Your father was charming and intelligent and attractive, of course," she began. "I know you adored him, and he adored you. And I loved him. But what you don't know is that he was never more than superficially in love with me, or his love dimmed quite early. Oh, he genuinely cared for me, and we enjoyed each other's company, sharing intellectual interests and having a good social act. But in the end, I don't think I ever truly knew your father. I don't know if anyone did, even himself. So when he left, it wasn't as shocking as you thought. It wasn't as though he suddenly became an unrecognizable person. He was just moving on with a younger woman who would respond anew to his charms. The old story. But part of it was my fault. I didn't know what I needed from him any more than I knew what he needed from me. Or not soon enough. And I think the same thing was true of him. We weren't honest enough with each other, or with ourselves. And that's what I'd change. I'd have pushed your father to be more emotionally honest, not all surface charm and intellect. Or I'd have married someone who was more emotionally accessible. And, even more important than that, I'd have been more emotionally honest with myself. Yes, it was difficult for me, starting over. But it might surprise you to learn that I'm glad I did it."

Rebecca stared at her mother. Glad? She had thought they were so close and candid. No deep secrets. But then . . . she had never asked.

Adrianna took a sip of tea. "And I suspect you are quite like me in this. You've always been so savvy and known what you wanted. But don't be too sure that you *do* know what's good for you. You might get what you *want*, but not what you *need*. That's an ancient adage. Nonetheless true. We all confuse wants and needs when we're young. And we might not know what we need until we have it, or until it's too late to get it. I had an inkling, by the way, that Richard was more of what you *wanted* at the time than what you *needed*. But I don't think you would've believed me if I had told you then."

Rebecca blinked but didn't answer. Her mother had seen through her before and was closing in now.

"Since you are now open to these things, may I continue this homily and offer a little motherly advice to a daughter still young but no longer a child?"

Rebecca waited.

"Life often tricks us by playing to our expectations and strengths instead of to our true needs. This makes us think we can win. But then, when we're convinced we're at the top of our game, we can discover that we've lost by winning. You know the cliché that when God wants to punish us He answers our prayers."

A 'good' cliché, Rebecca thought, but said, "I don't follow you."

"I'll spell it out. Don't play to your strengths all the time to get what you want. Go against the grain sometimes, if I may use that cliché. We can't change who we are, but we can discover things in ourselves that we didn't know were there. And these can turn out to be the most important things. Some of our deepest needs can get hidden by our wants and our very aptitudes. So sometimes we have to go against the grain of surface successes to find our true needs and natures. And that can save our lives."

"Have you taken up pop psychology?"

"In my fashion, I suppose. But you asked what I would change if I could re-live my life. That's what I'd do. I wouldn't have been so confident that my life would work out as I thought I wanted it to. I'd have taken some sharp turns instead of going straight ahead. I don't mean merely taking risks. That's not the point. I mean not always making the choices that come easily and naturally and that seem to fit. I'd go against the grain, at least sometimes. Pay the price, if necessary. But get the rewards. The truth is, we can pay a heavier price for living a life that comes easily and runs smoothly than for one that doesn't. We just don't notice right away because we pay that heavier price over time in smaller installments as we satisfy our immediate wants and fail to see our true needs. That might be a platitude. But discovering the difference between our wants and needs is one of the deep secrets of life, ancient adage though it might be. And it can take practically a lifetime to do it."

Rebecca furrowed her brow. "Do I know you?"

Her mother laughed. "Don't let a parent's platitudes and pop psychology throw you. I can honestly say that in some ways my life gets better all the time."

"Oh? How?"

"Well, in some ways, I've probably been more alive in the years without your father than I ever was in the years with him. You might be shocked at what your aging mother has grown capable of." Adrianna took a hearty swallow of her rummy tea.

"What are you saying?"

"*Oh, my dear,*" Adrianna replied with drama in her voice and a twinkle in her eye that told Rebecca she should long ago have seen much more in her mother than she had seen. "Let's just say my travels are more adventurous than the brochures promise, and my life at home more lively than its appearances."

"What? Lovers?" Rebecca blurted out.

"Lots of things. And most of them good. Not always easy. Not predictable. But good—for me. Now, let's leave it at that for the moment," Adrianna said, being deliberately provocative and tantalizing.

Reeling from her mother's revelations and hints of more, and dumbfounded at her own blindness, Rebecca downed the last of her tea. Yes, her mother had seemed quite contented, even gay—in the good old definition of the word—for a long time. But Rebecca had chalked that up to Adrianna's resilient nature. How insensitive of her not to have seen more, or not to have asked, while routinely thinking of herself as sensitive to other people.

"That's hardly fair—to stop with a cliff-hanger," she said, pouring herself another half glass of iced tea.

"Later."

Rebecca knew her mother wasn't to be swayed. So she acted on another curiosity. "OK. But tell me this. You've said before that you didn't marry again after daddy because the right man didn't come along. Is that the real reason?"

"Probably. But don't make it so definitive. Who knows, I might still do it one day, whatever my age. Although I get choosier all the time. And marriage is not something I *want* or *need*. Or not anymore. My life is very full." Adrianna flashed an amused smile.

Rebecca pondered her mother's words, struggling with herself. Then she said hesitantly, "I recently met a man who would agree with much of what you've been saying." She hadn't planned to mention Alex, but now it seemed unavoidable.

"Aha! Who is he?" her mother reacted with alacrity.

"A writer I met professionally for a friend. We've spent a couple of evenings together socially."

"And?"

"Oh, he has some of Daddy's qualities—intelligent, charming, interesting, attractive—incidentally, he praises my parents' verve in giving me my name. But he makes me uncomfortable. He likes to affect poses, and over-dramatize everything. I don't know if he takes anything very seriously. He could also be a womanizer. He's not like me at all. Or not . . . ." She faltered, refusing to speak of her "old self."

Her mother interrupted. "Could be a good thing. I don't mean to be callous, dear," she said, deciding her daughter needed a push and would survive it, "but, as I said, Richard was probably *too right* for you. And so have been many other things in your life. I must tell you that ever since you left childhood behind—when you used to get extremely upset over the loss of a pet and other sorrows, which you've long forgotten—you have perhaps managed your strong emotions and your life too well, controlling them too much and playing too much to your strengths. But you may *need* more than that. You should go against the grain more. What have you got to lose?"

Rebecca sat in silence. Her mother was playing an uncommon role today. Sympathetic and loving as always. But more revealing and provocative than normal. Adrianna hadn't wanted to do hand-holding. Not that Rebecca had wished her to. But her mother seemed determined to rock the boat. 'Go against the grain. What have you got to lose?' Those clichés were her most consoling words! Yes, clichés. But were they . . . *good clichés*? Rebecca's mind balked at the question.

Seeing her daughter sinking into herself, and having said all she thought should be said right now—which she recognized should have been said years ago—Adrianna decided it was time for a change of subject. She polished off her drink and said cheerfully, "Why don't we go in and fix dinner? I got a lobster for salad and made a key lime pie. I know you like that. Then we'll relax and watch a movie. You didn't bring work, did you?"

"Yes," Rebecca answered distantly.

"You're shamefully diligent." Adrianna gave her daughter's shoulder a gentle squeeze as they got up and went inside.

"Blame yourself," Rebecca retorted sarcastically. "I got it from you and Daddy. Like my other failings."

"On second thought," her mother shot back with a wry smile, "*don't* have children. They blame you for everything." Mother and daughter shared a restorative laugh.

The weekend proceeded pleasantly from there, as it normally did with Addy and Rebecca. They walked and talked and cooked and read and watched old movies and enjoyed each other, revisiting the sobering subjects of Saturday afternoon only briefly. Adrianna revealed as much about herself, and offered as much advice, and prodded Rebecca as much as she thought appropriate. Rebecca dwelled on her mother's revelations about her colorful and gratifying post-married life, thinking: how little we know of other people, even those closest to us, and how little we know of ourselves. At the same time, she pushed queasy thoughts about herself into that secluded place where she had always confined unwanted creatures of her inner life. A place that had become a crowded cavern. And there they stayed.

Until she was on the train back into the city. Watching the countryside flitting past out the window, she let her mind wander inward. And there she saw those creatures begin to rise, monsters from the deep murmuring malevolent sounds up through the emptiness inside her. But then she heard her mother saying *Go against the grain. What have you got to lose?* What exactly would that mean, for her? she wondered. Maybe she could turn this question into a problem to be solved. She had always been good at solving problems. In school and outside. And she had managed to turn most troubles she had encountered into solvable *problems*. But not the *dilemma* that had been with her more or less since the panicked night. Would her mother's words help with that?

Then *he* came to her mind. Is he what her mother had meant? Going against the grain? Rebecca remembered she had agreed to see him later this week to talk about his book proposal. What was she going to tell him? What was she going to *do* about him? What was she going to do about herself? Were these somehow the same thing? What did she want? What did she need? Platitude or not.

# 9

## The Moon Illusion

Walking into the crowded bar in the hotel rising above Battery Park and New York Harbor, Alex Rodgers was greeted by the resounding hum of countless conversations and the clinking of ice cubes swishing in cocktail classes. He had never relished these publishing events with their professional politics and bookish fashions and increasingly commercial atmosphere, but he knew their uses, and rather welcomed this one. He had arrived as late as he thought seemly, and now he girded himself and plunged in, contriving a smile and genial salutations to a few acquaintances as he eased his way to the bar for a drink and then outside onto the open deck overlooking the harbor. There he paused to take in the view—the Statue of Liberty standing prominently in the middle distance, the sun lowering in the west over New Jersey, and the Verrazano bridge to the south east framing the passage from Manhattan to the Atlantic Ocean between Brooklyn and Staten Island. How romantic, he said to himself with a smile. Swirling his drink, he turned to case the celebrants mingling outside and in.

He knew a few people—editors, writers, and his agent, Sarah—and he recognized others unidentifiable by name. Denizens of the publishing world at professional play, displaying all the manners of cocktail party animation—wagging heads, swaying bodies, steady smiles, staged laughter, lips periodically wetted with drinks, eyes casting about the room for better prey. He traded greetings with some who passed by, and he wondered if he should be politic and make the rounds himself. But he talked himself out of it. Then he heard a familiar voice nearby.

"How's it going, Alex?" It was Harold Rubin, a casual friend and a critic for the *Times*. "Rare to see you at one of these things. What's the occasion?"

"Oh, hi Hal. I've come to meet someone," Alex responded cordially. "What's your excuse?"

"I don't need one. I have to breathe this heady air. And you never know whom you'll run into."

"You have an insatiable social appetite, Hal. I'm in awe. And you always get your pronouns right."

Hal took the cue. "So, *whom* did you come to meet? Somebody I know? Somebody I *should* know?"

"Don't you know everybody already?"

"Not yet. Who is it?"

"An editor."

"Name?"

"Rebecca Winters. You know her?"

"The name has a familiar ring to it. Where have I heard it? I must have met her. Anyhow, are you pitching a book, or pitching woo?"

"Just a book idea. It wouldn't interest you. A novel."

"Don't be so sure. Will I be in it?"

"Never miss a step, do you, Hal. I suppose I could work you in, for a good review."

"Depends on how you depict me."

"Glowingly, Hal. I wouldn't do it any other way." Alex caught sight of Rebecca through the glass doors talking to a clutch of fellow bookies. "There she is," Alex said, gesturing in her direction with his glass. "I'd better catch her. Nice to see you, Hal. Keep your finger on the pulse." He started moving away.

"Aren't you going to introduce me?"

"Another time."

"Not fair. But remember to do me justice in the book."

"Justice is risky, Hal," Alex called back with a laugh. "Better ask for charity." They genially tipped their glasses toward each other, and Alex sifted into the crowd, returning inside past the bar while sharing more politenesses. When he reached Rebecca's circle, he assumed an attentive air and waited. She acknowledged his presence with a nod and mixed feelings. A man in a three-piece suit with an academic demeanor was talking about a book that had just been pulled from the press because of litigation over permissions. "Before long," the man remarked, "there'll be more lawyers in publishing than editors."

"There'll be more lawyers everywhere than anyone else," the woman next to him inserted.

"It's a peril of democracy," Alex chimed in. Eyes switched to the interloper. "Every conflict of interest in democracies will one day be resolved by the courts. The last bastion of presumed objectivity in subjectivity-besotted post-modern America."

"Oh, this is Alexander Rodgers," Rebecca spoke up with a trace of apology in her voice. "He writes on culture and politics, as you might have guessed. Mr. Rodgers, meet Catherine Ravitch, she is a precocious intellectual who teaches at Barnard—I edited one of her books—her husband George Martin, an attorney for Global Publishing, and Sanford Lieber, one of the most humane people in the business."

They exchanged greetings.

"Alexander Rodgers? I think I've read something of yours," Sanford remarked politely. "A *Harper's* piece on post-modern modernism, or some such historical depravity. It was good and nasty."

"I committed such an act. Thanks for reading it. But I didn't mean to intrude," Alex said. "Please go on."

"I was just reciting some of the woes of litigation in publishing," George Martin explained.

"A subject for John Grisham or Stephen King," Alex cracked. "Intrigue and horror in Rights and Permissions."

"Let the blood flow," Catherine laughed.

"Already does," George Martin added.

"Why don't you take it on, Mr. Rodgers?" Sanford asked. "You're keen on cultural mayhem."

"Not for me. I'm now leaning more to romantic mystery. Cheap, vulgar, fantasy. And I've come to talk to Ms. Winters about an idea for one."

"I see," said Sanford. "Well, perhaps we should let these literary negotiations go forward unimpeded. We'll leave you to your persuasions. Good luck with the mystery."

"And thanks so much, again, Rebecca," Catherine added, "for all you did for Gena. She's in heaven, and you're a saint."

"I'm glad it worked out," Rebecca replied modestly. "But don't start believing in saints. It could skew your critical judgment."

More polite laughter. Then Alex contributed his own appropriate manners, and the trio edged away.

"A triumph!" he boasted under his breath. "I chased them off."

"Was that your intent?" Rebecca said coolly.

"Not exactly," he replied, un-affected by her tone, "but I'll accept it. And what, if I may ask, was that about someone being in heaven and you being a saint? Do you perform miracles?"

"I only helped her younger sister get a job at my company. No miracle."

"Sounds like a miracle to me. I suspected you had hidden powers and a big heart. But now, can we depart discreetly to do our *business*," he stressed the word somewhat mockingly, "or do you still have to be sociable. Life is short. Parties long."

"You're being rather presumptuous, aren't you?"

"I apologize. I'll await your desires. But then please let's go someplace else to talk. This convivial throng would make it difficult."

She looked at him with ambivalence but admitted he was right. "I should speak to a few more people."

"All right. Then let's go down to the park and watch the sun set over the harbor while we talk, OK?"

She didn't answer, but glanced around the room. On a park bench? Why do that? It's hardly convenient. True, they would be far from other book people. And she could cut it short if she wanted to and take the subway home from there. Maybe it's not such a bad idea. Could be worth the chance. She relented.

"Good! I'll speak to Sarah and then loiter outside on the deck," he said. "Ten minutes? Fifteen?"

"Can't promise."

"I'll try to endure."

Rebecca merged into the murmuring throng. Seeing Sarah Rose leave a conversation across the room, Alex waved and walked over to her. He thanked her for arranging the invitation. "Don't mention it," she replied. "You gave me the best of reasons for your coming—to talk to Rebecca. She's a classy person and would be good for you, as your editor, or . . . anything else."

"Sarah, you are very sly. But I thank you for always thinking of my welfare. How many authors can say that of their agents?"

"All of mine. But you *are* special, of course, Alex."

"Requiring *special handling* I suppose."

"As I've said before, you have a rather whimsically willful temperament. And I think you're proud of it. I can *handle* you. But some people wouldn't . . . understand."

"I plead guilty. But it keeps life interesting. And it gives you a chance to scold me and try to put me under the influence of *classy* people like Rebecca Winters. I thank you for that."

"So how is that book proposal coming?"

"I gave her a few pages. We're going to talk about it after we leave here."

"You gave her something without clearing it with me?"

"It wasn't much. Not worth troubling you. When I write up the real thing, I'll get your imprimatur. You know I wouldn't make a serious professional move without you."

"See why you need *special handling*? But don't be careless with Rebecca. She won't put up with it. And she deserves better. So do I. I told her she should meet you. Don't make me look bad in her eyes."

"I'll do my best. But to tell you the truth, Sarah, she is, well, kind of mercurial, or maybe I should say unfathomable. I can't figure her out. One minute she's cordial and seems engaged, then the next she's bristly or on another planet. I don't know if this is just how she is with me or if that's her nature. Frankly, I don't think she's really very interested in my book idea. Not that it's much of an idea yet. But there is so much about her that I would like to . . . reach. Do you know what's going on with her?"

"As a friend, I'll tell you she might need some special handling herself these days. Please be careful with her. She's a very good human being, and deserves kindness."

Before Alex could dig further, another of Sarah's authors broke into the conversation, and after introductions and some gracious words, Alex excused himself, promising to be in touch with Sarah soon. He freshened his drink and went back outside curious about what Sarah had meant by Rebecca needing "special handling these days." Casting his eyes out over the harbor again, he was reminded what a wonderful place this harbor and Battery Park are. Following the Hudson river with his eyes to the north, he became aware that now he was seeing through open sky where the World Trade Center had stood a few blocks away.

He remembered the last time he had been there, a couple of years earlier. It was for a reception on the top floor of the north tower to honor restaurant designers, some of whom he had written about. It was a late afternoon in summer like this. And he had strolled from the reception room into the restaurant grandly named Windows on the World perched above the cityscape of Manhattan, which stretched out of sight to the north beyond a vast wall of windows. He had dined there a number of times, despite its being a tourist destination. And why shouldn't it be? he had thought. Everyone should get to see the romance of the city from up here over a candle-lit dinner.

He recalled then meandering down a hallway outside the restaurant into a busy bar above the harbor to the south. There, among the early barflies on their stools and fanciful standing light fixtures in the shape of skyscrapers arrayed around the room, a corner dance floor backed by two towering window walls had awaited late night swingers. Now he imagined dancing there, above the lights of the city and of ships sailing past the Statue of Liberty putting out to sea. Would Rebecca have liked it, he wondered? Or would she have thought it crass? Commercialized romance? He wished he could have had the chance to see it with her.

Musing on, he recalled himself making a circuit of that room, through the several bar areas, along the tall windows and out to the elevator lobby. There, near the entrance to yet another restaurant, he had stood in front of a sweeping curved wall painted dark blue and sprinkled with tiny electric lights. A starry night, in the shamelessly theme-park spirit of the place. Perfectly appropriate. And sort of pretty. Art and design can be "pretty" nowadays, he had thought, can't they?

But, he said to himself, now it's gone. All gone. And it is sad.

Absorbed in his melancholy reveries, he saw Rebecca approaching him. He snapped out of it. "Ah. You are liberated," he exclaimed. "I commend your courage." She disregarded his silly compliment, preparing herself for what she thought could be a strained conversation, although she still had little idea of what she would say or how it would go.

A few minutes later, they were walking in Battery Park at the southern tip of Manhattan. They stopped and sat on a bench along the harbor. Lovers cooed on other benches. Youths darted by on roller blades. Vendors sold hot dogs, soft drinks, and curios. Tourists roamed happily or gazed out into the harbor at the Statue of Liberty. Freighters lay moored in the outer bay. Tug boats churned up and down pushing laden barges or towing empty ones. Pleasure boats bounced over the wakes, and the sails of private skiffs bobbed on the swells. Ferries lumbered across the harbor from Manhattan to Staten Island and back, while others returned the last visitors of the day from Ellis Island and the Statue of Liberty. The statue itself was casting her lengthening late-day shadows across the glistening waters. The sky was nearly clear but for haze in the west that was just beginning to ignite in hues of red and purple, preparing the stage for the setting sun.

"You have to be grateful for air pollution," Alex said cheerfully. "You can't get great sunsets without it. Not here anyway."

"That's kind of a perverse idea." Her voice had a slight edge to it.

"Why do you say that?"

"Because," she answered in the same tone, "it's perverse to praise toxic causes for giving us pretty sights. Like Nero fiddling in the light of burning Rome."

"I'm shamed," he said archly to counter her earnestness.

"But we didn't come here to debate air pollution." She was now trying to be matter-of-fact without being edgy. "We have things to take care of."

"Yes. If we must." He knew he was being too off-hand, and she was not in a playful mood, much less in the engaging mood of their last evening together. Had something changed in her? But he was glad to be with her and had hoped to make this a short, light-hearted conversation leading to better things.

She had not looked forward to this conversation for several reasons. She had nothing good to say about his so-called proposal.

It was cavalierly unprofessional. And more than that, it reflected many of the things about him that annoyed her. The flippancy. The self-indulgence. The histrionics. The questionable motives. And she knew that he would want to drag her through them all again. Or some new version of them. And yet . . . there was that night after the theater, the look in the eyes, and the touch. She hadn't forgotten. Still, she wasn't sure what it all meant, and this made dealing with him more troubling than it should have been. She admitted that possibility to herself. Part of . . . her dilemma? Forcing these conflicting thoughts to the back of her mind, she hit on the protective tactic of pulling no professional punches.

"Well," she began, taking a breath. "Your book proposal. It's really not much, is it? Even as a draft. As I said when we first spoke about it, the idea amounts to a hackneyed psychological adventure. And now you've given me four pages of generic outline with no climax, no ending at all. You're not serious about this, are you? Why did you even bother?" Her voice trailed off at the end, and she felt some relief at having said what she had to say.

He was taken aback a little by the intensity of her reaction. But he decided to try a new gambit.

"Well, let's call it a work in progress," he said amiably, hoping to reengage her. "As to the ending, maybe you could give me some ideas. What should happen?"

She had half expected some kind of evasive reaction like this. And she wasn't going to be drawn in. "Look, Alex," she said with a note of tired exasperation. "If you want to write a book, get serious and write it." Then she dropped her voice again and turned away as she said quietly, "But I'm not the right person to take it on."

"Why not?"

She didn't answer.

"Oh, I know," he answered for her calmly. "You don't like to do novels. And besides, this one is too contemporary in the worst sense. Narcissistic. Exhibitionistic. Shallow. Fragmented. Clichéd. And it doesn't lead anywhere. Am I close?"

Her agitation was growing again. And her unsettled feelings of the other night were returning. All of that talk about romance and sadness, and even that momentary look in the eyes, were a pose, weren't they? It's all a game for him, isn't it? And he wanted to make her part of it. To cast her as a character in his personal romance. She wouldn't let him do it. The agitation was mounting. But it was mounting on the odd feeling she had noticed when first glancing at his proposal last Saturday: disappointment. Over what? Had she let herself expect too much? But what? And why? And was she now being unreasonably critical? He had goaded her into it, hadn't he? So, what was she going to do now, tell him she didn't trust him and let that be the end of it? But, why did it matter to her as much as it did? She remained silent.

She had withdrawn, he told himself. He had misjudged her and regretted it. He should have known better. Had he truly offended her with his half-baked book idea and his flippant manner? Had he been too *careless* with her, as Sarah had warned? Could he get her back—that irresistibly warm, unexpectedly revealing, and unintentionally seductive woman of the other night? He had to try.

"Rebecca," he said soberly, "I apologize. I was wrong to give you that so-called proposal. I didn't think you would take it so seriously. That was my mistake. I should have taken it more seriously myself. It was thoughtless and unprofessional of me not to. The thing isn't worth your time. And not worthy of you. Forgive me. I . . . didn't understand. And I allowed myself . . . ." He paused and turned to face her. "Rebecca, I will be honest with you. When we met, I did have a book idea in mind, but it was vague, and I was not in a frame of mind to do much more with it. Sarah had said you might *inspire* me. She is quite motherly, as you know. But then I was, oh, quite taken with you, for yourself. That's an old-fashioned way of putting it, but it's appropriate. You didn't try to do it, of course. You were, well, very cool, distant most of the time. Your mind on other things. A bit edgy. And you seemed a little sad. But you had this . . . . Oh, I can't describe it. Words fail me, believe it or not. You had this aura or something. A mystery and remoteness about you that made me want to know you, to find out who you are behind the intelligence and professional bearing and beauty. I've been trying to do that ever since. But not very successfully. Sometimes you have seemed at ease and willing to share yourself, but then you have withdrawn. It's my fault, I'm sure. I have not been as sensitive to you as I should have been. I will also confess that I thought you might stir my creative juices. But now that's the least of it. The last time we were together, just before we left the roof top restaurant after the theater, when I touched your hand and looked into your eyes, I felt a genuine closeness to you. Even an affinity. I thought you felt it, too. It lasted only a moment, but it affected me more than I could have predicted. I don't know why. But it made me want to be with you and share all kinds of things with you. And when we said good night, I . . . . Well, I still want that. And I would like to think it would not be only for me. But now I feel closed out again. Because I've been stupid and insensitive. I'm so sorry."

He did sound sincere again. And contrite. Was he? she asked herself. Or was this just another deft turn of his act? She didn't have the energy or desire to defend her doubts. Maybe she had taken his proposal too seriously, after all. Maybe all of this was more about her than him. But now one thing was clear. He wasn't here for a book. He was here *for her*. Or for something about her, and she might not want him to reach it. Could she trust him more for confessing the truth? Inexplicably, she wanted to.

"Let's forget about it for now," she sighed and sat back against the bench, giving him a pleasantly resigned expression.

"OK," he said. "Thanks." And heartened by what he regarded as a concession coupled with a veiled invitation, he shifted gears and moved on, telling himself to tread more cautiously around whatever it was in her that caused her to withdraw. "Now," he said, elevating his tone, "may I suggest talking about something more entrancing than anything I might ever write?"

She put the edginess and agitation behind her, but a certain uneasiness persisted. What was he up to now? She could just go home. Still, for some reason, she didn't want to. Her silence again gave him an opportunity.

"The sunset," he said, as he theatrically swept an arm across the western vista. "Of course, it does depend on how you look at it." He laughed self-mockingly. "One person's rapturous sunset is another's toxic air pollution." He glanced over to see her reaction. She had followed his gesture and was facing west. And she was thinking that he was at it again. Hardly missing a step. Back to his histrionics. But she let him go on. She was tired. And he was right—the sun, descending close to the horizon was striking. She would go along. Then she would go home. She focused on a sight she had seen many times but had never thought much about. The filter of haze over the western sky had now become a translucent scrim dropped in front of the sun, shading down from a vibrant orange at the top to a cool magenta near the ground, where the haze thickened. Behind the scrim, the crimson disk of the sun hovered over the edge of the world.

"Good show" he said, reassured that she was coming back. "The sun, when you see it like this, seems almost artificial, like a stage prop, much bigger than when it's overhead, doesn't it?"

"I hadn't noticed."

"The 'Moon Illusion' psychologists call it. Not astronomers, mind you. I read an article about this recently. May I tell you about it? I'm sure you'd be fascinated." She looked at him but didn't speak. He took that as a yes. "This is how it works. Our eyes see—actually our brains interpret—the moon and the sun to be larger when we see them down near the horizon like this than when we see them up higher in the sky. This has to do with the perception of distance. When the sun or moon are high in the sky we see them against the whole immeasurable infinity of the universe, which makes them appear relatively small. But when they come down to earth, so to speak, and we see them near the horizon, we unconsciously enlarge their size in relation to the finite world whose edge they are hovering above. Compared to infinity, everything gets smaller. Compared to our finite world, the moon and sun get larger. Our minds and eyes can't help it. Neat, 'eh? The Moon Illusion isn't in nature at all. It's in us. It's literally a way of looking at things."

He searched her face for a response to this nice proof of that prized notion. She shot him a mildly dubious expression, wondering if he was inventing this, but she conceded silently that the sun did look exceptionally large and the sunset was exquisite. Convincing himself that she was with him, he went on enthusiastically.

"I didn't make this up. And I have more to offer, if I may." He caught an inquisitive glance and continued. "Since the sunset is playing its proper role, and the evening light will be heavenly, could I persuade you to go for a ride on the Staten Island Ferry to see an even more sublime illusion? Manhattan is magical from out in the harbor at dusk when the lights of the city come up. It's illusion in reality, reality in illusion, touched by magic. And the ferry is only a five minute walk from here."

He was running fast with the small concessions she had given him. Now the Staten Island Ferry? What a quaint idea. She'd ridden the ferry a few times during the day but never at night. She had no inclination to do it now. She thought she was tired. But something was tugging her. Ambivalence tilting back and forth? Going against the grain? The summer evening? The sunset? She didn't know. But for some reason she didn't resist. She would go with it.

Within minutes they were standing on a ferry plowing through the harbor toward Staten Island. They leaned against the starboard railing on the west. Weary commuters slouched on the benches inside the cabin and out on deck. A cruise liner glided past, returning its load of happily sunburned tourists from some southern sea. Tug boats chugged alongside the liner, readying to tuck it into port. Wakes from the harbor traffic slapped against the ferry's hull. The torchlight of the Statue of Liberty began glowing against the evening sky as the ferry neared and passed it by.

They didn't say much, commenting casually on the harbor life. Was she, he asked himself, becoming once more the receptive woman he had seen briefly at the rooftop restaurant when their hands had touched, and their eyes had met, and whose cheek he had later given a shy caress when they had said good night? And will it last? Or will it slip away again?

She thought of nothing but the harbor and the close sight of the Statue of Liberty and the sunset that cast a warm radiance over everything, and that she had missed something by never taking the ferry in the evening before.

When the ferry docked at Staten Island, they were carried along by the crush of other passengers into the terminal, where they had a quick drink at a hotdog stand and then re-boarded. By that time, the commuters had gone to their homes leaving only a handful of pleasure-seekers onboard for the return trip to Manhattan. Alex and Rebecca proceeded to the bow for a full view of the skyline. There they were practically alone.

The sun, now below the horizon, still painted the scene when the ferry pushed out of the dock. And balmy summer air stirred in the shore breeze.

"Now we get to see the city's greatest magic trick," Alex announced with muted drama. "It transforms itself before your eyes. The work-a-day New York of energy, power, and hulking hard-edged buildings becomes a diaphanous city of glitter, fantasy, and romance."

"The loquacious tour guide has returned," she said. Her

voice had no edge in it, and her features were soft. She was going along. Against the grain. It was easier than she had expected.

He smiled. "It was more magical and spectacular with the World Trade Center," he added in a more subdued tone. "Not that those buildings were anything to admire architecturally. Quite banal in style and dehumanizing in scale. But they caught the sunset magnificently, and they dazzled in the twilight. I miss them for that. And I'm afraid they will be replaced by some misconceived memorial that will preserve the site as 'sacred ground' dedicated to the victims. That's what's been proposed anyway. Sure, there was a tragic loss of life, but New York deserves better than to enshrine that tragedy with a hole in the ground, a funereal monument to death and destruction. Ah, I seem to have surrendered again to the simmering anger I told you about. Still, a discreet monument to the lost, especially to the valiant rescue workers, yes. But the whole site should be rebuilt with exuberance and beauty and humanity as an affirmation of life and of New York. And to catch the sunset. Don't you think?"

She thought for a moment, observing the vacant space in the skyline. "They will build something," she said quietly, sensing a loss she hadn't identified before, "and it will be impressive."

"I hope so. But that won't matter as long as a big hole in the ground stays there dedicated to death and destruction, because then the place will be morbid, and terrorists can gloat. See, I am still angry. But enough of these maudlin and lugubrious thoughts," he brightened his tone again. "We have magic to see before us. Pay attention," he instructed playfully.

While they cruised toward Manhattan, the city brilliantly reflected the red and yellow and gold of the radiating sun as it sank out of sight. Then, as the twilight deepened, the Statue of Liberty seemed to raise her torch ever higher, as if to illuminate the way, and Manhattan's windows started to light up on their own, a spark here, a cluster there, dotting the skyline in a widening display. And as those lights came up against the darkening backdrop of the twilit northeastern sky, the city seemed to lose solidity, its contours vanishing in the enfolding dusk.

"See, Eros doesn't only build cities. He's a magician," Alex rhapsodized, "transforming the city from day to night, from fact to fantasy, reality to illusion through the twilight. A magical moment. We may not live for such moments, but we shouldn't live without them. Don't you agree?"

She didn't respond. She would probably have said *no*, she did *not* agree. That might be *his* view of life. It wasn't hers. But then, what was hers? She stifled the question. And as she watched the skyline dissolve into the nighttime lights while the ferry slowly approached it, she admitted to herself that it *was* kind of magical. An illusion in reality. She blinked away some moisture brought to her eye by the soft shore breeze, and swept aside a wisp of hair wafting across her face. Then she turned her head obliquely toward him and said softly, "You could be right."

Their eyes came together. And there they saw again the hints of hidden fears, and even more, the glints of unknown yearnings. This time they let the moment last. Glimpsing a slight sheen of dampness on her cheek, he gently wiped it away with the boyish stroke of his fingers that he had made once before, sentimentally imagining it was a tear of happiness. She did not move. He inched his fingers down to her chin. And lifting her unresisting face to his, he leaned nearer. His lips met hers with the lightest touch. The sensation gave him a thrill he hungered to hold. An ardor without urgency. To her it was a sensation feathery yet palpable. Real yet not real. There, but not there. It was a kiss she had not imagined she would want. It was a kiss he wanted never to end.

# On a Bridge of Dreams

(Continued)

Rebecca had no idea of the hour or the day when she was awakened by the doctor standing beside the bed telling her, "I have found your friend. He is alive."

"Thank God!" she exclaimed. Any god, she thought. She tried to sit up.

"But I must tell you he was badly injured."

"How badly?" She implored, shifting the pillow to prop herself up, ignoring the pain. The doctor bent down to help her.

"There were flesh wounds and some internal injuries. These have been attended to and now pose no danger. However, he also suffered head injuries and is still unconscious. That is all I know."

"But we were together. Why did he . . . ?"

"He must have been between you and the explosion. He could have been shielding you."

She remembered Alex pushing her in front of him. "Can I see him?" she pleaded again.

"Not yet. I will find out and tell you when it is time. I am sorry the news is not better. But it could have been worse. It was for many. He is lucky even to be alive. And so are you."

*Lucky? That word cut through her, slicing with bitter irony. "Will he . . . ?"*

*"It is too soon to say anything more," the doctor interrupted. "But I will let you know as soon as I learn anything. I promise."*

*Rebecca slumped back into the bed. The doctor attended to her dressings and instructed her to try to walk a little in order to prevent blood clots. It would hurt to do it, he warned, but it would be good for her, and she would get used to it. He gave her more anesthetic and repeated his promise to return with more news of Alex as soon as he could.*

*Rebecca's eyes followed the doctor as he moved on to other patients. Lucky? He had said they were lucky. Was that luck at the Taj Mahal?*

*Alex had spoken of their good luck again and again, and of the "benign coincidences" that had woven their lives together. It was one of his pet notions. He saw good luck and benign coincidences in all kinds of things. He could hardly stop talking about this during the weekend that had changed so much for them when they had gone dancing and had spent the night together and had then driven the next day to Atlantic City. But it had started at the horse races, hadn't it? Yes, the horse races. That was the first time he had carried on about their good luck. It was the first time for other things, too. Her eyelids closed, she forgot where she was, and she drifted off to sleep on bitter-sweet memories of their good luck that day at the races.*

# 10

## Gotta Horse Right Here

"Horse races?!" Rebecca's voice rose with incredulity, and the phone almost fell from her hand.

They had spoken a couple of times since the ferry ride and had planned to meet for dinner when her second hectic week was done. But this call surprised her. "Yes!" Alex replied spiritedly. "An impulse. And now that your stretch of over-scheduling has passed you can live again. Remember, we are having dinner tonight. And now, as it happens, I just got a gig that will take me away for two weeks beginning tomorrow. So I'm truly desperate to see you. Please take the afternoon off. It's Friday, and you said you often stay home that day anyway. I tried the office number just in case, and here you are. A mistake. Let's rectify it."

"I don't just play hooky on Fridays. I work. Sounds like you have some work to do yourself. What's the big project, if I may ask?"

"It's been in the works for a while. I'll be writing something on, let's say, the globalization of American popular culture and the decline of civilization. I'll be going to LA, Tokyo, and Shanghai. But never mind that. It's a gorgeous summer day. Made for the track, not the office. Especially on a Friday. And I have to see more of you before my exile. An afternoon of horse racing would make a perfect prelude to dinner."

"An ambitious trip. But, the race track? You're serious?"

"Sure. Have you ever been to Belmont Park?"

"Can't say that I have."

"You've been cheating yourself. Belmont is beautiful now. Leafy trees. Lush lawns. Flowers. You stroll around. Loll on the grass. Eat and drink. Pick your horses. Place your bets. And every half hour or so you get a minute or two of throbbing excitement. You'll love it. On the way back we can stop at the Riverside restaurant by the Brooklyn Bridge for dinner and a view of Manhattan."

"I can't just walk out of the office and go to the race track!"

"Why not? Nothing to it."

"You're nuts."

"There's another reason for you to come. You wouldn't want me to roam dementedly around out there by myself. I might have a streak of bad luck and run amok. Then you'd read in the newspaper about mayhem at the track that you could have prevented. Picture the *Post* headline: *Writer Loses Bundle and Mind at Belmont*."

"Is gambling among your compulsions?"

"Would that get you to come?"

"Nobody cures addicts by joining in their addictions."

"Who said anything about cure? You could bring me luck and save my life."

"Oh, that's very persuasive."

"Success!" he exulted.

"You missed the tone."

"This time I'd rather take you at your word. I'll pick you up in an hour."

"Not so fast."

Rebecca was hardly one to drop work in the middle of the day for a diversion, even now, when the satisfactions of work had dimmed. And to just get up and leave the office to go to the race track seemed like a joke. She tried to laugh it off. She could laugh, but not laugh it off. Her former responses were failing her. She stalled. Maybe she should go. She told him to call back in half an hour. She would see if she could do it, mad as it was. But made no promises.

"Another of your tempering delays. But it's a deal," he crowed. "Half an hour."

Rebecca hung up the phone. Horse races? How could she? Then the ferry ride came back to her. As it had many times since they had parted that night. And each time—at the office, at her weekend conference, at home—it had brought with it waverings of her ambivalence toward him, tilted increasingly by memories of the magical cityscape in the evening light, and of the kiss. She cleared her desk.

"So, are you going to save me from myself?" he cajoled through the phone exactly half an hour later, anxious as he was to see her and to keep the romance of the ferry ride alive.

"Please, no more phony appeals to conscience." She sounded more amused than reproachful.

"Conscience may be your weakness."

"Conscience would keep me in the office."

"Aha! The conditional *would* says yes. I'll be there at noon with a car."

"But . . . I'm dressed for work."

"Many people play the horses as their work. You'll fit right in."

"Among the Damon Runyon lowlifes? Thanks."

"No, no. Belmont's a classy place, as I said. Maybe not as classy as you, but you won't be slumming. I'll pick you up on the street in front of your office if that's all right."

Without having altogether consented, she was going with him again. Against the grain. To the horse races, no less. She couldn't resist a small smile.

⚮

Alex honked and waved from the waiting car to attract her attention as she came through the revolving doors of the glass and steel building on Madison Avenue that housed her publishing company. He had half expected her not to show up, since he had pressured her into this escapist outing without quite gaining her open consent, and her moods were . . . unpredictable. But there she was. Radiant in a bright floral dress and a light sea-green jacket. He reached over and pushed open the door. "You are summer itself!" he effused as she bent into the bucket seat beside him. "And dressed for summer at the track! Your horoscope must've told you what to wear."

"Can I blame the stars for this madness?" Her hesitant smile softened her words.

He wanted to kiss her right there, for her flowers and her colors and her joke and her smile—he reveled in the sensations. But the seats weren't made for it. Not like the old days, he thought. He reached for her hand. "Thanks for coming," he said with that note of unaffected sincerity that Rebecca had heard a few times before and liked.

"I can't believe I'm doing it," she responded with good-natured incredulity. "And nobody I work with would have, either. If I'd told them, they'd have brought out a net. I prevaricated and sneaked away."

"Congratulations on your agile deviousness. Damon Runyon would approve—and so would your namesake."

She laughed a little. Then a cacophony of horns swelled from impatient drivers behind who refused to go around him.

"Ah, New York," Alex sighed and released her hand. He shifted into gear and hit the accelerator. The car lurched forward and swung around the corner. Soon, they had fled Manhattan's traffic through the Mid-Town Tunnel and were zipping along the Long Island Expressway in Queens. Buoyed by the day and her company, Alex started rhythmically patting the steering wheel and singing lightly: *I gotta horse right here, his name is Paul Revere, and there's a guy that tells me if the weather's clear, 'can do, can do,' the guy says the horse 'can do.'"* He glanced at her. "You know—Frank Loesser, *Guys and Dolls.* Puts you in the mood for the track."

"Always. Very infectious," she said sarcastically, giving him a slightly strained but pleasant look.

He resumed drumming the steering wheel and repeated the performance. Then, admitting that this was all of the song that he knew, he switched on the radio. Facetiously feigning disappointment with a conscious act of sociability, Rebecca requested an encore. Facetiously feigning shy reticence with delight at her invitation, he turned down the radio and complied. *"I gotta horse right here, his name is Paul Revere, and . . . ."*

Within an hour they were entering the shady grounds of Belmont Park just across the city line on Long Island. People were milling about lazily. Some munched hotdogs at snack bars. Others lounged on the grass picnicking. Television screens hung here and there in the trees for those who chose to watch the races without leaving their grassy leisure.

"Civilized, isn't it?" Alex asked. "Not what you might expect."

"I'll grant that. Not the Damon Runyon version."

"There are plenty of those types around. They're probably off 'handicapping the ponies,' as they say."

"Handicapping the ponies? I'm afraid I haven't read enough Damon Runyon to know the jargon."

"Trying to figure out which horses are the most likely to win. Which ones to bet on. Haven't you ever seen a horse race, even on TV?"

"The Kentucky Derby a few times. But I did ride horses as a child. Does that count for anything?"

"Well, it's an apprenticeship. But now you get to learn the good stuff. The game. First we get a *Racing Form.*" He stopped at a vendor and bought a fat tabloid newspaper. "Would you believe there's a national daily newspaper devoted entirely to horse racing? It tells you all there is to know about every horse running at the major tracks all over the country. Horse racing's a whole culture. As Damon Runyon knew."

"So it seems."

They went inside the Grandstand and sat among the motley spectators, many of them studying the *Racing Form*. Alex paged through it to the headline "Belmont Park."

"Here are today's races at Belmont," he explained. "It lists every horse in every race and shows how they finished in their previous races. That's literally their *track record*. You no doubt offer book contracts based on an author's "track record" sometimes, don't you? Well, this is the real thing." He spread out the pages displaying dense charts of numbers.

"I trust you will decipher all of this," she said. "Looks as complex as stock market listings."

"I'll do what I can. Here's the first race." He ran his finger down one of the charts. "It goes a mile and an eighth for three-year olds and older. Now, this horse, *Jersey Joe*, has won four of his nine starts and come in second or third—you know, Place or Show— three of the other times. A good track record. There's at least one race most days, incidentally, for horses who've never won a race. So whoever wins, it'll be for the first time. It's called a 'maiden' race, even though most race horses are male—and the fillies usually race only against each other. Sexist, but that's the tradition."

"So the guys start as maidens and end as studs?"

"Ha! Clever. I knew you'd catch on fast. Should I go on?"

"The scales are dropping from my eyes." Her tone was genial. But she couldn't believe she was there.

"The track record also shows you the distances the horses have run. Most races in this country are around a mile. A mile and a half is probably the longest, and it's rare—on the dirt, if not the turf, or grass. It's the length of the Belmont Stakes run here the first Saturday in June to complete the Triple Crown."

"Of course I know of the Belmont Stakes and Triple Crown."

"Did you know that this year a 70 to 1 long shot won the Belmont? Named Sarava. The longest odds in Belmont Stakes history. Paid practically $150 on a $2 bet."

"Can't say that I did. Did you win?"

"I won Show money on him. Not bad. But back to the track records. Good track records in short races don't tell you much about who can 'go the distance' in longer races—especially for three year-olds, like the horses in the Triple Crown. Which is why the favorite in the Kentucky Derby seldom wins. It's a mile-and-a-quarter, and the young horses in it haven't raced that far before. An extra quarter mile can make a big difference in a horse race. And the Belmont Stakes is a killer because it adds yet another quarter mile to the Derby. That's why it knocks off so many Triple Crown contenders who've won the first two races, as happened last month with the big favorite, War Emblem, although he stumbled coming out of the gate. But remember Secretariat?"

"By reputation. I was a bit young for the races back then."

"Maybe the greatest race horse ever. When he won the Triple Crown he finished the Belmont leading by thirty-one lengths. And in record time. He proved he could 'go the distance' and then some. OK, now," Alex returned to the *Racing Form*, "what else do we need to know? Oh, yes. Serious handicappers also check the track records of the jockeys and trainers, which you can find here, and, naturally, the pedigrees of the horses to find those with winning parents. And they go to the paddock area before a race to see if any horses are sweating hard and to get other clues to how they might run." He paused. "Well, that's pretty much all I know about *handicapping the ponies.*"

"An enlightening introduction."

"Always willing to serve enlightenment."

"So I've learned."

"Is that offensive?"

"How could enlightenment be offensive?"

"It is if you're a religious fundamentalist, which you obviously are not. I like your mind. And your generosity."

Going back to the chart, he noted that *Jersey Joe* was the favorite with odds of 2 to 1. "He'll probably be in the money again, but he won't pay off much. We might make a dime if he wins. But take this horse, *Sleeper*. He's been in the money only three times in thirteen races. A long shot at 50 to 1. He'll pay off nicely if he does come in."

"What do those odds mean?—2 to 1, 50 to 1. And who decides what they are?"

"Aha! Got your curiosity. Can you stand another groping explanation?"

"I'll try. Should I take notes?" She almost chuckled with an unexpected ease.

Persuaded she was making a sporting attempt to give herself over to this outing, he revved up his enthusiasm. "Nice gesture. But I might not be coherent enough for that. It's very complicated. And more interesting and revealing than you would expect. From what I understand, it works like this. Start with gambling odds in general and games of sheer chance, like throwing dice or flipping a coin. Those games have what are called 'natural odds.' That means the odds of winning never change. They're always one-out-of-the-total-number-of-possibilities. When you flip a coin, for instance, the odds are always 50-50 that you'll get heads or tails, no matter how many times you flip or how many times one side comes up more than the other. We tend to think the odds change the more often one side of the coin comes up than the other, but they don't—theoretical statisticians struggle with this and try to counter it. Believing natural odds change is a fallacy. It's known as the 'Monte Carlo Fallacy'. And it's cost people plenty of money—and heartache. I don't suppose it ever got to you?"

"I'm not much of a gambler."

"You're more of a gambler than you think. Everyone is. Anyway, in games that don't depend on sheer chance alone, like sports, including horse racing, the odds aren't 'natural' and constant, as in flipping a coin. They change. And they change because there are many variables influencing the outcome beyond the finite number of possible outcomes. In a football game, for instance, there may be only two possible statistical outcomes, one winner and one loser, as in flipping a coin. But if one team is clearly better than the other it has better than a 50-50 chance of winning. Horse racing is like that but more complex because there are many possible winners. And the best horses in a race have a higher probability of winning than simply one out of the total number of horses running. This is where handicapping comes in. A subject you now understand thoroughly."

"Oh, yes. Thoroughly—thoroughbreds obviously demand it."

"How droll. Is that a pun or a commitment?"

"A rhetorical indulgence. Do continue." She was kind of enjoying this. It was sort of a test, an intellectual challenge.

Yes, she is getting into it, he said to himself. "OK," he resumed buoyantly, "long odds on a horse, say, 50 to 1, mean roughly that the handicappers figure this horse—because of pedigree and track record—is so much slower than the others in the race that he has fifty chances to lose against only one chance to win. For some reason they state the odds negatively, maybe to discourage gambling, and the numbers themselves are kind of arbitrary as far as I know—how odds makers decide a horse's odds are 50 to 1 instead of, say, 30 to 1 is a mystery to me. Anyway, short odds, like 2 to 1, mean that the horse is probably fast enough to have only about two chances to lose against one chance to win. Occasionally a horse will come into a race with a good enough track record to get odds better than 50-50 to win. The great horse Cigar, who won sixteen races in a row not long ago, went off in his next race at 1 to 10—one chance to lose out of ten to win—and he lost."

"I guess that's what makes for *a horse race*. No sure thing."

"You've got it. It's always a gamble, whatever the odds. Unless a race is fixed, as they sometimes were in the old days. And listen to this, you should like it. In those days when a race was fixed by the jockeys for some gangster, only one of the jockeys in that race would be riding to win while all the others would be subtly holding back and trying 'shoo' his horse ahead of them across the finish line without anyone in the stands noticing. That made the fixed horse, who was always a long shot, a *shoo in*—a sure thing. Charming anecdote, don't you think? And a good metaphor."

"I'll keep it mind. So, who decides the odds?"

"The original odds, or the 'morning line' odds as they are called, are set by the professional handicappers based on track records and so on. But once the bettors get into it, they create betting odds that may or may not match the morning line track odds. Here it can get very confusing."

"Don't quit. I want to see how it comes out." And she did want to. It was becoming more and more one of those puzzles she liked to solve.

"I'll take you at your word, even if you're kidding.

"I'm not kidding."

"Well, in pari-mutuel betting—where the winning bettors share the pool of money bet on all of the horses in a race—the more money that is bet on a single horse, the lower the betting odds and the payoff for that horse, regardless of the 'morning line' odds. That's why if you've got a hot tip on a horse, you shouldn't tell anybody, because they'll bet on him and drive down the odds and the payoff. The actual payoff, though, depends on the total pool of money bet on all the horses in the race, so you can't accurately predict it from the odds, and I honestly don't know the formula—although winnings often turn out to pay approximately the betting odds for each dollar you bet, if you bet one dollar on a 10 to 1 shot who wins you might get about ten dollars back. But that rule doesn't apply to horses with very short odds. As I said, a 2 to 1 winner will pay only a pittance. By the way, did you ever see *The Lemon Drop Kid*?"

"About a candy addicted child?" She gave him a playful look.

"You are witty today. It's a funky and sweet movie of the early Fifties with Bob Hope based on Runyon stories about a guy who eats lemon drops all the time and runs afoul of some gangsters by touting horses at the track—giving false tips to sway the betting odds away from the horses he bets on himself. Unknowingly, he touts a crook's girlfriend off of a winner, so the crook loses and goes after him. Then the Kid cooks up a scam to pay off the bad guy with dough he raises for an old ladies home he sets up. But he winds up helping instead of defrauding the Old Dolls, as he calls them, and foiling the bad guys. The Christmas song 'Silver Bells' comes from that movie. And a horse named *Lemon Drop Kid* actually won the Belmont Stakes a few years ago. Life inspired by art."

"The horse was inspired?"

"Horse racing's full of surprises," he joked. "But anyhow, that's the best I can do on the odds. From here on I'm all ignorance—and luck, good or bad."

"I'm impressed. How blinkered I've been." She shook her head in friendly self-mockery.

"How nimble you are. And you know more about horse racing than you let on." She was warming for sure, he thought happily. Had she forgotten the office and put their previous tensions behind her? Had she changed since the ferry ride? Or would she regress again? He could only hope. "But now," he said brightly, "let's see how well you do picking the ponies." Spreading the chart of the race in front of her, he scoured the statistics. "Here's our race. It goes a mile and 1/16. It'll take about a minute and a half. And, look at that!" He pointed to a line. "There's a filly in this race! Running against the guys! That's not common. Her name is *Maisie Knew*. Has to be from that Henry James novel *What Maisie Knew*. A literary owner. But what did Maisie know?"

"I think it was some secret about a seduction in the family. But with Henry James there's no sure thing."

"Ha! Touché. Let's see now, her track record. Three Wins, one Place, and two Shows out of ten races. And at respectable distances. Pretty good. But they give her only 13 to 1. Pure sexism. They figure she can't beat the guys. But I think she *knows* better, if I may say so. And I'd say she's a sure bet for us. What do you think?"

"I'd say your pun on her name is a stretch. But she deserves a bet to win anyway. She'll show the guys and show up the odds makers." Rebecca recognized she was irresistibly getting drawn in.

"Is that a political statement?"

"A vote of confidence."

"Fair enough. I'll join you. Do you mind if we pool our bets? Then we both win or lose together."

"Why not?"

"How much confidence should we give her? The standard bet is $2."

"I'd say $5."

"Well, I like your spirit. And she should, too. Now, the Place bet." He scanned the track records of the other nine horses in the race—*Jersey Joe, Rusty, Goforbroke, Fred's Café, Hopeful Tunes, Stormy Weather, Feather Duster, Sleeper,* and *Bygones Delight.* "There! *Bygones Delight.* Been in the money over half of his dozen races. They give him 15 to 1. There'll be some money in it. And I like the name, don't you? What do you think? *Bygones Delight* to Place?"

"Fine."

"Now, to Show. We could do *Sleeper.* That name could be a good sign—he's a sleeper in the race, a hidden threat. Or the owner has a sense of humor. But I guess the odds makers consider him truly somnolent at 50 to 1."

"How about *Hopeful Tunes?*" she said. "A horse with such a name deserves a bet."

"Nice idea. And a reasonable long shot at 25 to 1. Been in the money six of fourteen times, but two wins. Not a bad bet. So *Hopeful Tunes* to Show. And let's do a Quinella."

"A what?"

"A Quinella. It's a bet on two horses to come in first and second in either order. A fun bet. Why don't you chose. I've got a hunch you'll be lucky today."

"I wouldn't count on that. But OK." Then she searched the names. "You know, I think I'd say *Maisie Knew* again. I like her, and we'd have her for both first and second."

"Let's go for it."

"Well then . . . *Goforbroke*? Sounds like an appropriate gamble." A peculiar sensation came over her, and she was amused that she had said it.

"Hey, I like that. You've got style. And he's the second favorite at 5 to 2. Been in the money most of his eight starts. A good choice. Now, let's check the betting odds." He pointed to the large posting board across the track from the Grandstand. "See, every horse in the race has its total betting pool posted along with its betting odds, and you can see them change as bets are placed. *Maisie Knew* is actually dropping to 11 to 1. Other bettors are getting onto her. Bad for the payoff. *Hopeful Tunes* is getting shorter odds, too. But the odds on *Bygones Delight* are getting longer, 20 to 1—something going on there we don't know. And *Goforbroke* is now about even with *Jersey Joe*. Do you want to make any changes or shall we stick with our bets?"

"I'm the novice here. But we might as well go with them."

"OK. So now it's time to get our action."

"Action?"

"*Get our action.* Gambling jargon for placing a bet, getting in the game. If you're not in the game, you've got no action. No chance of winning. No excitement. You're not alive. But if you've got *action*, you've always got a chance. A chance of winning—at anything. That keeps you feeling alive."

"That's either a breezy philosophy of life or a prescription for an addiction to gambling."

"Oh, it's all philosophy, I assure you."

They shared a little laugh and hiked the Grandstand stairs to join one of the lines winding to the betting windows. Surrounding them, bettors tucked raveled *Racing Forms* under their arms and fingered rolls of bills—fives, tens, twenties. Some had grizzled faces and rumpled clothes. Others looked like customers waiting in a bank line. A bizarre mix, Rebecca reflected as she observed a dignified older woman shuffling her betting slips while she stood in line behind a Latino male in an undershirt flexing muscles by clenching his fist around a wad of bills, and in front of him a scruffy little character who could have lived in a cardboard box.

"Here's your Damon Runyon scene," Alex whispered in Rebecca's ear.

"Such a culture."

"I told you. It used to be richer than it is now, but we're doing our part."

"Anything for culture."

He was very glad she was here.

After placing their bets—$5 on each, as they had decided at the window, to heighten the *action*—they found new seats in the Grandstand above the Finish Line. The great oval of the track below them encircled a lawn and two blue ponds. Ducks floated on the water and flowers bloomed alongside.

"Now, isn't this the right way to spend a summer afternoon?" Alex gloated. "Vastly better than the office."

Mention of her office sent a twinge of guilt through her. She suppressed it. Somehow, she wasn't really sorry to be here after all.

"Doesn't that depend on the races?" she answered noncommittally.

"Not really. Once you've got your action, you get an incomparable day of excitement, as I said, in one- or two-minute doses, alternating with half-hour periods of civilized leisure. Ah! Here they come."

The horses were ambling onto the track at the far end of the Grandstand. "The post parade," Alex remarked. "They'll all come past and then go out to the starting gate." Ten lithe horses carrying their riders, accompanied by their stable ponies and outriders, trotted toward the Grandstand. "There's *Maisie Knew*. See, Number 5. And, hey! the jockey's in sea-green! Goes with your jacket. I knew you'd be lucky. It's in the stars for sure."

"I'd say a mere coincidence."

"*Mere* coincidence? No such thing."

"A cryptic remark."

"A Pandora's Box. But I won't open it now."

"Thanks."

They picked out their other horses in the post parade—*Hopeful Tunes* #3, *Bygones Delight* #6, *Goforbroke* #8—and watched all ten horses canter to the starting gate placed near the first turn of the mile-and-a half track. Metal doors slammed behind the horses one at a time, locking them into their slots.

When they were all in, a voice came over the loudspeaker: "They're in the gate . . . AANND . . . THEYYY'RE . . . OFFFFFFF!!"

Alex and Rebecca could make out no more than a herd of horses galloping away at the turn. The announcer's voice calmly narrated the pace: "*Jerrzzyy Joe* off to a good start to take the early lead, with *Fred's Café* and *Feather Duster* running next. Then it's *Rusty, Goforbroke,* and *Bygones Delight,* followed by *Maisie Knew* and *Stormy Weather*. Bringing up the rear around the turn, it's *Hopeful Tunes* and *Sleeepperr*."

Taking a breath as the horses began stringing out beyond the turn, he picked up the pace. "Passing the quarter pole, it's *Jerrzzsey Joe* at twenty-three-and-a-half, then *Fred's Café* a length behind, with *Feather Duster* at his side. *Goforbroke, Rusty,* and *Bygones Delight* another length back, tailed by *Maisie Knew*.

Then it's *Stormy Weather* and *Hopeful Tunes*, with *Sleeepperrr* trailing the field."

The horses were now galloping along the far side of the track. "Dowwnnn the back stretch," the announcer resumed, "*Jerzzey Joe* is showing speed, opening a three-length lead on *Fred's Café* and *Feather Duster*. *Gohforrrbroke* and *Byyygones Delight* are hanging close in third. Then it's a length to *Russsty*, with *Mayysee Knew* and *Hopeful Tunes* on his heels. *Stormy Weather* leads the trailer *Sleeeperr* by two. It's the half in forty seven."

"What's forty seven, and how can he tell one horse from another this far away?" Rebecca asked, as the announcer's voice purred on and she riveted her sights on the far side of the track to keep up with the line of horses moving along the rail.

"It's the time of the lead horse for the first half mile," Alex answered rapidly. "And he identifies the jockeys' colors through binoculars. He's also had plenty of practice."

"ROWNNNDING the far turn," the voice proceeded seconds later, "*JJJerrrzzyyy Joe* still in command with the three-length lead on *Fred's Café* and *Feather Duster*. *Goforbroke* presses on the rail. *Maisie Knew, Bygones Delight*, and *Hopeful Tunes* are bunched another length behind. *Rusty* has fallen off the pace with *Stormy Weather*. And at the tail it's still *Sleeepperrr*."

The horses came into view around the last turn, hurtling toward the home stretch.

"OK, MAISIE!" Alex shouted. "Time to MOVE!"

"AAANNDDD THEY TTURRNN FOR HOHMME!" the announcer's voice proclaimed, getting louder and faster with the pace of the racers. "It's-*JERZZYY-JOE*-on-the-lead-by-three-lengths-trying-to-go-wire-to-wire. But-*Goforbroke*-is-now-hitting-the-gas-and-pulling-ahead-of-*Feather-Duster*-along-with-*Fred's-Café*. *Bygones-Delight*,-*Feather-Duster*-and-*Hopeful-Tunes*-are-dueling-another-length-back. *Mayyzzeee-Knew*,-a-stride-behind-them,-moves-to-the-outside.

AND-NOW-FROM-THE-OUTSIDE-WIDE-OFF-THE-TURN-OUT-OF-TRAFFIC-COMES—*MAYYZZEE-KNEW!*"

Alex leaped to his feet. "C'MON MAISIE!!" he yelled. Rebecca hesitated then stood up beside him. She heard herself mouth the words, "Come on Maisie." Then she repeated them aloud. For a second she was self-conscious. But as the horses hurtled along the track with *Maisie Knew* on the outside, her voice grew louder. "C'mon Maisie!" she said firmly, "C'mon, c'mon," while Alex cried: "C'MON MAISIE!!!" DO IT! DO IT!!"

"AANNDD . . . DOWWWNNNNN-THE-STRETCCHH-THEY-COME!" the announcer called out.

The roar of the crowd swelled tumultuously as the horses flew down the home stretch toward the Grandstand, all but drowning out the announcer now hurriedly reporting how *Maisie Knew* was picking off horses, rounding at once *Bygones Delight, Hopeful Tunes,* and *Feather Duster,* catching *Fred's Café* and *Goforbroke,* then pulling ahead of *Fred's Café along* with *Goforbroke,* and the two of them chasing *Jersey Joe,* gaining on him together with every stride. From three lengths to two-and-a-half. Then two lengths. A length-and-a-half. A length. Half-a-length. A stride. A neck. A head.

The announcer shouted that *Maisie* and *Goforbroke* had now caught *Jersey Joe,* but he was holding on, and they were all running side-by-side.

Impulsively, Rebecca's voice kept rising until she found herself shouting almost as loudly as Alex: "C'MON MAISIE! YOU CAN DO IT! DO IT! RUN! RUN!"

The three jockeys crouched tightly on their horses, lashing whips against haunches again and again, harder and harder, trying to get another burst of speed as the trio thundered together toward the finish line neck-and-neck.

Rebecca and Alex were now jumping up and down, shrieking together, "GO MAISIE GO! GO! DO IT! DO IT!!" amid the cacophonous chorus of urgent cries all around them.

With only yards to the finish, the three horses were locked neck-and-neck, their bobbing heads momentarily thrusting one in front of the other, hooves pounding, jockeys whipping, spectators delirious. Rebecca was yelling so hard her throat hurt. "YES! MAISIE! DO IT! YES! YES! YES!!"

As the three horses crossed the Finish Line in a blur, the announcer called above the crowd: "IITTT'SSS . . . A PHOTO FINISSHH!"

"Did she do it!? Did she win?" Rebecca cried out breathlessly, pulling at Alex's arm.

"I don't know," Alex gasped, pointing to the board across the track posting the race results. In large bold letters it read: PHOTO FINISH. "A photo finish with all three!!" he panted. "Unbelievable! What a great race." He gulped a few breaths. "Exciting to be in the *action* isn't it?"

She was breathing too hard to answer.

They waited anxiously, catching their breath with expressions of astonishment in a nearly hushed Grandstand. One minute. Two minutes. Then the posting board went blank. When it came on again it read:

1st #5

2nd #8

3rd #2

"SHE DID IT!!" Alex whooped above the erupting crowd. "SHE WON!!"

"SHE DID IT!" Rebecca joined him. "GOOD GIRL!!"

"AND *GOFORBROKE* CAME IN SECOND!" Alex cheered. "WE GOT THE QUINELLA, TOO!! WE WON TWICE WITH *MAISIE KNEW*!!" He hugged Rebecca to him, pulling her off balance. "Sorry," he apologized, releasing her and calming himself. "I got carried away. But what luck! The green jacket must've worked! See, you were meant to be here! And maybe Maisie knew. Ha! A lucky day! Having a good time?"

"It *is* exciting, I'll give you that," she answered, still breathing hard, and passing over his remarks about luck and her jacket. "At least when you win. What happened to our other horses?"

"Don't tell me you're disappointed not to win all three. But look," he pointed to the board that had added the forth finisher. "*Hopeful Tunes* came up to finish fourth—in the money for the horse but no betting payoff. You know we picked three of the four money horses?! Amazing! You're a natural horse player. You really shouldn't waste your time in an office." He poked her gently.

"But what happened to *Bygones Delight*?"

"Let's see. Oh, sixth. Dare I say it?"

"Let bygones . . . ?"

They shared a short laugh. "At least we didn't put anything on *Sleeper*," Alex added. "He lived up to his name too well. Probably still running. Hey!" he pointed again to the posting board where some numbers had just popped up at the bottom. "The payoffs. *Maisie Knew* will pay $19.30 for $2 to win. That means we'll get about $50 for our $5 bet. And the Quinella will pay $28.80 for $2. That's about $70 for our $5. Together that'll be around $120. Subtract the $20 we bet and we still come out about $100 ahead. A terrific start. If the whole day goes like this, we're in clover."

"You always this lucky here?"

"Nope. You brought it. You and your jacket. But I don't come to win necessarily. I come for the *action*."

"Of course. But don't count on the jacket."

"It's already done enough. Let's go get our payoff and have a drink to celebrate."

"Why not?"

They collected $119.25, bought soft drinks and pretzels, and went out to the tree-shaded grounds. Selecting a quiet spot on the grass, they toasted to their good luck, munched their snack, and started choosing their next bets.

The afternoon wore on. They picked horses. Strolled the grounds. Won and lost. Snacked and drank and lolled on the grass. When the last race ended, they collected a few dollars from their final bets and went to the car, tallying their winnings and losings for the day.

"$85.50 ahead," Alex boasted. "Quite impressive. Practically where we were after the first race. A super afternoon. Good times, and we made a profit, to boot. I give you and your jacket all the credit. No *mere* coincidence at all. And the bundle'll buy us a good bottle of wine at dinner, if you don't mind squandering our pool on a celebratory libation."

"Not at all."

"Great! Aren't you glad you played hooky? I am. Thanks. You made the day."

She smiled at him enigmatically. She did feel oddly good about it. The day. And she sensed a kind of lightness inside, as if something had gone out of her. Thinking about this, she traced it back to the first race. Now she wondered, was she simply running away from herself? Or had something actually happened to her? If it had, how far would she let herself go with it? And would she regret it? She decided to go with it. A gamble? She smiled.

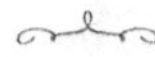

The car crept into the stream of traffic inching from the parking lot. By the time they reached the restaurant on the East River, it was the same hour of early evening that they had last spent together. They sat at a window table by the water, and saw leisure boats speeding past and a dinner cruise yacht making its leisurely way downstream toward the harbor where the Statue of Liberty rose just beyond the southern tip of Manhattan. Nearby, the Brooklyn Bridge arched high across the river toward the cityscape of lower Manhattan rearing up before them against the western sky.

Alex selected a bottle of Montrachet. "How about this? A gift from *Maisie Knew*?"

"She has good taste."

They studied their menus, compared comments, and ordered. After the wine was poured, Alex lifted his glass. "To *Maisie Knew*. Whatever she knew. But I think she knew you'd be there in her colors."

Rebecca cocked her head skeptically, and they clinked glasses.

"Speaking of Henry James," he said after taking a drink, "he gave us something else worth drinking to besides Maisie."

"What's that?"

"One of his best lines. He said: *Try to be one of those people on whom nothing is lost.*"

"Another of your *nice phrases* and *good clichés*? But wasn't he giving advice to novelists? And didn't Oscar Wilde have the decadent Lord Henry use the same line to corrupt Dorian Gray?"

"Oh, you're way ahead of me. How do you know such things?"

"I edited a book on styles of Decadence a while ago. You'd probably love it."

"I'd better read it. Can always use some pointers," he made fun of himself. "But the source doesn't matter. It's the idea that counts. It shows how to live. That's worth drinking to, isn't it?" He extended his glass again.

Instinctively, she started to pull back at this new mention of *how to live*, but she stopped herself. She let her glass meet his once more. After sipping briefly, Rebecca set her glass down and fingered the stem while she looked quietly out the window. His eyes followed hers. The sun was setting on the far side of Manhattan, silhouetting the darkening pinnacles of steel and stone in front of them against the reddening sky whose colors spilled onto the water. Offices were lighting up, beginning the city's evening transformation from hard workaday reality into nighttime fantasy, and strings of lights along the cables of the Brooklyn Bridge etched their graceful swooping flight across the river into the metamorphosing Manhattan skyline. Yes, Rebecca admitted silently, he could be right.

"Eros's magic trick again," Alex said. "But different when seen from this side of the city. You know, I've often wondered why so many office lights are on during the weekends. Surely there aren't that many people working on Friday night."

"You live a protected life."

"You mean people are in fact working there? I'd hoped the lights came on because the building owners were contributing to the romance of the night. One more of those 'seductive illusions' that you said get crushed by 'brutal truths.'"

"Don't blame me for your disillusionments—or quote me." She flashed a thin smile.

Dinner arrived, and they studied the items artfully arranged with minor variations on each plate. A circle of vegetables, a pyramid of greens, a mound of sculpted potatoes, a slice of fish set at an angle garnished with a sprig of rosemary. Surgically disassembling the chef's creations, they joked about the current trend in "food art." Then Alex laid down his surgical instruments, took a drink of wine, paused, and said, "Uh, continuing the theme of not letting anything be lost on us, I've got another proposition for you."

"Should I brace myself?" she said cautiously, working on her food art.

"No. Be open to it. A true adventure."

"Such as?" She sliced into her fish.

"India," he said, with self-conscious nonchalance.

"What do you mean?" she responded, undistracted from her meal.

"I told you I want to go there later this year. And now that you're an aficionado of Indian art, a seasoned hooky player from work, and lucky at the track, you should be tempted to come with me."

She looked at him dismissively.

Fearful of pushing her away at the end of this fine day, he changed tack. "OK. Something closer to home. Hmmmm." He scanned the skyline. As his eyes came to where the World Trade Center used to tower over lower Manhattan directly to the west, he recalled the whimsical bar he had visited there with its dance floor overlooking the harbor where he wished he could take her. "That's it!" he exclaimed. "Dancing amid the stars." He leaned over against the window searching up the river. "You can't see it from here. But it's there somewhere beyond the Empire State Building. The Rainbow Room at Rockefeller Center. You've been there, surely."

"The Rainbow Room? I was there for a party once. But isn't it for tourists and people from New Jersey?"

"It's for everyone with a touch of romance in their hearts. Where else can you dance the night away like Fred Astaire and Ginger Rodgers in art-deco elegance sixty-five stories above the city? You've seen *Swing Time*? One of their best movies of the Thirties. The set was probably modeled on the Rainbow Room, which had just opened, gleaming with polished *moderne* sophistication. And it hasn't changed much."

"You write advertising copy for them?"

"I could—although not for any management that opens it to the public only on weekends, as they do now."

"I'm tempted to ask, you can take a stance, but can you dance?" She blushed at her silly wordplay.

He picked up the gag to reward her playfulness. "I could say, 'when I get a chance,' but that would be too much doggerel. No, I'm not much of a dancer, although I've tried. But in that place you don't have to be. The setting inspires you. I'll wear black tie. You'll be magnificent, whatever you wear. And it'll give me a thrill to contemplate while I'm away for the next two weeks. You saved me today by coming to the track, and you can save me again by agreeing to go with me to the Rainbow Room when I come back. You know what they say about saving someone's life—you're responsible for them thereafter."

She faced him and shook her head slowly with an expression intended to convey friendly criticism of his excesses. He can't stop himself can he? she thought. But he is resourceful. Rooftop restaurants in the middle of the night. Ferry rides at sunset. Horse racing in the afternoon. Now it's dancing at the Rainbow Room. More of his theatrics, casting her as a character in his romance? Maybe. Still, this had been a good day. The best since . . . when? Why? That lightness? Drawn by those thoughts, she wound up saying, "I couldn't possibly decline such an ingeniously lavish invitation." Her face wore the naturally warm smile that melted him.

"Oh, thank you. I said conscience could be your weakness. I'll be back in two weeks for *you and the night and the music*," he crooned.

"Shhhh," she whispered, noticing people turning their way, and reminding herself that she didn't know what in him was real and what wasn't.

"Sorry." He lowered his voice. "I got carried away again. But let's drink to it."

They clinked glasses. Then reminiscences of the race track, talk of Alex's impending trip, and chitchat took them through the rest of dinner and dessert of chocolate confections erected in the shape of the Brooklyn Bridge, prompting more jokes about food art. Afterwards they went out on the pier to enjoy the mild summer air and the full view of the nighttime city with its lights reflecting in undulating patterns on the water. Caught up in the scene and the moment as they stood at the railing along the river, Alex felt another urge to take her in his arms and kiss her. But he resisted, fearing he might overstep and cause her to withdraw. Instead, he put his hands on her shoulders from behind. Then, he bent forward and put his cheek next to hers and said softly, "This was one of those days when nothing was lost—on me." She almost said it was true. She turned her face slightly toward him. He brought his around. A kiss came as softly as the first one had on the ferry. When it ended, just as tenderly, they said nothing and walked hand in hand to the car for the drive across the bridge to Manhattan.

If she was only a character in his romance, she was thinking, he was at least playing his role very well today.

⌒⌒⌒

"Would you like to come in?" she asked rather sleepily as they drove up to her apartment house and discovered an available parking space in front. "I don't know what I can offer you. Coffee? Brandy?"

She sounded like she was being more than polite despite the sleepiness. And she was. But she was a bit nervous about asking him in, remembering her last late-might episode with a man in her apartment when she was trying to get away from herself. Was she still?

"A little brandy would be nice," he answered. "I won't stay long. You've been a very good sport today, and I don't want to wear out your good nature. Besides, I have an early plane tomorrow."

When they went into the apartment, Rebecca switched on a light, and Clarissa raised a sleepy head from her spot on the sofa as though she hadn't moved since Alex had seen her there before. The room was unchanged. Everything in place. Including the cat.

"I'll see what I've got," Rebecca said, laying her jacket on a chair and going into the kitchen just off the living room.

"Will this do?" she asked a minute later, showing him a bottle of cognac from the cupboard.

"Sure." Seeing her standing in the doorway holding the bottle, with a sleepy warmth on her face, Alex hungered again to go over and embrace her and kiss her long and hard. But again he didn't. She opened the bottle and poured a glass for him and got a little for herself. Then they sat on the sofa, taking care not to inconvenience Clarissa, who eyed them through nearly-closed lids.

"You have to envy cats," he remarked. "So impassive, indifferent, imperious."

"You never win an emotional battle with them, that's for certain."

"To the impassive power of cats," he said, raising his glass. She joined him.

Sitting beside her sipping his cognac, Alex began yielding to accumulating desires. He laid a hand on her shoulder, and setting his glass on the coffee table, he came close to her. Tentatively, she came to him, questioning herself how far he would go and how far she would let herself go. They kissed. Softly. As before. Then the kiss gently deepened.

When their lips parted, Alex started to speak, then he kissed her again to prevent himself from saying inane things—the dead clichés of romance that he feared would flatten, not enhance, the moment for her. The kiss went deeper and lasted longer, without becoming heated or hard. It seemed to both of them that he was trying to sense her desires and to share them, rather than to arouse them, or to yield to his. This gave her a sensation of mildly exciting, but uncertain intimacy. She had no regrets—yet. It gave him a sensation of tranquil romantic intimacy that, like their very first kiss, he wanted never to end.

Withdrawing a little, he sighed, "Rebecca, its been a wonderful day for me. But, alas, I really must go. Or I won't be able to. And I wouldn't want you to have to throw me out. That would be too humiliating to endure." He smiled.

She couldn't tell whether he honestly had to leave, or was boyishly trying to be chivalrous to her, or was play-acting to solicit a request to stay. When he pulled back farther, finished the cognac and got up, she felt relief mingled with a trace of surprise.

"Thanks for the day, Rebecca," he said seriously as they walked to the door. "You made it, well, unforgettable. You brought good luck in every way."

"Thank you, Alex. It was a . . . very nice day. And if I lose my job, now I know I can at least spend my afternoons at the track playing the ponies." She smiled softly with a tinge of sleepiness in her eyes.

"Charming idea. I'll join you there any time. Bring your green jacket."

They chuckled sociably, kissed once more lightly, and said good night.

Alex promised to call from California, and went down to the car tasting the kisses and reliving the day, and thinking, now she *was* with him, at last.

Rebecca rinsed the glasses in the kitchen sink, feeling again the pleasant lightness of earlier, and yet a bit flustered. How unexpectedly fine the day had gone, and how well it had ended. No tension. No fuss. But what now? Was she letting herself get drawn into something she didn't understand? Was it for escape? Was it more than that? Where would it lead? Where did she want it to lead? She couldn't say. Setting aside her doubts about both him and her, she concluded she could live with that uncertainly for a while. What did she have to lose? And today, she told herself with a warm inner smile, she had won.

# 11

## Two Weeks

A couple of days later Alex called from Los Angeles to tell Rebecca again how lucky he had been to be with her at the track, and that he regretted leaving her so early that evening and being away so long, and that the prospect of being with her again was the only thing keeping him going. She laughed at his extravagance and equivocated about her feelings. But she did it in a way that made him hunger to see her all the more.

Then he called from Tokyo with more emotional profusions and with caustic remarks on the garishness of the Ginza and the imitative genius of the Japanese and their lust for all things American. She questioned his vaunted sense of urban romance and kidded him about his New Yorker's chauvinism and losing his sense of humor. He pretended to be chastened and promised to consult her at every step to keep from going astray.

Another time he called from Shanghai bemoaning the distance between them and reporting how fast that city was being reborn amidst flourishing commerce and ubiquitous construction with a forest of towers rising in formerly undeveloped Pudong across the Huang Pu river from the row of stately pre-war European buildings along the Bund. "Doesn't feel like it did when I was here ten years ago," he said. "It's getting to look like every other big city. And the American stores and fast food outlets have turned Nanking Road into an American main street. This is the future of the world. Communism can't repel it. Even the most traditional cultures will eventually submit and disappear. No one can stop the juggernaut of American commercial culture. That's what Islamic fanatics are fighting against—some Christian fundamentalists, too, for that matter. I despise their theocratic convictions, but I do at times understand their rage."

"A mite overstated and humorless," she jibed, suspecting he was trying to get a rise out of her. "It's not all that bad. And what would your romantic New York be without modern commerce? You're also idealizing traditional cultures. Don't most of them live in poverty and oppression and superstition, and treat women as chattel? That's no high standard of civilization and humanity. And doesn't the spread of modern commerce improve peoples' lives economically and help to promote human rights politically? Is any of this going to be in your article?"

"You keep springing surprises on me. Now you're a global cultural critic," he answered jokingly. "Maybe I could get you to write the piece with me. I'll put off the deadline so we can work on it together—in India. You probably thought I'd forgotten about that, or hoped I had. But I haven't. You could open my eyes and save me from clichéd perceptions."

She passed over his arch maneuver and asked him to give her a better impression of Shanghai.

"I actually like Shanghai," he confessed, "despite what is happening to it. So far it still has some of its own character." He told her about walking along the Bund and exploring the old city and visiting the new art museum and eating wonderful food and talking to officials and intellectuals and some young people about life in their transforming city. "But the most memorable thing," he said, "is The Old Jazz Band at the Peace Hotel, which was originally the grand Cathay Hotel built in 1929 on the Bund. They're a bunch of old guys in a ground floor bar who play everything from vintage jazz and pop songs to 'Home on the Range' in the same exuberant Dixie Land style. I love it. And that reminds me. It won't be long now until we'll be dancing to some of those tunes at the Rainbow Room. You can see I count the days."

She chuckled and commended his more upbeat report. He promised to call again soon and be even more upbeat in the happy anticipation of seeing her. After this conversation, she thought how these phone calls kept her periodic ambivalence toward him tipping back and forth. She couldn't get over the suspicion that even when he seemed to reveal sincere emotions, he was possibly just trying to draw her into his personal romance. But when she relived the ferry ride and the day at the races and their warm parting, and she thought of his fine masculine features and indisputably stimulating mind and her inklings of a genuine and sensitive human being beneath the histrionics and insouciantly debonair manner, she was drawn to him. The kisses proved that. And her questions about him invariably blended seamlessly into repetitious questions about herself. Was he becoming for her a kind of flight from herself, against the grain, not a step toward anything?? What did he want from her? What did she want from him? Would he be a way out? Her questions went in circles. She continued to leave them unanswered.

Her vacillating disengagement at work continued, too. But instead of emotionless vacancy, she now periodically seemed more preoccupied, as if she were thinking of things far removed from what she was doing. Some colleagues even thought she had more light in her eyes and life in her voice than she had had for quite a while.

Meredith, with her keen sense of telling details, had first caught signs of a change the day after spotting Rebecca and Alex leaving the party together at Battery Park. Later, Rebecca's gently evasive response to Meredith's questions about him had displayed less blank indifference than a hint of emotional awakening. And Rebecca's confession, under Meredith's dogged questioning, that when she had abruptly left the office at mid-day that Friday she had actually gone with him to the horse races convinced Meredith that much more was indeed going on in Rebecca than she was willing to confess. Of course, Rebecca wasn't likely to exhibit her feelings very conspicuously. A tone of voice, a look in the eyes, would be more like her. Meredith observed them, slight as they were, and waited to see what would come next.

Sarah also picked up on a change when Rebecca reported that Alex had promised to rework his book proposal, and she acknowledged having seen him a few more times not clearly related to the book. Sarah said she appreciated Rebecca's persevering with him despite her original reluctance. And she repeated that Rebecca was bound to have a good influence on him, adding with a smile, "and who knows, he might do something good for you, too." Rebecca chided her for the wayward thought, but left Sarah happily unpersuaded.

The lightness inside that Rebecca had begun feeling at the horse races subsided, but it didn't entirely go away. She wasn't sure where it had come from. But she didn't think it had come from Alex. It had somehow come from that day itself. As though something had happened to her at the races. She tried to hold onto the lightness, not knowing quite what it was. And when, after her long days of work and frequent evenings of professional socializing that she endured to keep from thinking too much about herself, she went to bed expecting her haunting visitors she found herself now fending them off not with thoughts of workaday routine but with remembrance of that lightness and with questions about Alex and herself. She couldn't answer those questions, but they gave her a reprieve. And some of them even gave her an unbidden pleasure, as they chased the demons away and led her to sweet sleep.

⁓

Alex thought he had broken through to her. Didn't the kisses prove that? At the same time, her voice on the phone continued to shift from warmth to remoteness when he said such things as that he was surviving only on the promise of seeing her soon, and that she should come with him to India. So he wasn't at all sure what she was feeling, despite the kisses, or what he would find in her when he returned.

He admitted to himself that this was a rare romantic adventure for him. Rebecca's very resistance had provoked him—to find out who she was, what she was holding back, what she feared, what she wanted, and to win her over, to bring her into what he liked to think of as the romance of his life. He had gotten very good at this kind of thing. Not that he had contrived it. It was his reality. And most women he had pursued had gone for it, whatever had happened with them after that. But she was different. She kept him off balance. Still, intentionally or not, she had allowed enough allure to come through to capture his interest, stir his curiosity, fuel his pursuit. Then he had seen something in her eyes that one night that had made him feel unusually close to her and uncommonly vulnerable himself, for a moment. After that, the ferry. And the races. And the kisses. Yes, he was reaching her, and she was coming around, if only part of the time. But there was more to it than that. She was *getting to him.* The mystery of her. The very keeping him off balance. The supple mind. The irrepressible warmth beneath the recurrent coolness. Yes, he was succumbing *to her.* Maybe she was even leading him on for some purpose of her own. But so what? The adventure of it all. The texture. The romance. With her, and her mystery, and her ambivalence, and her Renoir smile. How delectable. Who knows where it will lead?

# 12

## Eezzee to Luxx

Alex rang the bell thinking this was quaint. An old fashioned black-tie date. In this informal age. When Rebecca opened the door, he beamed like a boy. There she stood in a glistening black dress flaring slightly from the waist to the knees and hugging her curves in a silky sheen from the waist up over the sleeveless shoulders to a high neck that set off her luminous face, her large, lively blue-green eyes, and the glint of a gold necklace and matching gold shell earrings mirroring the gracefully descending curve of her hair. He had not seen her quite like this. Entrancingly sensuous, elegantly sensual. And simply, heart-stoppingly beautiful. In that Renoir way. And then some.

"Rebecca . . . you are sublime," he breathed. "You'll mesmerize the room."

"And you are a shameless flatterer. But thank you," she said modestly, inviting him in and observing silently that he was quite dashing himself tonight, trim in his tuxedo, slightly graying hair, and perpetual tan.

He stepped inside yearning once again to gather her in his arms and kiss her. But he held back as he had done before, discreetly cautious of making a wrong move. He was never certain what mood he would find her in, or how quickly she would change. This was not a time to presume, or to risk offending.

"No flattery at all. The plain truth. But if you *would prefer not to* hear it, I could just say, 'Nice to see you.'"

"*Ah, Bartleby. Ah, Humanity,*" she responded with the wryness that had come to mean so much to him. He heard it as a good omen. She collected her evening jacket from a chair.

It had been two weeks. He had looked forward to this night more eagerly every day. And now he was here, with her. And he felt like a shy adolescent boy.

She still didn't know how she felt about him. Or how she wanted to feel. But in recent nights she had been able to slide into sleep by thinking that, for all of her doubts about both of them, she would be glad to see him. And now he was here. And she *was* glad.

As she returned with her jacket, his eyes embraced her. He came close and took her hand. "Before we go," he said peering intently into her eyes, "I have to say it—It is *wonderful* to see you."

She smiled.

He melted. He risked it. He kissed her lightly, trying not to smear her lipstick. The risk was worth it. She shared the kiss. His blood raced. His heart leaped. Her ambivalence tilted. They separated with a blush. And they went out.

The maître d' welcomed them into the Rainbow Room on the sixty-fifth floor of Rockefeller Center. Wide twin stairways curved grandly from the entrance down around the revolving dance floor below. From there, semi-circular tiers of tables, only half occupied at this hour, ascended to the windows, which vaulted to the ceiling another twenty feet high, draped with gauzy curtains and set against the majestic backdrop of the dazzling city and the night sky. Alex requested a table at the windows and subtlely pressed a $10 bill into the maître d's hand. Following a whispered instruction, a tuxedoed escort led them down one of the stairways, across the dance floor, and up the tiers on the other side to a table at the windows facing south, where the lights of the Chrysler and Empire State buildings rose not far away, and the towers of lower Manhattan sparkled in the distance.

"Very nice," Alex said approvingly to the escort, who floated away. They sat down, viewed the city outside, and took in the room, suffused with a lush luminosity from discreetly recessed overhead lights, amber wall sconces, and pink table candles.

"*Izznn't . . . itt . . . rowmmaanntic?*" Alex sang softly, then continued the tune with la-dee-das while rhythmically swaying his head back and forth. "That song could have been written for this room," he said, dropping the impromptu performance. "Same vintage. Rodgers and Hart. Early 1930s. I think Maurice Chevalier first sang it in a movie."

"You are a wealth of arcana. I won't say trivia. Did you dig that up for this evening? Or do you keep a supply on hand for any occasion?" She gave him an ingratiating smile.

"Both," he laughed. And seeing her smiling face in the roseate light of the room, he said to himself: Here she is—the Rebecca Winters he had fantasized being with in this place, tonight, like this. Radiant and warm. A Renoir to die for.

"Shall we have some champagne? I want to celebrate."

She casually expressed assent, and he ordered a bottle of Crystal, ignoring the price. Then a serious air came over him. He reached across the table for her hand and entwined his fingers in hers.

"Rebecca," he said earnestly, "It does makes me *very* happy to be here with you, tonight, like this. Truly. A fantasy come to life. And that makes it even better." He knew he was coming close to being as banal and repetitious as he sometimes warned himself against. He felt boyishly awkward and fell silent.

Quashing an editorial question over whether his 'it' in that last sentence referred to fantasy or life, she said amiably, "I'm happy to be here with you, too." Then she added with a winsomely tentative smile, as if to keep him off balance, "—I think."

He was almost relieved. With all of his eagerness and expectations for tonight, he wasn't sure how she would be. Would she be the Rebecca he had left two weeks ago who seemed to be *with him*, or would she be the one who unpredictably withdraws?

The waiter interrupted the silence with the champagne, set up the ice bucket, poured two tall flute glasses, then departed. The fizz effervescing from the glasses glinted in the air as it fleetingly caught the candlelight and dissipated.

Recovering his confidence, Alex said, "Let's drink to . . . *you . . . and the night . . . and the music.*" He sang the lyrics to this old song.

"Oh my," she sighed, shaking her head and smiling. And as the "ping" of their glasses meeting dissolved into the room with the effervescing fizz of the champagne, and they felt the tingle of the first sips on their tongues, the orchestra, nestled between the curving stairways, tuned into the first bars of *Isn't It Romantic?*

Alex tossed his head back and cupped his ear theatrically. "Hear that?"

"Did you arrange this?"

"No need. They know the role they're supposed to play. And we have ours." He took a bold swallow of champagne, stood up, and stretched out his hand. "Shall we dance?" He smiled at the familiar phrase. "It can be hazardous here when it gets crowded, so we'd better take advantage of the space while we can."

She sipped from her glass then lifted her hand, and he led her down the tiers and out onto the circular revolving dance floor. Two or three couples joined them.

"You ever take ballroom dance lessons?" he asked as they came together.

"Years ago."

"What did you learn?"

They made a few false steps, then started fitting into each other's moves.

"How to follow a lead."

"That must've chafed."

"Not at all. I had no desire to lead."

"I'll remind you of that some day."

"And you?"

"I did once. At Fred Astaire, no less. To no great success. But I did learn that there are about eight standard dance steps. Waltz, foxtrot, swing, rhumba, tango, salsa. I've forgotten the rest. All other steps are fads or free style. Rock music? Not for real dancing. I wanted only to do graceful ballroom dancing, but I discovered a basic flaw in much of it."

"Oh?"

"Yes. That's because the most graceful and romantic dance steps," he said, leading her with growing confidence, "especially the waltz, as well as the foxtrot and even the swing, are all basically in 3/4 time. But most of the classic songs played for ballroom dancing, and that you want to dance to, if you're old-fashioned like me, are in 4/4 time. Like this one. This song makes you want to waltz. But you can't do it. So you have to improvise or resort to a two-step, like we're doing."

"The composers probably wrote for singers, not dancers," she said.

"No doubt. Of course, Fred Astaire could dance elegantly to any kind of music, but he went beyond ballroom dancing. You have to be a pro to do what he did. I'm no Fred Astaire, but are you game for some old-fashioned amateur improvisation?"

She looked askance at him and said a little tentatively, "OK."

And with that, he tightened his arm around her waist and pulled her closer to him. She gripped his left hand with her right and pressed the other against the back of his shoulder. And they pushed off into a 4/4 step, part waltz, part foxtrot, part swing. They staggered a little, bumped their toes, and then glided gradually into the Rodgers melody set to the Hart lyrics sung by an aging baritone in a white dinner jacket who sounded like he could have been there when the room first opened. Alex pressed his cheek to hers as much for balance as romance. And with an eye to avoiding collisions, they swirled and lilted and looped their way around the floor until they ended with a deep dip that they sustained through the final beat and the last measures of melody mellifluously fading in the air.

"A triumph!" Alex said, panting as they rose upright. "Very well done. You're a natural at this—along with picking horses."

"Hardly," she replied with a quick breath. "But I admire your terpsichorean facility."

"Ha! You made it possible."

Returning to the table, they toasted their dance-floor improvisations, and with the orchestra taking up the tom-tom prelude to *Night and Day*, they ordered Oysters Rockefeller, to honor the room, and a rack of lamb for two.

Seeing her face in the candlelight again, he wanted to be close to her and to share everything with her, all their fears, all their longings. He had to tell her. "Rebecca," he said, resuming his seriousness, "I have to tell you this. Something . . . extraordinary has happened to me. Or . . . it's still happening. I mean with you. And I've got to talk about it."

She didn't speak. Was this more of his theatrics? Or questionable self-revelations? Or unwanted interrogations? Oh, well, she said to herself, let him talk, if he wanted to. She would play her part as far as she was willing. She gave him a *willing* expression.

"It's . . . like," he began rather dreamily, "sailing on a rudderless ship blown by the wind. I don't know where it's going, and I can't guide it. But it's thrilling. And I want to sail it to the ends of the earth."

Yes, it was his theatrics. She almost laughed.

Reading her response and realizing he was over-dramatizing, he started over. "Maybe I'm being . . . well . . . juvenile—but you do have that effect on me sometimes. Let me try a literary allusion. Remember how Tolstoy has Anna Karenina and Vronsky get enraptured in their love affair like they're sailing on an unnavigable ship? They know it's dangerous, and they don't know where it'll take them, but they can't stop."

That's the second time in the past several weeks, she thought uneasily, that someone had commended Anna Karenina to her. She didn't like it the first time, and, although this was different, she didn't welcome it now either.

"There's a romantic grandeur in their voyage," he went on confidently. "It gives a passion to their lives that makes everything else seem limp and gray. I feel kind of like that. And I love it. Even if it makes me seem . . . juvenile at times." He paused for a drink, uncertain how she would take this.

She waited before speaking. What could she say? She didn't feel anything like what he described—not that she wholly believed he did either. But she didn't want to say so directly. She decided to question his literary allusion.

"I don't really think Anna and Vronsky were all that thrilled. They had a desperation in their passion that tormented them both. And it led to misery and tragedy. Remember, Anna deserts her husband and son and eventually gets so depressed she throws herself under a train. That's not grandly romantic. It's the sordid tragedy of someone who loses control of her life and ruins the lives of other people as well." Her voice had started evenly but gained an edge.

The reaction surprised Alex. He had wanted to open himself up to her and beckon her farther in. Now he seemed to have pushed her away. He chastised himself. But why did his words have that effect? Didn't she understand him? Did his manner mask his honesty? He wasn't ready to give up. The waiter interrupted with the oysters. When he left, Alex carefully picked up Rebecca's theme as they ate.

"You're being pretty hard on Anna, aren't you? Sure, she's not a particularly admirable character, but she's starving emotionally. Would the slow death of a loveless marriage be better than her . . . romantic tragedy?"

"It would've been a lot better for the people she hurts," Rebecca answered almost as edgily as she had left off. "And for her, too. Her married life might have been dull but it wasn't terrible. Her husband might have been a boor but he wasn't a monster. And she had a child to care for. She had no true justification for what she did. A desire is not a justification. She didn't have to wreck her family—or neglect the illegitimate child she later has with Vronsky, or kill herself for a passion . . . . She had other options."

She was feeling curiously uncomfortable as that last sentence fell from her lips with a diminishing tone. She wasn't sure why. The dark topic? The idea of *other options*? And didn't he see what he was doing to her? Taking her somewhere she didn't want to go?

Still surprised at her intensity, but noting her change of tone, he tried to bring the conversation back to where he wanted it to go without stepping on her toes. "Let's forget Anna Karenina," he said solicitously. "I can see she is doing me no good. What I mean to say is that life is, well, unpredictable, and largely unplannable. The most deliberate decisions don't always take us where we want them to. They might even send us astray—isn't that the theme of *War and Peace*, by the way? But leave that aside, too. So sometimes life works best—here comes another metaphor, I'm afraid; I can't seem to avoid them—when we cut anchor, let the winds blow, and, as Nietzsche said, sail our ships into uncharted seas. I feel like I have set out on a voyage like that with you. I didn't expect it. And I don't think I could now control it. Frankly I don't want to. That's more my style than yours—rudderless ships, uncharted seas and all that. But, Rebecca, isn't something like that happening to you, too? Even if you wouldn't describe it as melodramatically as I do? And even if you didn't exactly want it to happen?"

As he ended, she was thinking he was flying high now, pitching phrases and flinging metaphors, juggling the heartfelt and the histrionic. Did he know the difference? Did he care? But even as she questioned his theatrics and his motives, as she had before, she recognized that his was not the only voice saying some of these things to her. He waited patiently, sensing her self-reflections and not wanting to interrupt. She put down her fork and faced the window in silence. Soon she lost herself in the infinite moonlit night sky and the twinkling cityscape of Manhattan. *Eros and Aphrodite, cities and the night.* The words swam in her head, and the feeling of lightness began lifting her again. Yes, something had happened to her. She didn't know what it was or where it had come from, but she knew she had to tell him about some of her feelings, and about her ambivalence toward him. After waiting while the table was cleared for the next course, she finally turned toward him and spoke slowly.

"I'm not much inclined to talk about my feelings. Maybe that's because it's uncomfortable for me or because I haven't trusted them. And to be honest, I've never really cared to hear much about other people's emotions, either, especially if they confess them too easily."

"Particularly men?" he interrupted.

She paused. "Oh, possibly," she said somewhat defensively. "When most men talk about their emotions they seem to be trying to convince women that they do indeed feel what they believe women want them to feel. So I've preferred men who haven't tried be very openly 'emotional' at all."

"I guess that lets me out." He smiled.

She returned the smile slightly, sipped some champagne, and said reflectively, "To tell you the truth, Alex . . . I don't know quite what to make of you. You aren't like any man I've ever known before."

"I hope that's a compliment." He raised an eyebrow. "But go on anyway."

She thought for a moment and then spoke carefully, determined to be as honest as she could. "You are quite aware that I've, well, resisted your histrionics, your fantasizing, your aestheticism, and so on. These things all run together in you into a rather confounding mix, and it can all seem like a continuous performance. You do it very well. But I often get the impression that, for you, the performance and talking about things is as important as actually doing or thinking or feeling them. Maybe even more important. That makes it hard to know if what you say expresses genuine beliefs and feelings or if it is all part of your performance—for yourself as much as for anyone else. And, in spite of my . . . good feelings for you, this still causes me . . . unease might be the right word."

Alex was preparing to defend himself against this surprising candor when the waiter presented each of them a plate under a silver dome, and then ceremoniously lifted both domes in unison. "Bon appétit," he said and backed smoothly away to a duet of "Thank you" from the two diners.

"Such theater," Alex said. "But what does he really *feel*?"

She acknowledged his jest with a knowing glance, and they sampled the lamb with murmurs of approval. The break gave Alex a chance to collect his thoughts, sensing that he had broken through another barrier with her. Then he resumed without defensiveness.

"You're right, Rebecca. I might seem to view life as a performance. And I grant that talking about things, including emotions, may be as important to me as the things themselves. No, probably not. But let me explain." He continued nibbling intermittently while speaking, which made his words less solemn than they otherwise would have been. "My emotional life depends partly on how I think about it, and how I put it into words. This is true for everyone to some extent, I would guess—although you evidently would disagree. I don't mean that we can't feel without thinking or talking about it. But emotions aren't just lying around waiting for us to feel them either, any more than beauty is waiting around to be seen or heard. We have to learn to feel the depths of our emotions in some measure like we learn to use our senses to perceive beauty. We do the same thing with the imagination and the intellect. We have to learn how to awaken them all, inspire them, improve them. And that means, for one thing, talking about them. It's like those silver domes dramatically lifted from the plates—*cloches*, aren't they?"

She gave him a puzzled look.

"Well, the *cloches* don't just keep food warm. They embellish dining—if they're used judiciously, of course, and don't become a mere cliché of pretentious restaurants." He chuckled, alluding to a previous conversation while making fun of himself. "Emotions can work that way. They get better with attention, and even with occasional dramatic presentation."

"But emotions aren't artworks or performances or food presentation," she interrupted emphatically. "They're not something you polish and present and stand back and admire. And because you think they are I don't know what in you is real and what is performance. As I said, that makes me uneasy." The lightness within her had dissolved

"I appreciate your honesty," he said seriously, then added breezily, "I'm having a great time, by the way. And that's the *unembellished* truth."

She went on without acknowledging his attempt at humor. "Has it ever occurred to you, Alex, that you treat emotions, and practically everything else, as art and performance because then you don't have to *do* anything with them? You can simply observe life at a distance and cultivate that *hard gem-like flame* instead of living directly, like the decadent aesthete who said, *Live? Our servants will do that for us.* The truth is, Alex, aesthetes are cowards—even if they claim to *live dangerously* and do rash things like chase juvenile delinquents in cars who make life ugly for them. It's all for show. Not real life." She stopped, her emotions in a tangle. She'd gone farther than she'd intended. But he had pushed her to it, again. And yet, she wasn't sorry. She needed to say something like this to him. Then she felt that she had actually circled back to her uncertainties about herself.

He held his eyes on her as she dropped hers to return to dinner. Had he upset her? he asked himself. Or had she willingly opened a window on herself? He would take it as a window. "Nice lines," he said. "You do come up with them. But haven't we been down this road before?" He gave her a pleasant smile and went on eating and talking. "I guess I'm not very persuasive. I've tried to explain that I'm not simply a poseur observing life. I just want to shape my life on my terms and not let the world have its random way with me, as though there were some fine integrity to that. So when good feelings come to me I want to make the most of them. I want to feel them and, yes, observe them and talk about them." He put down his knife and fork and tried to see into her eyes. "This is happening to me with you, Rebecca. I truthfully don't know what all of these feelings are. But I know I have to talk about them and that nothing has ever been more honest and more *real* to me. I wish I could prove that to you. And make you feel less . . . threatened."

"Threatened?" Her voice was thin and almost nervous. "I said uneasy."

"Another of your nuances. But why else would you keep vacillating between cold and warm, inching toward me, then pulling away?" Emboldened to go straight to the questions he had wanted to ask her for so long, he said with a forcefulness unnatural to him: "Rebecca, what are you hiding? What are you afraid of? It isn't only me."

The fork slipped from Rebecca's fingers and clanked against her plate. She reached for her napkin and brought it to her lips, her eyes avoiding his. He saw her discomfiture and regretted pressing her. Had he gone too far—again?

"Forget I said that," he retracted. "This isn't the place or time for such talk. I've so looked forward to this evening. And now I'm being clumsy. Sorry." He resumed eating and fitfully turned the conversation to other subjects—the view, the food, the room, the dancing couples. His retreat appeased her, and she went along. But a persistent disquiet nagged her. And after the meandering conversation lapsed into a quiet look outside, she stunned him, and herself, by saying: "Why don't you tell me, Alex. *What are **you** hiding? What are **you** afraid of?*"

"What? Where did that come from?" he reacted.

"From you," she answered. She was tightening inside. But she made herself go on. "Ever since that night after the play when we talked at the rooftop restaurant, I've suspected you were afraid of something. I saw it in your eyes. You conceal it with your glib, debonair style and loquacious talk. But it's there. And if you want my emotional honesty, you'll have to give me yours, and not play over your defenses." She was nearly trembling, knowing that she had opened an assault on herself.

He could hardly believe what he had heard her say. Trying to dissolve the tension, he said with a grin, "Listen to you grilling me about suppressed emotions and hidden fears! The best defense is a good offense, 'eh?"

She took a breath and managed a slim smile. "You started it."

"All right," he said. "But if I play it your way, you have to play, too."

She wanted to pull back. This was no game. She wasn't going to reveal herself for his entertainment. But for some reason she also wanted to go on.

"It's not a game," she said calmly.

"Depends on how . . . Never mind." He hoped for a little levity.

"If we are going to do this, Alex, you have to be serious and honest and not just indulge in theatrics."

Undaunted he quipped, "What if I make things up?"

"Are you going to do this or not?"

"Of course. Sorry again."

"If you don't tell the truth, in the end you won't get anything out of it, and I would likely know. And you won't get anything out of me."

"So it *is* a kind of game. A gamble even."

"You don't get it. Let's . . ."

"Yes, yes, I do," he interjected, gesturing apologetically. "But if I start and I play by your rules, you've got to end it."

He doesn't get it, does he? she said to herself. The truth. Reality. What had she gotten herself into? But she nodded faintly and tightened more inside.

He drank more champagne wondering, was this the same Rebecca Winters, the woman of Renoir beauty and resistant mystery, the reluctant player in his personal romance who had nevertheless captured his heart, who was now pressuring him to reveal *his* secrets? How was he supposed to act? No, that's just what she did *not* want him to do—*act*.

"All right," he said, abandoning his frivolous tone. "I don't know if I can satisfy your high standards of integrity, but I'll do what I can."

"Sail your ships into uncharted seas." She made herself say this with a smile to needle him and to ease herself.

"Touché," he replied, gratified that she *was* playing along.

The waiter attentively refilled Alex's nearly empty champagne glass and topped off Rebecca's. Alex took another swallow as if to fortify himself. Then he stared at the glass in his hand thinking of how to begin. "I'm sure I have subterranean wounds and fears that I can't see," he started softly, nibbling as he went on to give himself time to think and to distract from what he was saying. "That's what defenses are for, aren't they?—to protect us from ourselves as much as from other people. Isn't this where we left this subject that night on the rooftop? Anyhow, besides those hidden fears, I can own up to another kind that I have long been able to see. It's the fear of getting stuck in a life that I don't want, but that I can't escape. It could be a professional routine, or unwanted obligations, or submission to authority, or even unwittingly becoming someone I don't want to be. That might be the worst—to be trapped in the wrong life and not know I'm trapped. That's not blissful ignorance. It's death in life."

Rebecca's stomach tightened still more. Did he know about *her*? Did he see *her* fears? Her life? Was he playing with her? Her eyes focused hard on him. "Where does that come from?" she asked tensely.

"Oh, it probably goes back to my youth in that small Midwestern town outside of Chicago where everyone was the same. Or they seemed the same to me. They were contented, but I saw myself dying a long slow death of monotony. The distant whistle of the train passing in the night called to me. That's an American cliché, I know. But it's still alive for me—every time I hear a train whistle."

"So you're just a traditional American boy chafing to break free," she said, regaining her poise. "Another Huck Finn, or more likely Walter Mitty."

"Something like that," he shrugged. "I don't claim novelty. I may be a cliché through and through—although you kindly said I was not like the other men you have known."

"Alex, for all of your love of clichés, you're no cliché yourself." She said this with a half-smile that encouraged him to tell her what truths he had to tell.

He laughed. "I'll take that as a compliment." He had a bite and put down his utensils to speak without distraction. "The harder truth is, Rebecca, as far as I can understand and describe it—which I've never admitted to anyone, but you demanded honesty, and I'm doing my best—the harder truth is that at bottom what I fear most is . . . that I might not be able to save myself. That may sound melodramatic and phony, but I don't know how else to put it."

"Save yourself from what?" she asked with a mixture of curiosity and trepidation, wary of where this would go.

"A life I don't want. I've always dodged the standard male roles—the macho stuff of power, status, domination. I have no desire to impose my will on the world. And I don't have the temperament for it. But to be more painfully honest, I doubt that I have the strength of will or whatever it takes to do it, even if I wanted to. That could be why I indulge in what you've complained about—the histrionics, the fantasizing, the aestheticism. I know this makes me seem like Walter Mitty or worse, maybe Emma Bovary, living in fantasy because there you can be what you want to be. But actually, for a fictional role model I'd take—and I've said this before, too—Don Quixote, because he didn't merely escape into his fantasies, he lived them out to become the noble knight he wanted to be, follies and all. There is a kind of strength in that. Not that I'm trying to be anything noble. I might, as I said, just be compensating for my incapacities and defending myself against threats from the real world. But this Quixotic quality, I guess I'd have to call it, also makes me who I am, for better *and* worse. This is the person you see in me—and may not like. I don't think I could be anyone else. I've sometimes tried, but it didn't last." He paused. "But now, because of you, something new is happening to me, and I don't quite know what it is, or where it will take me." He slowly drank some champagne. "And I don't care."

She gazed at him. And she saw something different from what she had before. She had seen flashes of sincerity now and then. But this was more than that. He knows he's not what he seems, after all, she thought. And yet, in his way, he is exactly what he seems. That's a nice irony. What was she going to do with it?

"In fact," he continued, "since you induce me to be searingly truthful, I'll give you some more grim biographical details. They go back to my early adulthood, and to the Vietnam War."

"You in the military? You didn't tell me. It's hard to picture."

"I pictured it too vividly to go through with it." He fiddled with his remaining lamb while seeming again to be sorting his thoughts. "I was in college," he went on. "And although the war was winding down, and luckily my draft number hadn't come up, I decided to make myself undraftable. So I got married and went to graduate school—not only to skirt the draft, but it worked—and started teaching. I didn't think very thoroughly about any of this, and while it shielded me from the draft it sent me into a misbegotten marriage and a misguided career. And when the threat of military service ended, I soldiered on in the life I had created for myself. But I wasn't really alive." He finished eating, had more champagne, glanced out the window, and played with his glass as he continued. "Then one day when I was writing an article for a magazine—I did that occasionally—I interviewed that Vietnamese woman I once mentioned who told me she was always sad. Her words rocked me. I saw that I had become too much like her. And I had no good reason for it. Unlike her. By laziness and cowardice—you're right about that, I concede—and habits of mind, I had all but lost my life. The very thing was happening to me that I had feared most: not living my own life at all, and being blind to the fact." He lifted his glass to his lips, muffling the words: "Then I kind of snapped."

"Snapped, did you say?" Bleak memories sprang to her mind.

"Uh-huh. Not psychotically. But I more or less stopped in my tracks. I couldn't stay on that path. I quit teaching and withdrew from everything I didn't want to do—fortunately, I had some money from an inheritance to get by on. Before long my wife left me, less angry than baffled, convinced that I didn't need anyone. And I couldn't blame her. She deserved better. I was living for myself alone, or trying to. I started traveling more and writing more and felt better about myself. And I vowed not to let passivity or sadness or other bleak ways of thinking consume my life, whatever the cost. And that's what I've done ever since. But," he set down the glass and spoke directly to her, "at the time I met you, Rebecca, I felt my life almost slipping away again. Not in the same way as before. But I needed a change. I didn't know what kind. Writing a novel and going to India were to be part of it. But I certainly didn't foresee it involving you. And yet . . . I think it does. See, you can't plan life. And it's why the image of being with you on a rudderless ship driven by the winds appeals to me. That's trite and melodramatic. And it's probably predictably male. But there it is." He sat back, drained his glass and smiled, a bit sheepishly it seemed to her. "Now you know me as well as I do, for what that's worth."

She wasn't certain whether he was telling the truth or mixing fact and fiction for effect. But she found herself inclining to believe him more than not, because now she saw through the romantic bravado to a self-doubting boy. And she felt herself loosen, and that pleasant feeling of lightness begin to return.

"Isn't it time for another dance?" he said, his aplomb reviving as he put his confessions behind him.

With the melody of *I Could Have Danced All Night* swelling from the band, she agreed and slid her chair back from the table.

They worked their way onto the dance floor now crowded with starry-eyed young lovers, wide-eyed tourists, and seasoned hoofers.

"That's how it should be done." Alex nodded toward a statuesque gray-haired couple agilely sidestepping through the other dancers with the insouciance of pros. "But it takes years of practice. Every Saturday night."

"Is that romantic or obsessive?"

"It depends on how . . ." He gave a hushed self-mocking laugh as he wrapped an arm around her. "This song makes you want to dance all night for sure," he said as they dodged elbows and sashaying hips, "but it's in that vexing 4/4 time. It should be a waltz. Even a polka, like *Shall We Dance* in the *King and I*. Oh well, shall we give it a literal whirl? Warn me if we're about to collide."

"I'll sound the alarm."

Clasping each other, they swirled into the eddy of dancers, inventing steps in time with the tune, and moving with increasing assurance, swooping here, diving there, and spinning into the open like dolphins surfacing for a sporting leap. They were not the most graceful swimmers in this sea. But they became quite at home in it, an occasional wobble and bump scarcely detracting from their flair. Then, with a buzz of dizziness in their heads, and a flush on their cheeks, they wound up with a final tight spin and a swoop on the song's last notes and lyrics, which Alex softly sang, "*I could have danced, danced, danced all night.*"

"Very nice!" he exhaled. "No serious injuries, I hope."

"Nothing life-threatening." She was enjoying herself now more than had seemed possible earlier.

"Considering our conversation, that's good news."

Catching their breath, they left the dance floor. And when they sat down at the table, Alex said with his typical zest, "'We must have Baked Alaska for dessert. It's de-e-e-llectable. Ice cream and cake and meringue and flaming brandy. Another piece of drama that goes with the room. And, in fact, an apt metaphor."

"How's that?"

"You'll love this," he chortled with a self-deprecating grin. "First, the hot flames from the brandy leap up over the looping meringue." He sculpted the forms with his hands. "They attract you, but they can burn. When they die down, you slice though the meringue into the ice cream underneath, and then into the warm cake in the middle. It's all fire and ice, hot and cold, charred and sugary. Always surprising, kind of mysterious, and a little dangerous. Like romance. And—to get all I can from the image—it's kind of like us. You allow yourself to approach the flames but the heat drives you away. I'm more willing to get burned, so I rush right into the fire for the delectations it holds—like riding that rudderless ship into uncharted seas. And then . . . ."

"Enough. Enough," she waved a hand at him with a laugh. "You've lost me. Too many metaphors."

"You'll see." He ordered Baked Alaska for two. The waiter emptied the champagne bottle into their glasses. "We'd better have a couple of champagne cocktails," he said over Rebecca's protest that she couldn't drink any more champagne. "Two pink champagne cocktails, please," he instructed the waiter. "You don't have to drink it," he goaded her. "Just admire it. They're pretty, and they'll go with the room, as well as with the dessert."

She gave him a mockingly exasperated look.

"And now," he said in a more serious voice, "since I have revealed my fears and foibles to you, it's your turn. That was the deal." He leaned toward her. "So. What are *you* afraid of Rebecca Winters? And what is happening between us, *for you?*"

She couldn't get away this time. And she didn't altogether want to. She had brought it on herself. She would play this game with him, if that's what he wanted it to be, even though it wouldn't be just a game for her.

She took a drink of water from the glass beside her champagne. "All right," she began tentatively, "I've . . . told you that I've never quite trusted what people say about their feelings. Or people who live for them. But . . . ." She hunted for suitable words. She couldn't find them because she didn't know where she was going. So she let her words follow her thoughts. "Truthfully, as I hinted earlier, I've probably never entirely trusted feelings in themselves, either. Or not for a long time. They're fickle and often hurtful. I saw my mother deeply hurt by my father when he left—or I thought I did. Now I'm not so sure, from what she's told me. Anyway . . . I was hurt by him. Maybe more than I knew, or wanted to know." She paused, following a skein of ideas that felt new to her. "My mother told me recently that as a child I seemed to feel emotional hurts more acutely than she would have expected—the loss of pets and so on. I do remember times like that, but she said she saw me increasingly manage to suppress such feelings. I don't know if that's true. I suppose it is. I've never thought much about it. In any case, I know I made an adult life for myself that gave me, well, self-control and emotional comfort. Was that an unconscious defense against strong emotions I didn't want or couldn't handle well? Maybe. But it worked for me. I've succeeded at more or less everything I've set out to do, and I've had everything I thought I wanted." She sipped more water.

"What about your marriage?" he broke in.

Rebecca leaned her elbows on the table, eyes cast down at her finger lightly tracing the rim of her champagne glass. How much was she willing to tell? "Oh, it was a modern marriage," she said slowly. "Two careers. He was a lawyer. Richard. A fine man. We grew apart. And eventually, very amicably after about six years, we decided to live separate lives, which just added a chapter to the lives we were already living. This happened a few months ago. A divorce made in heaven."

"Another nice phrase. Oscar Wilde? And another economical autobiography. I'm sorry about the divorce, although honesty compels me to say I'm grateful for it, for my sake. And it sounds a bit like my own divorce. Another coincidence. But weren't you ever in love with him?"

She started to pull back, but made herself go on. "I thought so at the beginning. Or maybe I never really thought about it, like other things. We were very compatible and comfortable. I was happy enough. And it ended well. Richard and I are now like old friends. That's probably all we were ever meant to be. Possibly that's all I wanted. Do you ever see your ex-wife?"

"Not for many years. She re-married, and happily as far as I know. But we're not talking about me now. Didn't you have any pain or regrets about the marriage?"

Rebecca sensed the tightening inside again, and a quaver in her stomach. She lowered a hand from the table and pressed it against her stomach, hoping he wouldn't notice. The quaver receded. The tightness remained.

"Are you all right?"

"Yes, yes. Just the champagne," she evaded, and was relieved to see the waiter arrive. His tray carried two full pink champagne flutes vigorously effervescing from sugar cubes at the bottom, and a small cake covered in curling peaks of white meringue browned at the tips. After setting down the glasses, he placed the cake in the center of the table, splashed some brandy on the plate surrounding it, struck a match and waved it over the plate. A whoosh of blue flames leaped into the air. Rebecca jerked back. The flames quickly subsided into flickers.

"See—appealing but dangerous," Alex cracked. "Like romance. And there you go backing away."

She arched her eyebrows at his labored metaphor. With a flame or two still flickering from the brandy, the waiter cut into the puffy desert and served half to each of them. He plucked up their first champagne glasses and withdrew.

"Another toast," Alex proposed, holding up his pink champagne cocktail. "To Baked Alaska. Romance. And emotional honesty."

She felt a quiver of nervousness as they clinked glasses. They tasted the bubbly drink and then forked through the snowy, singed meringue into the ice cream to reach the cake at the center. Balancing portions of the hot and cold, scorched and sweet confection on their tines, they took a bite.

"Honoring the spirit of honesty," Alex announced. "I have to say that Baked Alaska is better as drama and metaphor than as dessert. But then, many things are better in fantasy than reality."

"That again?"

"Never mind. Where do we go from here?"

Dabbling with the frothy meringue on her plate, Rebecca answered distractedly, "To a side show?"

"You're a comedienne. But you can't get away with laughs alone. You have more to tell."

Rebecca had another bite and continued toying with the meringue. She would have to speak of things she hadn't even been able to think about, or not clearly. How could she be honest with him when she didn't know for sure how to be honest with herself? And how much could she make herself say? She parted her lips, but words wouldn't come. At last she said haltingly, "After I got divorced . . . ." Fingering her champagne glass again, she felt herself tightening inside once more. She started over. "A few months after Richard and I separated, and not long after the divorce this spring, I had . . . a . . . frightening emotional experience. It wasn't *because* of the divorce. Something had been happening to me for a long time before that. I don't know for sure how long, possibly a year or more. I wasn't actually aware of it. Then . . . September 11th seems to have compounded it, or brought it closer to the surface. Whatever the reason, I . . . I was becoming disengaged from things. The marriage. Work. Life." She put the champagne to her lips and wet them. Setting the glass down, she left her fingers on the stem, keeping her eyes on it as if in a trance. She took a deep breath and sat up, avoiding looking him in the eyes. "Then . . . one night I saw myself in my mind. And what I saw was . . . ." Her stomach knotted. "*Nothing. I saw nothing.*" She spoke softly. "I didn't feel anything. No pain. *Nothing!* I didn't care about the marriage, or the divorce, or work, or anything. My whole life . . . was a blank. I didn't know why. And when I saw this in myself, I . . . I panicked."

"What . . ." he started to interrupt.

"Wait," she silenced him with a raised finger. "I have to finish." She strengthened her voice, resolving to tell the whole story. "I collapsed in a cold panic, and woke up utterly bereft, vacant. The panic had gone, but all I could feel was an empty loneliness and a lonely emptiness, and the fear of being hopelessly lost and not being able to do anything about it because I didn't understand it. Except that I must've brought it on myself, simply by being myself, by living the only way I knew how to live. And that's pretty much how I felt when I met you, which was only a few weeks afterwards. And it's what you observed in me."

Alex reached across the table and touched her hand.

"I'm not quite through," she said with renewed determination, removing her hand from his and having another taste of cake and a sip of champagne. Then she fingered her glass again as she spoke. "That night after the theater . . . and then on the ferry ride . . . . I think something started happening to me, too. I didn't know what it was. It felt good, but . . . . Anyway, when we went to the horse races, something else happened. Somehow I felt that a kind of weight had been lifted from me. Maybe it was all that screaming, so unlike me. But whatever it was, since then, I have felt, not all the time but sometimes . . . I don't know . . . a sensation of lightness inside. The emptiness and fear haven't wholly gone away. But I have been able to shut them out better and to relish that new sensation when it comes." She stopped and had more champagne.

"I'm so glad to hear that Rebecca," Alex said soberly. "You . . ."

Before he could say more she continued. "But in all honesty, Alex," she said firmly, "if I hadn't been in that disoriented, desolate state when I met you, I would never have been willing to spend time with you. You . . . you are so different from me. As I've said, I have never trusted your theatrical poses and so forth, and that has made me question how much I can trust you."

He opened his mouth to speak, but she held up a finger to stop him. "Because I was in that state, and I thought that I must have caused it by being myself, I guess I kind of started taking the advice of my mother when she told me to go against the grain of myself. I didn't do it deliberately. I wasn't even sure what she meant. But the idea was in my mind when I went with you on the ferry. You were very much *against the grain* for me." She stared directly into his eyes. "And yet, I . . . I've come to see something else. I've come to see, in spite of myself, and especially tonight, that for all of our differences and my resistance to your theatrics and romanticizing and the rest, deep down in our fears and in our defenses and in our longings, somewhere in our deepest selves, *you and I are very much the alike, Alex.*"

Rebecca's words echoed back and forth across the table. She hadn't expected to say this. She had never even thought it. It just came at the end of the thoughts she was following. But now that she had said it, she felt a release. The tautness inside dissipated. And that benign lightness began lifting her, stronger than ever. Perhaps the champagne, she said to herself. But champagne had never done this.

He hadn't anticipated anything like this, either. He had been probing her well-managed exterior for weeks trying to find a path to her heart. He could not have exactly explained why, except for the romance of breaking through to this subtly alluring woman who made their every encounter an enticing contest that he never wholly won, yet never quite lost. But now, she had seen through him and the differences between them, and had been honest about what she saw. And what she saw was close to a mirror image. He did not know what that meant to her. But whatever it meant, she had made him feel light as air.

"You are perceptive and honest and courageous, Rebecca," he said quietly. "I would never have thought . . . or dared to say . . . ." He stumbled. "Well, as you said, aesthetes are cowards. But for you to say we are alike makes me very happy. And," he brightened his tone, "it not only makes me happy. It gives me an exalted and liberated and delectably dangerous sensation. This is more than romance. It is—may I say it?—love. And I'm not play-acting."

Rebecca studied his face. Was he sincere or . . . ? He did seem genuinely happy. Still rather boyish but not as brash and debonair as usual. She liked him this way. For a change. But she doubted it would persist, and she knew he was wrong to say she was perceptive and honest and courageous—that's just what she had not been with herself for so long.

He raised his glass. "One more toast," he said. "To your penetrating eye and honest heart, and to our deepest affinities and what is happening to us . . . together." She smiled and joined him, touching her lips to the champagne while Alex finished his off. Then they sat in silence as if absorbing what they had said to each other here tonight, and what had been happening to them both, although it was not entirely the same thing. Until, as if on cue, Alex cocked an eyebrow and raised a finger in the air to mark an alert. "Listen," he said, re-donning his cavalier air. "They're playing the perfect song for one last dance. 'Easy to Love.' You up to it?"

"I guess so," she answered softly.

"This may be our last dance of the night," he said, taking her hand as they stood up and started down the steps. "But it'll be my first dance with you as I confront the danger of dangers."

Rebecca shot him a quizzical glance, as if to say, "What now?"

"I mean my first dance with you as a man in love, sailing for the first time into uncharted seas on a rudderless ship because . . ."—he completed the sentence, as they swept onto the dance floor, by whispering melodically into her ear his rendition of the song welling from the band—"*Yuuu **arrr** soh **eeeezzeeee** to **luuvv**, soh **eeezzeee** too eyye-dol-eye-zzz . . . .*"

He was playing again. But Rebecca was willing to believe he wasn't altogether playing. She knew his games now. And why he played them. And now, in her way, she was playing, too.

# 13

## Sentimental Intimacy

They spoke little during the taxi ride from the Rainbow Room through the quieting city streets to Rebecca's apartment. They had talked enough. They knew something had changed between them. And they knew more would come. And they would let it.

Walking into the apartment, Rebecca switched on the hall light and then a living room lamp, hung her jacket in the closet, and slipped off her shoes. Alex wandered into the living room and greeted Clarissa, who lay imperturbably in her place on the sofa.

"Would you like a drink?" Rebecca asked, shuffling across the room toward him, her shoes dangling from two fingers.

"Nothing thanks. The champagne's still carrying me." As she came near, he reached out to her. She slowed. He drew her to him. The kiss began softly. Her shoes fell to the floor.

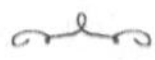

Warm summer air wafted through an open window languidly stirring the sheer curtains as the pale light cast by the street lamps outside played shadows across the ceiling and filtered down onto the sheet draped loosely over the two bare figures lying lightly entwined on the bed. The only sounds came from the distant rumble of an occasional car on the street outside, and from their own barely audible breathing and halting swallows.

Rebecca had long regarded sexual intimacy much as she had the good men in her life. Pleasing. Sometimes more than that. A nice part of life. Like Richard. But this night, she had felt an unusual sensation of romantic arousal, as well as an undertow of uncertain expectations.

Alex had not known what to expect from physical intimacy with this irresistible, yet often mystifying, woman any more than she had known what to expect from him. He had probably thought about it more than she had, but that had not answered his questions. How would she respond? Would it bring them closer? Or would he become self-conscious and clumsy? Would she withdraw behind her defenses? Would it all go awry and leave them blushing and more distant from each other than before?

But when their lips had met in her living room, a tide of desire had begun rising in both of them. A slow tide, but calmly inexorable. And they had ridden it, and it had not ebbed. They were riding it still, lying together in the semi-darkness. Their desires had not been driven by the urgent, unconstrained passions of youth. It was as if they had been orchestrating their emotions to the end of time, dissolving their uncertainties with every tender touch and kiss.

Following another gentle, loving kiss, Alex breathed, "Rebecca . . . I do love you . . . and . . . please believe me . . . it is the first time that I have loved anyone . . . in this way."

She had heard similar words before. But these sounded different. Almost like a plea. Yes, she told herself, they are different. She reached an arm around his neck and held him close. And he held her. Seconds passed. A minute. An eon in the reckoning of love. Finally she sighed, "And I you."

When they relaxed their embrace, Rebecca lay back, and Alex raised up a little to see her face in the dim light from the street. He lifted a hand and brushed her cheek with the back of his fingers. What a self-consciously tender gesture this was, she thought. Contrived, and yet it had come to seem quite natural to him, like so many of his affectations. He felt a trace of moisture on her cheek, as he had once before, and he wondered if it was perspiration from their long embrace or a trace of tears. He wanted it to be tears. Happy tears. That would say what no words could.

He leaned over and kissed her once more. The kiss was light, like the first time on the ferry. They held it, remembering.

Drawing back a little he whispered, "Tell me . . . something . . . beautiful."

Puzzled by the request, and far from expecting a conversation now, she replied softly and quizzically, "Beautiful? What do you mean?"

"Tell me something beautiful that you've seen, or that has happened to you, or that you like to think about. A scene. An image. A feeling. An incident. Anything lovely."

"Your aestheticism acting up again?"

"Could be. But I want to hold onto the emotions of this moment. Try it, will you? Remember something beautiful. Or invent it."

Another of his games. But she would try to play. To go along. For him. And maybe, in some way, for her too. She closed her eyes and started searching back along the pathways of her memories. All she could see was haze. Then a pair of familiar images began faintly forming. The blank book and the flickering screen. She tensed and threw open her eyes. How thoughtless of him to do this to her. How rash of her to let him do it. The sweet emotions were drifting away. She swallowed hard and, trying to conceal her uneasiness, she said with a broken voice, "I can't . . . ."

"You might be trying too hard," he reassured her. "It doesn't have to be anything elaborate. Just a lovely, memorable thing that you can recall or imagine. Let's see," he thought for a few seconds. "Here's one. Sometimes on a summer night when the air is clear and still and the moon is so full its brightness dims the stars and you can see the whole night sky into infinity, a thin, wispy cloud will appear from nowhere, and will drift slowly into the moonlight and across the center of the moon like a slender, translucent gray feather, white at the edges. And while you watch it pass, inch by inch, you think nature must have created this scene for its beauty. The artistry of nature exhibited for us to see."

His soft tone and the nice image soothed her. The warm feelings were returning. "Charming," she murmured. "But . . . I can't say I've ever seen what you describe. New York doesn't much lend itself to such a sight."

"I hope you will see it some night, somewhere. But that's just an example. It needn't be aesthetic beauty. It might be an experience that touched you . . . beautifully." He leaned up on an elbow. "Have you ever read *The Tale of Genji*?"

How odd, she thought, that he would bring up literature now. Or . . . maybe not. "In college," she answered. "It was too long. Needed a good editor."

"Always the consummate professional, aren't you. But you've got a point. I love it anyway. That's what it's really about, you know—the beautiful moments that we capture fleetingly on the 'bridge of dreams' that is our life. Moonlit nights occur in it again and again. There are even moon-viewing events. Genji's favorite nights come in January when the full moon in the clear crisp winter air glistens off the snow creating a starkly elegant black-and-white painting. The book teaches you to see the moonlight, and to appreciate all kinds of beauty like that, if it does nothing else."

"So it teaches you to be an aesthete?"

"Well, maybe. But, as I said, beauty isn't confined to the aesthetics of the senses. It's a way of thinking and feeling. Can you indulge me and try once more? Forget aesthetics. Just tell me about something that gave you a beautiful feeling. I have that kind of feeling with you now. *Beautiful* is the word for it. And I am not going to let it go." He caressed her cheek once more. "Please."

She didn't want to try again. She feared this game would dispel, not enhance, the good feelings. But then it struck her that she should force herself. That she should face down her fears of what she might see—the blank book and flickering screen and the shudders they could cause, even now. She had to do it. She had to find something *beautiful* in the past beyond her fears. She had to. Pursing her lips, she closed her eyes. Haze filled her mind again. Traces of the book and screen began to appear. She tensed once more. But she made herself look through them. She strained to see something. Shadows started gathering. She recognized everyday activities, the office, friends, her mother, Richard. But she could see nothing that she would call "beautiful" in the way he was talking about. She closed her eyes tighter, determined to succeed.

Some faint new images formed. The ferry. The kiss. Dancing. This amorous night. They were *beautiful*, weren't they? But they were all with him. That wouldn't really count, would it? While she was thinking about this, another image started emerging in the background. A child. Walking along a sidewalk. Gradually, she could see the child clearly. A long-forgotten memory began gathering in her mind. As she thought about it, a mild pleasure came over her, tinged with other, more amorphous, emotions. Had she done it?—seen through her emptiness and her fears and found a *beautiful* experience in her old life? It felt like that. She would tell him the memory, if she could.

"Okay. This might not qualify," she said tentatively. "A trivial piece of autobiography."

"Your autobiography couldn't be trivial." He lay down again, his head next to hers.

She put her head back and looked meditatively at the ceiling and spoke diffidently. "Once . . . when I was a child, maybe five or six years old, my parents gave me a doll for my birthday. She had curly hair and a frilly dress with lace and bows. I was very proud of her. I named her Alice, after *Alice in Wonderland*, which my parents had read to me." She paused. "Oh, this is embarrassing . . . ."

"Not at all," he intruded. "I'm an avid audience."

"Well, I was taking her to a friend's house to show her off. And while I was walking along the sidewalk admiring her and tinkering with her ribbons, I stumbled and fell, and the doll tumbled from my hands. As I started to get up, I saw her lying face down in a puddle."

"Your beauty would be grim realism," Alex interrupted.

"Don't complain. I'm playing your game."

"Sorry. Please go on."

"I broke out crying. With tears running down my face, I sat up and saw an old man coming toward me from a nearby shop. He had evidently heard me cry and had come out to help. He lifted me up and, seeing that I wasn't hurt but that I was weeping over what lay in the puddle, he picked up the dripping, muddy doll and invited me into the shop, where he described the situation to a gray-haired lady at the counter. She brushed the dirt from my knees and dress and assured me that everything would be all right. She asked the doll's name, and after I told her she said something like—and I can almost her words—'Oh, Alice is a beautiful name. And she is a beautiful doll. She just needs a bath and some clean clothes. May I do that for her?' I mumbled yes, and the lady took the doll in her arms and went into a room at the back of the store. A few minutes later, she returned with the doll fresh and clean in a new dress. 'That wasn't so bad,' she said. 'Alice is just fine.' She put the doll into a box on a bed of tissue paper and put a top on it, 'to keep her safe on her way home,' she explained. She handed the box to me, and the old couple escorted me outside. 'Be very careful as you walk,' they said. 'And take good care of Alice.' I timidly waved goodbye and went on my way, watching my steps and cradling the box cautiously in my arms, very happy." Rebecca hesitated. "But . . ." Her voice cracked, and she went silent.

Alex tightened his arm around her waist. "What a remarkable memory you have. A very *lovely* story. And you are such a good storyteller. I knew you could do it. But it sounded like you weren't through."

She cleared her throat. "I'd forgotten about this ages ago. I don't know why I remember it now, and very vividly. It's a sentimental memory. Even treacly, I'm afraid. But it is . . . *beautiful*, at least to me. And the beauty in the memory isn't my feelings for the doll. It's the old couple. They were so kind. The old woman must have given me a new doll just like mine that she had gotten in the back room. My mother had probably bought the first one there. I kept the new Alice for years, not knowing . . ." Her voice faltered again.

"It *is* beautiful. And you needn't apologize for the sentimentality. What would literature and movies and love affairs and life itself, for that matter, be without it? Sentimentality is the candy of the heart. Everybody needs it sometime. Besides, beauty and sentimentality can be hard to untangle. One person's aesthetic beauty is another's cheap sentimentality. Only critics fuss over the difference."

Rebecca didn't want to debate this or anything else. But she replied anyway. "You think so? What about anyone trying to be honest about their emotions?"

He removed his arm from around her waist and sat up farther. "For the sake of the honesty you keep extracting from me, I must make a distinction. There is such a thing as honest sentimentality. That's not an oxymoron. Honest sentimentality is a genuine and pleasurable emotion of beauty—aesthetic or moral—that makes us *be good* as well as *feel good*. Cheap sentimentality is different. It only makes us *feel good*, and *feel* that we *are good*. Your memory has honest sentimentality. And it says good things about you."

She wasn't really listening. She didn't care about his theory of sentimentality. Not now. She was thinking of her *beautiful* memory—and what she had not told him about it. She wanted to tell him. With a teary voice, she said, "I didn't finish the story. You see . . . ." She swallowed. "I now remember . . . that I . . . didn't thank them." Her voice faded.

He looked into her eyes. This time he saw small tears. He wiped them from her cheeks with loving fingers. "You are a beautiful person, Rebecca," he said, "in many ways." He bent over and kissed her softly. Then he laid his head back on her shoulder and put his arm around her.

She didn't speak. She just wanted to lie there with her memories and feelings, sentimental though they might be. And her gratitude. These were all sweet and deep and strong, and yes, she admitted, *beautiful* . She was lost in them. Then a question came to her: Could this be a clue to her "crisis"? Had she feared giving herself to emotions, bad or good, because she had sometimes felt them too deeply? So she had protected herself, but too well and had finally gone empty inside? Possibly. But she didn't want to think about that. She wanted to stay pleasantly lost in her *beautiful* feelings.

Alex sensed her wishes, if not her complicated thoughts. They both closed their eyes, silently absorbing their sentimental intimacy.

When Rebecca opened her eyes again, sunlight was glinting through the window shades, and Alex was leaning up watching her.

"Good morning," he said, smiling, and touching her cheek with the back of his fingers.

"Good morning," she replied, rubbing sleep from her eyes. A twinge in her shoulder reminded her where he had slept part of the night. She massaged the stiff joint.

"Sorry about that," he apologized. "You make a heavenly pillow. I've got a few aches and pains myself. Honorable wounds. Emblems of love."

She smiled.

"I have to tell you," he said with quiet earnestness. "If you will indulge me yet again." She almost laughed. He continued. "Rebecca . . . you make me . . . very happy. Not just because of last night. But . . . because . . . I care for you . . . more than . . . for myself." He took a deep breath. "That's a completely new thing for me . . . . I've never really given much of myself to anyone. I guess I've never wanted to–except for the romance of it, as you know." He flashed a shy smile. "Now I do. And that makes me feel wonderfully . . . free and happier than I've ever been with a woman. And I want that to go on forever. I hope . . . ."

She raised up and kissed him softly before he could finish, not fully knowing what he meant, but convinced that he believed it, and somehow glad he had said it. Her mind drifted back to their intimacy of last night and to their talk about beauty. She told him what she was thinking. "Last night," she began haltingly, "was, well, beautiful, as you would say. You were . . . very tender and sensitive and loving. More than any man I have known before. I felt very close to you. I still do. But physical intimacy was only part of it. And our *sentimental* conversation was . . . uh, moving and . . . revealing to me. It will take me more time to sort it all out." She paused, "But you have made me very happy too."

She said no more. He kissed her again. Not a kiss of passion. Or one of his ethereal kisses. But a kiss of simple, honest, understanding endearment.

⌘

They lay for a few minutes in the sunlight now pouring through the window shades, brightening and warming the room on this early August day. Then Alex abruptly sat up and said ebulliently, "I've got a great idea. Another adventure."

She gave him a puzzled look.

"Atlantic City! It's a balmy Sunday. The drive takes only a couple of hours. We could be back by dark. Don't tell me you have a better way to spend the day. Surely not work!"

"There's always work. But Atlantic City? What for?"

"It's on the ocean. And it's pure vulgar Americana awash in gambling. Who knows, we might strike it rich. We were lucky at the races. Why shouldn't it happen again?"

Assuming his theatrical air, he launched into song: *"Luck be a lady tonight, la da, dee-da-da, dee da.* Remember, Marlon Brando sang that song," he said, "not very well, in the movie of *Guys and Dolls.*"

"You regaled me with a song from that show as a prelude to gambling once before as I recall," she responded.

"Well, it worked. And it's a good show. Besides, I'm a true amateur, you see, in song and gambling, no less than in other things—I do them just for the love of it; that's the *amour* of the true *amateur.*"

"More of a gamboler than a gambler?"

"Oooh! Never too early in the day for your puns?"

"We all have our weaknesses."

"Anyway, we can't lose. Whatever happens at the casinos, we'll have the day. Forever. It's a sure thing."

"A shoo in?"

"Aha! You don't miss a trick. I'll take that as a yes." He hugged her. "I'll go home and change and get a car. It'll take me about an hour and a half. Is that enough time?"

Surrendering to his enthusiasm, she nodded with a small smile.

Looking into her face, framed by the puffy pillows, he thought she was more glowing than he had ever seen her, untouched by the make-up she had washed away last night. Nature's sensuality. "I love you Rebecca Winters," he said seriously. "Thank you for that." He bent over and kissed her with that newly-born endearment. Then he said cheerily, "Don't get up. I'll let myself out." Before she could react, he leaped out of the bed. Quickly donning his clothes, he tucked his tie and cummerbund in pockets, slung his tuxedo jacket over his shoulder, and pranced to the bedroom door. There, he made a theatrical twirl then tossed his head and shoulders back, turned his face toward her, and tipped a nonexistent top hat to her as he crossed the threshold as if exiting a stage while singing *Luck be a lady **today*** . . . .

"Don't quit your day job," she called out.

"Don't want one," he shouted back as he left her apartment.

Rebecca lay on the bed facing the windows and the blue sky over Central Park. She felt warm inside and out. A novel feeling. It went with the sunny summer day, she thought. And, yes, with that long, beautiful night of dancing and sentimentality and loving. And more. Her eyes strayed to the ceiling, now bright with reflected sunlight, where she had seen nightmarish images so many times. They weren't there now. Would they return?

Shaking off the disquieting question, she took hold of the bed sheet and pulled herself upright. Casting it aside with a sweep of her arm, she pushed herself off the bed, padded to the kitchen to feed Clarissa, and then got in the shower. The steamy water gushed over her, splashing to the floor, soothing her skin, and obscuring from any ears but her own the soft sound of her singing, *Luck be a lady* . . . .

# On a Bridge of Dreams

(Continued)

She was walking now, painfully and with crutches, but she was walking. And growing impatient to see Alex. A few days had passed since she had first awakened here, as best she could tell. She marked them by the afternoon visits of the doctor, whom she always pressed for news of Alex. Today he told her he was able to find out that Alex had had surgery for the head injuries but was still unconscious.

"Surgery?" she exclaimed fearfully. "What kind of surgery?"

"To relieve bleeding under the skull."

"What . . . now?

"We must wait and see. As I said sad before, he is lucky to be alive."

Lucky? That cursed word again. She didn't want to hear it. She wanted to hear that Alex would recover. And that they could leave. And live.

"You might be interested to know," the doctor added after giving her this latest prognosis, "that they captured the terrorists who set the bomb at the Taj. Hindu fanatics. They want to force Muslims out of there and all of India. Evidently they had planned to cause an international incident at the Taj while the foreign leaders *were visiting, but they couldn't get close enough because of security. So they did it the day after, when you were there. Bad luck."*

*Listening indistinctly, Rebecca heard "bad luck" and thought the doctor had at last got it right. She had to see Alex. She had to talk to him, even if he couldn't hear her. The doctor said they could not let patients wander around the hospital visiting each other. And it was too soon for both of them. It might even upset her more than console her. She argued. She coaxed. She pleaded. He conceded. At least he would try to get her in to see Alex as soon as possible. Only for a minute. But he would try. She pressed her own hands together in a gesture of gratitude.*

*When the doctor left, Rebecca turned her thoughts back to the explosion. That's luck for you Alex. All bad. As the doctor had said. Alex would likely make some glib remark about the irony of religious hatred and violence erupting at the Taj Mahal, that peerless monument to love. And he would carry on about the dramatic unpredictability and coincidence of their coming back here a second time—after their first visit was thwarted—to be caught up in it as part of some cosmic pattern! He'd make some crack about their karma, too. But this wasn't some game of his. It was all too terribly real. And it could end for her what had become much more than a way out of her dilemma—or had it?*

*If only they had foreseen any of this when, after their first night of intimacy with its many sentimental and beautiful moments, they had gone to Atlantic City and had joked about their good luck and good karma and benign coincidences, and they had visited a palm reader. And Rebecca had surprisingly agreed to come with him to India,*

# 14

## Against the Odds

The two-hour drive south to Atlantic City passed swiftly on the felicity of their mood while the radio played classic show tunes and an all-Sinatra program swinging from brassy razzle to mournful saloon songs. They chatted about the poetry of good old-fashioned lyrics, the salubriousness of the summer weather, and the goofiness of what they were doing. They laughed easily and touched affectionately. Alex was tempted to delve further into the night before, plumbing what it meant to him, and to her, and to them. But he didn't want to risk deflating their balloon. This was a day for diversion, not delving.

Their happy mood was still elevating them as they arrived at the wall of buildings on the backside of Atlantic City's Boardwalk hotels and casinos, all facing the ocean on the other side. A sprinkling of people strolled on the sidewalks, a couple of dogs cavorted, and a few cars drove by, but there wasn't much life this early Sunday afternoon that they could see. Not much of a city. They parked the car in the first lot they saw and walked hand in hand toward the casinos, Alex singing one more time about luck being a lady. A flight of steps flanked by a pair of high windowless walls led them up from the street to the Boardwalk. And there they stepped onto the Atlantic City stage.

Before them a vast sandy beach tapered away into the low surf of the shimmering Atlantic Ocean. To the right and left, the Boardwalk ranged out of sight, bordered on one side by the beach and on the other by the garish facades of hotels and casinos and the tawdry fronts of gaming arcades, cheap eateries, and curio shops. Sunday swimmers, sunbathers, and idlers lazily animated the scene.

"Picturesque," Alex observed.

"Pure Americana," she acknowledged. "You could use it in your article."

"I said you'd be an inspiration."

Ambling off down the Boardwalk, they chuckled at gaudy souvenirs, marveled at industrial-size salt water taffy pulls in candy stores, and kidded about the tasteless excesses and wondrous vulgarity of it all. Coming upon a bearded man in a circus outfit swallowing a sword beneath a sign promising fantastic side-show acts, Alex stopped and blurted out, "Rebecca! You're psychic! See! You knew we'd be here. You said so last night."

"What do you mean?"

"You suggested at dinner that we go to a side show."

"It was an evasion, not a suggestion."

"Well, here we are. A telling coincidence."

They moved on, letting the sword-swallower suffice as their side-show. A boisterous arcade opened beside them. Hawkers were touting their games. "Step on up! Evvverreeebboddddyyy wins!" Shoot a row of flying ducks. Throw a ring around a peg. Collapse a stack of bottles with a ball. And a dozen more.

"You ever play one of these old games," Alex asked.

"At a local carnival as a child."

"Ever win?"

"No. You?"

"I won a fat stuffed bear once at a fair by slinging a plastic loop over a bowling pin at ten feet or so. A highlight of my youth."

"Downhill from there?"

"'Not exactly. Remember the horse races. But these things are all rigged, of course, so it's almost impossible to win anything. The bottles are made of lead. You need a bulldozer to budge 'em. Stuff like that. But shall we try our hand at something for fun anyway?"

"To get some action?" She smiled.

"You're wonderful." He hugged her around the shoulder.

They ventured in. "How about that contraption?" Rebecca gestured toward a glass case standing about six feet high and four feet wide half filled with small stuffed pandas. A metal claw dangled loosely over them. "You see these things everywhere these days, even in grocery stores. I've wondered why."

"It's because, as the great American philosopher P.T. Barnum proved, 'There's a sucker born every minute.' These things were invented for suckers. I confess I've been a victim. I'd warn children against them. But it's a place to start. I'm hopeless at coordination games though. Could never hit a baseball except by blind chance. You'll have to play. You might get lucky. We've seen your luck before. And for fifty cents a try how much can we lose?"

"OK. What am I supposed to do?"

"Just take the handle," he placed his hand on the *L*-shaped object protruding from the front of the case, "and move it to position the claw above one panda like this." He manipulated the handle in her hand. "Then you let the claw drop by pushing this button over here, and at the right moment you pull the handle to close the claw around the bear. The claw lifts up and if it's got a bear it's yours."

"Seems too easy."

"It is. It's all but impossible. You'll see."

Waving away his proffered coins with the remark that this was her game, she took a few quarters from her purse and slipped a couple into the slot. The arm rose jerkily and the claw opened predatorily above the pile. Rebecca maneuvered the claw to where the head of one panda rose above the rest. "Now?" she asked.

"Go for it."

She pressed the button with a finger of her other hand, and the claw dropped. It bounced off the panda and slid into the pile, its claws collapsing limply as she pulled the handle. The empty claw lifted on its own to its original position. "No good." She muttered.

"Not so easy after all, is it? You have to coordinate the drop with the grab. Pull back at the just right time or you miss. Even if you don't miss . . . you'll see."

She inserted more quarters. Edging the claw above the target, she pushed the button. The claw fell. She pulled the handle. Snap. The claw closed on air before it reached the pile, then jerked back up again. "Damn!" she cursed quietly.

More quarters went in, and again she steered the claw into position. She pushed the button, the claw dropped, and as it reached the panda she pulled the handle. The talons closed around the panda's head, and the arm began lifting the panda from the pile. "Got it!" she rejoiced. But before she had liberated the panda it slipped out and settled back into place. The claw waggled and returned to its post.

"That's not fair!" she exclaimed. "I had it. The claw is too weak to hold anything. What a cheat."

"I told you it's a fraud. You might get a panda if you tried long enough. But you could buy one at a store for less money than you'd spend doing this. Of course, it's not the bear that matters, it's the game, the gamble, the action."

"But this is supposed to be a game of skill, not of chance."

"That's where they get you with all of these games in here," Alex said as they left the pandas and started wandering through the arcade, passing an array of contests they declined to try. "We think it's skill. And we bet that our skill can beat the odds. But what we don't know is that the house has fixed the odds against us by rigging the game. So it's less a test of skill than a game of chance, a gamble, against long odds. Like life."

"Dare I ask what you're talking about?"

"OK. Here it is. We think that with skill we can make life work for us as we want it to. But we can neither predict nor control it. And the 'house'—God, nature, existence, call it what you want—fixes the odds against us in ways we don't know. So we're always more or less playing against the odds in life. That's why, if you're not a gambler at heart, the *action* of life can discourage you instead of exciting you. To play or not to play, that is the question, as Hamlet said. Didn't he? All of this makes the panda game not a total fraud after all. It's a metaphor of life. And worth in philosophy what it costs in quarters. Atlantic City is a philosophical place."

"You just make these things up as you go along don't you?" she said with a laugh. But some of what he said had a resonance for her that didn't come from him. She didn't want to think about that.

"A casino will clinch the case. The more garish the better." They returned to the Boardwalk, and he scanned it up and down. "There. That's it. The Taj Mahal." He pointed to a casino not far away whose glaring onion-domed architecture vulgarly imitated the historic Indian shrine.

"Wins the prize for garish," she remarked.

They wove through the accumulating pedestrians on the Boardwalk—mainly packs of vacationing teenagers and families out for a day at the beach—and pushed through the wide glass doors of the casino. "Say goodbye to the day," Alex quipped. "It's always night in here. An underworld where people live like moles, gambling around the clock. This is the real *action* of Atlantic City." They stood for a moment adjusting their eyes to the low artificial light. Then they surveyed the cavernous space extending farther than they could see. A bright red and gold carpet ran down several steps and on through the seemingly endless room. Rows of slot machines marched uniformly out of sight. A constant chorus of whirs and chings and coins spilling from machines rang in their ears. Flashing colored lights and clanging bells signaled winners and blared enticements to bet, and gilded mirrors on the ceiling above gaudy chandeliers redoubled the glitter. Alex and Rebecca set off through a row of slot machines, eyeing the dedicated bettors who concentrated on the devices in front of them, methodically, even mechanically, sliding quarters or dollars into the slots then pulling handles or pushing buttons.

"Do you think they're enjoying themselves, or is it compulsion?" Rebecca asked. "Some of these people look like robots." She pointed toward a middle-aged woman in a sequined dress who sat transfixed on a stool, inserting one dollar bill after another into a machine. After each bill went in, the woman pressed an illuminated button to spin the machine's three wheels of icons. Then the woman watched without visible emotion while the wheels spun and snapped to a halt, hoping each time for three identical icons to line up in the window and prompt the machine to cough up a jackpot.

"Probably both," he answered. "The odds are so bad with most slot machines that you have to be pretty compulsive to play them much. Oh, they'll give you small payoffs now and then to seduce you. But it's the chance of winning a huge jackpot, even against long odds, that keeps hardened players going. I prefer roulette. Doesn't pay off like the slots do on rare occasions, but it's not as chancy or mechanical either. It's fun to play and has an old-world elegance to it—suited to gambolers as well as gamblers." He winked at Rebecca recalling her remark of earlier that morning. "It's a straight-forward game of chance with 'natural odds.' And those odds aren't bad. Always 38 to 1 on the individual numbers—36 numbered squares and two spaces of zeros. Unless, of course, the wheel's manipulated, like Humphrey Bogart did at Rick's Place to help that young couple in *Casablanca*."

"That's illegal!"

"Yes, but crime can pay—it's another gamble." As they wended past the slot machines and black jack players, he asked if she wanted to know more.

"How could I not?" she answered with light sarcasm. "Now that I know all about playing the ponies, why not roulette, too?"

He chuckled. "All right. In roulette you can improve the natural odds by betting on combinations instead of individual numbers—rows of numbers, numbers that touch each other, the odd or even numbers, black or red numbers, and the top or bottom half of the board. That can lower the odds down to almost 50-50—although the green zeros still give the house an edge there. But low odds give a low payoff."

"Not enough action?"

"Right. The best you can do is double your money, but that's better than 50-50 odds payoff in horse racing—or in the stock market."

They reached the roulette tables and stood at one of them behind the seated players. The croupier whirled the tiny ivory ball in its groove rimming the large wheel embedded in the table at the head of the playing board. Then he sent the wheel spinning. Late bettors hastily placed their chips—each player using a color different from the others—covering about half of the board's thirty-six black and red numbered squares arrayed in twelve rows of three, with space on the sides for bets on red and black, odd and even, and topped by the green 0 and 00. The croupier waved an arm across the table, signaling no more bets. The bettors stood soundlessly. As the wheel slowed, the ball rolled out of its groove and bounced from one number to another, clattering across the frets between them. It came to rest.

"Nuummberrr Niiine! Red," the croupier called out.

No winners. The croupier smoothly swept the chips from the board. The players laid out more chips. A young couple standing next to Rebecca and Alex, twitching like honeymooners, giddily played number 25 for some sentimental reason. A woman of a certain age, heavily made up and wearing a blonde wig, leaned from her chair with the cold determination of a seasoned gambler to stake chips on half-a-dozen numbers. A nervous pair of tourists, he in a plaid sport coat and mismatched shirt, she in a flowered dress with short puffy sleeves, tentatively placed a couple of chips on the spaces for red and for the even numbers as though afraid of losing the family inheritance. A cautious older couple consulted each other and then carefully arranged chips on a corner position. A dapper man in his sixties wearing a well-tailored jacket and complementary tie sitting with a detached air, insouciantly laid five chips on number 11. A few other bettors arrayed chips on much of the rest of the board. The croupier repeated his moves. The ball whirled. The wheel blurred. The players watched.

"Nummmberr Eee-ll-evv-enn. Black," he announced and swept the board, except for the chips on eleven and a couple of chips on black. The croupier stacked and pushed forward thirty-five chips for each one on the winning number, and one chip for each on the winning color. The dapper man impassively gathered his winnings. The game repeated. He played 11 again.

"Why would he do that?" Rebecca whispered to Alex. "The same number won't come up again soon."

"Ah, there's some of the philosophy," he replied in a hushed voice. "It's a variation on the Monte Carlo Fallacy of believing that natural odds change. As I said, in roulette the natural odds are 38 to 1 with every play. But luck can change those odds in a kind of metaphysical way. Some bettors count on it, looking for lucky numbers that come up against all odds, at least for a while. They'll play those numbers over and over. If a number's lucky, it'll keep coming up. If it's unlucky, it won't come up."

"So the Monte Carlo Fallacy isn't always a fallacy."

"It's not if luck is on your side. Good luck always changes the odds, and beats them."

They watched three more spins that turned up no big winners. The dapper man kept playing 11. The honeymooners gave up on number 25 and drifted off. The nervous couple clutched their sparse winnings from betting on the colors and happily vacated their chairs.

"Ready to give it a shot?" Alex asked Rebecca.

"Sure." They settled into the empty chairs.

He put a twenty dollar bill on the table and, observing roulette etiquette, slid it over to the croupier. Rebecca pulled another twenty from her purse and did the same.

"Uh, you want separate chips?" Alex asked her.

"No. Let's share the *action*. It worked at the race track."

"How sporting of you."

They requested one-dollar chips. The croupier counted out forty green ones and slid them back across the table.

"Our lucky color, too." Alex said gleefully. "Now, what numbers do we want?"

"Try 15 and . . . 29," she said tentatively.

"OK. And some corner bets." She placed chips on 15 and 29, and he put a couple at the corners connecting 2, 3, 5, 6, and 20, 21, 23, 24. Other players placed their bets, some cautiously, others confidently. And the dapper man played 11 again.

A few last-minute chips went down, the croupier waved, and all eyes fastened on the wheel. It sped 'round and 'round as the ball rolled, then bounced from number to number. When the wheel slowed and the clattering stopped, disappointed sighs met the sight of the ball lying below a green space on the number the croupier announced as "Duubbble Zeeerohh!" He cleared the board.

"Bad luck there," Rebecca said.

"Gives the house that edge in the odds."

They placed more bets and lost the next time. And the next. And the next. There were some small winners, and the dapper man lost each time on 11.

"Luck's not a lady yet," Rebecca murmured.

"That'll change."

"The Monte Carlo Fallacy?"

"Good luck's not a fallacy, only misjudging it is." He lowered his voice and said, "Let's try 11. At least a corner of it. The guy who keeps playing it must know something we don't."

"But he keeps losing, ever since that first win."

"That might not mean anything yet. I like his confidence."

Alex put chips on 7, 18, 29, and on the corner connecting 11, 12, 14, 15. She bet on 3, 17, 23 and 27. Other bets went down, the wheel spun. The ball careened and clattered and fell into place. Eyes found the number.

"Nummmberr Eee-ll-evv-enn! Black," called the croupier.

"Hey!" Alex nudged her. "See. He does know something."

The croupier swept the losers from the board. Then he piled winnings on eleven: thirty-five for each of the dapper man's five chips, and eight on the one that Alex had placed at the corner.

"Experienced gambler's say every table has its own luck on a given day or for a period of time that beats the odds," Alex commented as they sorted their modest gains. "It could be a series of numbers, or a part of the board. And it can take a while to discover it, but they watch for it, like lucky individual numbers. Now we've seen proof it's true. And at this table it's not just number eleven. I think the table's favoring the low end of the board overall. How many times has a number higher than 16 won since we've been here?"

"I hadn't noticed."

"I'd say about twice."

"Well, the high numbers have to hit sometime," Rebecca said. And she set chips on 19, 30, and the corners of 31, 32, 34, 35, and 22, 23, 25, 26.

"Ah, the Fallacy's getting to you. But you're playing it against the luck of the table. I'll go with the luck." He put chips on a couple of low numbers and on two corners, including 11. The croupier spun the wheel and cut off the betting. When the ball came to rest it lay on number 8. The woman of a certain age collected the only winnings.

"Still in the low numbers," Alex needled Rebecca.

"Not forever." She bet again on high numbers.

"You just don't believe in implausible, inexplicable luck, do you?"

She didn't answer.

They played on for nearly an hour, losing more than they won, but winning often enough even with their small bets, to keep going, and buying more chips when the winnings dwindled too low. Low numbers kept coming up more often the high numbers. Alex carried on his patter about gambling. Their fellow players changed periodically—some carrying chips, some empty-handed. The dapper man won on 11 more often than any odds would permit, and they shared his luck a few more times, disinclined by caution to follow his lead with every play.

"That's got to change your view of life," Alex said after the dapper man put his entire stash on eleven and won again then finally left carrying a bag full of chips.

"His luck hasn't rubbed of on us much."

"Maybe we're being too timid," Alex responded. "Not risking enough. That guy won a lot because he bet a lot. Counting their remaining chips, they saw they had only fifteen left, out of eighty they had purchased altogether. "Why don't we blow the rest on one last shot? Three bets. Five chips each. You pick one, I'll pick one, and we'll pick one together. Whole numbers. No combination bets. If we lose, we'll have had our money's worth of *action*. If we win we'll celebrate. And I have a premonition our luck has been waiting for us to take the chance. Against the odds. What do you think?"

She made a cavalier gesture with her hand and said, "Go for broke." Recalling the horse of that name they'd won money on in their first race at Belmont Park, she smiled to herself.

"Excellent! OK, I think I'll try 7, a venerable lucky number at the low end of the board."

"Still playing the Fallacy for luck, eh?" she joked and stacked her chips on number 35.

"Yup. And you're still playing it against luck. But what'll we pick together?"

"How about today's date?"

"What is it?"

"I think it's . . . the eleventh."

"No kidding? August 11th. You know, a month from today it'll be one year since . . . . But let's not think about that. Maybe the gods are making amends with a perfect coincidence. That's why the number's been lucky today. And that guy was onto it. I hope he didn't take that luck with him. We should've known and followed his instincts more boldly. Maybe he was sent here by the fates for us. After all, this should be a lucky day for us because," he whispered in her ear, "it's our first day after . . . ." He gave her a quick hug.

They placed their bets on 7, 35 and 11. The croupier performed his routine. The spin of the wheel, the roll of the ball, the wave of the arm. The whirling. The waiting. The clattering. And expectant silence.

"Nummbberr Eee-ll-evv-enn. Black"

Rebecca and Alex gaped at each other.

"It worked!" he exulted. "Luck beat the odds. The gods are with us." He threw his arms around her and she lightly embraced him. Releasing her he said, "This might be a sign to quit. The table can't stay lucky forever."

"Are you retreating from your gambling philosophy?"

"No. Just ready to take it someplace else. Shall we go out to the Boardwalk for some fresh air and sunshine?"

She agreed, and they gathered up their winnings of one-hundred-seventy-five chips along with the five they had bet on 11, gave twenty to the croupier as a tip, and went off to the cashier, Alex singing in a muffled voice, "*Luck is a lady today. . . .*"

Eighty dollars richer than when they had come in, they wove back through the casino. "Just as lucky as at the track," Alex boasted. "I'm never going to gamble without you." She smiled. Pushing through the glass doors onto the Boardwalk, they blinked as the bright sun blinded them.

"I forgot it was mid-day," she said, squinting and shading her eyes.

"Yeah, this natural light is a killer." They stepped into the shade. "So, what'll we do with this huge fortune?"

"Let's keep it and walk a while." They roamed along the Boardwalk, sharing jokes over purple-haired adolescents with safety pins through their cheeks, laughing at more grotesque curios, and tarrying at a vendor where Alex bought a large spool of pink spun sugar on a stick.

"You really like this stuff?" she groaned.

"Another childhood memory. It's pretty, don't you think? But, yes, better as a memory or an idea than a reality. Like so many things."

She rolled her eyes and declined his invitation to buy something for herself or to sample the sticky treat. Alex munched the frizzy sugar as they wandered on. Suddenly, he stopped and pointed to a sign propped on the Boardwalk ahead of them. "Look." He read the sign aloud: "'Madame Raja: Palm Readings. Astrology. Tarot Cards, Psychic Readings. $10.' You ever had your palms read?"

"No. Have you?"

"Sure. Everybody should do it. Not to learn your future. But your nature."

"You don't say. What did you learn?"

"I've long forgotten. But no palmist tells you bad news. And what they see can open your eyes. How about it? Shall we go in?"

"Get our palms read? Aren't fortune tellers phony? Making predictable guesses and telling you reassuring things that everybody wants to hear?"

"Some may do that. But a good palm reader is in touch with cosmic forces. Better by far than a shrink. And you have a bit of the psychic in you—remember the side show?"

"Are you serious? Palm readers? Cosmic forces? Lucky numbers? Lucky colors? You are downright superstitious."

"No. I simply respect coincidences. I might even say there is a law of coincidences."

"Oh, my," she laughed. "More of your impromptu philosophizing?"

"It's not impromptu. But can you bear it?"

"When have I refused to hear any of your imaginative inventions?"

"I do love you—and not just for that reason. See, the law of coincidences isn't superstition because it isn't about causes-and-effects. It's a law of inexplicable patterns in events—repetitions of the past, intimations of the future, symmetries in events, a horoscope that fits, good luck that goes against the odds. Like the number 11 winning so often today on August 11th, and our winning big when we bet on it as today's date. Or your green jacket matching the colors of *Maisie Knew*, who gave us a big win at the track. Or our winnings that day and today being almost the same. Or even you and I coming together at this juncture of our lives. I wouldn't presume to explain or predict or try to control such things. That's superstition. If your lucky number keeps coming up, does that mean there's a definite cause for it? I don't know. But at least it's a benign coincidence. Such coincidences add a mysterious and delectable texture to life. Go with them. The same with palms. Do your palms accurately reflect your nature and your past and foretell your future? I don't know. But there are a lot of coincidences. Palmistry is an art of coincidences."

"Alex," she said with affectionate astonishment, "you are remarkable. I'll bet you made all of this up because of that sign."

"Aha! You're getting to be a gambler despite yourself. Well, I didn't really make it up just now. I only adapted it to the occasion. Remember at the races I said there was no such thing as a 'mere' coincidence? And I said I'd explain that some other time. Well, now I've kept my promise."

"I'd forgotten. But ingenious as your notion may be, you make a dangerous distinction. The path to superstition is paved with the likes of your 'law of coincidences.' When people start believing coincidences are more than 'mere' they can get very superstitious."

"That happens if they mistake coincidences for causes and effects, or the work of God or part of some cosmic design. I just see them out there for what they are and appreciate the patterns they reveal—for aesthetic reasons I suppose—and I make use of them to add texture and mystery to life. No superstition there. But why not let the palmist prove it. You might discover more coincidences and patterns in your life than you knew were there or could imagine. We might even learn how to read our own palms. What better way to spend some of our winnings on this lucky day? An entertaining investment in the future."

She balked. Cheap performers prying into your life with commonplace predictions, random guesses, and mumbo jumbo? Superstition, coincidence, what's the difference? But, then, if it's only that, she didn't have to take it seriously, did she? They can't really see our lives in our hands, can they? What did she have to fear from a mere palm reader? Especially now, after last night? Why not go along. Against the grain. Against the odds. They could be the same thing. She gave in.

He disposed of his sweets and rinsed his hands in a fountain. And they headed toward the sign.

15

# Palms and Coincidence

"Good afternoon." The salutation came from a portly Indian woman swathed in red and gold silks inside a small windowed vestibule at a doorway on the Boardwalk. She was sitting alone beside an empty chair and a diminutive table that held books and a sewing basket. A curtained archway rose behind her.

They returned her greeting, and she said in a soft, inviting voice: "I think that perhaps you wish to learn something from me, but you are not sure." An impish smile stole across her face, as if to say: 'I see you are intelligent, skeptical people who doubt fortune tellers and palm readers, so let's start off with this little joke about my insight.'"

They smiled back. The joke had done its job.

"We'd like to have our palms read," Alex spoke up. "And we would like you to explain how you read them."

"So you desire to learn *my* secrets as well as your own?" she asked with a wink.

"Something like that," Alex answered with a laugh.

"Well, we shall see," she said slowly, looking at the two of them. "I think you have both read many books, yes?" They nodded. "But you do not read the hands as you read a book. There are no words in the hands, only signs. You can learn what signs to look for, but to truly understand what you see you must use *psychic powers.*" She stressed these last two words in part to play on her customers' skepticism. "Not everyone has these. And no two palmists read the hands exactly alike, because psychic powers differ from person to person. These powers don't conflict, they just tell different parts of the same story. In the end it is all one."

Alex was intrigued. Rebecca remained skeptical.

"So you will describe how you read ours?" Alex repeated.

"Be patient. I will tell you only what I care to tell." Her voice was pleasant, but firm.

"Fair enough," Alex agreed. Rebecca made no response.

Without moving, Madame Raja said, "I can see that you do not wear wedding rings. That tells me you are not married. Here I am revealing my secrets already." She gave them another impish smile.

They rather shyly acknowledged her accuracy.

"Married people rarely come in," she continued. "And almost never together. Either they have no questions about themselves and each other, or they want to keep their secrets hidden. And that is usually wise. The palms can be shamelessly honest." She smiled broadly. "Do you wish to remain together for the reading?"

"I have no secrets from the lady," Alex said, glancing at Rebecca. "But she will decide for herself."

"I think the lady," Madame Raja directed her words at Rebecca, "is doubting that she should be here at all."

Rebecca flushed. "No. I'm . . . I'm interested," she responded diplomatically.

Concluding that they were willing enough, if skeptical, customers, Madame Raja closed the door to the Boardwalk, positioned a sign in the window reading, "In session," and led them toward the curtain. "Come this way. I promise no harm will befall you." A bell attached the curtain tinkled as they went through. On the other side, they could make out almost nothing but a dim light and the smell of incense. As their eyes adjusted to the dark, they could see an electric candelabra standing on a small round table in the center of the room. A crimson cover draped from the table to the floor, and the same fabric billowed from the ceiling down the walls. An elaborate gilt-framed mirror hung on the wall behind the table, and pictures of bearded gurus ringed the room. Madame Raja sat with her back to the mirror, gesturing for them to be seated on two small chairs across the table from her. A suitable stage set, Alex thought. Hokey, thought Rebecca.

"I will read the gentleman first because he is eager," Madame Raja said, "and then the lady can decide. Even I cannot predict," she added with a glimmer in her eyes, "what she will wish to do. Give me your left hand please," she instructed Alex, while brightening the light of the candelabra and pulling herself up to the table. "I will return it undamaged." She smiled warmly again.

Alex politely acknowledged the smile and leaned forward, reaching out his hand. She took it with both of hers, inspecting it on both sides briefly. Then she opened the palm with one hand and fingered its surface with the other. She studied it silently. The electric candles eerily illuminated her face, etching lines and casting shadows that evoked in Rebecca's mind an ancient sooth-sayer reading the entrails of birds. Madame Raja then asked Alex for his right hand. More study. She returned to the left hand. When he asked what she was looking for, she said reflectively, "To read the hands you must be patient. It takes time. You must read the whole hand—the shape, the fingers, the mounts, the lines large and small—and read both hands. The left hand tells us more of the past and of our nature and our inner selves. The right hand tells more about how we act on our nature, and about the present and possibilities for the future. So the left hand is usually more revealing. If you are left-handed, this can be reversed. But you are not."

She glimpsed his inquisitive eyes and raised a hand in front of him to indicate he should listen and not speak, then she went on. "And you should understand that the palms go with the stars. Your palms and your star chart say much the same about you. So you should know them both, because your life is in the stars, as well as in your hands." She gave him a friendly look, then turned to Rebecca, who had her eyes on Alex's hands.

Resuming her examination, she told Alex, "You have complicated hands. They tell me many things. First, they say you have an active intellect and much curiosity and imagination. And you relish pleasure and beauty, and you want to live your life with strong feelings."

He tried to speak, but she raised a hand again to deter him.

"You also appear to others to be very capable and confident. But you do not want to have the ambitions and responsibilities that other people expect you to have. You would rather be independent, and follow your impulses and pursue pleasures, or possibly even ideals. So you do not always live up to your abilities. But you do not care about the consequences. Or you want people to think you don't care. This also implies that you do not give yourself easily to others, because you live very much for yourself."

"Please," Alex broke in. "Where do you see all of this? What are you looking at exactly. Can you explain as you go along?"

She answered with a note of genial resignation, "Do not be so impatient. I said you are impulsive, did I not? But as you wish. Although I will explain only what is most important."

"That's all I want."

"First the shape of the hands. Yours are conic, we call them. They are a little wider at the center and taper slightly to the ends of the fingers. And you have rather short fingers, each one also tapering to the tips. Your thumb is low and opens wide. You might not see any of this, but I do. And all of these traits go with imagination and idealism, as well as with romance and fantasy and independence, impulsiveness, impracticality. Is this not you?" She looked up at him with that impish expressions.

He smiled self-consciously and shifted in his chair, glancing at Rebecca, who leaned just perceptibly toward the table.

"And now the lines and mounts. This line here," she traced the line curving across the top portion of his left palm, "is the Heart Line. It shows your emotional tendencies and your relations with other people. Your Heart Line in this hand is curved but not deep, telling me that you have a large capacity for love and sentiment but that you have never fulfilled it. In the right hand, your Heart Line curves even more and is deeper, saying that you are becoming more giving and even tender-hearted. Perhaps a new love. You would be disappointed if I didn't see this, would you not?" She caught his eye and winked. He smiled. She reverted to his left hand.

"Your Head Line—this large one running across the middle of your hand—is also quite strong, showing that you are a person of intellect, and that you are curious. But the distance between it and your Heart Line, and the curve of your Heart Line down toward it, shows that your Heart Line influences your Head Line more than the other way around, which signals willfulness and often being guided by emotions. And because the Head Line slopes down here and ends on the Mount of Luna, the Moon Mount"—she touched the fleshy part on the far side across from the thumb—"it is even more clear that you are exceedingly inclined to imagination and fantasy. Conical hands often have these markings. So you see, the same traits appear in many places. Then up here"—she touched the area between the ring finger and the little finger—"you have a strong Mount of Apollo and a relatively long Apollo finger, the ring finger, above it, with a Line of Apollo coming up to it, also saying that you like beautiful things and pleasures, and that you have some artistic talent. These are all Apollo attributes. And because your Mount of Apollo is close to the Mount of Mercury under the little finger, you clearly have verbal abilities, a Mercury trait. That, and a little fork down off your Head Line, tells me you are probably a writer of some kind."

He was impressed.

"But," she continued, "your Fate Line, or Career Line, coming up the center of your hand from the wrist, is wavy and has many breaks, saying your work has never satisfied you for long."

She caught his eye again, seeking a confirming sign. "Go on," he urged, exchanging glances with Rebecca.

"So impatient!" Her genial expression belied her reproach. "But perhaps the most revealing part of your left hand is here." She ran her finger over the puffy area at the base of his thumb down to the his wrist. "This mound is the Mount of Venus. Yours is large and lively with color. That reveals energy and emotion and passion and more love of pleasure. These are good qualities. But they need to be held under control. The strengths in your Head Line should help you do that, but," she cast him a cautionary look, "as I said already, they do not do it enough. And that could cause you trouble."

He nodded.

"And here is the most important line for you, and for everyone." She traced a deep line beginning near the outer edge of his hand between his index finger and his thumb. It arched down around the Mount of Venus to his wrist. "The Line of Life or Life Line. It reveals many significant things, particularly in the left hand. Our energy and vitality. The past course of our lives. Even how we feel about life. It has been said that the meaning of life is simply the feeling that our own lives have meaning, and we can get that feeling in many ways, and we should get it in every way we can. That is true enough. And this truth always appears in the hands, and especially in the Life Line. Your Life Line is generally strong and goes wide. That shows vitality and a love of life. And because it starts here on the lower part of the Mount of Jupiter under your index finger, it suggests you also have many physical appetites, like a taste for highly seasoned foods." He and Rebecca shared a chuckle. "And this small line coming down near the bottom of the Life Line at your wrist says you like travel, probably for escape." He turned to Rebecca, who was sitting closer to him now, visibly curious and enjoying this. "But," Madame Raja added in a darker tone. "I also see a few signs that are not so favorable."

He noted the change. "Yes?" he inquired.

She held his right hand up under the light and searched it closely, then shifted to his left hand, then back to the right. "Because you are impetuous and independent and want to enjoy life," she went on, "you take risks and maybe gamble. I think this is why you have come to Atlantic City." She shot an amused expression at both of them. "But you have doubts about yourself as well—the inconstant Fate Line in your left hand shows that. And in the right there are indications of possible dangers ahead."

"Where?" he prodded.

"This small mark here on the Life Line, like an *X*." She pointed to a place on the lower part of the line which he could barely discern. "It represents an obstacle or an accident. And this similar cluster of crossing lines on the Head Line also says there could be an injury. So you should be especially cautious until the marks go away."

Straining to see these signs, he asked, "So the lines come and go, and we can change them by changing what we do?"

"How could it be otherwise?" she said gently, raising her eyebrows. "The lines change all the time. Just as we change. Your Life Line might always have some danger markings on it because you want to be free and impulsive. But individual markings come and go, and the lines and mounts themselves alter as we do. I am told that the Life Line even fades when a person remains in a coma for a long time. You see, our lives are in our hands more than you would think." She winked again and released his hands. "Come back in a year and your palms will be different. Then you will understand and believe me."

He started to ask another question, but she cut him off.

"That is enough. I have told you all of the secrets that I choose to reveal." She turned toward Rebecca. "Now the lady?"

Rebecca vacillated. She didn't want any fortune teller probing into her life and speculating about it, even if she didn't believe in *psychic powers*. Still, this woman was more intelligent and intuitive and kindly than Rebecca had expected. And she had captured Alex perfectly. But if she truly could read lives in the palms, the possibility stirred in Rebecca as much trepidation as curiosity. Would Madame Raja see too much in her hands? Things she had not wanted to see in herself? Or had she banished these things last night by seeing through her fears? Would Madame Raja bring it all back and revive those fears? Or would this astute and engaging palmist find hopeful signs? Summoning her curiosity and courage and hopes, Rebecca brought her chair up to the table and gingerly offered her hands.

Madame Raja reached for them and examined both sides as she had Alex's. Then she took the left hand and bent the fingers back to expose the lines and mounts as she studied them in the light. She did the same with the other hand.

"Your hands are simpler than the gentleman's. Not so messy," she said with a twinkle in her eye.

"Glad to hear it," Rebecca replied, a hint of nervousness in her voice.

"Do you wish me to explain what I see, as I did for the gentleman?"

"Yes," Alex answered intrusively.

Madame Raja ignored him, casting an inquiring look at Rebecca, who nodded assent. "Very well," Madame Raja said. "But for you I can be more brief because you will remember what I have already explained." She held both of Rebecca's hands. "Now, first, the shape. Your hands are close to what we call broad or square hands. The palms are wide and nearly square, and although the fingers are a little longer than the palms, the fingertips are more flat than pointed. These hands tell me you are very practical and dutiful and productive in your work, and you do not like to be distracted from pursuing your worldly goals—although your slightly longer fingers suggest a degree of sensitivity to others." Rebecca's interest was growing.

"These prominent qualities also appear in your palms themselves." She concentrated on Rebecca's left hand. "You have a deep Fate Line that reaches the Mount of Saturn under the middle finger, showing that you have professional ambitions and a successful career—although some alterations near the top show something else. I will get to that. And because your Head Line is stronger than your Heart Line, and meets it under Jupiter and Saturn where they begin in your hand—although some palmists say the Heart Line starts on the other side—you follow your intellect more than your emotions, and you have the Saturnine qualities of caution and self-control, as well as practicality, unlike the gentleman." She threw Alex a sunny glance then faced Rebecca. "This does not mean that you do not have strong emotions, only that you usually prefer not to display and act on them. Your Heart Line is also more straight than curved, indicating order and directness rather than sentiment in matters of love—although it curves slightly in the right hand." She exchanged a glance with Rebecca. "And your Mount of Mercury is full under your little finger, telling me that you have a very verbal intellect. These things fit together. I would guess that you work with books—a teacher or librarian or editor." Rebecca raised her head in startled confirmation.

"Now," Madame Raja said, spreading Rebecca's left palm, "the Line of Life. Yours begins high on Jupiter. That is another sign of ambition. It also meets your Head Line in a way that says you are naturally prudent and cautious, as we would expect from the other signs. But your Life Line itself is quite small and thin, and comes relatively near your thumb—I see some other things in it that I will get to shortly—and your Mount of Venus is not large for a hand like yours. These signs fit with the others I have mentioned telling me you are diligent and engage mainly in mental and practical activities, and you do not wish to yield to emotions that could disrupt your life. This shows up in Apollo as well, where you are not very strong, revealing less attraction to pleasure and beauty than to productive work, again unlike the gentleman." The three of them momentarily locked eyes.

"These are good qualities," she added, looking directly at Rebecca, "because they give you the ability to accomplish what you set out to do, especially professionally. But . . . ." She paused. "They also suggest that you could be rather self-protective or passive, accepting what comes easily and feels comfortable in your life. So you might not always get the full satisfactions you expect, even from your professional success. And"—her tone was deepening, as it had with Alex—"there are specific markings that suggest you have recently had a loss or confusion and even some pain."

An apprehensive expression crossed Rebecca's face. She flashed back to Madame Raja's remark about the meaning of life being a feeling that shows up in your hands, and she didn't want to hear that 'her whole life had been wrong.' Madame Raja detected her anxiety, but also sensed a desire to learn more. She heeded the desire.

"Some of this is clear, some is not." Madame Raja now traced Rebecca's left hand with a finger as she spoke. "Back to the Fate Line. It has some crosses and islands, or boxes, near the top here, showing a period of troubles and doubts starting a while ago. Islands on the Head Line also reveal confusion, and this dot on the same line marks an upsetting or even a traumatic experience. Then the Life Line has a break here"—she fingered a place near the middle of the line. "This shows a severe illness or loss of energy not long ago." Madame Raja looked up. "I saw signs like this in the hands of many people who work in New York after

September 11th. Perhaps some of this in your hand goes back to that time too, but I think most of it is more recent. The same things appear in your right hand, although not as clearly. And there are a few indications there of possible danger ahead, as in the gentleman's hand. But they are not so pronounced, probably because you are more cautious. And I can also see what could be positive signs of change, especially around the Life Line in both hands."

"Yes?" Rebecca asked hopefully, despite her skepticism. "Where?" Alex leaned over the table with her under the light.

"Down here in the left hand, the Fate Line running alongside the Life Line near the bottom may be giving support to it. And this little line going down off the Life Line at your wrist foretells new directions, or perhaps travels. There also seems to be activity in the Life Line itself and in the Mount of Venus, especially in the right hand where they have a little more color than in the left. These signs are faint, like the curve in the Heart Line of your right hand, but they hint at changes now or soon in your life. These could be on the outside or the inside—remember, the Life Line reveals not only how we live our lives but how we feel about them. I cannot tell what these changes will be or what you should do. But I believe you will know."

She released Rebecca's hands and sat back, folding her arms and saying "That is enough." The reading was over. Rebecca reacted slowly, thrown off by the woman's ingratiating manner and remarkable observations. She had described Alex, for sure. And, yes, Rebecca, too, or some of her. But what about those signs of the future?

Alex tried to ask more questions, but Madame Raja declined to answer, inviting them instead to re-visit her, repeating her prediction that their palms would look different later and adding with a smile that she suspected their palms would then even be more alike. Accepting the invitation, they thanked her for the instructions and advice.

"I think you will not take my words very seriously. Your Head Lines are too strong." She laughed gently. "But do come back one day. Then you will see the truth of what I have told you. And more." She offered them another warm smile. And it seemed to them to be surprisingly knowing, even wise.

She ushered them back through the curtained doorway into the vestibule, where they handed her $50—much more than her posted fee, because she had given them more than a palm reading. She accepted graciously, saying she thought she had seen generosity in their hands, but hadn't said so, and now she was sure of it. Then they bid her goodbye and stepped outside. Squinting again in the glare of the sun, they started off down the Boardwalk.

"Well . . . ?" Alex said, leaving the question unfinished.

Rebecca was asking herself what she thought. The readings had hit so close. How was that possible? Just good guesses or a clever formula? Or maybe this Atlantic City soothsayer really could see people's lives in their hands. And the future? What did she mean by 'changes in your life'? The question brought echoes of: *What did it mean to her, this thing she called life?* This last question resonated eerily. Rebecca's mind was clouding. She shook her head to clear it. A fresh and pleasing idea came to her. She slowed her pace and said, "Let's go walk on the beach. Wade in the surf. Gather some sea shells."

Alex swiveled toward her. "What? You want to frolic on the sea shore?"

"Why not? It'd be refreshing to go barefoot in the sand and water."

"You think this is the kind of *change* she meant?"

"Could be worse."

"Let's do it."

They found a stairway leading down to the beach where they sat on the bottom step while Alex took off his shoes and socks and rolled up his pants, and Rebecca slipped the sandals off her bare feet. Steadying each other, they wobbled through the warm sand, passing between the low dunes and dodging sunbathers, to the ocean. There, timidly at first, they waded into the foam of the shallow surf lapping and ebbing on the shore. The water threw a chill into them. But, adapting to it, they started strolling.

"So tell me," Alex asked at last, "what do you make of Madame Raja?"

Rebecca continued kicking her feet through the sand and the foam before answering. She bent down to pick up a shell and then said quietly, "I was . . . surprised at her. She was . . . not what I had expected. Quite convincing. Especially about you."

"So you're a convert?"

"I didn't say that." Her tone was again softer than her words.

"Well, are you going to take her advice? Besides spontaneously walking barefoot on the beach?"

"To do . . . what?"

"Oh, something wildly different."

"That's your version. And she warned you to be cautious. Are you going to do that?"

"These could come down to the same thing. Your fortune and mine. Two versions of the same life. You said last night that we are much the same. And she said our palms could become more alike—I'll bet they're doing that already. It's the ultimate coincidence—the stars and the palms, cosmic forces and our private lives in harmony."

She laughed. "Superstition."

"Benign coincidences. Give it time."

They meandered along, picking up and tossing away clam shells and remnants of starfish lying among strands of seaweed, and letting the higher waves splash up their legs, wetting the roll of Alex's trousers and the hem of Rebecca's cotton skirt. After a while, Alex said, "Why don't we go get something to eat over there?" He motioned to a long pier ahead of them running out from the Boardwalk into the ocean. "We can sit on the deck and nibble fried shrimp and fathom the mysteries of palmistry and life. And we've still got winnings to spend."

She liked the setting and the prospect of lunch, having had no breakfast. They made their way back to the Boardwalk, brushed sand off their feet, and put on their footwear. Soon they were sitting at a table over the water at the end of the pier from where the beach and the Atlantic City skyline spread behind them, and the ocean with its low-breaking surf rolled before them to the horizon.

"It's oddly quiet out here," Rebecca observed. "Few sounds but the surf. You could forget where you are."

"True. We could be on a movie set depicting a peaceful seashore backed by false facades of casinos and shops and arcades along the Boardwalk. But this is better. It's real."

"You extolling reality over artifice and fantasy? That's a change."

"Not really. I like to live out my fantasies. Like this weekend with you. Dancing. Talking. Loving. And luck. And we've learned how to read our lives in our hands. It's all a beautiful romance of fantasy and reality, don't you think?"

She didn't answer. Her eyes and mind were on the rolling sea.

"And now," he said, playing over her silence and assuming a theatrically serious tone. "Let me see." He took her right hand in his, opened her fingers, and studied her palm. "Ah, yes. It is as Madame Raja said. Changes of life. Choices to make. What will they be? Hmmm. Here, I think I see it . . . in the little line going down off the Life Line at the wrist. Travel. She said that. To where? Wait. Ah, yes. I see. I see. It's . . . It's . . . to . . . India!"

"Ha!" Rebecca burst out and gently withdrew her hand. "You're a comedian. Ingenious, but comic."

"But Rebecca," he said with rising enthusiasm, "it's in your hands. And in the stars. The coincidences. We've already made forays toward India. Think about it. There was our first evening together at the Asia Society and the Indian restaurant. And now the faux Taj Mahal here where we won a bundle. And the Indian palm reader who saw our lives in our hands. We must be intended to go to India together for *real*. And you'd be following her advice, making a change in life."

"You're droll superstitions are running away with you."

"Not at all. And I'm not trying to be funny. I'm serious. The benign coincidences are falling into place. We can't let this opportunity be lost on us. We have to go—together. I wouldn't want to go without you. Not now."

Rebecca stared at him incredulously. He wasn't just playing. He *was* serious. Or it was a rendition of his serious play. She didn't say anything. Instead, she turned silently back toward the ocean. And lost herself there. The palm reader came to mind, followed by memories of the night before and of other surprisingly affecting times she had shared with him going back to . . . . A balm began washing over her. It came as if from the sea, sending her buoyantly off on its waves with a new fizz of the lightness she had felt from time to time for a while and so transportingly last night. She was floating far away, dizzied by the fizz and the undulating ocean and the warm moist salty air, and carried possibly, she conceded, just possibly, by benign coincidences. She fizzed and floated on until a high ocean swell, rare in this place, splashed against the pier, casting a fine spray over them and returning her to the present, still pleasantly light-headed. She massaged the spray into her arms.

"You cold?" he asked.

"No, no," she muttered. "Just . . . thinking."

"And where were your thoughts taking you?"

Still looking toward the ocean, she sighed, "Nowhere, really." She let time pass. Then she said softly, "Or . . ." She inhaled deeply and turned to him. And through a quizzical, wistful smile that Alex had not seen on her face before and couldn't interpret, she breathed, "possibly to . . . India?"

# 16

Had she really said it? Rebecca asked herself as Alex clapped his hands and gave a cheer. Had she actually agreed to go with him? At least intimated it? Taken the first step? How could she have let herself get drawn into this fantasy of his? The very kind of thing that had made her so uneasy with him. And yet, here she was all but saying yes.

Alex claimed victory. But he knew it could slip away. She had answered him ambiguously, hadn't she? 'Possibly to 'India?' she had said with the upward inflection of a question and a curiously quizzical smile. That gave her a ready out. She could say he had willfully misinterpreted her. To reel her in, he assured her she would have time to get used to the idea. They could plan the trip together. They'd go in late October or early November between the monsoon and the tourists. Be gone for only a couple of weeks, if that would satisfy her work ethic. She could change her mind, too. But he said she shouldn't.

On the ride back to the city, they listened to their own thoughts against the background of more show tunes and classical popular songs.

. . . Would she really go? She kept asking herself. Why? Especially during the busy fall book season when she always had so much to do. Or didn't that matter anymore? But could she break away? Yes, she deserved it. She hadn't been out of the office for more than a week at a time since . . . when? Perhaps Madame Raja was right. She should make a change. Would this be it? And would she do it just to 'go against the grain' and to bet 'against the odds'? Were these the same? To what end? Her mind was swimming.

. . . Would she do it? He wondered. Or was this merely a temporary concession of her wavering moods brought on by the romantic night and the pleasant day and the lucky gambling and the engaging palm reader? No. Surely, things had changed between them last night. But why did it matter so much to him to have her go? Was it because she would be sharing his romance? Or because she saw through it and accepted him, so that he didn't have to pretend for her? Or was it because with her he could now pretend freely and share everything, and now he needed her for that?

. . . Perhaps, she told herself, she might go with him because he didn't unnerve her as he used to, with his romancing and theatrics. She knew him better now, and trusted him more. And when he had opened himself up to her, and tenderly made love to her, and had said he loved her, she had believed him. Yes, that was part of it.

. . . It's true, he admitted to himself, he needed her more than she needed him. But why was it that this woman, who could be so restrained, and who could make him feel so childish, could also make him so happy by seeing into him and saying that they were alike in their deepest selves and could elate him by even hinting at agreeing to travel to the other side of the world with him? Was it because she was only part of his romance? Or was she *real life* for him! Yes. That's what she had become. Not a fantasy. Not a contrived romance. *Real life.* Rebecca Winters, herself, with her sharp mind and playful wit, her perceptive eye and cutting honesty, her supple voice and Renoir smile, her slowly unraveling enigmas and irresistibly melting warmth. She was *real life* for him. At its most *unimaginable.* He didn't wholly understand it. But he didn't want any life without her.

. . . Is it possible, she reflected, that this man, who in every manner and every idea had seemed so unlike her, but who, she had then discovered, beneath their differences was, paradoxically, like her, and who had helped her face down her fears and see through them? Is it possible (by some benign coincidence, he would say) that she should take the gamble (yes, he'd say that, too) of traveling halfway around the world to an exotic, chaotic country for no better reason than to do it? Is all that possible? Not likely. But then why go? There had to be better reasons. Would she go without entirely knowing why?

. . . She has to go, he told himself. How could he go without her now? Should he pressure her? No, she wouldn't like that. She should go because she wanted to, on her own. But will she really do it?

. . . What a strange sequence of events, she thought. Last year, or who knows how long ago, she had started unconsciously drying up inside and slowly descending into a vague depression. Then not quite three months ago she had collapsed in panic when she had discovered that somehow, maybe, her "whole life had been wrong." Later, she had let him enter her life. And, despite the tensions between them, things had happened that had given her new sensations and emotions. The horse races. The ferry ride. Then last night they were talking and dancing and sharing intimacies—confessional, sentimental, physical. And they had said they were in love. Today they were in Atlantic City gambling and having their palms read. Now she was thinking of doing something she could never have imagined she would do. Even two weeks ago. And she was thinking of doing it for no clear reason. What had really happened? Yes, it was all very strange.

In the weeks following their jaunt to Atlantic City, as the hot hazy days of summer became the cool clear days of autumn, Rebecca and Alex still sparred over their differences, but they understood them now. And their affinities brought them closer. They also teased each other about the palm reader's revealing readings and how they should act on them. And she agreed to go with him to India. They made travel plans, joking about the implausibility of going off to such a place together just like that, disregarding the bad timing for her, which her boss submitted to because she seemed to need it. Yes, she would go, if without completely knowing why. Except that something was urging her. And it wasn't only him.

Meanwhile, her doubts about herself and him faded, without completely vanishing. Had she honestly found a way out of her dilemma? Or was she deceiving herself once more? And if she had found a way out, what exactly was it? Was she just falling in love as never before? That old cliché. Could be. Alex was certainly in the midst of what was changing in her. But other things were going on inside, too. There was the lightness that had become an agreeably recurrent companion. Where did that come from—the horse races?? What did it mean? What did it all mean? She still couldn't say.

For him, the emotions were clearer. They were all about her. Yes, he still indulged his fantasies shamelessly, and she still chided him for his excesses. And he knew she saw through him. But he was becoming dependent on her for his very life. Or so he told himself, and her. And he loved this because it made him feel more *real*. He tried to explain this to her, but couldn't quite succeed—he couldn't even entirely explain it to himself.

And in the privacy of their nights together, their intimacy became ever more free and *beautiful*, as Alex liked to say, but no less sentimental. Theirs was not a youthful passion of the flesh flaring brightly and dying fast. They wanted it this way. They would let it grow with shared thoughts and feelings as a slowly intensifying flame. With attentiveness and tenderness, he was trying to bring her ever closer to him. With attentiveness and tenderness, and without trying, she was bringing him ever closer to her.

⁂

"I've got a new metaphor for you," he said one night while lying beside her after an hour of beautiful intimacy. "That rudderless ship sailing into uncharted seas . . . . I'm not on it anymore."

"That's a relief," she sighed facetiously.

"I'm still riding the sea with you, but no ship at all."

"Yikes! That sounds even more ominous."

"Not really. We're riding rolling waves on a rising tide. No danger any more. Only loving bliss, floating toward some Edenic place. Or could it be that you don't like the idea of riding the sea with someone who has my feeble grasp on reality?"

"That's all pretty dopey."

"I grant that, but I can't help it. Can you come up with a better metaphor?"

"I'm not much good at metaphors."

"Humor me."

She thought a moment. "Well, you could at least give us life preservers. Then we could survive if the sea gets rough. That's silly, but I told you I'm no good at this."

"Rough seas? Life preservers? There's the realist again. But I applaud the gesture. I'd just add a line between us so we couldn't drift apart, and we could save each other. You've done that for me, you know, as I've said before. Saved my life. In many ways."

She gave a slight laugh, thinking how indefatigably fanciful he was. But she asked herself: had he saved her, too?

"Who knows," he said, "the metaphor could be useful in India."

She shook her head. "I hope not."

# On a Bridge of Dreams

(Continued)

She almost jumped from her bed when the doctor and a nurse who had compassionately attended her regularly arrived with a wheel chair. He had been true to his word a couple of days after he had submitted to Rebecca's pleas and promised to get her in to see Alex. And he told her that although Alex was still unconscious there had been some slight signs of improvement since the surgery. Rebecca's heart leapt.

"You can go up to see him now," the doctor said, "but very briefly. And you must use the wheel chair."

Rebecca thanked him profusely and, with the nurse's assistance and considerable discomfort, eased into the chair. Rolling past the rows of beds, down a cluttered and crowded hallway to a creaky elevator, Rebecca thought what a scary place this was. Unintelligible voices, patients everywhere, peeling paint, and probably antiquated equipment. The bomb victims must have added to the disorder. How could anyone survive here, even if the doctors and nurses are kind and competent? She knew she was being uncharitable, but she couldn't help it. She was afraid.

As the nurse wheeled her out of the elevator, Rebecca observed that this hallway was quieter and cleaner. No patients visible. Only a few medical people methodically carrying out their duties. At least they know something about intensive care, she reassured herself. And she chastised herself for her condescension.

The nurse consulted someone at a desk and then pushed Rebecca down the hall. Near the end, they stopped at a closed door. "The doctors insist you can stay only a minute," the nurse said in a hushed voice. She opened the door and maneuvered Rebecca inside. The room was quiet except for the beeping and clicking and wheezing sounds of medical machinery. Curtains concealed two beds. The nurse slid the closest curtain aside and moved Rebecca toward the human form lying under a sheet connected to tubes, his head wrapped in bandages and facing her as she had seen Alex the last time. Rebecca strained to study the face. Was this the man she knew? The features were there. The thin outline. The high cheekbones and the strong straight nose. The dark eyebrows and long eyelashes. The finely etched mouth and smoothly contoured lower lip. It was a fine masculine face, with a touch of femininity. She hadn't been aware of the femininity before. Or not consciously. Possibly it had unconsciously attracted and comforted her. And yet now, framed in bandages as it was, this face, pale and motionless, seemed more a mask of Alex than Alex himself. If there were signs of improvement, she couldn't see them.

She slumped in the chair, and the nurse began pulling her back toward the door.

"No, no," Rebecca objected. "Not yet. Please. I'm all right. May I be with him alone, just for a few moments?"

The nurse assented, and stepped outside the curtain, sliding it closed behind her.

Rebecca wanted to get closer to him. Her torn and trussed body made it difficult, but she inched the chair near the bed and leaned forward. Raising one of her hands to her lips, she kissed the fingertips, then laid them lightly on his cheek. "Come back Alex," she whispered. "Come back." Withdrawing her hand, she thought of when, seemingly yesterday in Khajuraho, they had traced each *other's features with their fingers after they had made love. A fountain of emotions welled up in her. She didn't want to cry. She wanted to scream. To hurl vituperation into the heavens.*

*Why did we come to this chaotic, savage country anyway? she screamed in silence. It was madness. No, that's wrong, she corrected herself. It was wonderful in so many ways. But why did we have to come back here, to this place, after the first time? Just for him to get into the damn Taj Mahal so he could have some kind of romantic experience? A heartless trick of fate—or of bad luck! or of malign coincidence! She scarcely knew what she was soundlessly saying.*

*The nurse drew open the curtain. "We must go now," she said softly. Rebecca wanted to stay longer, but the nurse backed her chair away. Rebecca kept her eyes on the sleeping face, and held back burning tears.*

⁓

*"Your husband is very handsome," the nurse said as she wheeled Rebecca down the hallway.*

*"He . . . He is not my husband," Rebecca replied distractedly.*

*"But you will marry when he gets well, yes?"*

*Rebecca responded equivocally to the nurse's confidently optimistic question. But she reflected on it after returning to her bed, and the nurse had gone. They hadn't really talked about marriage. Not in so many words. It had never seemed important in itself. They had so many other things to talk about. Tensions to dissolve. Thoughts and feelings to discover and explore and share. But they had come to believe their lives were now entwined. This trip to India had sealed that belief, from its first day, until . . . .*

# 17

## *Sweet Irony*

A scattering of lights twinkled below as the plane circled for its late night arrival in Bombay. How sparse those lights appeared, the two travelers remarked, for a city of many millions. Nothing like the sea of lights in New York or Los Angeles or London or Paris. Then they remembered reading about the 'hutments"—acres of shanties packed together like boxes in and around the city, where millions of people live with scarce electricity. Alex and Rebecca braced themselves for their entry into the Third World, acknowledging their "politically incorrect" Western perceptions.

The long seventeen-hour trip from New York through Frankfurt had left them aching and tired at nearly eleven o'clock at night. But anticipation now awakened their energies as the plane landed and taxied toward the terminal. It slowed to a halt, and the passengers disembarked down a portable stairway onto the tarmac into a blast of hot humid air, half a world away from the chilly late October night Rebecca and Alex had left behind in New York.

After getting through passport control, collecting their bags, and clearing customs, they left the customs area to be confronted outside by an intimidating but ebullient mob greeting passengers from behind a tenuous rail. "RODGERS/WINTERS" read one of the hand-written placards waving above the eager faces and gesturing arms. Alex signaled to a large dark man in a white shirt holding it. The man's face broke into a wide smile.

"Please come with me," he said courteously, taking their baggage cart. Leading them through the cheerful tumult, he reached a small white car parked at the curb. He tucked the bags into the trunk, ushered them into the back seat onto a clean white cloth cover, and got into the front beside the driver.

The car inched out of the parking lot. "Your first visit to India?" the guide asked with friendly deference in the lilting Anglo-Indian accent they would hear wherever they went.

"Yes, I'm sorry to say," Alex answered, and then asked, "Are you from Bombay, or rather Mumbai."

"I am. And yes, it is Mumbai now. The nationalists have changed many city names back to those before the British. But many people still call this Bombay. It is a lively city. But there is much poverty. You will see as we drive in."

Within minutes of the airport they saw what he meant. With startled Western eyes, they stared out the window as the car careened along a bumpy road lined with what appeared to be piles of junk—broken crates, tangled wire, shards of concrete, mounds of refuse. People were idling about even at this hour, others were sleeping on the ground. Mile after mile the spectacle unfurled, until they came to a more dense urban region of substantial buildings and shuttered shops, where people still loitered as though it were mid-day. Making a turn, they swung out of the congestion onto a broad brightly lit highway arcing around a crescent beach fronted by modern, if weathered, high-rise apartment houses.

"Marine Drive," the guide said proudly. "We call it the Diamond Necklace because that is how it looks at night. Chowpatty Beach is here. On the Arabian Sea." He waved an arm out the window. "It is very popular." Only vacant darkness lay in the direction he was waving. "If you go that way," he pointed to the end of the illuminated crescent opposite from where they were heading, "you come to the Malabar Hills, where rich people live. At the other end, is Nariman Point, the modern business center of the city. Bombay Harbor is on the other side of the point. Your hotel is there."

"Pretty boulevard," Rebecca observed.

"Like Rio de Janeiro," Alex added. "Bombay's Copacabana."

They sped around the crescent and across Nariman Point to Front Bay, home of the harbor, and to the grand old Taj Mahal hotel, which they had chosen for sentimental reasons and for its rich history as an Indian-owned hotel opened in 1904, and because it was still the most elegant hotel in the city.

Once in their shuttered room, barely aware of their surroundings, Rebecca and Alex gave themselves over to an exhausted but erratic, jet-lagged sleep, their bodies craving rest that the clock would not permit. At some uncertain hour, Alex found himself wide awake. He could see almost nothing in the darkness, but, judging sleep impossible, he got up, leaving Rebecca undisturbed and groped his way to the window. Pushing open one of the heavy wooden shutters, he was pleased and a little surprised to see dawn already breaking. On the far side of the bay large shipping cranes in the harbor were silhouetted in the twilight. On the near side by the hotel an imposing structure was taking shape in the ascending light. It appeared like nothing so much as the Tower of London, turrets and all. As the light grew, he recognized this as the Gateway of India, a triumphal arch built on the waterfront to commemorate the visit of King George V in 1911, the only British monarch to set foot in India before it gained independence in 1947. An ironic vestige of the Raj, he thought, still claiming prominence in post-colonial Mumbai.

A few minutes later he heard Rebecca's sleepy voice say, "You're up early."

He turned toward her. "You awake? Come and take a look."

She crawled out of bed and joined him at the window,

rubbing her eyes. They watched the morning light bring the harbor to life all around the Gateway. Pigeons swarmed, rowboats bobbed, beggars gathered, children frolicked, hucksters staked their positions with trained dogs and monkeys and cobras in baskets, and vendors began laying out fabrics, brass, and souvenirs, all preparing for the tourists who would soon arrive to see the Gateway or to take the ferry from there to Elephanta Island, an hour away, for the gigantic cave sculptures of Hindu gods.

"Glad you came?" Alex asked, putting his arm around her shoulders.

"Ask me when I'm conscious." She yawned. "You getting ready to start your novel?"

"What novel?" He hugged her.

After returning to bed and extracting a little more restless sleep from the early morning, they had breakfast in the hotel and then boarded a ferry to Elephanta Island. There, in the mouth of a huge cave on a hillside, they stood before a massive dancing Shiva carved in stone and reminisced about their first argument over Shiva's dance, when they had barely known each other and could never have imagined themselves here together.

"It's still the perfect metaphor of the romance—or better—the marriage of art and religion," Alex said. "God dancing."

"The patron deity of aesthetes?" she joshed.

He wrapped an arm around her. How glad he was that she was here. They went on to other sculptures, lingering at the massive three-headed figure of the divine triumvirate Shiva, Vishnu, Brahma.

"It's as though we've done this before," Alex said, "and were destined to come here after that first evening at the Asia Society. Our lives do seem woven together in a pattern of benign coincidences. Repetition and all."

She raised an eyebrow and gave him an affectionate poke in the ribs.

For the next three days, they explored the city, riding with their guide through choking traffic and drenching heat to visit Hindu temples and Victorian monuments, cricket fields and open bazaars, affluent areas and squalid neighborhoods, dusty museums and the immense outdoor hand laundries that they were told keep the city's clothes cleaner than could any machine. They walked along crowded crumbling sidewalks, balked at fetid smells, inhaled floral scents, joked about the ubiquitous posters boosting the latest movie melodramas made here in "Bollywood," ate excellent Indian food (which Rebecca had now acquired a taste for), drank cocktails on their classic hotel's open verandah—an Indian word, so they were also told—overlooking the harbor and the Gateway, and watched the sun set beyond the Arabian Sea one night from Marine Drive. The city was madly eclectic and unapologetically commercial, and for all of its poverty not as alien as Rebecca had expected. Not after New York. And it felt reassuringly unthreatening.

"That is because of Hinduism," their guide explained in response to Rebecca's question as their last Bombay day ended and they were on the way to the airport for a flight to Agra. "Hindus are supposed to be peaceful and not crave material things. So we do not have much stealing and violence on the streets. But unfortunately we are having more crime and corruption than in the past. It is mostly hidden in dark places and in old practices, like the captive young prostitutes on Falkland Road. And there is political terrorism. The Muslim and Hindu fanatics both do crazy things, especially in the north because of Kashmir and disputes over sacred sites. A bus was bombed near Delhi yesterday. Twenty people were killed. You should be cautious while you travel here."

"How do we do that?" Rebecca asked nervously.

The guide shrugged.

Exchanging perplexed glances, Rebecca and Alex mumbled thanks for the advice. They stared out at the shanties flitting past, and at the prolific wreckage of vehicles indifferently strewn along the roadside. And they grasped each other's hands as trucks and buses and cars repeatedly roared toward them passing one another two and three abreast on this narrow two-lane road and speeding within inches of their car. They understood the wreckage. What is there to fear from terrorists, they agreed, compared to Indian drivers?

The two-hour flight to Agra delivered them in the wilting late afternoon heat to a smoggy humid city on the flatlands a hundred-and-twenty-five miles south of New Delhi. As they rode from the airport, their new pre-arranged guide pointed toward an area of thick haze hovering over the fields. "The Taj Mahal. But you can hardly see it today." They strained to discern the dome barely visible in the distance.

"We'll go tomorrow," Alex said.

"Tomorrow it is closed. Every Monday," the guide announced matter-of-factly.

"What?" Alex shot back. "The travel agent didn't tell us about that! Can we still go today?"

"It will close soon, but you can try."

They decided to chance it, and the car sped up, bouncing noisily along the rough road, dodging a mélange of buses, bicycles, oxcarts, and animals. In twenty minutes, it pulled around a stand of trees into a cramped street clogged with pedestrians, tour buses, touts, and curio stalls, and jerked to a stop. The guide told them they would have to walk from there to the entrance at the end of the street sixty or seventy yards away, where a high wall blocked all sight of the fabled monument.

The two visitors got out of the car with the guide and were

immediately surrounded by hucksters of all ages peddling postcards, models of the Taj Mahal, and necklaces made from colored stones. Alex and the guide did their best to push them aside and clear a path. "Not now, not now," Alex sputtered, "we're in a hurry."

They freed themselves from the first battery of peddlers only to be besieged by others while a flood of tourists streaming toward them from the Taj blocked the way. "Oh great," Alex grumbled. Led by their guide, they muscled through the crush until they could see the ticket booth in front of the high wall. A sign on it read: Hours: 600 to 1900. "That's seven o'clock," Alex said, checking his watch. It was almost 6:00 PM. "Looks like we've made it."

As they counted out rupees to purchase their tickets, a sign went up in the ticket window with words printed in several languages and boldly announcing in English: CLOSED.

"But it's not time yet," Alex protested.

Their guide took them to the window around a string of other disappointed ticket buyers. "Why do you close now?" he asked the ticket agent."

"To prepare for state visit."

"What? When?" Alex reacted.

"Top government officials from several countries coming from New Delhi for meetings and ceremonies this week. Open again Thursday." He closed a shutter. The guide resignedly hunched his shoulders. "That's Indian bureaucracy for you."

"How could they do this to us?" Alex spat out. "We leave Tuesday."

"Calm down." Rebecca put a hand on his arm. "Why don't we go someplace where can see it from a distance. Maybe we can get a drink and watch the sunset."

He scuffed a foot in the dust and swore. Then he muttered, "We'll have to see if we can stop on the way back from Khajuraho at the end of the week. But," his voice lifted, "you do have a nice idea." He kissed the hand she held on his arm. "You're wonderful. Let's find that view with the sunset and a drink."

They put their request to the guide, who said he knew just the place. After re-threading through the tourists and touts, they were back in the car creeping down the thronged street, then bouncing along another dusty road. Before long the car abruptly swerved down a gravel driveway and stopped in front of a sign reading "Vista Hotel." There wasn't much of a hotel—a modest two-story building with peeling white paint.

"You wait," the guide said, and darted inside. He emerged shortly with a well-dressed older man and beckoned them out of the car. Introduced as the proprietor, the older man invited them through an arched doorway to a path up a grassy hill behind the hotel. At the top, several wire tables and chairs were sprinkled around, and clusters of people sat with drinks.

"This is the closest place to see the Taj from outside," the proprietor boasted. "Every other place is much farther away, and no new construction is permitted closer than one mile."

They responded admiringly and chose a table.

Less than half a mile to the west, against the hazy orange sky, rose the domes and minarets of the Taj Mahal, seen here from the eastern side, unlike the familiar frontal view from the south.

"Well done, Rebecca Winters," Alex congratulated her. "A brilliant idea. And now, although I know you don't much like beer, shouldn't we order a couple of bottles of Taj Mahal? It'd be symbolic, and sentimental—celebrating our being here and honoring our first evening together at the Indian restaurant in New York and our luck at the faux Taj Mahal in Atlantic City. All in the pattern of benign coincidences."

"Aren't you over-doing this theme?" she said with a laugh. "But I guess this is the place for it." She conceded silently that something like that could be true. And she consented to the beer for symbolic reasons.

When the drinks arrived, they toasted symbolism and sentimentality. And they sat back to contemplate the view.

"You know," Alex said pensively, "there is a melancholy to it, the Taj Mahal."

"Melancholy?"

"Uh-huh. Shah Jehan built it for his favorite wife, Mumtaz, after she died giving birth to their fourteenth child, I think it was. Then they say he had the hands of his best craftsmen cut off so they could never build anything so beautiful again. Later, one of his kids overthrew him and locked him up for the rest of his life in his palace up the river. Finally he was buried in the Taj beside her. That's all quite melancholy."

"That's hardly in the spirit of the moment. And it doesn't sound like you. I thought you liked to be a sentimental romantic not a melancholy cynic."

"Scratch a romantic and you'll find a cynic, scratch a cynic and you'll find a romantic. See, you've found out another of my dark secrets."

"I prefer the romantic. And I'll stick with the beauty and sentiment of the Taj."

"Aha! Beneath your realistic exterior you're a true romantic. I'll drink to that." He raised his glass toward her and downed a hearty swallow. She sipped her beer and turned back to the view.

They watched the sun lower behind the tomb, silhouetting its elegant Persian domes and accentuating the ornamental minarets that seemed awaiting a muezzin's sonorous summons of Islamic faithful to evening prayer—then they faintly heard that call and remembered reading of a small mosque beside the Taj Mahal constructed for visiting and local Muslims. A flock of blackbirds flew across the sky and alighted on branches not far away, their dark angular figures in striking contrast to the graceful curves of the domes behind. As the sun sank, Alex remarked how the Moon Illusion had never displayed itself to better effect than here. A huge golden orb silhouetting the Taj Mahal. As the sun slowly disappeared, it sent colors skyward, followed by the evening's gray gradually descending like a curtain.

They waited until the light in the sky had dimmed, thanked the proprietor with a wad of rupees for his hospitality, and returned to the car for the drive to their hotel.

"To tell you the truth," Rebecca said as they lurched onto the bumpy highway, "I'm not sorry we didn't get in. What we saw was so . . . peaceful and enchanting, almost magical, like you said of New York on the ferry as the city lights came up. The conventional picture postcard view of the Taj Mahal that everyone has seen is lovely but more commonplace. Are you sure we should take the trouble to come back and go in with crowds?"

"You *are* a romantic."

"I just don't need the commonplace view. This was memorable enough. That's all. But if you want to change the schedule, go ahead."

"I think we should. Otherwise the trip would be frustratingly incomplete. Tomorrow we'll go up to the Red Fort where Shah Jehan was imprisoned and see the Taj from there like he did. Maybe that'll change your mind about it."

"I don't want to change my mind."

"You want to leave your romantic illusions intact?"

"You should approve."

"I'm dumbfounded." He laughed.

After arriving at the hotel, Alex set in motion the change of plans to stop briefly in Agra again on their way back from Varanasi and Khajuraho to Jaipur, Udaipur, and Aurangabad—to see the miniature Taj Mahal built there by Shah Jehan's grandson and the spectacular Buddhist cave art at nearby Ajanta and Ellora—then on to Bombay for the flight home. They showered, put on fresh clothes, and had dinner beside the azure blue light of the hotel swimming pool at a candle-lit table while a sitar player sitting cross-legged on a silk carpet sent the ragas of India into the sultry night. They ate and talked their way through the buffet of Indian breads and chaats and curries and byrianies and tandoories and vindaloos. They drank a little more symbolic, sentimental beer, and occasionally they caught a look in each other's eyes that awakened warm memories and made them feel alone together in an enchanted world, and this was what they wanted to feel.

From the palatial Red Fort on a plateau five miles behind the Taj Mahal across a low, wet plain where the Yamuna river winds its way down past the Taj to meet the Ganges at Allahabad, the tomb seemed to hover over the river, quivering in the heat and haze. Standing in a high terrace alcove of the Fort, Rebecca and Alex took in the scene. They were told that Shah Jehan had spent many hours here during his seven-year imprisonment mournfully observing the translucent white marble of his beloved wife's distant mausoleum as it changed hues in the light of the sun and moon passing overhead. They could almost picture him where they were, shedding sorrowful tears at the sight.

"When you see the Taj from here," Alex said, "it's not only melancholy. It's ironic."

"Here we go again." She rolled her eyes.

"Well, listen. First Shah Jehan and Mumtaz have all these children. And Mumtaz dies having one too many. So Shah Jehan builds the most beautiful monument in the world to memorialize her—practically bankrupting the kingdom and cutting off the artisans' hands when it's finished. Then his son Aurangzeb seizes the throne and locks him up here where he can only sit and brood longingly over Mumtaz and the Taj lying far away. Later, one of Aurangzeb's own sons builds a small version of the Taj for his mother in Aurangabad when his lousy dad, who named that city for himself, refuses to do it. Besides all that, Aurangzeb becomes a religious fanatic, breaking with the Mughal tradition of tolerance, and starts razing Hindu temples and fomenting the religious hatreds that persist today, and he winds up sending the great Mughal Empire itself into decline because he was such a wacko. The Taj Mahal symbolizes not only what Shah Jehan loved but what he lost. And he lost everything. That's the irony of it."

"I don't buy that," she replied. "Your history's too pat and cynical, and probably wrong—I don't believe that about the hands. Besides, Shah Jehan didn't lose everything. The Taj Mahal survives as a monument to love and beauty for the whole world. That's what it will always be. You should like that."

"Whaaat? Rebecca Winters, the cold-eyed-realist-who-insists we see-things-as-they-are-not-as-we-want-them-to-be is now not only a romantic but an idealist?"

"Don't get carried away. I just don't accept your cynical irony. You may be kidding, but that kind of irony can erode belief in anything while presuming to be so wise. And it doesn't become you, Alex." Her words spilled more feeling than she had intended.

"I suppose I should take that as a back-handed compliment. But, in fact, I have a rather ironic view of life, you know, especially of myself—the clash of appearances and reality and all that."

"Is that how you see me and us? The irony of it all? You the romantic, me the realist, or the other way around, or whatever it is that you really think—it's hard to know sometimes? So that you can knowingly smirk at the irony and not take it seriously? Or is this one of the pretenses that masks who you are, or maybe a persona that you don as part of who you are? Anyway, I don't much care for it." Her voice trailed off.

He brought his eyes to hers. "Where did that come from?" He paused. "I'm sorry if I . . . over-stepped. But surely you know me well enough to know that I love you honestly, with no pretense or irony. Don't you?"

She didn't truly doubt his feelings. But his excursion into cynical irony unexpectedly grated on her. This was not one of his airy flights into fantasy. She had grown used to those, and understood them, and could play along with them. But she didn't want to think this was a dark, cynical attitude underlying them. She would rather think it was another of his innocent games. Still, this was one she wouldn't play along with because she feared it wouldn't lead to anything good. Unless, it now came to her, she could beat him at it and lead his dark irony into the light.

"Yes," she said softly. "I know." She slid an arm through his and turned with him toward the far away tomb. "One thing I will concede on irony," she said affectionately as they gazed out over the winding river through the hazy sunlight. "Here we are, in this of all places, arguing about love and the Taj Mahal. That *is* ironic—but not cynical. Let's make it sweet." She kissed his cheek.

He was taken off guard. And loved it. She made him feel so alive. Her agile mind. Her strong character. Her goodness. Her warmth. Yes, he thought again, how glad he was that she was here with him. And he admitted to himself that she was right in every way about irony.

Leaving the terrace, they retraced their steps through the chambers of the Red Fort to the car where their guide was waiting. With time on their hands, and at their guide's urging, they decided to visit the shops outside the city where craftsmen—some of them said to be descendants of those who built the Taj Mahal—make artful objects from the same translucent white marble and semiprecious stones that give the mausoleum its luminescent and colorful splendor.

After fending off the merchants' pressures to purchase carloads of marble artifacts, Rebecca finally bought some inlayed marble coasters for herself and as gifts. As the merchant began wrapping them, he paused to show her a small white marble elephant adorned with similar inlays. He pointed out that white elephants are sacred in South Asia, and because of this the Kings of Thailand used to reward loyal noblemen with the gift of a white elephant along with sufficient land to feed and display it; and they would punish disloyal noblemen with the same gift but no land. Unable to support or dispose of the sacred creature, the punished noblemen would be ruined. "White elephants can be a blessing or a curse in that way," the merchant concluded with a smile. "But this one is sure to be a blessing, bringing you wisdom and good fortune, as blessed elephants do."

Charmed by the tale, and by the little white elephant, Rebecca added it to her purchases.

"You're buying a good luck charm?" Alex said incredulously. "You keep surprising me. But you could regret buying it. You can never get rid of it."

"I'm not worried. I think he's cute. He's not just a burdensome 'White Elephant.' He can bring wisdom and good fortune. And I'm not buying it for me. It's for you."

"Me? Why?"

"For wisdom and good fortune, of course."

"I need that, eh?"

"Don't we all?"

The next morning, while they packed for the mid-day flight to Varanasi, Alex read aloud from a guide book. "*The sacred City of Shiva, Varanasi is among the oldest cities in the world, inhabited since the days of Babylon. And it is one of the holiest sites in India. Here all Hindus should come at least once in their lives to pray and bathe in the Ganges to insure good karma and to open the door to nirvana.* No cynical irony there," he said self-mockingly.

"You can find it anywhere, if you try," she replied casually, closing her suitcase. "It's just a way of looking at things." She shot him a knowing glance.

He shook his head and smiled. She's stealing my lines, he said to himself. And she's using them against me. Sweet irony.

# 18

## *City of Rebirth*

The bicycle rickshaw, or trishaw, dodged and wove through the crush of traffic—cars, pedestrians, cows, chickens, goats, dogs, and other trishaws—moving along Varanasi's jumbled streets in the early dawn. The age-old city, long-known as Benares, was coming to life at first light before nighttime's cooling reprieve began dissipating and the morning heat closed in. Merchants laid out their fruits, vegetables, fabrics, brass wares, and curios on the dusty roadside. Votaries preparing their morning prayers shuffled toward the hundreds of Hindu temples tucked into the ancient tangled urban maze. And Hindu pilgrims headed for the Ghats, the stepped landings leading down to the Ganges where they go to pray in the holy waters at least once in every lifetime.

After arriving the previous day, Rebecca and Alex had visited a few temples and other historical sites around the city. Now, at dawn, the best time to do it, they were headed for Varanasi's sacred heart—the Ganges riverfront. They lurched back and forth on the narrow seat behind their wiry driver, who rose up and down with the peddles, sometimes heaving his whole weight on one peddle with both of his leathery bare feet to pull the trishaw over humps or through patches of mud. Finally, pressing his heels against the brakes with all of his force, he brought the vehicle to a skittering halt on a walkway sloping down to the central Ghat. The passengers climbed out, handed the driver some rupees, and started toward the river with their local guide, who had ridden another trishaw. A bony cow roamed lethargically past in front of them, munching blades of grass plucked from fugitive shoots in broken pavement and cracked walls. Blanketed forms of sleepers lay along the walk. And holy men dusted with ashes sat still in yoga positions unseeingly facing passersby.

As Rebecca and Alex reached the top of the Ghat, they saw the Ganges flowing past, thirty or so broad steps below them, still swollen from the monsoon and measuring possibly a hundred yards across. The guide explained that during the summer monsoon the Ganges expands almost as far as the eye can see over the flat plain on the far side, then shrinks to a river only a few rowboat-lengths wide before the next monsoon. Pilgrims knelt in solemn prayer on the Ghat, or stood waist-deep in the river, ritualistically bathing themselves, as worshippers have done here for thousands of years. Near the pious pilgrims, others seemed to be lounging on the Ghat and in the water, while vendors hawked vials of the holy river, children splashed and swam, women scrubbed clothes, and boats rowed past carrying tourists awaiting the sunrise or merchants waving handicrafts to sell from their floating shops.

"Who's worshiping and who's not?" Rebecca wondered aloud.

"To them there's probably not much difference," Alex speculated. "It could all be worship of some kind."

Following their guide down the steps, they found an available rowboat, and their boatman pushed out into the dark, turbid water. The sounds from the shore waned until all that could be heard was the squeaking of the oars rubbing against the oarlocks, the low rhythmic splash of the oars dipping in the water, and the soft slapping of ripples against the boat's wooden hull. Across the river from the Ghats, the crest of the sun began rising above the horizon and radiating through the thick mist, casting a filtered beam that shimmered in a broken line on the water more like moonlight than sunshine.

Amidst this peaceful dawn on the Ganges, Rebecca suddenly gasped and clapped a hand to her mouth, her features frozen in wide-eyed shock.

"What is it?" Alex reacted with alarm.

She was staring at the water on one side of the boat. Breaking the surface just beyond a dipping oar floated the motionless features of a human face. The eyes were closed. An arm's length above the face the fingers of two hands poked through the water, and a body's length below the toes of two feet did the same.

"Is that . . . ? Is it . . . ?" she stuttered.

"Just a holy man," said the guide nonchalantly. "In a trance. They can do that for hours, with almost no breathing."

"My god," she exhaled heavily. "I thought it was a corpse. It's hard to believe he can do that."

"Such willpower could be useful," Alex remarked.

They watched the seemingly lifeless figure recede as their boat drifted on. The calm returned. They oared on past one Ghat after another, some jammed with people, others nearly deserted. Above and alongside the Ghats, a skyline of ornate weather-beaten structures alternated with the conic domes of Hindu temples whose finials spiked into the brightening sky.

"Over there is a crematorium." The guide indicated a gray area on the shore. "They bring bodies here to be purified in the Ganges and then cremate the bodies. If you look closely you can see some of them wrapped and lying on the side waiting to be put into the water. And bundles of wood for burning. After cremation the ashes are scattered on the ground and in the river. That makes the ground white, as you see."

Rebecca and Alex peered into the hazy, rising light to see the shrouded forms lying near the crematorium, ashes all around, and mountains of sticks piled against a wall where a stubby smokestack sent thin white curls into the dawn air.

"Quite an industry," Alex observed.

"A creepy one," Rebecca muttered.

The boat cruised out into the middle of the river and turned around for the trip back. From there the full length of the shore-line unfolded before them.

"It's Breughelesque," Rebecca said meditatively. "Everything thrown together. Sacred and profane, human and divine, flesh and spirit, life and death."

"How philosophical you are," Alex commented. "By the way, what do you think of reincarnation, the transmigration of souls? We've never talked about it. I really should know."

"Why?"

"Because we're surrounded by devotion to it. And because reincarnation is not a bad idea. It could be one of those patterns of repetition in human life. And it lets you live life over and over and over until you get it right."

"*Get it right*? But when Hindus 'get it right' they leave life altogether. They enter nirvana and that's the end of it."

"I'd rather think of it as getting another chance. Reincarnation is one of those rich religious metaphors. It's a metaphor of rebirth, rejuvenation, renewal, whether you believe in another life or not. It could even be the *metaphor of metaphors*, since metaphors are things changed into other things, or they make one thing play the role of another. And they can change us, too. That's a kind of reincarnation, a change of our lives from one thing to another."

Rebecca was hardly listening to him going off on another of his imaginative tangents. Her eyes were panning the shore where the Ghats were now teeming with people in a quiet bedlam of prayers, ablutions, cleansing, swimming, and who knows what else. Rejuvenation? Renewal? Rebirth? But that's not really what they want, she thought. They want the cycle of rebirth to end. To *get it right, and get out, for good.* Find extinction in Nirvana. But what would that mean, to get it right—for her? The question gave her a start. She still couldn't answer it. But it didn't frighten her as such questions had done months earlier. It even roused an unthreatening curiosity. And looking at the countless figures on the shore and in the water trying to *get it right* so they could *get out*, like millions of others had done over the centuries, she began to feel small and insignificant. That's what Hinduism is about isn't it? she asked herself. And Varanasi, too? To make earthly life and its trials seem insignificant? With those questions in mind she marveled at the Brueghelesque scene. And felt pleasantly insignificant.

The sun was now mercilessly pouring heat through the haze, and humidity was raising sweat on their brows and making clothes cling to their backs. The boatman dug the oars more deeply and rapidly into the water, causing the shoreline circus to pass by in a cinematic montage. Finally, he navigated through the mass of bathers, swimmers, and worshippers to the base of the Ghat where they had started. He threw a line to a comrade who wrapped it around a post. The passengers jumped out of the rocking boat, paid the boatman, and hiked back up the steps. When they reached the top of the ghat, they stood and passed their eyes once more over the panorama of life and death on the Ganges. Reflecting on the scene and absorbing that pleasant sense of insignificance, it came to Rebecca that maybe rebirth is not a bad idea.

Captured by the moment, she said, "How about going off on our own for a while? Explore the old city by ourselves. Learn it's secrets."

Taken aback, Alex looked at her and replied, "You mean without the guide?"

"Yes," she answered. "I don't think we could get very lost. And if we do lose our way a little that could be a spiritual experience. Only the lost can be found."

"That's goofy. Sounds like something I might say."

"It is."

"Well, I love your daring. India's getting to you."

"Many things are probably 'getting to me,'" she said to herself.

After paying the guide and pressuring him to point the way and leave them, they struck off down one of the narrow shadowy lanes branching into the maze of the oldest part of this ancient city. As they slowly ventured deeper into the maze, much of it covered overhead, they felt that they had again left the known world behind.

The scent of incense thickened the damp air, mixing with the odor of dung from the cows that roamed as casually in the dark, narrow alleys here as they did on major thoroughfares outside. Beggars crumpled in the shadows feebly stretched out crippled limbs for coins. Peddlers proffering bottles of Ganges water announced promises of purification and good health. Merchants in tenebrous shops held out silks and brass objects to lure customers. Children sitting on the primeval path played timeless games with sticks and stones. Armed soldiers stood guard at the barbed-wired gate to a hemmed-in mosque defiantly erected long ago on the ruins of a Hindu temple and now protected by government decree from Hindu fanatics threatening to rectify the historical injustice. And practically every other doorway opened into a tiny shrine bedecked with images of Hindu gods— Shiva, the patron deity of this city, usually at the center with smoldering reeds of incense at his feet. Through all of this, in the penumbra of overhanging eaves and impinging walls, Rebecca and Alex moved on, squeezing their way past the oncoming traffic of cattle, carts, children, beggars, worshippers, tourists, and residents whose families have called this warren home forever.

Making a turn into an alley that seemed to end in an open marketplace possibly some forty yards away, Rebecca grabbed Alex's arm and pointed. "Look!" Ahead of them a sign leaned against the wall:

## MADAME RAJA
### Readings

Their eyes locked together.

"Well!" Alex exclaimed. "You can't say that's a *mere* coincidence."

"Could be a franchise," Rebecca joked. "But we have to go in."

"*You* pressing *me* to go to a palmist?! What next?"

"Who knows?" she answered. "Maybe we'll find out."

She led him to a low doorway strung with twined strands of colorful silk thread. The stone path in front had been swept clean of the dirt and detritus littering the rest of the alley. They pulled the strands aside and peeked into a small, tidy, room. In one corner sat a diminutive, wizened female figure wrapped in a gold sari wearing glasses and holding an open book in a shaft of light falling through a small window above onto a table in front of her.

"Oh, come in, come in," she said, beckoning them toward her. She took off her glasses, marked a page in the book and closed it.

They bent down and stepped inside where Alex's head almost touched the ceiling. Their eyes, already accustomed to the shadows in the alleys, could see that the room was almost bare. The table, covered with a gilded red cloth, held a lightless lamp. Two plain wooden chairs were lined against the opposite wall. Foot-high brass vessels adorned three of the corners, and a short statue of Shiva stood on a pedestal beside a closed door. The musty smell of mildew mingled with incense, but the room was kempt and cooler than the alley outside.

"Please." The woman motioned toward the chairs. Sitting down, the visitors received a youthfully bright smile from the woman's aged coppery face. A comely face, they both thought, and her smile filled the room.

"You have come from far away." She spoke in confident English with just a trace of Anglo-Indian lilt and in a tone that could have been either a statement of fact or a question. Her voice sounded younger than her apparent years

Alex waited for Rebecca to answer. This adventure was, after all, he happily said to himself, her idea.

"Yes," Rebecca said and went on rather shyly. "We are from America, uh, New York. And . . . well . . . it happens that a while ago we visited a palm reader near there whose name was, uh, the same as yours. So when we saw your sign we were . . . surprised and curious."

The woman laughed softly. "Oh, there are many of us. With so many lives to live, we must sometimes share the same name." Her eyes glimmered in a ray of sunlight. Déjà vu swept over both Rebecca and Alex. "Now you wish for me to read your hands to see if she was right?"

"Well . . ." Rebecca responded, glancing at Alex, "I guess so."

"And you want to be together for the reading?"

"Yes," Rebecca said unhesitatingly.

"That is a good sign," Madame Raja responded genially. "You have nothing to hide from each other, even though I gather you are not married."

Rebecca smiled with an increasingly woozy sensation of re-living the past.

Madame Raja invited them to bring their chairs closer to the table. She switched on the lamp, put on her glasses, and reached for Rebecca's already outstretched hands. Drawing the left one into the lamplight and splaying it open, she ran her fingertips back and forth over the surface, studying every line and shape. Then she shifted to the other hand and studied it even more intently.

"Very nice hands. And interesting," she said, raising her eyes as if reading Rebecca's face along with her hands. Which she was. Returning to Rebecca's left hand, she described many of the same traits that her namesake in Atlantic City had seen—intelligence, ambition, success, discipline, practicality, caution, self-control, emotional wariness, and so forth. After completing this portrait, she looked up again. "I think you were told these things before, yes?" Rebecca nodded. Taking both hands, Madame Raja laid them flat to accentuate the lines. "But there are other things in these hands," she resumed soberly. "Much that is not easy to read. And these things may be the most important."

"Yes?" Rebecca prodded.

"First, I can see you have been through some troubles. Not too long ago. Possibly illness, but probably more emotional than physical. Upsets, conflicts, doubts. They seem to be in the past, but perhaps you have not put them all behind you." She examined Rebecca's face again. It confirmed the message of her hands.

"And where do you see that, if I might ask?" Rebecca inquired. Alex raised his eyebrows.

"A curious lady, indeed." Madame Raja smiled again, bringing Rebecca another flood of déjà vu. "But why should you not be?" She continued as if pleased to have been asked. "Here is one place," she said, tracing the line running up the center of Rebecca's palm. "It is the Line of Saturn. Same call it the Line of Fate. There are breaks and marks on it that show turmoil and change. This might be in your profession, but I would say it is not only that. Also, these dots on the Line of the Head." She touched the line running across the middle of Rebecca's palm. "They show emotional upsets. But the most significant signs are here." She fingered the line around the mound beneath Rebecca's thumb. "The Line of Life—perhaps you know this. In your left hand, it is rather thin, suggesting a certain thinness of life or of your feelings about it. And it has marks and a break on it, telling of troubles or difficult times not so long ago. It is not clear how much these difficulties are still present. But I think the line could be changing. Parts of it might be deepening and moving outward. Your Line of the Heart is brighter, too. It will take time to tell. Your right hand is more active with many signs. Some easy to read, some not."

Rebecca leaned closer, and Alex came with her. "Can you show me?" she urged.

"Such curiosity. Here," Madame Raja pointed, "this break in the Line of Life appears to be growing together. And the Line has more color and could be getting stronger after the break than before it. Smaller lines also seem to be branching out beside it on Venus—the mount beneath your thumb—which would help to strengthen it. And, as in your left hand, your Line of Life might even be deepening and moving outward. These are very good signs. But, since you seem to want to know everything, I must also tell you there are some markings of possible troubles to come. These signs appear mainly on the Line of Life and the Line of the Heart here and here—she pointed to a few new irregularities in the lines."

"What kind of troubles?" Rebecca broke in.

"They could be events, emotions, decisions or all of these. They might continue some of the troubles you had before, I cannot say. But you should be aware of them to help you be strong, as everyone should do, and to follow the good signs to change the bad, as everyone can, to fend off troubles, or at least overcome them." She gave Rebecca a beneficent look.

A bit concerned by the negative signs, Rebecca repeated a question Alex had asked in Atlantic City. "So, we can make all of the lines change?"

"Oh, yes," Madame Raja affirmed. "If not completely. For when our lives change, our hands change. That is how we make our karma. You know about karma?"

"Some," Rebecca answered.

"But you do not believe in it?" She looked at them both.

"We're not Hindu or Buddhist," Rebecca answered.

"You do not have to be. Karma is our life. Our life is our karma. For everyone. If our karma is good, our life is good. But we do not always know what our karma is. This is one reason to read the hands." She pressed her fingers tenderly against

Rebecca's palms. "Your hands seem to be changing. If they are, your karma will, too. It will likely be for the good. But that is for you to decide. As you live. Some people do not believe we can change our karma during our lives this way, but I do. Someday you might be able to see this change in your hands yourself." The two women's eyes met and held in silence. Then Madame Raja released Rebecca's hands saying, warmly, "Yes, you will know."

With that woozy déjà vu in her head, Rebecca withdrew her hands and placed them self-consciously in her lap rubbing the palms together. She was tempted to examine them herself. Would she be able to see anything in them? Would she see the good and the bad? Could she change them? Would she see if she were *getting it right*?

Madame Raja turned to Alex. He came closer and stretched out his left hand, provoked by what he had heard her tell Rebecca. She took the fingertips and leaned over, studying his palm. She did the same with his right hand. Then she described what she saw, and at his urging, identified where she saw it—the signs revealing that he worked with his intellect, that he was independent and emotional and reckless and a dreamer, that he enjoyed beauty and much in life, but that he had not followed a regular career, and that he had doubts about himself and his life, along with other details that the first Madame Raja had also seen. She added, "Like the lady, you may have changing karma. The curving Line of the Heart suggests that you are growing closer to people. Maybe you are learning to love. This is good karma." She glimpsed Rebecca. "But," she paused, "also like the lady, there could be some troubles ahead." She touched what she said were crosses and dots on the Line of the Head and the Line of Life, and reported their possible meanings. "You should not take risks during this time. Wait until the marks go away. And try to make your karma good. Then they *will* go away and good will things come to you and to those close to you."

"So if two people are close to each other, in their hearts and in their lives," he asked, "do they share the same karma?"

She sensed an expectation in his question. "Oh, no. We might share part of our karma, but not all of it. We each have our own, from the many lives we have lived. But not even the palms can reveal it all. The palms can tell us many things, but they cannot tell us everything that we would like to know about ourselves and our lives, or about what we should do. These things remain a mystery until we have lived. And this is good, I think, don't you? Otherwise there would be no reason to live. Even one life." She smiled broadly and released Alex's hands.

The reading was over. They sat in silence for a moment. Then Rebecca asked Madame Raja, "Would you . . . tell us something about yourself? How you came to be here and . . . to read palms?"

Madame Raja sat back in her chair and smiled. "You want to know *my* life? An unusual request. But you are very inquisitive and sensitive, and perhaps this is what you came to learn from me, more than what is in your hands. I should have seen this, shouldn't I?" Her eyes sparkled.

"I had not thought of asking before," Rebecca replied. "But now I would like to know. If you don't mind."

Madame Raja folded her arms and reflected. "I will tell you what I think you would most want to know."

"Thank you," Rebecca said. She and Alex leaned forward to hear.

"I am very old now, as anyone can see," Madame Raja began. "When I was young, my father was an official with the British in New Delhi. I had two brothers, and we had a good life. But my mother hated the British. She was a proud woman from a high caste family, and she resented British rule. Nevertheless, both she and my father wanted us children to learn English and be well-educated so we would have a better future. Someday the British will be gone, they would say, and then the educated will rule, and knowing English will help. So we attended schools for the children of Indian government officials. Later my brothers became soldiers. And . . . both of them were killed in the war, fighting the Japanese. My mother hated the British for that, too, although my brothers had fought willingly and honorably. I married a man I met during the war. He was a Muslim. I am Hindu. My parents did not object. But his parents did. We married against their wishes. Then in the bloodshed after independence during the partition of India and Pakistan in 1947, my husband was killed. He was a lawyer and one of those trying to maintain order. My father also died, and we lost our home in fires set by rioters. No one knew if Hindus or Muslims were responsible. It was a terrible time. My husband's family moved to Pakistan. I did not marry again." She paused as though pondering the past. "Ah, such a long time ago," she sighed. "A lifetime."

A little embarrassed that she had caused Madame Raja to revisit bad times, Rebecca said a little awkwardly, "I'm sorry. I didn't mean to . . . ." Then collecting herself, she asked, "Do you have children?"

Madame Raja's eyes brightened. "Oh, yes," she said glowingly. "A beautiful daughter. Pavi. A gift to my life. I think of her every day. She died when she was ten years old. Of polio. Thank you for asking about her."

Rebecca's throat tightened. She shouldn't have asked. Now, she wondered somewhat guiltily, how could this woman, who had lost so much, who had so little, not resent her life for its tragedies and losses, and instead be so serene, and even be grateful to speak of her beloved daughter who, in the bitterest of losses, had been taken from her as a child? Tears began welling in Rebecca's eyes. She drooped her head and dabbed them.

"I'm sorry," she said again in a murmur.

"Do not be sorry for such a feeling," Madame Raja replied solicitously. "It is a good feeling. Be sorry only when you cannot feel it." Rebecca couldn't help herself. Tears ran down her cheeks. She pulled a tissue from her bag and muffled the sounds of crying. Alex could only guess at the causes. He reached an arm around her shoulders.

"Forgive me," Rebecca said, sniffling. "It's just that you . . . seem . . . well . . . ."

"Perhaps you do not understand," Madame Raja interrupted. "Of course I am sad to have lost many loved ones. But I am more grateful and happy to have had them. And Pavi most of all. She was so important to me. To speak of her makes me very happy and grateful. Does feeling grateful in this way not make us happy?"

Rebecca wiped her eyes and repeated the question to herself, without answering it.

The question brought to Alex's mind the woman who had told him, "I am always sad." Perhaps gratitude can lessen sadness, he said to himself.

Seeing the two visitors shuffling their thoughts, Madame Raja proceeded. "I will explain it this way. A teacher of mine, who wore his Hinduism lightly, once told me that we cannot be truly happy unless we feel gratitude, because gratitude helps us see the things in life that mean the most to us—especially, perhaps, if we have lost much. He also said that gratitude makes us compassionate and kind and generous because it reminds us what we owe to the compassion and kindness and generosity of others. Time has proved to me that this is true. And is this not where our good karma—or, I could say, our humanity—comes from? You see, these are all one. Hinduism teaches this, but we Hindus do not always live up to it." She changed her expression. "Oh my. Here I am, an old woman, presuming to be a guru."

Her face still glowed. From an inner light, Rebecca thought. And her words took Rebecca back to the night last summer when she had told Alex the sentimental and *beautiful* reminiscence of herself as a child ending with the words, "But I never thanked them." She held back tears.

"And now to the end of my story," Madame Raja began again. "If you wish to hear."

"Please," Rebecca said, collecting herself.

"After Pavi died, and then later my mother, with whom I was living, I came here to work as a translator and to study philosophy at the university here. Benares, or Varanasi, is a historic center of Hindu learning, as you may know. In time, I taught there myself. Now I am too old for the university. But I continue to teach what I can, through the hands, and the stars. And sometimes a little philosophy." She chuckled. "It is all the same." She beamed her enfolding smile.

Rebecca and Alex did not speak. Both had an intimation that they had somehow been led here—through a curious pattern of coincidences.

"This is possibly what you came to learn," Madame Raja said with that ambiguous inflection coupling a statement and a question.

"It is not . . ." Rebecca answered haltingly, "what we would have expected."

"We seldom get what we expect," Madame Raja replied with an amused and knowing glint in her eye. "Only in the end what we deserve. That is our karma." She sat up in her chair. "But I have been talking too much. And now, I must rest and then go to the temple."

"Thank you for . . ." Rebecca stammered, "for everything."

"Oh, not everything. That is *too much* gratitude." Madame Raja responded with a gentle laugh. "And I am grateful to you for coming here from so far away, and for letting me share my memories. For an old woman like me, this is a gift."

"We will not forget you," Alex said in a voice softer than usual.

"That is the best kind of fortune telling." Madame Raja's smile and eyes were bright. "Because you can make it come true for yourselves just by trying."

They nodded at her and stood up. Rebecca laid a pile of rupees on the brass tray.

"No, no," Madame Raja objected. "Too much again." She pushed half of the rupees away. "You have given me enough. Others need them more. Give them to the poor."

Rebecca reluctantly gathered them, and, after reiterating their gratitude and pronouncing their warm farewells, the couple passed through the doorway into the alley. Somewhat disoriented, they moved off dreamily in silence toward the light of the marketplace. At its entrance a beggar held out a withered hand. Rebecca gave him the rupees. Through the profusion of activity typical of Indian marketplaces, they could see at the far side a few tables and chairs arrayed in front of a shabby café.

"Let's go get a drink or something," Rebecca suggested.

Alex eagerly agreed, and after weaving through the merchants and shoppers and animals they chose a table and ordered Pepsi Colas, which came in bottles labeled in some Indian script and were said to be reliably safe to drink for Western visitors.

"Well," Alex said as they sampled their beverages after cautiously wiping off the lips of the bottles, "you have to believe in the law of coincidences now. The repetitions and symmetry of it all. Two Madame Rajas! Similarly intelligent and kind—they could be sisters. And virtually the same palm readings. Except that this one saw more change in your hands. Is she right?"

"I don't know," Rebecca said meditatively. "But what an extraordinary person."

"She seemed to have quite an effect on you. Why?"

Rebecca sorted through her feelings. "Oh, I guess because of her gentleness and thoughtfulness and . . . humanity and . . . strength. She had lost so much, and yet she seemed so . . . so . . . serene. And when she said, 'I had a daughter. She died . . . . Thank you for asking.'" Rebecca's voice dropped. "I felt so spoiled and selfish and . . . trivial."

"You're not any of those things. And I think you are more like her than you know."

"No." Rebecca pensively shook her head. "Far from it. I'm not . . . . You know, she reminds me of what George Eliot said at the end of *Middlemarch*."

"Which is?"

"I memorized the words once in school. And never quite forgot them. This is not exact, but she says, '*The growing good of the world depends in part on unhistoric acts, and . . . that things are not so ill with you and me as they might have been . . . we largely owe to those who have lived faithfully a hidden life and rest in unvisited tombs*'."

"I'm impressed. A good memory. And a good thought. That you keep it in your mind proves not only my point once again about nice phrases punctuating our lives but about you having affinities with this Madame Raja."

Ignoring his remark, she went on. "She's one of those people—making the world better by living faithfully a hidden life of unhistoric acts. And what she said about gratitude . . . is surely true."

"Probably. But, could I add something?'

"Don't spoil the moment."

"I'll try. You know gratitude isn't always a good thing. It can be a mark of deceptive submission to power, or fate. Anyone with power over others, even abusive power, can extract gratitude from them by bestowing favors. Think of bread and circuses. And the Stockholm Syndrome. And religions exploit gratitude by promising heavenly freedom from suffering through belief and rituals. Hinduism has done that for millennia."

"That may be," Rebecca replied with a note of irritation. "But don't get cynical on me again. Her gratitude is genuine and true and good."

"I was just . . . . Yes, her gratitude is what you say. And, if I dare say it, her kind of gratitude is one of the best ways of looking at things."

Rebecca cast him a critical eye. "You can't reduce gratitude to mere perception. It's an authentic emotion."

"I don't mean that it's not." He hadn't intended to upset her sympathetically contemplative mood. But he couldn't resist going on. He leaned over the table. "Consider this. Madame Raja said gratitude can help us see what matters most to us in our lives. Doesn't that make it a way of seeing the true value of things for us, and of 'appreciating' that value, just as 'art appreciation' in school teaches us to *appreciate* art in school? Gratitude is, after all, a kind of *appreciation*."

She shook her head. "That's facile. But her gratitude isn't art appreciation. It's a true feeling of indebtedness to others for the good in her life. And it has given her a humanity, as she called it, and a serenity, that I have never seen in anyone before."

"OK. But didn't she say we have to learn how to find gratitude and humanity and serenity and the rest of it for ourselves? They don't come instinctively. Just like we have to learn how to feel many of our other good emotions."

Rebecca didn't answer. She had heard this line before. But she had to admit that it had a different ring now.

"In any case," he said, focusing his eyes on hers and speaking earnestly, "I'm grateful to her for what she did for us. And I'm deeply *grateful* to you for all that you have done for me. This makes me very happy, for all of the reasons she said gratitude can give us happiness." He paused. "When I think about it, she was right about everything." He put a hand on Rebecca's. "Now," he perked up his tone, "Why don't we go back to the hotel for lunch and a swim. Later we can drive out to Sarnath to see the Buddhist shrine there and talk more about gratitude and . . . the meaning of life"

Rebecca smiled and assented, letting their debate about gratitude go, but not the feelings that Madame Raja had stirred in her.

With the mid-day sun now beating hard through the thick muggy air onto the congested streets and smelly markets, they made their way past chickens and goats and cows and children and vendors and pilgrims to a street, secured a ramshackle taxi, and rode back through the urban maelstrom to their hotel. Drained by the heat, and weary from their pre-dawn rise, they cooled themselves in the pool, lunched on fruits and raita, then collapsed on the bed in their air-conditioned room and let time drift peacefully away.

Later, after the sweltering midday sunshine had descended into late afternoon shadows, they ventured out with a car and driver to the Deer Park at Sarnath, where Siddhartha Gautama had given his first sermon as the Buddha. The quiet parkland with its archaeological digs, its somber monument on the spot of the Enlightened One's epochal pronouncement, and the saffron-robed monks sitting in motionless meditation, all seemed worlds away from the welter of life and death and rebirth on the Ganges and from the maze of crowded alleyways in Varanasi. There was tranquility here. And transcendent Buddhist detachment on life's bridge of dreams. They wandered around, paused at the Buddha's monument and rested beneath a Bo tree said to be descended from the one that had shaded Siddhartha as he became Enlightened. And they absorbed the tranquility.

But that night, back at the hotel, as they tumbled weight-lessly into clouds of sleep, it was not the Buddhist tranquility of the Deer Park that went with them. Nor was it the Breughelesque spectacle on the Ganges. It was that *coincidental* palmist in a tiny room off a narrow alley amidst the penumbral maze of Varanasi who had read their lives in their hands, and who, with her irreparable losses and enduring gratitude, and her gentle humanity and invincible serenity had given them unforeseen gifts in the ancient city of rebirth.

# Serene Elation

The flat plains and mountainous outcroppings of Central India unfurled below as Alex and Rebecca flew off late the next morning to the village of Khajuraho, famed for its exquisite temple sculptures, and infamous for its sculptural celebrations of sex.

After checking into their hotel, they made the short dusty drive to a gated park. There a guide led them along footpaths through lawns and shade trees to the dozen or so temples ascending from plinths, or platform terraces, to conical peaks a hundred feet from the ground. He explained that Khajuraho had been the religious capital of a sprawling kingdom a thousand years ago, but then the kingdom had for some unknown reason rapidly collapsed, most of the temples had crumbled, and foliage had claimed them until the British stumbled upon the remains in the nineteenth century. "Its history is much mystery," he concluded with a broad grin at his erudition and euphony.

Mounting the terrace steps of the first temple, which the guide said was named Lakshman and which was one of the oldest and grandest, they walked around the platform examining the exterior wall up and down, craning their necks to see the upper levels, and stooping to examine those below. The walls swarmed with a myriad of finely wrought and fetching sculptured human figures about two feet high. Some exuded sublime composure and divine dignity. Others were dancing, playing music, or engaged in mundane pursuits like farming, applying cosmetics, and plucking thorns from their feet. But those that most strikingly caught the eyes of these travelers, like most, exhibited varieties of erotic ardor. Amorous embraces and salacious couplings, coy peepings and coquettish exhibitionism, acrobatic sexual acts and group orgies. Yet they were mostly depicted with an air of what Rebecca and Alex agreed was a kind of serene elation.

"Eros was the builder of these temples for sure," Alex murmured, then turned to the guide. "Hindu art often shows eroticism, but why so much of it here?"

"There are many interpretations," the guide answered. "Some of the erotic sculptures may illustrate the Hindu scripture *Kama Sutra*. But most of them probably show Tantric exercises. Tantra teaches how to sustain arousal without completing it. This self-restraint takes us to a higher level of being."

"So they aren't about sensual pleasure," Alex queried, "but about restraining that pleasure to reach nirvana?"

"Yes, possibly," the guide replied. "But I should tell you that an inscription on one of the ruined temples here honoring the marriage of Shiva and Parvati, says: 'May the laughter of Shiva, with his beloved wife Parvati, be for your welfare.' Some scholars say all of the temples here celebrate that wedding and Shiva's loving laughter for all of us. Is that sensuality? Probably. No one knows."

"Some wedding," Alex cracked. Rebecca just looked at the sculptures.

Approaching the north face of the temple, the guide signaled them to follow him into an alcove. There he pointed to a rough-hewn figure of a man and a woman performing a contortionist erotic act. "Look at this," he said, smirking slyly and laying a hand on a small ornamental elephant standing next to the couple.

Coming nearer, they saw that, unlike the many other elephants in the same frieze that faced outward, this one had its head turned in profile. It was watching the adjacent sexual performance. An unmistakable smile curled up its cheek.

"An elephant voyeur," Rebecca remarked.

"The laughter of Shiva in another form," Alex responded.

Rebecca studied the quirky elephant and found herself returning to that dim hovel in Varanasi where Madame Raja had smiled at life. Slowly she raised her eyes up the temple's surface from figure to figure over the profusion of human forms. They seemed to come alive. Musicians playing. Dancers dancing. Damsels primping. Voyeuses peeking. Lovers loving. Gods and goddesses embracing and performing Tantric exercises. It was a carnival of life for divine and human purposes. She felt a strong fizz of that pleasant now-familiar lightness that lifted her, and, as if suspended in air, she watched the carnival with awed delight. Then, as her gaze descended and the sensation lessened, the figures went still, restoring their composure in stone. She brought her eyes down to the smiling elephant. Madame Raja would like him, she thought. How amusing lovers are, he seems to be saying. Let us smile at them, and laugh with the loving Shiva, and share a generous humanity.

"Amazing," she heard Alex say, as he surveyed the cornucopia of sculptures.

"Yes," she sighed, roused from the daydream but still floating. "And this little character," she touched the elephant, "could be the clue to it all. And more."

"What do you mean?"

"I'll tell you later. Let's go see the other temples. Then. . . ." She didn't finish but smiled broadly and took his hand. He arched his eyebrows and let her lead him. They went on to revel in the sacred carnival of religion, art, and life from temple to temple until they had seen each one. The mid-afternoon sun was now beating down on them, and they decided to return to the hotel. Once there, they stretched out on the bed in the coolness of the room.

"So," he said, "are you going to tell me now what you meant about that elephant?"

"Well," she answered quietly, "it seemed to symbolize the joy and humanity and even laughter of love. And I . . . wanted to share that with you here." She kissed him. And they made love with a joyous passion, a divine ecstasy, and a serene elation new to them. Their tide was running higher than ever. And they were riding it, with Shiva's loving laughter.

After their raptures lulled, they lay together, delicately tracing with their fingertips the contours of each other's faces and lips. Rebecca whispered, "Thank you." Alex kissed her fingers, and mouthed her words. And they both knew it was not just for their erotic transports that they were grateful. It was for being together in this far-away, complicated land that had opened their eyes and hearts to so much, and where they were sharing life and love and laughter and the happy humanity of the blessed, and the serene elation of the gods, and thinking they would never again be quite who they had been before.

Early the next morning, still borne on their bliss, they returned to the temples to partake once more of the bounteous celebration of life and love and humanity there. That's what Khajuraho means, they agreed. All of that.

Later, as they watched the temples dwindle into miniatures below while their plane headed out across the flatlands to the west on the short flight to Agra where they would make their brief belated visit to the Taj Mahal, both felt they were taking all of that with them.

When the last sight of the temples faded from view, Rebecca turned her face from the window where she was sitting to Alex. He was lying against the headrest with his eyes closed. But his features were not those of someone sleeping, whose muscles go lax and lips droop downward. His expression was too lively, the lines at the corners of his eyes and mouth tended upward, betraying daydreams of a fondly remembered past, or of delightful times yet to come, or of fantasies only he could imagine. She wondered where he was, what images he was playing among. She could ask. But that would end the sweet moment for him.

She laid her head back, shut her eyes, and let her own images form. She saw the temples again, and that funny elephant, and the palm readers in Varanasi and Atlantic City, and sunrises and sunsets, and arguments, and love-making. And she saw Alex, charming and irritating, romanticizing and fantasizing, extolling beautiful things and spinning fanciful theories, hiding his shyness and loving selflessly, and becoming part of her. A slight motion moved upward from the corners of her lips. Was this what she had seen on his face? She rolled her head toward him. And let the images play, with serene elation.

Alex saw them all. All the images she was seeing, and more. Pleasures, places, feelings, fantasies. And she was always there. He wanted her there. Everywhere. In everything. Because he cared more for her than for himself. Or he couldn't think of himself without her. This is the woman who had pierced his fears and revealed her own, and who had seen how, for all of their differences, they were kindred beings. This is the woman who could argue with him over anything, and cry over a memory of kindness in childhood and over a fortuneteller's gratitude, and philosophize over a smiling elephant, and make love like a goddess. This is the woman whose intelligence and honesty and slowly unfolding emotions and irrepressible Renoir warmth he had come to depend upon to feel alive. This is the woman he loved more than he had thought he could ever love. Selflessly. He had a life with her now. Real life. Their life. He wanted it no other way. And he soared on the feeling, with serene elation.

He opened his eyes a crack and angled his head toward her. And he wondered what she was thinking behind that soft hint of a smile.

# 20

## Romance and Reality

Early that afternoon, they were racing along the road in Agra again through the perennial industrial haze for their close-up view of the Taj Mahal. When they pulled into the narrow roadway leading to the entrance, they were met by the same crush of tour buses disgorging hordes, touts flogging curios, and merchants hawking artifacts that they had seen before. The driver stopped at the edge of the swarm, and Alex and Rebecca plunged in with their guide.

Crowding through the tourists and peddlers, they eventually reached the ticket booth. After paying the fee, they decided they wanted to go in by themselves without the guide and, leaving him behind, they handed their tickets to a functionary at the entrance in the outer wall and went through. There they found themselves in an expansive space separated from the Taj itself by another high wall, where an imposing ceremonial gateway stood surmounted by ornamental cupolas. A queue of visitors wound to a second checkpoint at the side of the gateway. They joined it and submitted to military officers' assiduous search of every bag and parcel carried by everyone.

At last they made it down a passage that opened onto a broad porch overlooking a wide tree-lined garden. There a reflecting pool directed eyes straight to the peerlessly beautiful monument some three hundred yards away, its white marble lustrous under the November sun, and the sublime symmetry of its shapely domes, alcoves, and four slender minarets set dramatically on a terrace at the end of the garden to stand out against the sky above the low valley behind and throw a bright reflection onto the pool. Prepared as they were for this sight from photographs, they were not ready for its effect in actuality.

"It's almost too perfect." Alex said.

"Nothing can be too perfect," Rebecca replied in a mocking tone. "'Perfect' is an absolute term. You can't have more or less of it."

"Thanks Madame editor. I just meant it looks too perfect to be real. It's almost artificial."

"Is that a metaphysical or an aesthetic judgment? I'd expect you to go for the aesthetics."

"Such a philosopher. Well, maybe you've changed my view of the world."

"I doubt that," she laughed. "But I warned you about coming back for the post-card view."

"Oh, I'm not sorry we came. But let's go see what it's like in the flesh, so to speak."

They went down a bank of steps and set off with a stream of tourists alongside the pool toward the tomb, which seemed to rise up before them as they approached it. When they arrived at the base of the terrace where the Taj stands, they put on obligatory foot coverings dispensed by another functionary and climbed a flight of stairs. At the top, they raised their eyes to take in the resplendent monument ascending in quiet grandeur to the pointed finial of its sensuous central dome. Now they could see bright semi-precious stones—lapis lazuli, coral, vermilion, malachite—inlaid in the white translucent marble flaring out in floral patterns across the walls up to the dome, and arching around the towering entry vestibule in flowing Arabic calligraphy from the Koran.

"I've never seen the inlays distinctly in photographs,"

Rebecca said, awed by the colors and artistry. "The place seems more real now, and yet still kind of magical."

"Is that metaphysics or aesthetics, irony or paradox?"

She ignored his question and went over to touch the marble and the inlays, half expecting a guard to prevent her. "How soft it feels," she murmured. "Your white elephant is like this."

"I'll caress it and keep it always," he responded with a smile.

Merging with a clutch of tourists at the vestibule, they squeezed through the doorway into the cramped interior burial chamber. As their eyes adapted to the dark, they could perceive faint rays of sunlight filtering through the translucent marble walls. In the center of the chamber they discerned a filigreed white marble barrier encircling the sarcophagi of Mumtaz and Shah Jehan. Moving toward it, they spotted a turbaned figure furtively summoning them. Curious, they followed him to an uncongested spot on the far side of the circle. There he bent an arm through an opening in the filigree and held a small flashlight behind one of its inlaid panels. The marble panel lit up like a light bulb, and the semi-precious stones of the floral inlay burst with color—reds and greens and blues. "If all of the walls were this thin," he declared, "they would be this bright. Like a rose window in your European cathedrals." Withdrawing his arm, he proffered a hand to receive a reward for his expertise. They gave him some rupees and continued around the circle, viewing the two sarcophagi through the filigree. Soon they were back outside.

Squinting in the glare, they took shelter in the shade against the side of the tomb and moseyed along, tracing the entwining inlays and admiring the artistry. Noticing some of the inlays missing, Rebecca rued callous treasure hunters and the vandalism of time.

From there they wandered around the terrace, loitering here and there, visiting the mosque and the corresponding "guesthouse" bordering the terrace on opposite sides—both later additions to the architectural symmetry—and watching from every perspective as time passed and the sunshine and puffy clouds cast evanescent patterns of light and shade across the monument's luminous dome, colorfully inlaid walls, and the four stately minarets at the corners of the terrace. Eventually, they sat down on a bench in the lengthening shadow of one minaret at the railing above the Yamuna River fifty feet or more below. Barely visible through the haze up the winding river, they could just make out the parapets of the Red Fort.

"I grant that the Taj Mahal is more ironic from there than from here," Alex said, gesturing toward the distant fortress. "Or I'm losing my sense of irony."

"Don't lose it. Just use it well."

"How poetic." Turning from the fortress back to the mausoleum, he went on. "Aren't you glad we came back?"

"I didn't need to. But I'm not sorry we did. To walk around it and see the inlays and touch the marble does enliven it as no photograph or distant view can."

"Well, I needed to come back. And you're right. When you see the Taj up closes, it is magical, like it was the first night, and yet real, too. Now I'm beginning to think Shah Jehan built it not only from his love and longing for Mumtaz but from his gratitude to her for all she gave him in their lives together, as well as for his memories of her. That makes the Taj a metaphor of many good things. There is both magic and reality—and gratitude—in a love like Shah Jehan's . . . . I know." He kissed her hand softly.

The same Alex, she thought. Playing with sensations, feeding feelings, dramatizing incidents, stretching the meanings of things. He had to come back here, to this historic, romantic place, to have one of those moments that he could milk for all it was worth, creating more of the romance he lived for and insisted on sharing with her. But his performance was quite endearing now. And she knew it was not just a performance. She laid a hand on his and said, "I like the sentiment, even the sentimentality. Better than any irony."

Then it was time to go. They had to catch a plane for Jaipur. Standing a final time behind the tomb, they gazed once more toward the Red Fort.

"Ah, irony," Alex muttered, "eclipsed by sentimentality."

"Works for me," she said and nudged him.

Hand in hand they meandered to the front of the tomb, went down the stairs, doffed their shoe covers, and walked slowly beside the long reflecting pool toward the exit.

"It's too bad they don't let you in here at night to see it under the moon," Alex lamented. "Did you ever read Richard Halliburton?"

"Can't say I have."

"A young adventurer and travel writer of the Twenties and Thirties. He wrote a book called *The Royal Road to Romance* where he tells of climbing over the wall here one night to swim in the pool in the moonlight. I read it when I was young. Never forgot that episode. Or the book. Wonderful title. He later disappeared on another adventure when a historical schooner he was sailing across the Pacific vanished."

"Sad ending."

"But romantic."

"I can see why you were taken with him. A role model?"

"Only in nostalgia. His world is gone. Overrun by tourists—like us."

"That hasn't dimmed your penchant to romanticize things."

"No. But you've changed the way I do it."

"What do you mean?"

"You have taught me the romance of reality."

"Come again?"

"You are real life to me, as I've said and as I have never known it before. That makes our romance more real to me than anything has ever been. It also makes reality more romantic than

I had ever thought it could be. The romance of reality and the reality of romance. The Taj embodies that. You create both of them for me. And, you know, you've been sounding like quite a romantic realist yourself lately. Ah, how alike we have become. Sweet irony."

There he goes rambling on again, she thought. She shook her head and smiled. But she sensed that somewhere in those ramblings he was possibly right—about the two of them.

They strolled on beside the reflecting pool chatting about where they were and how they had changed since they had met each other, and how India could change anyone. When they reached the end of the pool, they went up the steps toward the massive departure doorway in the surrounding garden wall. There they turned back towards the tomb. Before leaving, they wanted a final look to cap their lasting memories of the romance and reality of their time together here.

"Yes," Rebecca sighed. "It might be too perfect when you see it like this. Beautiful, but artificial."

"Didn't you say that nothing could be too perfect?" Alex replied.

"Well, perhaps it could depend on how you look at it."

"Ahh," he reacted with a smile, "you *are* stealing my lines."

They shared a knowing laugh and gave each other's hand a loving squeeze and went through the doorway.

# On a Bridge of Dreams

(Concluded)

The good news came from an American attaché who had previously visited the American victims of the bombing while Rebecca had been too disoriented to grasp much of what was going on. It wasn't the news she had hoped for, but it was good. They were going home. Arrangements were being made to fly the remaining American victims on a military plane, complete with a medical team, from Agra to Frankfurt and then to Andrews Air Force base outside Washington, D. C. They would be back in the U.S. within the week. Rebecca's heart pounded. This was the first encouraging thing that had happened since everything had gone so unbelievably, nightmarishly bad. Soon they would be in New York, where the hospital can give Alex the care he needs, and her own doctor can be there, and the nightmare can end. The idea boosted her spirits and gave her a clear purpose. She could make plans.

She managed with the help of a particularly sympathetic nurse to make some calls—she reached her mother and Sarah and her office—and to retrieve the baggage that she and Alex had stored in an airport locker for their short stopover in Agra. And she gave a bunch of her own things to the kindhearted nurses. That made her feel useful.

*Finally the word came. They would depart the next day.*

*Remarkably, no Americans had been among the twenty fatalities of the blast. Mostly Japanese in a large tour group and Indian soldiers on security detail. But a number of Americans had been hospitalized and several were still there with serious wounds waiting to go home—a honeymooning couple from Pennsylvania, a pair of catholic priests from Chicago, some members of a tour group from the Midwest, and Rebecca and Alex, who was the most gravely injured American survivor. They had all become minor celebrities in the American news media as victims of a brazen terrorist attack at one of the world's most revered monuments and popular tourist sites. Some American journalists had even come to Agra for interviews. Rebecca had not participated. She was not about to parade her emotions and injuries on the front pages of newspapers and on the nightly news. And she wasn't sure she could control what she would say amid her hurt and sorrow and anger and fear.*

*Nearly ten days after the bombing, tending their wounds and with relieved exhaustion—except for the still comatose Alex, seemingly oblivious to all around him, whose gains, she thought, only doctors could yet see—the handful of Americans landed at Andrews Air Force Base for their private journeys home, and out of their collective tragedy.*

*How vivid her memories of the past few months were, down to her conversation with Alex at the Taj Mahal before the tragedy. And how happy most of those memories were, dimming what had happened to her that night before it had all begun with him. At last, Rebecca was leaving her bridge of dreams, if not her nightmare. What would happen now?*

# 21

## Give Me Paradise

Clouds hung low in the gray November sky as Rebecca accompanied Alex into a medical van for transfer to another plane that would take them from Andrews Air Force base to New York. She had forgotten the season. And, exhausted from the prolonged ordeal, weak from her injuries, and drained by the journey, she was oblivious to the weather. The nightmare wasn't over. But soon she would be home.

The short flight passed in a fog. Half asleep and hoping she was now finally flying away from the tragedy of her life, she let her mind stray into other-worldly thoughts. For some reason she remembered reading somewhere that the English word 'paradise' came from the ancient Persian word for garden, *pairidaeza*, and that this was the paradise of Islam described in the Koran—a garden of fragrant flowers and verdant grasses and cooling shade and honeyed nectars bubbling from pristine springs. Paradise as a garden. She dwelled on the soothing image. Shah Jehan had probably graced the grounds of his wife's beautiful mausoleum with gardens for that reason—or so Rebecca imagined—although she didn't want to think about that. Let the Christians have their heaven and hell, rife with judgments and punishments and rewards, she thought, and let the Hindus live their many lives trying to *get it right* so they can *get out* and enter the nothingness of *nirvana*. The Muslims have it better. They go to repose in a bounteous garden paradise forever. Who needs a vague heaven or a vaporous nirvana? her dreaming voice said as she dozed off. Give me paradise.

Rebecca awoke from her dreams when the plane neared its landing at the Marine Air Terminal near La Guardia Airport. She stiffly clambered out onto the tarmac with the aid of a military medic and was led on her crutches to an ambulance that would take Alex and her on the last ride of their half-way-around-the-world journey to the New York Medical Center on the east side of Manhattan. Beside the ambulance stood Adrianna Winters.

She and Rebecca had spoken by phone a number of times during the agonizing Agra days. Adrianna had wanted to go there to help, but Rebecca had dissuaded her, saying she could do more by making arrangements on this end. Although Adrianna had not met Alex—that was to come this Thanksgiving— Rebecca had told her enough since the first mention of him that afternoon in June that Adrianna felt she almost knew him. She had arranged everything along with Alex's agent, Sarah, who managed his professional and financial affairs. Alex had no family of his own anymore, Rebecca had explained to her mother. Or none she knew of. He had said that a brother had been killed as a youth, and that his parents had both died not long after he was forty. It had seemed odd to her that he never talked about his parents, except to say, while joking about the American myth of the unencumbered male loner, that the best parents make their influence invisible, and that his parents had been very good at that, and that he owed them more than he could ever have repaid. He didn't even seem to have close friends besides Sarah and Conrad, the psychotherapist whom she had met once with Alex at dinner. He had many social and professional acquaintances, of course, but he had no keen appetite for idle socializing. She had concluded that he must be more or less the loner he had said he was.

Rebecca had telephoned Sarah from Agra first with the tragic news, and later to tell her they were coming home and that Adrianna would contact her about the hospital arrangements. But Rebecca wanted only her mother to meet her at the airport.

Now she and her mother were together. Adrianna suppressed her distress at seeing Rebecca so gaunt and colorless, her eyes sunken in dark rings, her hair disheveled as it had never been. They fell into each other's arms, both grateful that Rebecca had survived, and yet both grieving—Adrianna grieving that her daughter had suffered so much, and Rebecca grieving that the man now in her heart and her life was possibly dying. But Rebecca felt relief that she didn't have to be so alone in the crisis anymore. Addy could manage everything. She always could. Rebecca had emulated her in that. But this was not the time to do it.

When they arrived at the hospital, they waited at the emergency room while Alex was admitted. Adrianna had planned this through their own doctor, Raymond Carey, who had been with the family ever since Rebecca's birth in New Haven, where he had been a resident before going on to important positions at the New York Medical Center. Sitting there waiting, Rebecca heard her mother say that now Alex would get the best medical attention possible. And she could visit him. This gave Rebecca some comfort, but not relief. Then Doctor Carey came through the Waiting Room doors. He drew Rebecca tenderly to him.

"Rebecca, Rebecca. You've had such an awful experience. I am so sorry."

She thanked him for his concern and for arranging to have the hospital receive Alex. In his best doctorly manner, he assured her that everything would be done for Alex that needed to be done. First a battery of tests, X-rays, EKG, EEG, MRI, CT Scan— "the alphabet of modern medicine," he said in a fatherly attempt to lighten the gravity. But it would not be until at least the next day that they would have full results—a diagnosis to describe, a prognosis to give. "Meanwhile," he said firmly but affectionately, "let's take care of you. I want to be sure you have been properly treated, and to see what we can do to speed your recovery."

Without thinking, Rebecca said she was fine.

"*Fine?*" he reacted incredulously. "*Fine?* If I may say so, Rebecca, my dear, you don't look *fine*. You look like you have been through hell, which you have."

Yielding to his demands and leaning against his arm, Rebecca went with him to an adjacent examining room where he inspected her injuries, approved of her overall treatment, replaced some of her dressings, and prescribed medications to stave off infection and to assuage pain if she needed it. He also prescribed an anti-depressant to get her through emotional downswings. Injuries and illnesses, as well as emotional traumas, often leave residual depression, he explained, and she might as well fight it instead of giving in. He said she *would be fine* once she got some rest and her strength returned. Caring Doctor Carey, the Winters family had called him. A role he liked to play. The Winters family had loved him for that, and had counted on it.

But was that all there was to it? she asked herself—this feeling of anguish and loss in the depths of her heart? Pills would fix it? Rest and strength would banish it?

"I just want to have a bath," she said finally. "A real bath. That's all. Can I do that?"

"It's not the usual thing to do at this stage with injuries like yours," he replied. "You shouldn't get the dressings and injuries very wet. A sponge bath would be more suitable. But under the circumstances, it'll probably do you more good emotionally than harm physically. I'll refurbish everything when I see you next, and maybe I can remove some stitches. Call me tomorrow to tell me how you are and to set a time. I should have learned by then about Mr. Rodgers. Now the only thing you can do for him is to take care of yourself. Will you do that?"

He was, Rebecca thought, trying to be paternal. This was reassuring. But she could only answer, "Yes," unconvincingly.

When they rejoined her mother, Rebecca said to him earnestly. "Thank you for being here, Raymond. And for everything you've done for us."

"Yes, thank you Raymond," Adrianna added. "I don't know what we would have ever done without you today, or over the years."

"Knowing you, Adrianna, I'd say you might have *become* a doctor." He gave her a quick hug.

Rebecca and her mother said goodbye to the doctor and went outside where they found a taxi at the door. The driver dumped Rebecca's and Alex's suitcases in the trunk. Rebecca handed the crutches to her mother then gingerly slid into the seat. Adrianna got in the other side, and they drove off to Rebecca's apartment. The sky was getting dark, but Rebecca paid no attention to the time, or the day.

Adrianna had told Rebecca that she should go with her to Connecticut to recuperate, but Rebecca had been determined to stay in New York so she could see Alex. And she wanted to be home with Clarissa. Understanding all of that, Adrianna had insisted on remaining with her for at least a while. "Mothers have to impose their good sense now and then," she had said, "or their children, at any age, forget how good it is." This was one of those times. Rebecca was glad.

As they entered Rebecca's apartment, Rebecca breathed deeply. She *was* home. A bouquet of fresh flowers bloomed in a vase on the coffee table. Her mother's welcoming touch. So like Addy, Rebecca thought. Knowing what you want without asking, as on the day—Rebecca flashed back to her adolescence—when her mother had bought an album of Rebecca's favorite pop singer and had laid it unannounced on Rebecca's bed as a gift, for no reason other than to make her daughter happy, even though Adrianna hated the music. Rebecca pressed her head against her mother's shoulder in a tender gesture of thanks, blinking back a child's tears.

Clarissa sauntered toward her and stretched welcoming paws up to Rebecca's knees. Adrianna had taken the cat while Rebecca was away and had brought her back the previous day when preparing the apartment for Rebecca's return. Balancing against her mother, Rebecca lifted Clarissa up and petted her comfortingly. It was good to feel that friendly fur and hear that happy purr. Maybe Doctor Carey's homey prescription for recovery would work after all.

Setting Clarissa down, Rebecca hobbled, with her mother's support, to the bedroom and began pulling off the loose beige blouse and khaki skirt she had been wearing ever since retrieving her clothes in the Agra hospital and giving most of them to the kind nurse. Adrianna drew a tub of hot water. Rebecca cautiously stepped in. Wincing as the heat briefly scalded her bare feet, she slowly sank down and lay back, resting her head against the porcelain rim and letting hot water lap the ends of her hair. The wetness seeping through her new but lighter bandages stung. Then tingled. Then numbed. How delicious to have this womb-like, salutary warmth embracing her. She stirred the steamy water with her hands and watched it roll back and forth from one side of the tub to the other in mesmerizing, desensitizing waves.

Half-an-hour or more later, almost anesthetized from the hot water, and wrapped in a thick terry-cloth robe, with her mother's helping hands she slid into the cool clean sheets of her bed. The sensation was as sweet as the bath. She hadn't slept soundly since the bombing. Now she closed her eyes and sent herself sailing off on cottony clouds to a garden paradise.

# 22

## A Deeper Well

When she opened her eyes, she didn't know where she was. The hospital? A hotel? Then it came to her. She was home.

Groggy, stiff, aching, muddled, and still damp, she sat up and grimaced at the pain. Oh, yes. The nightmare. How long had she been asleep? What day was it?

She pulled herself onto the edge of the bed and saw a fresh robe laid out for her by her mother on the chair beside the table. Another thoughtfulness. Holding onto the night table, she stood up, telling herself she could do it without help. She slid out of the robe that she had slept in and picked up the fresh one and slipped it on. Aided by the chair and her crutch, she limped to the door and opened it a crack. She could see her mother in the living room. At the sound of the door opening, Adrianna turned from the sofa where she had slept and was now reading.

"My dear! You've revived. I was beginning to wonder if you would sleep forever." She came to her daughter, and helped her to the sofa.

"What time is it?" Rebecca mumbled.

"Close to two."

"Good God!" Rebecca burst out. "I have to call Raymond. Why didn't you get me up?"

"Don't worry. I spoke to him a while ago. He said I should let you sleep as long as you could."

"But . . . ."

"He told me an attending physician had reported that they needed to do some surgery to ease the effects of the head injury. He said there would be no point of your going today. Besides, it's getting late. You can go tomorrow."

"Surgery? More surgery? Addy . . . I have to . . . ."

"Rebecca, there is *nothing* you can do today, except take care of yourself. And hope for the best."

Rebecca slumped into the cushions of the sofa, wincing at the pain in her leg. "Hope? Hope isn't enough," she exhaled and closed her eyes. She thought of praying. Not to call upon the gods figuratively, as she had done before, but to beseech an actual, living, divine being to intervene for Alex—and her. She would promise future devotion to this God, if not her whole-hearted worship. She recalled a facile remark Alex had made more than once about God being a metaphor for a power we cannot have, a perfection we cannot achieve, and a hope we cannot live without, or some of us can't. Yes, she must at least have hope, she told herself, as she prayed, in her way, to God. Any god.

Led by such thoughts, her mind returned to the night, seemingly so long ago, when her "old life" had ended right here, on this sofa. The night when those frightening images of emptiness had filled her mind, and the abyss had opened, and the panic had seized her. That was her first living nightmare. And now she was living a second nightmare. But this was different. For one thing, it wasn't hers alone. The events at the Taj Mahal were a public tragedy that she had only been part of. She couldn't help recalling the events of September 11th, also a public tragedy that had affected her, but more indirectly and in ways she could never quite put her finger on. Still, while the new tragedy had been shared by many, it did have consequences all her own. Partly the fear of losing Alex. But equally the fear of losing herself again. As she followed this unhappy mental trail, she sensed the abyss yawning inside once more. And from somewhere deep within her, an eruption gathered force, welled up, and engulfed her in sobs.

At first she felt she was reliving that awful night in a terrible *déja vù*. Amidst her sobs, she braced for the panic of that night. But it didn't come. Gradually she became aware that these tears were not the same as those back then. They were flowing from a deeper well, with a flood of feelings she had never known. And these feelings weren't all bad. She covered her face with her hands and let the torrent flow.

Adrianna Winters had always suspected that her daughter's seemingly unflappable self-mastery, her icy control in a crisis, her tidy life contained more complicated and powerful emotions than Rebecca had ever wanted to show, or to know. Adrianna had seen signs of this occasionally in Rebecca's childhood, but fewer of them over the years. And she had tried to lead Rebecca to understand this in their conversations last summer. But Adrianna recognized that this eruption, so heartrending and encompassing, came from someplace deeper and with greater force than she had even expected.

When the sobs finally abated—nearly depleting a box of tissues that Adrianna had set at Rebecca's side while waiting, with loving sorrow tinged by perplexity, for the emotional outpouring to run its course. Finally Rebecca wiped her face dry and coughed. "I'm sorry," she apologized, her voice breaking. "I don't know . . . ." She couldn't complete the sentence.

"After what you've been through and are still suffering," Adrianna said consolingly, "anyone would need to cry."

Rebecca pulled the last tissue from the box and blew her nose while her mother replenished the supply. "It's not only that," she said, beginning to collect herself. "I don't really understand it. I don't know what's going on inside. It's a muddle. Sorrow . . . loss . . . fear . . . anger . . . even traces of . . . good feelings, and I don't know what else . . . emotions steeped in memories. But the anger . . . ."

"Anger?"

"Yes. Anger at the madmen who did this, and at Alex for taking us there, and at myself for going. At everything. I know I'm not being rational. I'm being disgustingly narcissistic and self-pitying. But I can't help it." She pressed her hands to her face to hide the grief. Her mother laid an arm gently around her shoulder.

"Rebecca, you don't have to be rational and in control of yourself all the time," Adrianna said sympathetically. "And this is an appropriate time not to be. You deserve some pity and anger. Venting anguish and rage can be cathartic. Better than holding them in where they can embitter you or do other evil things. Besides, you can be free with me. You know that."

Rebecca wasn't listening closely to the words. But her mother's voice was pacifying. It always had been, whenever Rebecca had needed it. She had sometimes wondered if she would herself be able to do that one day for a child. Could she be that patient and empathetic and understanding and caring? Or was she too self-possessed, self-disciplined, "task-oriented" in the jargon of an aptitude test she had taken in high school and never forgotten? Get over it! Get a grip! That had been her advice to people. Especially to herself. Until . . . .

"And you are in no condition at the moment," she heard her mother going on, "to know what you should feel or do. You have to take more time. And Alex might well recover. Then you can pick up where you left off."

Rebecca wiped her eyes again. "I don't know what . . . that means." She choked as she rasped out the words, and her mother went into the kitchen for a glass of water. Rebecca drank half of it and cleared her throat. She spoke with confessional solemnity. "It's . . . it's as though I don't know if . . . I have a past that I want to pick up, or that I have no future I want to enter." She sniffled and drank more water.

"That's rather confusing, for sure. But why do you feel that way?"

Rebecca thought a moment, took another drink, cleared her throat again, and said, "You remember last summer . . . when I told you I felt . . . empty and desolate because . . . I had looked into myself and seen something that scared me, and that it had been coming on for a while?"

"Yes, of course."

"You said I should try to get over it not by relying on my usual self with its strengths and comforts because this could have been a cause of my . . . crisis. I should instead 'go against the grain,' as you put it. Well, I sort of did that. It wasn't that I set out to do it. It just happened. It was Alex. He was nothing like me. Or that's what I thought at first. His manner irritated and unnerved me. But I guess I let myself 'go against the grain' with him. You are to blame for that." Rebecca smiled wanly. "And eventually we came to see that we were actually very much alike . . . inside. Hidden fears, secret defenses, unspoken yearnings, and such. I could never have predicted that. From this came an emotional freedom and honesty and an intimacy that I have never had with anyone else. He said he hadn't either. I told you about some of this when it was happening. But . . . it gets worse," Rebecca flashed a self-deprecating look. "He said I had saved him by giving him a purpose to live for besides himself. He was being characteristically melodramatic, but I suppose I could have said something like that myself, juvenile as it sounds. It's possible that he did literally save my life at the Taj Mahal." Her voice caught. She lightly blew her nose into the tissue. "Maybe he saved me in other ways too. I don't know. But in truth . . . it wasn't just him. Things were happening to me that he was only a part of. I didn't know quite what these were or why. But I was starting to feel differently about . . . lots of things . . . myself . . . my life. Of course I could have been kidding myself. Anyhow, now . . . here I am . . . lost and . . . drowning in feelings, somehow both bad and good, that I don't understand or know what to do with." She sniffled. "Oh, I'm being so . . . childish and mawkish and selfish."

She laid her head against the back of the sofa and pressed her hands to her eyes. Emotions swirled within her. "What should I do," she breathed, as if talking to herself, "with all of these feelings now?" A quiver ran through her body, leaving her fingers trembling over her teary eyes.

Her mother spoke more consoling words. But she doubted they would help. She knew Rebecca was suffering from the accumulated effects of a shattering trauma, physical and emotional. And that it wasn't over. She was reasonably confident her daughter would pull herself together again once she had rested and recovered her strength, as Doctor Carey had said. And yet, Adrianna Winters could not deny to herself that this woman weeping beside her was not the same Rebecca Winters she had known as her daughter for nearly forty years.

# 23

# Death Mask

Sleep did not come as irresistibly to Rebecca that night as it had the night before. Her feelings roiled and confounded her. They were as new to her as the heart-wrenching sobs earlier. They didn't arise from an abyss of emptiness. They came from that deeper well of grief and anger, love and loss, heartache and helplessness, yearning and despair . . . and something more. . . . Finally, enervation gave her release. She again slept hard and long.

She awoke to morning light slanting through the window shades. At least that night was over, she told herself. But what about today?

Limping foggily out of her bedroom, supporting herself on one crutch and anything she could reach, she found her mother sitting with breakfast ready at the dining table. Adrianna greeted her daughter warmly and hugged her gently, searching for signs of renewal.

"You look a little better," she said, trying to be upbeat but not falsely cheerful. "And it's still morning. How do you feel. Do you want to sit at the table or on the sofa?"

"Let's try the table," Rebecca mumbled. She shuffled over and cautiously eased herself onto a chair. And she noticed that in fact she did feel better physically—less pained and more limber. Her mother poured her a glass of juice and a cup of coffee and laid out some fruit and croissants. Rebecca took a swallow of juice. Its tartness dispelled some of her grogginess.

"I spoke with Raymond," her mother reported, knowing this would be first on Rebecca's mind. "He said the surgery went fine and to come about two o'clock. He'll attend to you and tell you everything there is to know about Alex."

Rebecca peered at the clock on the wall—10:30. She had slept well over twelve hours again. That's one way to escape, she thought. To sleep forever. But what's the point? Numbly picking at the fruit and croissants, she apologized again for her emotional drama of yesterday. She still didn't understand it, but she didn't want to talk about it. Not now. So they alternated desultory conversation with silence as they ate until Rebecca said she should call her office. That heartened her mother. It was a sign of normal life.

Rebecca returned to the bedroom to make her calls from the comfort of the bed. First she tried Sarah but had to leave a message confirming that Alex was being cared for at the hospital and thanking her for making the arrangements. She would fill Sarah in on the details as soon as they could speak.

Next it was Meredith, whom she had called briefly from Agra, and who had wanted to meet Rebecca at the airport and take care of her and had been disappointed, but understanding, when Rebecca had said her mother would play that role.

"Rebecca, this is all so ghastly," Meredith cried. "When can I see you? I have to see you. What can I do?"

Such a good friend. Always ready to give of herself. But Rebecca wasn't ready to see anyone socially. She thanked Meredith for her generosity and told her that the whole saga, including the long trip home, had drained her physically and emotionally, and that her mother would be with her for a while. But she did promise to see Meredith in a day or two, as soon as she felt up to socializing.

Rebecca hung up the phone grateful again for Meredith's friendship. She had said the expected things, but Meredith could tell this wasn't the poised, resilient Rebecca Winters she knew. The trauma must have gone deep. Had it propelled Rebecca back into the depression, or whatever it was, that Meredith had seen deepening in her last spring, which Rebecca had never fully explained but which she had then seemed to come out of, more or less, before so uncharacteristically going off to India this fall with that most unlikely new man in her life? Or had it done something else to her? Whatever it was, Meredith vowed to do anything she could to help Rebecca out of it.

Then Rebecca reached her boss, Henry, whom she had also managed to reach from Agra to report the tragic events and to say she didn't know when she would get home or into the office. He had expressed sympathy, in his fashion, aware that her commitment to work had become intermittent for some time, leading to this autumn adventure during their profession's busiest season—but he had given his consent hoping that the break would mend whatever was distracting her and restore her previous professional dedication. Henry tried to be suitably sensitive. "Take as much time as you need, Rebecca," he offered. "When you're ready we can shoot some manuscripts over to you. It'll stave off boredom. Boredom is death, you know."

Rebecca practically threw down the phone. Did he think that was funny? When actual death hovered so near? "Thanks Henry," she replied sarcastically. "You're always very thoughtful. I'll let you know when I can use your prescription."

They said their goodbyes, and Rebecca was relieved to have that obligatory conversation over with. She didn't want to talk about work, or herself, or the past, or the future. She didn't want to talk about anything. Or think. She lay on the bed, shut her eyes, and succumbed to an undertow of emotional and physical fatigue.

When Rebecca's bleary consciousness revived, she saw that it was time to muster her will for what was to come—the hospital, and the uncertain fate that awaited her there, and thereafter. Then a prosaic question insinuated itself. What to wear? How trivial that she should think about such a thing at a time like this. But she had to go out, and that meant deciding what to wear for the first time since she had put on the khaki skirt in Agra. What season was it? she asked herself groggily.

Laboring to the closet, she pulled open the door. There she saw her autumn outfits freshly cleaned and hanging neatly, accompanied by a few items she didn't recognize. Her mother again, always anticipating and doing thoughtful motherly things. Rebecca nearly cried. Selecting a new wool tweed skirt that that would be comfortable over her injuries, and a new brown sweater, both bought for her and placed conspicuously together by Adrianna, along with a pair of comfortable low heels, she staggered with them to the bed and put them on carefully, despite the pains that had definitely lessened. The hot bath and rest must have done some good, abetted by the pain killers. Making her way to the bathroom, she glared in the mirror at the haggard face and the mop on her head—unattended since she had washed her hair in the tub two days earlier. She wetted the hair, toweled it off, put the blow-drier to it, and brushed and arranged it, finishing with a gesture of futility at a lost cause. She applied make-up to her face, lending needed color and concealing the rings under her eyes, and drew a line of lipstick across her lips, routinely pressing them together. Satisfied, if not pleased, with the results, she switched off the light and hobbled with a crutch into the living room.

"Well done, my dear," her mother greeted her. "You're practically your old self."

The words stung. Rebecca shrugged off the painful compliment and thanked her mother lovingly for the new clothes and for cleaning the others.

"What are mothers for?" Adrianna replied. "Speaking of that, I should make you have more to eat. It'll give you energy. There's plenty of time. A taxi will take us only about twenty minutes."

*"Us?"*

"Of course. You're not thinking of going by yourself"

Rebecca was virtually an invalid, her mother declared. And she would want company at the hospital. Rebecca objected that she could get there by herself, and she could handle the hospital alone. But Adrianna gently insisted. Rebecca finally yielded to her again. Secretly, Adrianna was glad Rebecca had resisted, seeing it as a mark of revitalized will. Secretly, Rebecca was glad her mother had prevailed.

A few minutes later they were getting into a taxi. Rebecca had brought just one of the crutches, relying mainly on her mother's arm and convincing herself that she could do without those clumsy things. Once settled in the cab, Rebecca leaned back and focused on the street life as the taxi whisked them downtown on another gray autumn day. Those streets could be so many things. Dirty. Crowded. Noisy. Entertaining. Eye-opening. Invigorating. Romantic. Yes, even romantic, she allowed sadly. But not today.

⌒⌣⌒

"Rebecca, you look much more yourself," Doctor Carey encouraged as he met her in his office. "Admirable progress. You have Adrianna's spirit, as I've always known."

She smiled politely and passed over his observations. "What about Alex Rodgers? Please tell me?"

"As I told Adrianna, the surgery went well. I'll explain everything shortly. First I want to take care of you."

"Can't we . . . ?"

"No, we can't," he countered unequivocally, leading her into an examining room, while Adrianna waited in the office. When they returned, Rebecca had fresh dressings and fewer stitches, which gave her a lift, and the doctor's reassurance that she would be on her own feet soon. That reassured Adrianna. But Rebecca's mind was elsewhere.

"Now," he said somberly, "I assume you want me to be completely honest about Mr. Rodgers."

"Yes. Please. You must."

"All right. First the good news. Although his wounds from fragments in the back were fairly serious, there were no critically damaged internal organs. Nothing life-threatening once they were treated. Now the . . . less good. The head wounds. They put him in a coma, which signals a brain injury of some kind. Those wounds also caused what is called a subdural hematoma. That's bleeding from a membrane outside the brain. It can result in clots and put pressure on the brain that can be lethal. That pressure had to be relieved surgically. It's actually a fairly simple operation. They did a version of it in India, which certainly helped. But the bleeding evidently resumed and surgeons here had to do a more thorough job."

"Will he . . . ." she interrupted, unable to complete her question.

"Time will tell. Head injuries like this have notoriously unpredictable consequences. He could remain unconscious for a time and then come around and recover. Many people do. How long it takes depends on the extent of the injury. But some of his neurological responses do look promising."

"Like what?" she interrupted. "They said that before, but I couldn't see anything."

"Oh, he can open his eyes, and he can make sounds. Maybe other things. We hope there will be more. But, I have to tell you that even if he does wake up he could have some residual effects. And, in all honesty, Rebecca, it is possible that . . . ."

"Oh, God!" she blurted out, as his last words slashed through her.

Adrianna put an arm around her. Doctor Carey leaned forward and placed a hand gently on her hers. "We'll do everything possible, you know that."

"Can I see him?" she asked in a trembling voice.

"I thought you would want to do that. But don't expect . . . ."

"No," she cut him off. "I won't expect anything. I just want to see him."

"You know," Doctor Carey said as they went to the elevator, Rebecca depending more on the crutch and his arm than she wanted to, "you and Adrianna seem to be about the only people who know he is here. Doesn't he have any family?"

"Oh, damn" Rebecca cursed under her breath. She had neglected to call Conrad Goldman. How thoughtless. "No," she went on disjointedly. "No family. Not any more. Friends, of course. One of them made the arrangements here with Addy. She'll be coming to see him when it's appropriate. But I've failed to call another close friend. I must do that."

When they got to the Intensive Care floor, the quiet efficiency of the staff and the hospital technology at once reassured her and stirred new anxieties. This was not India, but it was ominous. Doctor Carey introduced Rebecca to the taciturn surgeon who had led the operation on Alex. The surgeon expressed sympathy and confirmed that the surgery had been successful. They had removed blood clots and relieved pressure. And Alex was showing more neurological activity.

"What happens now?" she urged.

"We will monitor his condition and watch for more responsiveness."

"What kind?" Rebecca prodded, eager for something she could identify.

"Oh, reactions to speech, for instance, such as speaking words, and then any voluntary activity," he answered.

Rebecca brightened slightly and thanked him for his good work. Doctor Carey then led her to a door at the end of a corridor that reminded her too much of the ICU in Agra. She wanted to go in alone. He nodded and said it would have to be a short visit then pushed the door open. He helped her get to a chair by the bed and left.

A figure lay partially suspended at an angle and motionless

on the only bed in the room. His torso was wrapped. An arm and a leg were in splints. Bandages covered his head down to the eyes. An oxygen tube was attached to his nose, and other tubes ran from other parts of his body to bleeping machines and to bottles hanging from metal stands. She bent forward to look at his face. She had let herself forget how deathlike he had appeared before. Being on home ground had led her to believe he would look more alive. And the doctors had said . . . . She stared at him. No, this wasn't yet Alex. It was more like . . . a death mask.

Do they make them anymore? she asked herself with ill-ease. Death masks? A morbid practice to preserve semblances of the dead. Why did anyone ever do that? Who'd want to be reminded of someone's face with no life in it on the death bed? Museums, maybe. Idolaters. Fans. Not her.

How unreal this place seemed now. The antiseptic atmosphere. The impersonal room. The laboratory environment. The machinery. The foreboding sounds. Alex hooked up to tubes and technology. And the mask. It had nothing to do with him, or her. None of it did. There was no life here. Not for them. No life at all.

Such thoughts were running through her mind in a daze when, a few minutes later the door opened and Doctor Carey came in with a nurse. "I'm afraid we'll have to go now," he said sensitively.

"Already?" she asked, feeling only half-conscious.

"You can come back tomorrow," he reassured her.

She reluctantly went out with him. Observing her glazed eyes, he asked if she was feeling ill and wanted to lie down. She registered a remotely negative response and said she just wanted to go home. He escorted her back to the office, providing more instructions for her own recovery. She didn't hear much of what he said, but thanked him again for his attentions and his kindnesses and his generous friendship. She would come again tomorrow.

Rebecca and Adrianna went down to the street and found a taxi. During the ride home, Rebecca ignored her mother's consoling words. She faced the window in silence. But she saw no New York street life this time. She saw no life at all.

They returned the next day, and Rebecca was able to spend more time with Alex. She saw no change. Only a death mask. Doctor Carey reminded her to be patient. Improvement could be slow for a while. "There is room for optimism," he said. "The surgeon sees positive indications. So the odds are not too bad."

The odds? she sighed silently. Not bad? Her mind flashed back to Atlantic City and talking about the odds and playing against them and deciding to come here. She shook her head slightly. Then a thought intruded—they had won in Atlantic City, hadn't they? Against the odds. She resolved to hope that he beat the odds, whatever they were. That the death mask would come alive. She went back home with her mother, who could only guess what Rebecca was thinking.

# 24

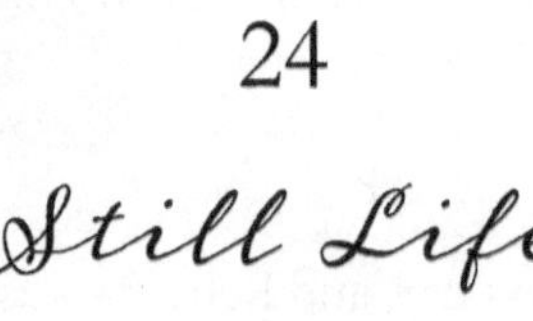

Over a week had now passed since Rebecca had come home. Physically she was recuperating, although eating fitfully and sleeping long. Emotionally she was still topsy-turvy, if not as distraught as at first. Grief and anger, self-pity and self-reproach, longings and desolation, broken by phases of dazed detachment and moments of unsummoned, even appealing, memories. This became the pattern of her waking hours, and of her tormented dreams.

What did it all mean? she asked herself. Was it all retribution? Punishment? Was the stark panic and emptiness that had seized her those long months ago a kind of retribution for having managed her life too well, and for not letting herself feel enough or care enough about anything? That would be unjust. She had felt and had cared about lots of things. Not enough? Or not openly? Too passively? Was that because she had feared intense feelings? And was she now being punished with more emotional disarray for letting herself feel too deeply and care too much? She lost both ways. Another dead end. Another dilemma. Self-control and losing self-control, feeling and not feeling, caring and not caring—they all ruined you.

But no, damn it! she cursed. No more banal *existential dilemmas!* More was going on in her than that. Doctor Carey had recommended anti-depressants, but she had rejected the idea. This was no post-traumatic depression, or whatever the label is, the kind of thing that had afflicted many people, probably her, too, after September 11th. This was not like that. No pills could alleviate it. Pills could deliver only a temporary drugged escape. They couldn't assuage or make sense of her consuming and confused emotions and the memories that fed them. And what did it mean that some of what she felt—as in the flood of tears after she got home—wasn't all bad? She needed to fathom it all, to understand. Then she might be able to manage it.

Her daily hospital visits had brought some salutary order to her days, but had added more uncertainty to her life. She continued to see no change in Alex's condition. And with each day of no change, she feared his chances of recovery dipped. To comfort her, Doctor Carey and others explained that *no* change was better than a change for the worse. Alex's vital signs were quite stable, and he was not sinking farther into a coma. In her anguish, *no change* started to seem good.

Sarah Rose came to the hospital with support to offer, along with the guilty confession that she had indeed set up that first lunch with Alex last summer for more than professional reasons. Rebecca thanked her for her kindness and for helping with the hospital arrangements and for taking care of Alex's bills, and so on. But she returned only a wan smile to Sarah's mention of her well-intentioned deed. Rebecca didn't want to go back to that beginning. Not now.

Rebecca also spoke to Conrad Goldman. When she had met him at dinner with Alex in the late summer, she had found him wryly charming, good natured, and prone to exchange friendly barbs with Alex. She liked him. He had anxiously followed the India story in the press and was eager to lend a hand to Alex and to her. They planned to get together at the hospital soon so that Conrad could at least visit Alex.

She saw Meredith, too, as she had said she would. Meredith

responded with delight and was her most appreciative, sensitive, and generous self. She would continue running interference for Rebecca at the office, keeping Henry at bay. And she would accompany her to the hospital any time, and would shop and cook for her once Rebecca's mother left. Rebecca had only to ask. Meredith also encouraged Rebecca to return to the office sooner rather than later. That would keep her mind off painful things and give her some bolstering company. Sadly, Rebecca's needs lay elsewhere. And no one could do anything about them—except herself.

With her body mending, yet her emotions still unsettled, Rebecca decided she probably had a better chance of getting a grip on those emotions if she were alone for a while. Convinced that she was well enough to take care of herself, she explained this to her mother. Adrianna resisted, not wanting to leave her daughter alone. Rebecca gently insisted. Heartened by this as a healthy assertion of will and a symptom of restarting a normal life—although she could not say what that normal life would be—Adrianna relented and prepared to go home today. They would speak often. Rebecca promised to ask for anything she needed and to come stay with her mother in Connecticut soon— which Adrianna knew would not likely happen until Alex's future was clear, one way or the other. Rebecca made another promise too. She would gladly use the stylish cane that Adrianna had bought to replace the crutch Rebecca disliked and was sure she could manage without, and that Adrianna assured her would lift her spirits while supporting her injured leg. How like her mother to do that, Rebecca thought. Adding a touch of style to mundane necessity. Alex would applaud. That thought gave her a bitter-sweet pang. With loving thanks for being the mother she was, Rebecca hugged Adrianna and said goodbye.

Now she began readying for her afternoon visit to the hospital, her first time alone. Surveying the closet for something she'd like to wear, her eyes fell on Alex's suitcase tucked in the back where her mother had stored it when they had arrived. It gave her a start. But instead of shrinking from the painful memories it might provoke, she wanted to touch the clothes in it, to be close to him and have good memories. There would be life there. Ignoring the physical discomfort, she bent down, lugged the thing from the closet and laid it down. Sitting on a chair, she undid the latches, pulled the zipper, and lifted the top. Rumpled shirts and a safari jacket lay on top. She placed a hand on them and smelled a whiff of Alex's familiar after shave. He *was* there. Alive. His presence and her fond remembrance of their months together, and of their . . . the word floated into her mind, *romance* . . . eased her. Her eyes then picked out a bright object through the netting in a corner. She couldn't tell what it was. Opening the compartment, she found the little white elephant from Agra. She took it out and held it, caressing the soft white marble and bright stone inlays, and remembering the merchant's ambiguous story. Was it a blessing or a curse? If it was a curse, was she to blame? No, she wouldn't be swayed by such morose superstitions. This white elephant was supposed to bring wisdom and good fortune. She would think of that, and maybe, she hoped, it might, like Ganesha, even bring an auspicious new beginning. The idea appealed to her now more than it ever had. She went to her dresser and set the figurine on it then returned to the suitcase, closed it affectionately, and pushed it back into the closet.

Resuming the task of dressing to go out, she started feeling, for no discernible reason, that something would change today. What would it be? Would it be for the better or the worse? And . . . would it be in him or in her? She looked over at the white elephant, and, determined to enliven the good feelings that had periodically flickered within her despair, she said to herself, Yes, something would change today. She would make it change—for the better. Somehow.

To start, she would wear something she hadn't worn to the hospital before. No skirt or dress this time. She would wear slacks, proving that she could get them on over her healing leg. She selected a pair of grey flannels, a black turtleneck sweater, a wool blazer, and comfortable loafers. Successfully pulling on the slacks, if with some difficulty, she was pleased with herself. She finished dressing and completed her cosmetic preparations in the bathroom, then passed back through the bedroom. Her eyes fixed on the elephant again. She walked over to the dresser, picked it up, looked at it affectionately, and gave it a hopeful caress. Somehow, she repeated, something *would* change today, for the better. She put it down and left the room

When she reached the front door she leaned down stiffly to stroke Clarissa, who had trailed her there with a plaintive meow, as if lamenting her departure or lending her sympathy or so Rebecca wanted to think. Then she drew the cane from the umbrella stand and looked it over. She would do the best she could with it. Fitting its chic handle into her hand, she tested its base on the floor. And went out.

Doctor Carey received her as comfortingly as always on these difficult days, and, tenderly taking her hand, informed her that Alex was continuing to exhibit some positive signals but had not awakened. Her hopes for the day slipped. He told her again to be patient. And, as he had promised earlier, he removed more of her stitches and bandages, approving her progress, but scolding her paternally for not eating enough to regain the strength and energy she needed. She pledged to heed his advice and, with an affectionate embrace, departed his office for the ICU. She used the cane as little as possible, gratified to be less medically trussed and weighed down. Maybe things were changing, for the better.

Known as she was now to the doctors and nurses in the ICU, she could make short visits on her own. She opened the door to Alex's room, agitated by the welter of emotions she carried with her. Approaching the bed, she saw again only the death mask. As before, she could scarcely find Alex in it. But this day she *had* to see more. Not the mask. *Him, himself.* Could she *will* it to happen? Yes, she said to herself, *will* is better than hope. Or, maybe, *will* adds something to hope. Yes, will gives . . . strength to hope. She liked the idea, trite as it might be.

She held her eyes on his face. Her mind drifted back to those moments when, on the medic's cot after the explosion, she had seen him open his eyes, and smile, and breathe the words "love you." She was sure he had done it. Would he now? "Wake up, Alex," she said quietly in earnest supplication. "Oh, please wake up." She repeated the words over and over, like a mantra.

Minutes passed. She had no idea how many. She repeated her plea. Then his features appeared to soften. And she detected a twitch in his eyelids. Was he dreaming? Was he waking? Was he coming to life? Did he know she was there? She saw quivers of sensation cross his eyelids and cheeks and lips. And his eyes opened a slit. She widened her own eyes. Was it happening? Or were these only her memories, or her wishes?

Shutting out everything around her and concentrating on this face, she could see in it again the living man she had come to love and to share more of herself with than she had ever thought possible, or even desirable, before knowing him. She wasn't sure how or when that had happened. The ferry ride? The horse races? The Rainbow Room? The night of sentimental intimacy? Atlantic City? Varanasi? She couldn't say. Conflicting memories and wishes and emotions flowed together, making her want to cry with sorrow and joy at once. She bent over him. "I love you, Alex," she whispered. She watched intently. After a few moments, she noticed him smile faintly and raise his eyelids slightly. Then she saw his lips move, and she heard him quietly echo her words. Yes, he did. She was sure of it.

Her heart skipped. She looked again. The face resumed its usual sleep. Another illusion? She waited to see. She saw the mask, but not for her a death mask now.

The door opened behind her, and a familiar nurse entered apologetically announcing once again duties to perform. Rebecca eagerly described what she had seen on Alex's face and had heard him say. The nurse said that was wonderful, and she tried to arouse similar responses. He did move his eyelids a little and make almost verbal sounds, but spoke no discernible words. Detecting Rebecca's need to believe what she was sure she had seen and heard, the nurse sensitively remarked, "You could be right. Those activities might be coming. We will observe him very closely. And hope that we all see more signs of life by your visit tomorrow."

Signs of life? Yes, Rebecca thought. They were there. She wanted to tell Raymond. And, yielding to the nurse's gentle insistence of tasks to perform—calling to mind the first time she had seen Alex like this in a hospital half a world away—she backed toward the door and paused in the open doorway. Her eyes locked on Alex's face. The relief of seeing him come to life, if only marginally, and even if partly illusion, renewed the presence of him that she had felt earlier at home. She held onto it. She inched backward into the hall. The door swung shut.

Rebecca reentered Doctor Carey's office at least half-convinced that Alex was awakening. She told the doctor what had transpired, and he said that was very encouraging, for it could indeed happen like that. Alex could start waking up with accumulating sparks of life such as those she had perceived. Things might well be looking up. But, he cautioned, if the nurse couldn't get the same responses, she shouldn't expect too much too soon. And in his best fatherly manner, he advised Rebecca to take a break from her worries. Go shopping. See a cheerful movie. Visit friends. Have dinner with someone. Try to have a good time.

Rebecca resigned herself to wait, if not to follow all of the doctor's advice. With Alex's living presence still with her, she went to the street and stood there foggily watching the traffic, uncertain what to do. She didn't want to go home. She'd be alone now. Not that being alone was the issue. She didn't really want to be with anybody right now. She didn't want to go to a movie or anything like that, either. Wondering what she did want to do, she noted the weather and the season for virtually the first time since her distraught homecoming. She recalled how dark and dreary that day had been. Today, the autumn sky was clear, and the crisp November air invigorating. Another good sign? An indistinct inclination gathered within her. She started to walk. She wasn't going anywhere in particular. Just walking. She wanted to do it, in spite of her physical handicap, which she admitted was eased by the cane that she was grateful to have. She crossed First Avenue and headed west. Her mind held onto Alex's presence, telling herself he was reviving, if only bit by bit.

But as she reached Second Avenue, troubled emotions began boiling up in her again. The grief, the anger, the self-pity, the confusion were crowding out the presence of Alex in her mind. Stop! she demanded and walked on, struggling to suppress them, searching for the *will* to make things change for the better today, as she had thought they were.

At Third Avenue, waiting as traffic raced past in a blur, she pictured herself stumbling off the curb under the car wheels. That would put an end to it all. No more grief. No more anger. No more loss. No more self-pity. No more futile hopes and failed will. But she didn't do it. She would be no Anna Karenina.

When the light changed, she moved unthinkingly with a phalanx of pedestrians across the avenue. And she became acutely conscious of them—intense professionals in business suits carrying valises locked with too many combination dials; tired delivery men hauling packages from trucks and offices; earnest young women conservatively dressed for a lawyer's or an executive's success, and flashy ones dressed for modeling or seduction; impeccably coiffed matrons in fine strands of pearls ending a day of shopping or socializing; and others whose busy purposes on New York's sidewalks had always eluded her. She didn't know why she had become so aware of them. But it took her mind off herself. As she observed them, she began detaching from everything. This was not the opaque, lifeless daze that had intermittently befogged her lately. She was oddly more alert than that. In a curious limbo and thinking herself all but invisible, she wandered down the avenue, remembering that Alex used to talk of walking in the city this way. A *flâneur* gliding along, seeing everything and everyone, and yet unseen, and letting nothing be lost on him. The recollection re-awakened his presence in her. It gave her a warm sensation. Drifting along, invisible to everyone but herself, she absorbed the sights and sounds of the city—the bustling people, the congested traffic, the attractive shop windows—as a panorama animated for her alone.

Then, while waiting to cross a side street, she caught sight of her reflection in a store window. That broke the spell. She stared. The reflection showed a thin and rather slouched but not unkempt woman leaning on a cane. She moved closer. Can that be me? she asked. She didn't want it to be.

But instead of turning away, something led her to make the reflection vanish by peering through it. Refocusing her eyes, she gradually dispelled her image and discerned inside the window a large painting on display. It depicted succulent melons and berries and peaches and plums dripping with juices and gleaming in a luscious luminescence. Dutch probably, she told herself, remembering art history classes that had extolled the copious folksy Still Lifes of seventeenth-century Holland.

She'd never cared much for them. But for some reason, this one appealed to her.

She noticed the shop was an art dealer, and a memory arose of going into a gallery on Madison Avenue with Alex in early September and seeing a painting quite like this one. She pressed against the window to read the name of the painter. Severin Roesen. Yes, he had done that other painting too. Not old Dutch at all, they had been instructed that day, but a nineteenth-century German-American who painted luminous Still Lifes, vibrant pastiches of the old Dutch. This had inspired Alex to launch into one of his fanciful monologues. A Still Life like this, he'd said, might show the artist's skill with form and color and light, but it's really about the good life—delicious food, hearty sociability, homey warmth, goodies and good things. And he'd summed up his typical over-interpretation with a phrase she heard now as if he were speaking it. "A good Still Life is a love story of the good life." He was proud of that pithy, euphonious snippet of spontaneous art criticism. Another of his imaginative versions of art and life. She had laughed. She did not laugh now. Tears moistened her eyes. But they were not all melancholy tears.

Gazing at the painting, she visualized Alex lying comatose in the hospital. Another Still Life. She shivered. He'd probably relish the affinity. The *coincidence* of it all. And yet, it occurred to her, there is *still . . . life* in him, and he *will still live.* He'd go for the tangled puns. But it was true. She'd seen it in his face and heard it in his voice. She felt her will reemerging.

An impulse seized her. She straightened up, turned toward the street, caned her way to the curb, and flagged a taxi. Settling herself into the back seat of the cab more easily than she had done before, she told the driver emphatically: "Battery Park, please."

# 25

## *Into the Fantasy of the Night*

The late afternoon November sun was throwing long shadows through the near-barren trees and across fallen leaves in Battery Park when Rebecca got out of the taxi. She had come here for reasons she could not name. It was as if something had beckoned her.

Making her careful way along the park's winding footpaths, she passed plowed-under flower beds awaiting winter's snow, around the circular brick fortress pock-marked by British gunfire in the War of 1812, past the corroded bronze statue of Giovanni da Varrazano, who had "discovered" this harbor in 1524, and neared the somber, dignified rows of tall concrete slabs memorializing American soldiers lost to the Atlantic in World War II. There she found a vacant bench facing the water and sat down.

Tugboats, ferries, and barges churned back and forth, sending their cresting wakes across the sparkling, choppy waters to splash against the sea wall a few yards away. Vendors on the promenade peddled hot dogs, soft drinks, pennants, T-shirts, miniature Statues of Liberty, and the like to dawdling tourists. Early departing office workers marched toward the subway or

318

to the Staten Island Ferry on their diurnal journeys home from one more long, industrious day in the city. Visitors and lovers strolled by, pausing to take in the scenic waterfront and the clear blue skies and golden earthen colors of autumn in New York.

How vivid it was in her memory. She and Alex coming here that afternoon from the party over at the hotel to a bench near this one. This could even be the same bench. He'd love that, she thought. Another of those romantic, sentimental, benign *coincidences* he reveled in—always wringing lush emotions and far-fetched meanings from any occasion. Then they had taken the ferry across the harbor and back. And they had watched the city's twilight magic-show come up and perform on the sky-lit stage. And they had kissed. That first time. And nothing had been quite the same since.

She had shied from it all at first. His indulgence in anything that made life more delectable. That was one of his words. *Delectable.* It suited his creed as an aesthete who invents pleasures and feeds *beautiful* emotions for their own sake, and as a romantic who lives for enchanting moments, and as a fantasist who tries to live the life he imagines and over-interprets everything. It all belonged to his *way of looking at things*, as he never tired of saying. Like that "Moon Illusion" he had made so much of here. But, she conceded, she now found it all rather endearing.

She also knew he didn't unequivocally believe everything he said, or even in himself. He'd confessed it—that he'd conjured up this life of delectation and romance in part to compensate for his fear that he hadn't the temperament or the strength to impose his fantasies—or his will—on *real life*. Still, he believed in this quixotically invented life of his as much as he could believe in anything. He'd said that too. And what was he thinking in those horrifying moments when he had lunged at the terrorist, and had then grabbed her and shoved her ahead of him into the fleeing crowd, and had then been hit by the blast? He was probably thinking it was so dramatic! And romantic! And ironic. Love and loss—at the Taj Mahal, for God's sake! Yes, it was probably something like that.

She clenched her fists. Her vacillating moods were swinging again. Why couldn't he simply do things honestly, unselfconsciously? Why did he always have to dramatize everything and watch himself living, as though his life were a fictional romance, as though nothing in it had effects outside himself? But this . . . *this*, his fate, is no romantic melodrama. No airy *way of looking at things*. It is *real life*. He had said *she* was *real life* for him, but that was just a figment of his romance, wasn't it? Not like this. *This is real life*, and it could bring—death.

An abyss began opening inside her once more, resounding with renewed fears, and with her breaking heart. She pressed her fists hard against the wooden slats of the bench seat. It hurt, and she wanted it to hurt. Because, in her heart, she knew it wasn't really him she questioned. It was herself.

While she fought this renewed attack of fears and sorrows and self-recriminations, she heard within a muffled voice. *What did it mean to her, this thing she called life?* She stiffened. How many times in months past had she heard those words of Clarissa Dalloway asking her over and over what she had not been able to answer? How could she answer them now? Then another voice, soothing and kind, followed. *Thank you for asking.* Who is that? Asking what? About her life? *I had a daughter . . . . She died . . . . Thank you for asking.* Rebecca's throat tightened. The palmist of Varanasi. That remarkable woman returned, as if beside her. She who had lost so much, but who was so serene and so grateful for her life and for her memories, even for what it had hurt her most to lose. Rebecca felt tears gathering in her eyes. Sentimental tears, she said to herself. But she knew they were swelling from that deeper well.

The benign lightness she had not felt for a while began lifting her again. And a beneficent tranquility that she had never known descended over her, mingled with another emotion that she could not identify. What was it? She heard the soft echo of that same voice in her mind: *Thank you for asking.* Soon she heard a more familiar voice silently say: *But I never thanked them.* The childhood episode flashed back to her. Could that be it? Could that be the unidentified emotion? A kind of . . . *gratitude.* She held fast to the word, and the feeling.

Absorbing these healing emotions, Rebecca cast her eyes toward the southeast, where the harbor opens onto the Atlantic Ocean. A tint of indigo was beginning to brush the low eastern sky, signaling impending night. Bringing her eyes around westward, she saw the sun hovering above the horizon behind that scrim of polluted air, a great red-orange ball, illuminating the western sky with a vibrant iridescence before sinking out of sight. A scene made for obvious metaphors, she mused—the darkness of nature gradually enshrouding the east while the artificial colors of an air-polluted sunset brighten the west, complete with the visual trickery of the Moon Illusion. Nature passing the baton to culture, both giving us delight. Alex would have seen it that way. He couldn't resist finding metaphors everywhere. Life is made of metaphors, he'd say. Ideas and images, incidents and people, that come to mean more than themselves to us, revealing affinities and coincidences that give life texture and vivacity, and that sometimes even reveal what matters most to us. They're ways of looking at things. That's what he'd said. A hundred times. On a hundred occasions.

And . . . after all, wasn't Alex himself something of a metaphor? The thought surprised and intrigued her. He was going to call his novel *Metamorphoses.* And he'd rambled on about how metamorphoses and metaphors go together because metaphors change one thing into another, which is a kind of metamorphosis, and they can change us too, if we let them. *Metaphors of metamorphosis,* he'd called these. Another of his glib, over-reaching notions. Will he ever write that book? Possibly he never intended to. It was one of his metaphors for enhancing life, and changing it. Yes, that's what he was, too—a metaphor of metamorphosis. Something that changes one thing into another, and can change us by awakening us to what matters most. Had he done that for her? She held the thought, and realized that thinking of him like this brought no sorrow.

A cool puff of wind gusting in from the water as the sun disappeared beneath the horizon broke into her thoughts, reminding her again of the season and the early end of autumn days. She massaged her hands together to warm them from the chill. As she did that an obscure curiosity arose. Opening her hands, she held them side by side and lowered her eyes. The radiant orange-pink sunset reflecting from the high cirrus clouds overhead threw a rosy blush on her palms. She looked at the lines. A disturbing recollection hit her. Her hands and Alex's! Both Madame Rajas had seen foreboding signs there, hadn't they? Troubles. Dangers. Now . . . what would his hands say? Would the lines be . . . disappearing, as the first Madame Raja had said they might do for someone in a coma?

She shook off the ominous thought. Concentrating on her hands, she felt the lightness and tranquility resume. She spread her palms and focused on the lines. Do they actually change as we do? Do they tell the truth? Her fingers traced the long lines arcing around the fleshy mound of her thumbs. Could it be that this line in both hands *had* changed? In the left hand it appeared to have breaks in it, but both of them seemed larger and circled wider than she remembered them. Or was she just imagining it?

She wanted to know if she was right, and what might happen from here on—in her hands, and in her life. A question wafted into her mind. Was a trip to Atlantic City in her future? If so, would that show up in her right hand? The idea amused her. How Alex would love that. Then it dawned on her that she didn't have to wait for a palm reader to explain her hands and predict her life. She could—"take matters into her own hands," quite literally. The cliché and its pun came spontaneously, prompting a quiet laugh. But that's how it worked, didn't it? At least partly. We can change the lines in our hands by ourselves. Like life. As the palmists had said, we create our lives as we live them, intentionally or not, actively or passively. And, just as important, perhaps more, we determine how we feel about our lives, whatever they are, whether we know it or not. And our very "feeling for life" shows up in the Line of Life. She ran her finger along that line in her right hand again. She recalled that when the first Madame Raja had explained this to Alex, she had added something about how the very meaning of life is the feeling that our own lives have meaning, and that we should try to get that feeling in every good way we can. A platitude? Who cares? Is it *true*? And was that what Alex had been saying all along?—his so-called Buddhism of everyday life? Yes, she answered, it could all be true.

Lingering on that idea, she raised her eyes from her hands to the sky again and brought them around from the setting sun to the city skyline towering behind her above the trees. It was starting its twilight transformation from the prosaic working day into nighttime illusion. A twinge of sadness rippled through her as she thought of the loss that this magical scene, and this city, had suffered a little more than a year ago. Her eyes moistened. Oh, I do love it so, she said inside. The city, more than I ever knew, or let myself know. That must be why . . . back then . . . I felt so . . . . She stopped herself from returning to September 11th and its aftermath. She was not going to follow sorrow. A wave of warmth swept over her, and she sighed, "Thank you, Alex, for this place. And for . . . ."

Before she could complete the thought, a pleasing notion came to her. Why not go over to the hotel where they had met that night before coming here and go up to the bar overlooking the harbor? Have a drink and something to eat. Doctor Carey would approve. Go outside and see the dusk deepen over the harbor and the Statue of Liberty's torch light up, and watch the city lights finish arraying themselves for their fantastic dance into the dark. And summon memories to . . . make a new life, somehow. Alex would surely be there, she told herself. He'll always be there, in places like that, at times like this, in ways of looking at things that discover what is *beautiful* in them and arouse feelings that give meaning to life, no matter what. Others will be there, too—people, experiences, images: palm readers and good clichés, loyal friends and a loving mother, horse races and Still Lifes, sunsets and journeys, metaphors and coincidences, and who knows what else—all with gifts to give, and with gratitude to awaken, even for what it hurts most to lose. She was beginning to understand . . . . Oh, how much she owed to so many, she thought. They will all be there with her, she repeated to herself, if she can find them, whether he lives or . . . .

She thwarted the foreboding intimation with a confident affirmation. "He *will* live," she whispered. Then she said aloud, "And *so will I*. I will find them all, and I will live for all that they give me . . . and for what I can give to them. And for life itself."

She heard only her own voice now. A new voice. The turmoil had dissipated and the confusion had dissolved. Lightness and tranquility lifted her again. Gradually it came over her that the *lightness* was . . . a kind of *freedom* . . . freedom from old fears . . . even from herself . . . a freedom from living too . . . passively . . . a freedom to feel, whatever that might bring . . . yes, that was it, a new sensation of freedom. And the *tranquility* was . . . what? . . . a kind of *gratitude* . . . yes . . . to him, and to others . . . and to life, for its feelings of both joy and sorrow, even sorrow for what it could hurt her most to lose . . . and for the imagination and the will to live anew with a hard gem-like flame even if . . . . Yes, she understood it all at last. Is that an epiphany, a rebirth? she asked herself. Dismissing the cliché, she shrugged. Why not?

But, what about work? The prosaic question intruded. She answered without hesitation. Her work could no longer be what it had been. It would have to be something different. Something she could *feel* as never before, or had not felt for a long time.

Yes, she would start over. A new beginning? Another cliché. But some clichés ring true. And she didn't need Alex to tell her that. Perhaps she would switch from editor to agent, seeking out promising new or neglected authors who have something good, perhaps something *beautiful*, to say. Help them say it, nurture them along, make both art and life work for them. And maybe, just maybe, she would write a novel herself one day. She knew the subject. She even knew the title. Would that make her a cliché or a metaphor?

The corners of her mouth inched upward. The dried streaks of tears cracked on her cheeks as a smile crept across her face in the brisk evening air. It felt good.

Giving her hands a sharp slap together, she opened her purse and fished out her compact. Squinting into the mirror under the dimming light, she wiped smudges of mascara from under her eyes, applied a brush of make-up and a line of lipstick, ran a comb through her hair, and patted her palms against her cheeks to brighten the color and efface the remnants of tears. Getting to her feet, with spirited resolve, she arranged her jacket, fluffed her sweater, smoothed her slacks, squared her shoulders, stood firm, and looked up at her lofty destination. Sweeping her eyes across the cityscape coming to glittering nocturnal life, she savored the sight. How . . . fantastic it was. Setting her course, she gave the cane a jaunty twirl, chiding herself for the silly theatrics, and, buoyed by her epiphany, or whatever it was, with a light and confident, if slightly listing gait, she strode smiling into the fantasy of the night.